Newton's Riddle

The Psalm 83 Conspiracy Revealed

Newton's Riddle

The Psalm 83 Conspiracy Revealed

by Neill G. Russell

Tate Publishing & *Enterprises*

This title is also available as a Tate Out Loud product. Visit www.tatepublishing.com for more information.

Published by Tate Publishing & Enterprises, LLC
127 E. Trade Center Terrace | Mustang, Oklahoma 73064 USA
1.888.361.9473 | www.tatepublishing.com

Tate Publishing is committed to excellence in the publishing industry. The company reflects the philosophy established by the founders, based on Psalm 68:11,
"The Lord gave the word and great was the company of those who published it."

Cover design by Lindsay Behrens
Interior design by Isaiah R. McKee

Published in the United States of America

ISBN: 978-1-60247-894-7
1. Fiction: Religious: Apocalypic

08.01.18

I dedicate this book to the wife of my youth, Cindy.
You have been a living example to me of
God's grace and unconditional love.
To God be the glory forever and ever!

Neill G. Russell

Foreword

With terrorism, international turmoil and uncertainty being instantly broadcast into homes throughout the world, people are turning to church leaders for answers as never before. As these teachers and pastors take their Bibles and explain how these events were foretold hundreds and thousands of years ago by the prophets, it reveals what is going on today, and more importantly, what is yet to come.

The timeliness of this book is perfect. Other authors have wetted the appetites for mysteries based on biblical events, be they heresies or based on truth, but there was a great need for someone to take the Bible, current world situations as they are unfolding, and the diabolical plots in the supernatural realm and put them into a perspective that we can understand.

Newton's Riddle is that book. Using the premise of an ancient code discovered by Sir Isaac Newton, Neill Russell pulls us through time and thrusts us into the future foretold in Revelation. The reader gets a look into the dark spiritual realm to see how the army of Satan's demons is structured and how they attempt to bring total destruction to Israel and Christian nations supporting her.

We also see into God's supernatural realm to understand how God's army of angels combats and outmaneuvers the enemy, providing protection, guidance and inspiration for God's people. The reader is held captive as these end-time events explode and conclude to reveal God's ultimate plan.

I encourage you to read this book and pass it on to anyone who is looking for answers and inspiration in these troubling times.

John C. Pringle,
Pastor, New Life Christian Outreach
Chester, Maryland

Prologue

The Middle Eastern Region of Moriah
1846 *BC*

Throughout the entire history of mankind, there have been few requests that were more difficult to accept, more agonizing to fulfill and carry out. For one man, such an unfathomable request of this magnitude would soon test everything he had ever believed, everything he had valued and held dear. The consequences of this man's decision were about to set in motion a historic chain of events that would shape the destiny of mankind until the very end of time.

For nearly three days, a small band of humans, three adult males and a male adolescent, and a small donkey burdened with a load of chopped wood, trudged slowly over hot rocky hillsides toward some unseen destination. The only relief for the four weary travelers was an occasional breeze ushering in slightly cooler air from the hilltops above. As the evening of the third day drew near, the group's leader, an aged man surprisingly spry for a human over a century old, stopped and gazed in the direction of a distant mountain. With tear-filled eyes, he turned to his two young servants quietly commenting, "We are here. We will stop and set up our tents for the night."

Alabar and Malzar stared at their master with a look of confusion. In all of their years of faithful service, they had never witnessed, not once, this type of emotion exhibited by the man they grew to love and respect not just as their lord and master, but as a father figure and trusted friend.

"Adoni, is everything all right with you?" Malzra asked his master with a voice of concern.

"All is fine." Abraham assured. He had been Alabar and Malzra's master ever since their births in the land of Canaan over thirty years ago. They were just two of over twenty servants responsible for attending to the needs of Abraham, his wife, Sarah, his young son, Isaac, his large flocks of sheep and goats and a sizable herd of cattle. Out of all his servants, Abraham had a special fondness for Alabar and Malzra. After all, they were the sons of his oldest and dearest personal servant, Eliezer of Damascus. After the death of this most trusted servant, Abraham felt a duty to consider the young sons of Eliezer as if they were his own and had them accompany him everywhere he went, especially now, on the most difficult journey of his life. Lagging somewhat behind the group was Isaac, Abraham's thirteen-year-old son.

Noticing the group ahead had stopped, the boy impatiently shouted out from a distance, "Father, are we there yet? Is it time to offer up our burnt offering to the Lord?"

As his son approached, it took everything within the old man to hold back his tears. Staring up at his father's aged, weathered face with youthful anticipation was Abraham's prized possession, greater than all of his wealth in gold, flocks, and servants. Isaac meant everything to Abraham. He was the miracle fulfillment of God's long ago promise to the childless couple of descendants that would one day cover the Earth as the grains of sand cover the seashore below and stars cover the skies above. To Abraham, Isaac represented an old man's reward for a lifetime of faithfulness to a God who called him to leave everything, his family and birthright, and journey off to some unknown, distant land of God's own choosing. Abraham's enduring trust in God's promises was his guiding compass to a lifetime filled with blessings and unsurpassed success. But now, some ninety years after he had started his initial life's journey with his God, his enduring trust was about to be tested like never before.

In spite of a breaking heart, Abraham found the inward strength to conceal his own internal anguish and calmly responded to his son's impetuous question. "Not today, my son. Tomorrow the two of us will journey alone to that distant mountain and offer a burnt offering up to God. For now, help Alabar and Malzar set up our tents for the night."

"I will, my father."

For Abraham, the morning could not come soon enough. All through the night he struggled with the same raging thoughts. *How could the God I've loved and trusted my entire life allow me to go through such torment? He has never asked anything like this before. How could he possibly ask me to do the impossible, to offer up my beloved son, Isaac, as a burnt offering sacrifice? Did he not promise that my descendants would someday make up a great nation? How can this be if my son is dead! Sarah and I are far too old to have another child!* Eventually, Abraham's troubled mind surrendered to the fact that regardless of how incomprehensible the request, the following day, God's will would be accomplished; and He would make sure that everything would turn out all right.

°

In the still of the darkness, sounds of hushed voices outside his tent roused Alabar from a light sleep. He was usually the first to arise and prepare the morning meal, but not this morning. Exiting his tent, Alabar found his master Abraham and son, Isaac, gathering up the wood for the burnt offering.

"Alabar, you and your brother stay here with the donkey," Abraham told the young man. Placing a gentle hand on his servant's shoulder, Abraham pointed in the direction of the rising sun and commented, "The boy and I will travel a little farther. We will worship over at that distant mountain, and then we will return no later than midday."

Abraham proceeded to place the wood for the burnt offering on his son's shoulders, while he himself picked up a knife and a bowl full of hot embers for the fire. For the old man, the short journey from their campsite to the base of the mountain called Moriah would prove to be the most difficult task in all of his 113 years. There was only one thought, one single word that kept Abraham from turning around and abandoning this agonizing mission with destiny. Over and over, every time a depressing thought would attempt to well up, Abraham would repeat the word "trust" until he regained a sense of assurance that God would somehow intervene and keep his son from any harm.

During their short journey to the base of Mt. Moriah, Isaac could sense not only his father's apprehension, but also, that something important was missing.

"Father?"

"Yes, my son?" Abraham calmly replied.

"We have the wood and the fire," said the boy, "but where is the lamb for the sacrifice?"

"God will provide a lamb for the sacrifice, my son."

Not another word was spoken between father and son until they arrived at the base of the chosen spot. Abraham paused and looked up toward the top of the mountain before him. After taking in a deep breath, the old man looked down at his son and said, "It is time. Follow me and I will show you where God wants the altar to be built."

With that said, Abraham led his son slowly up the rocky hillside to a place near the summit marked by a smooth outcropping of rock. Completely exhausted, Abraham sat down, placing the bowl full of hot embers and his knife on the ground beside him.

"It is here that God wants his altar built," the old man faintly commented.

Isaac knew exactly what to do. Ever since his earliest childhood recollections, he had watched his father faithfully construct altars for the sole purpose of submitting up burnt offerings to the Lord. Without questioning where the sacrifice to be cremated would come from, Isaac went right to work laying first a secure foundation composed of stones selected from the surrounding rocky surface. He then proceeded to completely cover the altar's surface with the cut wood. In only a few short minutes the job was completed. As the boy knelt placing the final wooden piece in place, he felt the strong presence of hands pressing down on his back and shoulders forcing his body to roll and lie flat on top of the altar of wood. Without saying a word, Abraham sat straddling the boy's body and proceeded to securely tie a twine rope around the boy's hands and feet.

Totally confused by his father's bizarre actions, Isaac watched helplessly, as if in a state of shock, as his father Abraham got up from his kneeling position and picked up the long knife that was resting along the edge of the rock.

Repositioning himself along the front side of the altar, Abraham placed his left hand over the eyes and brow of his son, pushing back on Isaac's forehead until his entire neck was exposed. Staring at the knife in his right hand, Abraham once again heard the word "trust," but this time, it was loud and audible. As he lowered the knife and placed its blade firmly against the boy's throat, Abraham looked up toward heaven and silently replied, *I trust you, Lord!*

Immediately, a thunderous shout came down from heaven, "Abraham, Abraham!" High overhead appeared a luminous being garbed in a brightly colored white robe, whose face, hands, and feet shone like highly polished brass. The light radiating out from the hovering spirit was so intense that Abraham and Isaac had to turn away from its brilliance.

With his head turned to the side, Abraham answered back. "Yes, I am listening."

"Lay down the knife," the archangel of the LORD replied. "Do not hurt the boy in any way, for now I know that you truly fear God. You have not withheld even your beloved son from God."

Abraham looked up and saw a ram caught by its horns in a bush. So he took the ram and sacrificed it as a burnt offering on the altar in place of his son. Abraham named the place "The Lord Will Provide."

Then the Archangel of the LORD called again to Abraham from heaven, "This is what the LORD says: Because you have obeyed me and have not withheld even your beloved son, I swear by my own self that I will bless you richly. I will multiply your descendants into countless millions, like the stars of the sky and the sand on the seashore. They will conquer their enemies, and through your descendants, all the nations of the earth will be blessed—all because you have obeyed me. Again I say unto you, the God of heaven and earth will bless those who bless your descendants and curse those who curse your descendants. This is my promise from now until the end of time."

Chapter One

"The folly of interpreters has been to foretell times and things by this prophesy, as if God designed to make them prophets. By this rashness they have not only exposed themselves, but brought the prophecy also into contempt. The design of God was much otherwise. He gave this and the prophecies of the Old Testament, not to gratify men's curiosities by enabling them to foreknow things, but that after they were fulfilled they might be interpreted by the event, and his own providence, not the interpreters', be then manifested thereby to the world. For the event of things predicted many ages before will then be a convincing argument that the world is governed by Providence."

Sir Isaac Newton (1642–1727)

Wednesday, December 25, 1642
Woolsthorpe, Lincolnshire

Even on a common day in late December, the winds off the North Sea blow cold and strong across the open farm fields of Lincolnshire, but today was not a common day. It was Christmas Day and an uncommonly bitter wind permeated every open space in this small hamlet of farmhouses forcing both man and beast to seek refuge in the protected shelters of either stable or home. *The exception to this cold deserted scene was three solitary hooded figures slowly walking down a narrow cobble-stoned road, seemingly undaunted by the harshness of the elements.*

"Do you two see that small stone farmhouse at the bottom of the hill?" the taller figure asked his two smaller companions. "Even now, cursed be the day, a very special Christmas gift is awaiting our arrival. So let's make haste. We cannot be late. I want the two of you present the moment it arrives."

Inside the dwelling was a scene of organized confusion. Two women, one robust in her middle fifties, the other, small framed, in her late teens, took turns running to and fro, alternating clean and used towels from the focal point of the activity, the back bedroom. A young woman, mid-twenties in appearance, cried out in painful agony as she lie semi-propped up in bed, pulling forward on straddled legs while expelling exhaustive heaves of short breaths. And yet, a fourth woman, hair wrapped in a light blue linen cloth, positioned herself at the right edge of the bed, coaching the young mother-to-be to push at ever increasing intervals with all of her might.

"Just one more time, Hannah. Now push!" commanded the midwife. "I can see the head!" The young girl again thrust forward, pulling her sweat-soaked body against her quivering, straddled legs.

"It's coming!" the midwife shouted as the other two women stopped everything and ran to view the spectacle being played out in the bedroom.

With one last push and a gush of fluid, a very tiny, premature baby was ejected into a perfectly positioned soft cloth towel.

"Hannah, it's a boy!" declared Sara Wallington, her neighbor and volunteer midwife.

"Hannah, you did it! You did it!" shouted Katie Ayscough, Hannah's younger sister. Turning to the robust woman in the background, Katie proudly stated, "Mother, you have a grandson!"

"Indeed I do!" the beaming grandmother declared.

"Here, Katie, carefully hold the baby in the towel while I cut the cord," Sara instructed.

"Mother, he's so small," Katie whispered as her concerned mother looked on.

"What a touching human scene," mocked Beelazad, captain of the demon spirits. "This little innocent baby will be your charge. Of all the

familiar spirits assigned to humans of the British Isles, you two have come highly recommended for this very special assignment."

"Who is this human, that two spirits are required?"

"Excellent question, Pythos!" declared Beelazad. "Listen carefully and you will soon find out."

"Here is your son, Hannah," Sara said as she gently handed the tiny baby, now wrapped in thick layers of linen, to his exhausted mother."

"Mother, he is so tiny, he could fit in a quart pot," Hannah commented in a voice of deep concern.

"He's a few weeks early, my dear, but he's going to be just fine," Sara quickly responded.

"You have our promise, we'll not leave this house until that beautiful son of yours is as plump and fit as King Henry's prize pig!" Hannah's mother reassured.

"I only wish his father was here to see him now," Hannah murmured tearfully.

"Where is the father?" asked Ronwe, the other familiar spirit assigned to the baby.

"Dead," declared Beelazad. "We had it arranged three human months ago. You two will be this baby's father and mentor from this day forward. Under your combined mentorship, he will grow up to possess one of the greatest human minds this world has ever known. Produce the same outcome as you did on your last assignment and you will both be promoted to levels of authority beyond your every dream! Fail at this assignment, you both will be reduced to cleaning bug dung off the floor in the lowest pits of hell. Am I clear?"

"Yes, Lord Beelazad."

"Hannah, have you chosen a name for your son?" anxiously asked her sister Katie.

"I have," Hannah declared. "I will name him after his father. His name will be Isaac Newton."

°

That premature baby, born on a cold Christmas Day in Lincolnshire England, did survive. He grew up to be one of the most recognized names not only in England, but also throughout the civilized world. For his achievements in the fields of physics and astronomy, Isaac Newton was thought by many to be one of the greatest scientists who ever lived.

During the latter years of his life, Newton turned his full attention to an earlier passion of his life, studying the ancient prophesies found in the Bible. Gifted with an extensive knowledge of ancient history and languages, Newton saw himself as one of those specifically chosen by God for the task of unlocking the mysteries of prophesies contained in Daniel and Revelations, two books he viewed as intertwined. With an exception of a few close friends, William Whiston and John Criag, Newton kept his writing on biblical prophecy private.

On May 27, 1725, Sir Isaac Newton suffered a severe lung infection and a bad bout of bladder stones. His failing health forced him to move into Kensington House in South London with his half-niece Catherine and her husband, John Conduitt.

Saturday, March 18, 1727
Kensington House, South London

"Oh no! God, no! John, please come up here! It's Uncle Isaac. He's collapsed on his bedroom floor!" Catherine Conduitt screamed to her husband at the bottom of the stairs.

"Bernard, go get Dr. Mead, immediately!" shouted John Conduitt to Bernard Smite, the Kensington House butler. "If he's unavailable, send for Dr. Cheselden!"

"John, he's burning up with fever," Catherine declared as she knelt down and touched her fallen uncle on his forehead. "Please, help me get him back into bed."

"Catherine, I'm afraid it's those damn bladder stones again," Isaac Newton whispered into his niece's ear as she and her husband carefully lifted him to his feet and back into his bed. "This time the pain is quite unbearable."

"Uncle, John sent Bernard for Dr. Mead," comforted his niece. "The doctor should be here promptly."

"Catherine, stay with Uncle while I go downstairs and get some wet towels."

Catherine Barton Conduitt, Isaac Newton's beautiful half-niece, remained at her uncle's bedside while her husband of ten years, John Conduitt, raced downstairs toward the kitchen. Though seemingly alone in an upstairs bedroom, two shadowy apparitions sat totally unnoticed in the far corner of the room. These were special spirits, assigned to remain with Isaac ever since his early childhood. Most humans were assigned just one, but for a chosen few, two spirits of such complementing specialties were matched to work in hideous harmony. Their names were Pythos, a demon spirit mastering in lies and rejection, and Ronwe, a spirit specializing in worldly knowledge and conceit. Combining their vile talents, Pythos and Ronwe attacked Newton in his areas of human weakness, pride and rejection, producing a lifetime of mistrust of fellow scientists and mankind in general. Mental instability took its toll on one who was recognized as the most eminent mathematician and scientist the world had ever known. Newton's mind was barraged daily with a lying concoction of self-pride and the fear of constant rejection, producing chronic fits of rage when criticized, and eventually two nervous breakdowns.

"Catherine, I want you to take a letter and send it to John Craig and to William Winston," an ailing Isaac Newton requested.

"Uncle Isaac, why don't we wait until later when you are feeling a little better?"

"No, no," Newton interjected. "It is imperative that we take care of this now. I want them to know that I have finally come to my senses."

"All right, Uncle, I have a pen and note pad. Whenever you're ready."

> *My dear friends,*
> *Upon rereading the verses in St John's Gospel and Colossians concerning Christ's deity, the spiritual blinders that I have inflicted upon myself for all of these wasted years have been lifted. I wish to inform you both that I have deeply and sincerely repented of this grievous sin and have rightfully placed our Lord and Savior Jesus Christ as the second person in the Godhead. It is my firm stance from now until eternity that Jesus Christ, my Savior, is God and fully God. God the Father, Jesus the Son, and the Holy Ghost are one!*

As Newton proceeded to confirm his declaration of faith in his Savior, the two spirits in the background started hissing and shrieking as their shadowy bodies began twitching and convulsing uncontrollably. At the very same time, a brilliant light radiated out from the center of the room so intensely that the two miserable spirits dropped face down to the floor and buried their heads with their trembling hands.

Standing tall and overshadowing the bedridden Newton and his grief-stricken niece stood a giant of a man, an angelic being dressed in a garment of brilliant white, whose face glowed as polished bronze and whose eyes glowed as burning blue flames of fire. The man proceeded to reach for his flashing sword that hung securely from his glistening golden belt. With one blinding swipe, the man sliced through each of the trembling spirits and in a puff of dark brown smoke, the spirits vanished. Repositioning his sword, the man walked to Newton, placing his massive hand on Newton's shoulder. Within seconds, Newton's pain-racked body totally relaxed and a sense of peace and tranquility filled the room.

"My dear Catherine, I have one more request for you to carry out," Newton continued. "Open my top dresser drawer and you will find a black notebook. It is imperative that this notebook gets into the hands of John Craig and him only. He will know what to do with it."

"I will, Uncle," Catherine promised.

Though his fever remained for the rest of the day, Isaac Newton was sensible and free from pain. Remaining bedridden, he was able to have long discourses with his physician, Dr. Mead, and his very close friend, Edmond Halley.

The following day, Sunday, March 19th, Isaac Newton never regained consciousness. He died without any appearance of pain on Monday the 20th at one in the morning at the age of eighty-five, and was buried in Westminster Abbey. All of London, both commoners and England's most eminent figures, attended Sir Isaac's funeral. English royalty and noblemen carried Newton's coffin, a funeral fit for a king.

Wednesday, March 29, 1727
Kensington House, South London

"It's certainly not going to be the same around here without dear Uncle Isaac," Catherine Conduitt sighed as she knelt down and carefully arranged another of her uncle's cherished books in an orderly pile up against the back kitchen wall.

"Indeed!" replied John as he passed by his wife holding another box full of her uncle's books.

"Done! These are the last of Uncle's books," John proclaimed as he carefully lowered the last of the boxes filled with volumes of scientific books and journals. "Sir Winston and Sir Halley will be by shortly with a royal coach to cart the last of these to the Archives of the Royal Society."

"Dear God, John, I almost forgot!" Catherine exclaimed as she stooped down and picked up an obscure black covered notebook from the volumes of books neatly stacked against the corner wall. "It must have been all the confusion with the funeral and all. When you ran downstairs for a wet towel for Uncle last Saturday, Uncle Isaac asked me to give this notebook to John Craig. He was very emphatic that this notebook be given to John Craig and none other!"

"Excuse me, Sir John and Madame Catherine," Bernard interjected as he stepped into the kitchen. "Sir John Craig is here to see you."

"Providence?" John replied as he turned to his wife. An equally surprised Catherine shrugged her shoulders.

"Please, Bernard, invite Mr. Craig into the parlor." Catherine requested. "We will be there directly."

"Catherine, I would like very much to look at your uncle's journal before you pass it on to Craig."

"Dear husband, I am afraid I cannot do that," Catherine carefully replied. "Uncle Isaac made me promise that I would pass the notebook onto John Craig and no other. I am obligated to honor Uncle's wishes."

"Very well, we'll attempt the next best thing," John conceded. "We'll ask Craig himself to interpret the notebook in our presence."

John Craig and Isaac Newton shared much in common. Both were considered England's preeminent mathematicians and were highly respected members of the prestigious Royal Society. They worked closely together on publishing original works in early stages of both calculus and optics. This commonality alone was enough to form a lasting friendship, but it was their shared zeal for probing Scriptures for what they felt were hidden universal truths that bonded a relationship that would carry on long after their passing.

"Mr. Craig, please forgive us for keeping you waiting so long," John Conduitt commented as he greeted his guest with an extended hand and a firm handshake.

"Not at all. You may not believe this, John, but I truly cherish these rare moments when I can catch a few moments of peace and quiet," Craig replied as he relaxed into the soft cushioned back of the parlor chair.

"Mr. Craig, you are truly a gentleman," Catherine Conduitt followed.

"I second my wife's opinion!" John Conduitt jokingly added. "Now, what can we do for such a grand gentleman as yourself on this fine day, Mr. Craig?"

"I'll get to the point," Mr. Craig began. "Your Uncle Isaac informed me not long ago that he was very close to completing what could very well be one of his greatest works, and he was about to share it with me just before his passing."

"Could this be it, Mr. Craig?" Catherine asked as she displayed before her guest a black bound notebook with unrecognizable lettering written on its top ledger.

"It's quite possible!" Craig exclaimed. "The lettering on the cover is also quite interesting."

"Middle Eastern?" Catherine guessed.

"Bravo, my dear!" Craig confirmed. "Hebrew to be precise."

"What does the title mean?" John Conduitt asked.

"It's a biblical expression," Craig followed. "In Hebrew, it is pronounced '*Barak Tikvah*,' translated into English it means 'Our Blessed Hope.' What I find so odd is that your uncle chose to write the title in Hebrew."

"How so?" questioned Conduitt.

"Well you see, the expression comes from a verse in the New Testament, I believe the book of Titus to be exact. What I find so odd is the New Testament was written in Greek, not Hebrew. Why would Isaac write the title in Hebrew?" Craig pondered.

Upon opening the journal and thumbing through the first several pages, Craig immediately displayed a wide grin as if discovering something very amusing.

"Did you find something of interest, Mr. Craig?" asked Catherine.

"Your uncle either had a great sense of humor or he didn't want anybody understanding the message in his journal."

"What do you mean, Mr. Craig?" John Conduitt asked as both he and his wife moved closer to Craig for closer inspection.

"Except for the title, your Uncle Isaac wrote the entire message of this journal in alchemy, a language of riddles understood only by a select group of chemists."

"Well, why do you suppose Uncle chose to write something so important in the form of unintelligible riddles?" Catherine inquired.

"On the contrary, the writings of alchemists are metaphoric, not unintelligible. Who knows why your uncle chose this style. One thing's for sure: he took his secret with him."

"Craig, are you able to decipher this gibberish, I mean these metaphors?" asked John Conduitt as he bent low to inspect Newton's writings.

"Mr. Conduitt, I'm afraid for me that's not possible." Craig smiled as he proceeded once again to thumb through the notebook pages. "I'm a mathematician, not a chemist. I am acquainted with a couple of alchemists, but without your uncle's presence, I'm afraid it could take some time."

"Well, Mr. Craig, what do you suppose is the true meaning of this journal?" Catherine asked. "Uncle was so emphatic that you and only you were to receive it. You must have some idea."

"To a degree," Craig admitted. "Your uncle was quite the master of keeping his research a secret until he was absolutely sure he had the answer. What was not a secret was Isaac Newton's passion for studying the hidden prophesies found in Scriptures. It was about a month ago when Isaac informed me that he had made a monumental find in the prophetic Scriptures and that he would soon be willing to share it with me."

Holding the black notebook in plain view, Craig continued. "If this is what I think it is, and I feel quite possibly it is, then what we have here in our possession could very well be the prize goal of Isaac Newton's lifetime. Something he spent more time searching and researching than any other quest: the date and time of Christ's return!"

Chapter Two

"It was revealed to Daniel that the prophecies concerning the last times should be closed up and sealed until the time of the end: But then the wise should understand, and knowledge should be increased (Daniel 12:4,9,10). And therefore the longer they have continued in obscurity, the more hopes there are that the time is at hand in which they are to be made manifest."

Sir Isaac Newton (1642–1727)

Monday, August 12th, 6 a.m. in the very near future.
The Digital Research Lab
Lower Ground Floor of the Cambridge Library
Cambridge, England

Located on a large table in the darkened recesses of the Cambridge Library's research lab, a nearly imperceptible light illuminates a rather ordinary box placed amongst a stack of similarly appearing packages yet to be opened and examined. For nearly three centuries, the contents within this package have never left the constant vigil of Ariel, Isaac Newton's former guardian angel. Since Newton's passing, it has been Ariel's new charge to both safeguard these documents and make sure they arrive securely to their final destination. Ariel was fully aware that loyalty to his Creator is the duty of a guardian angel, no matter how long or difficult the assignment.

As centuries pass, Ariel stood in unquestioning solitude guarding the contents of his task.

Little do humans realize or even comprehend the clandestine roles such spiritual entities play in their lives and surroundings. At the moment of birth, human beings are assigned spirits; at least one angelic guardian charged by the Creator to direct a human on a predestined path leading toward successful fulfillment in this world and eternal salvation in the next. The other, a spiritual malefactor, appointed and equipped by the powers of hell with an arsenal of lies and deceit intended to lead his assigned human down a path of destruction and everlasting shame. However, as in the story of the Garden of Eden, spirits only have the power to influence. Humans are solely responsible for the consequences of their own self-willed decisions and ultimately, their own destinies.

In a few short minutes, the contents within this box would become the center of rare excitement seldom, if ever, experienced within the halls of this usually mundane institution. With the flip of an electrical switch, the once-cluttered basement storage room of this centuries old institution instantly transformed into Cambridge Library's most innovative project, a 21st century state-of–the-art digital research facility, complete with computers, remote-controlled cameras, and a dust-free clean room. The stage was now set. All the technology necessary for analyzing such rare documents was in place. All that was needed now was the expertise to decipher its contents.

"It arrived late last evening as I was locking up the office," stated Professor Harrison Andrews, the head secretary of Cambridge University's Royal Society of rare bibliographies. "You have no idea how badly I wanted to open it right then. Needless to say, I couldn't sleep much last night."

"Nor did I when you called me, Harry!" replied Sara Newman, chair of Cambridge's technical research department. "To think of the possibilities of what this box might contain is quite mind-boggling!"

"Or even the odds of coming across a find like this after nearly three centuries," followed Professor Andrews.

The two distinguished researchers stood just inches away from the observation table staring down in childlike amazement at the inconspicuous box on the table. As if anxiously waiting to discover the contents of their first Christmas present, they had every right to be excited over such a find. The Reverend Geoffrey Edkins, Rector of Sampford Parrish, had recently informed the Cambridge University personnel that his family had long been in possession of several theological letters and manuscripts belonging to John Craig, a long time friend of Sir Isaac Newton. Reverend Edkins decided the manuscripts would serve a nobler purpose by being opened to the world and it was time he donated John Craig's manuscripts to the world's oldest and largest institution of public information, the Cambridge Library.

"Well, I have only one thing to say," Professor Andrews commented as he turned to face his equally mesmerized colleague. "Let's find out what Mr. Craig has been dying to tell us after almost three hundred years."

"I'm with you, Harry. Let's get started!"

The two British researchers had every reason to be excited. Besides being in possession of such an extraordinary find, this would mark their first opportunity to use their newly installed clean room. Before entering the twelve-by-twenty-foot stainless steel chamber, Professor Newman assisted Professor Andrews with the cumbersome task of putting on the required multi-piece clean suit. Once outfitted, Professor Andrews opened the first of two stainless doors. With his precious cargo tucked tightly under his arm, the professor first entered a very small four-by-four-foot airlock chamber. Within a few short seconds of entering, a green light positioned above a second door began to flash, informing the professor the chamber air was now clean enough for him to enter the main observation room. Like a child anxiously awaiting entrance into an amusement park, Professor Andrews couldn't wait for his first chance to enter this brightly lit room equipped with everything a researcher of antiquities would ever need to study such rare documents.

While Sara Newman viewed the video relay from her office desktop computer located outside the clean room, Professor Andrews positioned the sealed box on a stainless steel observation table directly under an overhead video camera. Next, he carefully opened the top flaps of the box, each sealed with Velcro. Inside the box appeared to be separate manuscripts sealed in transparent vinyl bags, one stacked securely on top of the other. In all, Professor Andrews removed three separate vinyl bags and carefully placed each on the table.

"Where do you suggest I start?" Professor Andrews asked his colleague, whose image was projected on the video monitor screen directly in front of him.

"Why don't you start first with what appears to me as bound documents on the right and work your way over to the unbound papers to your left. I'll get ready now and position my camera directly over each document just in case we strike gold."

Pulling back the Velcro strips on the first bag, Professor Andrews carefully removed the first document and placed it on the table. The first thing he noticed was that its aged leather cover was still remarkably intact. Leaning closer, the professor's eyes widened and his jaw dropped as he viewed a faded, but clearly visible Latin inscription on its cover.

"Oh, my!" Professor Andrews exclaimed. "Sara, I think we may have struck gold on the very first try!" The professor stepped back allowing Professor Newman to zoom in her image of the inscription. "Sara, look carefully at the inscription!" Andrews declared. "I believe this could be the original manuscript of *Theologiae Christianae Principia Mathematica* that Craig had published in 1699! If I can remember correctly, Craig believed there was some kind of mathematical relationship between Christ's return and the diminishing belief over time in biblical Truth. We have a copy of this text on file upstairs, but it's not the original."

"We bloody well do now! Harry, I'm too excited right now to take images. Why not just open all the bags and we'll go back and digitize them later!"

"Why not!" Professor Andrews soundly agreed. "It's a little before seven. We have all day!"

Carefully positioning the first set of documents to the far right side of the examining table, Professor Andrews placed the second bag directly under the overhead camera. This bag appeared to contain two items: the first, an unsealed envelope addressed to John Craig, and the second, a faded, but amazingly well-preserved black bound notebook. Professor Andrews first carefully removed the envelope from the vinyl bag.

"Harry, the writing on the envelope is not Craig's!" Sara Newman observed.

"I agree," Professor Andrews affirmed. "My impression is that it's a woman's handwriting. Here we go. I'm removing what appears to be a folded letter from the envelope."

Sara Newman pressed her face even closer to her computer screen, watching every move Professor Andrews made as he carefully attempted to remove the fragile contents of the envelope. "Harry, look at the date at the top and the signature at the bottom of the letter."

"It's dated Saturday, March 18, 1727. This letter is signed at the bottom by Newton, but it is definitely not his handwriting!" Professor Andrew declared as he carefully secured the four edges of the letter with safety clips. "I believe it was written by Catherine Barton Conduitt, Newton's niece!"

"Why would you think that?" Professor Newman questioned. "Well, according to John Conduitt's biography on Newton, it was Catherine Conduitt who remained at her uncle's bedside up until his death. Sara, Do you know what this means?"

"What?" Sara demanded. "What are you saying Harry? You're driving me batty!"

"I believe Newton dictated this letter to his niece while on his deathbed. He died on Monday, March 20th! Dear Lord, Sara. You are not going to believe this. Don't wake me up! Don't even wake me up!"

"What is it, Harry? What does it say?"

Professor Andrew stared directly up at the overhead video camera and smiled through his clear plastic visor.

"Sara, you know how we thought all this time Newton was a

bloody Unitarian and he didn't believe in the doctrine of the Trinity?"

"Well, Newton didn't come out and make that fact public, but I believe his writings leaned in that direction."

"Not anymore!" Professor Andrews declared as he pointed to the second line of the faded letter resting securely on the observation table.

"Let me see that!" Professor Newman demanded as she once again pressed her face against the computer monitor. Professor Andrews moved to the side of the overhead camera to allow his associate full view of the letter. Now it was Sara Newman whose eyes widen and bottom jaw dropped.

"Oh my God!" Newman shouted out. "Newton rescinded it on his deathbed! Nothing can top this. Not even an autographed copy of the bloody Ten Commandments!"

"I think we may have topped that, Sara," Professor Andrews commented as he once again stared up into the overhead video monitor. "You don't know how close your last statement was from the truth!" he declared.

"What are you talking about, Harry?" asked his giddy associate.

"I'm looking right now at the inscription on the front cover of the black notebook."

"Don't tell me it's bloody Hebrew," Professor Newman stated in a calm controlled voice. "I'll die!"

"It's Hebrew, Sara!" Andrews proclaimed. "And its translated '*Our Blessed Hope.*' "

"What in the world is Craig doing with a notebook written in Hebrew?" Sara asked.

"Let's find out," Professor Andrews replied as he carefully moved the remarkably well-preserved document's cover in plain view of the camera. "I am carefully opening the cover to the first page."

Silence.

"Harry, what's wrong?" Sara demanded. "Is there nothing there? Are the pages removed?" Again, Harrison Andrews stepped out of the view of the camera to give Professor Newman an unimpeded view.

"Oh, my God!" Professor Newman exclaimed with tears streaming down her face. Then, silence.

"It's Newton! It's bloody Newton!" Sara Newman shouted out with her arms wildly waving all about. "It's his handwriting and it's written in his damned alchemy! Please say I'm not dreaming!"

"You're not dreaming; it's his bloody writing," Professor Andrews confirmed looking again up into the camera. "Look at the top of the page. Newton signs all of his alchemy journals using a pseudonym he made up for himself, Jehovah Sanctus Unus—that is, Jehovah, the Holy One."

"Harry, isn't that a little chauvinistic or even blasphemic!"

"On the surface, one might think that," Andrews agreed, "but you must remember who Newton thought he was. He truly thought of himself as one of the chosen few—ordained at birth to receive God's special wisdom. He saw himself in the same class as Moses, Plato, and Galileo. The name Jehovah Sanctus Unus was simply a musing concoction of Newton's imagination. He didn't intend it to be blasphemous or disrespectful."

"Harry, can you decode Newton's alchemy?" Sara Newman asked.

"To a degree, but I am far from an expert," Professor Andrews admitted. "Tell you what, find me the phone number and email address of that Yank from NSA, Dr. Ezra Schroeder. We'll give him a buzz."

"Isn't he the American chap who was here last summer doing research into the theological papers found in the second edition of Newton's Principia?" Professor Newman inquired. "I believe he published a book on that topic."

"Indeed, a number one best seller," Professor Andrews replied. "He was also quite helpful in decoding some of Newton's alchemy journals for me. That is his full-time profession you know, analyzing secret codes for the Yanks."

"I'll get right on it, Harry," Sarah replied as she jotted down the name on a slip of paper.

"On second thought, Sara, just email him and inform Schroeder that we will be in contact. Don't say anything about our find. I'll call him at noon today," Professor Andrews interjected. "No need waking him from his sleep. It's only two a.m. in the States."

As this exciting drama unfolded, Professors Newman and Andrews were completely unaware that they were not alone in the research lab. Standing in the same room were two towering angelic beings. One, polished bronze in appearance, dressed in a brilliant white garment held securely at his waist with a golden belt, and the other, a mighty olive-skinned giant, dressed as a warrior protected by a highly polished golden breastplate, a golden belt with a securely attached, blindingly brilliant golden sword.

"Mission accomplished, Ariel!" proudly proclaimed the mighty warrior as he placed his massive hand on the shoulder of his fellow angelic companion. "Without questioning, you have patiently stood by and carried out your assignment to perfection. The Lord is well pleased with you."

"It is my sole honor and my duty to serve our God and Creator, Jesus the Christ," Ariel humbly stated as he bowed low on one knee before the mighty angelic warrior.

"You have qualified yourself highly for what is to follow and I promise you, Ariel, there will be no idle standing on this mission. The Lord has selected you for one of the most exciting and purposeful missions of any of His guardian angels. In this sense, your charge has not changed. You will continue your mission guarding and protecting the contents of Newton's notebook, but this time, you will be given new assistance. The Lord has promoted you to Chief Guardian Protectorate of His Prophetic Will. Along with your promotion, you will now be given divine insight into your mission's purpose. The prophetic message that our Lord gave to Isaac Newton contains a sealed code not to be revealed until God's designated time. Up until this very moment neither man nor spirit has knowledge of it. It is your mission to make absolutely sure that this prophetic code arrives safely in the hands of its intended interpreter, Dr. Ezra Schroeder. You are to protect him from all attacks from the enemy, for once God's plan

is revealed, Satan's wrath will be merciless. I am authorized by God on High to supply you with the complete assistance from four of God's most capable archangels, warrior princes specialized in their assigned command to attack and defeat the enemy."

As the mighty angelic warrior proceeded, three other mighty angelic beings made their appearance in the room. Each was a towering giant in his own right, garbed as the first with a golden breastplate, a golden belt, and a mighty golden sword, differing only in skin tones, facial features and hair color. One by one, each warrior stepped forward to raise his sword high in honor of their Lord God as their individual names and titles were announced.

Kiel, known as the Demon Slayer, was the first warrior called to raise his sword. Kiel was massive by any standards. His perfectly sculptured, muscular body was covered literally from head to toe with the most brilliantly shining golden body armor found anywhere in the universe. "Kiel can discern a demonic plan of attack even before they've conceived it themselves. He has charge of over a thousand angelic warriors at any given moment. Kiel will safeguard your mission."

Yahriel was the name of the next warrior called to step forward to raise his sword. "Yahriel is the prince of prophetic wisdom and worldly affairs. He has full knowledge of the present national and international earthly affairs and how they're aligned with our Lord's prophetic plans. Yahriel's angels are stationed in every nation, every capitol, and every city on earth. His wisdom is critical to the completion of your mission."

Muriel, Archangel and prince of Truth, was the next name announced. "Muriel is charged with making absolutely sure that the Lord's Truth is preached and communicated throughout the world in these end times. This directive is firmly established in God's word and Muriel and his angelic hosts are charged with fulfilling this mission. Once the contents are unsealed, you will require Muriel's assistance to communicate God's prophetic message to the world."

There was one final introduction remaining. The great warrior stepped forward and stood face to face with Ariel. "From this moment on, I, Michael, Archangel of the Living God, will give you my complete and unobstructed assistance. My orders come directly from our Lord God and

I am charged to carry out His prophetic plans. I am also the angel called to protect the people of the covenant and to secure God's covenant land, Israel."

Michael paused momentarily and proceeded to point in the direction of the remaining journal still held securely on the examining table.

"The message concealed in this human document contains the time of nation Israel's appointment with destiny. Ariel, I leave you now with this final charge for your mission."

As Ariel knelt before the great Archangel, Michael drew out his brilliant gold sword and proceeded to tap Ariel first on his right shoulder, then on his left. In a brilliant flash of light and vivid colors, Ariel's appearance instantly transformed into that of a great warrior angel, complete with a golden breastplate and a golden sword.

"Follow and protect the oracle who was chosen to decipher the sealed message contained in Newton's journal. Fulfill your mission to the glory of the Lord of Lords and the King of Kings who was, and is, and is to come, whose Kingdom has no end!"

Chapter Three

"For he shall give his angels charge over thee, to keep thee in all thy ways."

Psalm 91: 11 KJV

Monday, August 28th
8:45 p.m. Eastern Time
Baltimore Washington International Airport

For the past two weeks, an unusual series of strong tropical weather systems played havoc all up and down the Atlantic coast, canceling and delaying flights from Florida to New England. One particular flight, British Airways flight 228, originally schedule to depart from Baltimore's BWI at 8:45 p.m. on Friday, August 26th destined for London had to be cancelled and rescheduled for three consecutive days. Finally, on Monday August 28th, radar showed the entire Atlantic basin free of any tropical systems and British Airways flight 228, a large Boeing 767, took off on time for a seven-hour non-stop flight to London's Heathrow International Airport. The vast majority of the 250 passengers on board were vacationers, either American tourists heading for an exciting vacation in England or British tourists returning home after vacationing in the States.

There was one person onboard who fit neither category. An older, very distinguished looking gentleman, with snow white hair adorning the sides of his partially bald head, sat alone at a window seat admiring the spectacular view of the sun setting in the western sky. As the jumbo passenger jet banked toward a more easterly direction, the sky outside the window darkened. The older gentleman reclined in his seat and closed his eyes, dreaming of the exciting possibilities awaiting him when he arrived the next morning in England.

Tuesday, August 29th
9:05 a.m. GMT
Heathrow International Airport, London, England

"Dr. Schroeder! Dr. Ezra Schroeder," called out a voice with a familiar British accent from among the friends and family members gathered at the entrance to British Airway's arrival Gate 6. Stepping out from the anxious crowd was a stately gentleman, perhaps in his late fifties. Standing trim, over six feet tall, he wore a brown tweed suit and matching tweed cap that covered a full head of graying hair. His distinguished face was graced by a shadow of a gray moustache and a strong cleft chin.

"Harry Andrews!" Dr. Schroeder declared as the two men locked right hands and shook vigorously. Long after the crowds had come and gone, the two old friends from across "the pond" remained standing in front of the empty arrival gate still getting reacquainted.

"I was beginning to think this day would never come," Schroeder jokingly commented.

"Who would have dreamt two hurricanes and a new grandchild, all arriving in the same week!" Andrews stated as he continued to shake the hand of his friend from America. "How is the little tyke?"

"Perfect!" the proud grandfather replied. "Ezra Aaron MacDougal, eight pounds, four ounces, born at 3:22 a.m. August 16th."

"MacDougal!" Andrews declared with a big smile. "Now that is a strange Jewish last name!"

"Scottish!" Schroeder proclaimed. "My son-in-law Mark's grandfather was originally from Edinburgh, Scotland. Finally, after six beautiful granddaughters, I now have a grandson and he is named after me!"

"Mazel tov!" Professor Andrews congratulated his American friend with another handshake.

"And I believe Mazel tov is also in order for you and your library!" Schroeder reciprocated with a congratulatory pat on his English friend's shoulder. "Have you made the announcement about your find yet?" Schroeder asked.

"We were hoping that once you had time to study the documents, we could announce the findings together." Professor Andrews proudly proclaimed. "After all, Ezra, you are the star on the world's stage right now! Your book is quite the talk of England."

"I owe it all to you, Harry," Schroeder humbly stated. "If it wasn't for your help over the past few years, *Newton's Passion* would never have been written."

"Nevertheless," Andrews smiled, "you are the one with the gift of interpreting Newton."

"And you, my dear English friend, are the one with the car!" Schroeder commented as he jokingly looked down at his watch. "Why don't we continue this discussion on our way to Cambridge?"

"My dear American chap, I bloody well second that!" Andrews agreed with the nod of his head. "Let's go downstairs to pick up your baggage. The car is parked directly across from the terminal." With that said, the reacquainted friends left the arrival gate and walked promptly in the direction of the terminal escalator that led downstairs to the baggage area.

Once downstairs, Professor Andrew turned to his guest and commented, "Now, if you don't mind cafeteria food, we'll get a spot of lunch at the university before our afternoon appointment with Sir Isaac. If we leave now, we should be in Cambridge before noon."

Tuesday, August 29th
11:30 *a.m. GMT*
Cambridge University Library
Cambridge, England

The entire drive from England's main airport northeast to the town of Cambridge consisted of a blended maze of modern motorways and country roads. In a little over two hours, after weaving a course around a dozen or more picturesque English towns and hamlets, Professor Andrews and his American guest had arrived at their final destination, the college town of Cambridge.

Tourists from all over the world descended upon this quaint English town known for its wonderful fusion of English history and breathtakingly lush, green gardens built along the picturesque banks of the Cam River. The town's main attraction was its famed university. The University of Cambridge, a confederation of world-renown colleges, faculties, museums, and other institutions all bound within the city limits of the town of the same name, was one of the oldest universities in the world and one of the largest in the United Kingdom. Its academic fame had attracted a host of English noblemen and royalty throughout the centuries and had inspired some of the world's most influential scientists, such as Isaac Newton, Charles Darwin, Ernest Rutherford, James Clark Maxwell, James Watson and Francis Crick, Stephen Hawking, as well as over eighty Nobel Prize winners.

With most of the streets leading into the university closed to traffic for all or part of the day, parking spaces were limited to university faculty staffers and faculty. Fortunately, the library's head secretary had a reserved parking space positioned directly in front of the Cambridge University Library for Professor Andrews and his guest.

"Well, my good friend, we are back home," Professor Andrew proudly stated as he pulled back on the handle of his emergency brake and turned off the key to his late model Mercedes. Sitting back momentarily to reflect the magnificent structure before them, the driver asked his awestruck passenger, "Ezra, does this scene bring back any memories?"

"It doesn't seem possible that two years have passed by so quickly. It seems like I was here only yesterday," Schroeder admitted.

The Cambridge University Library, established during the late fifteenth century with fewer than 600 volumes, mostly religious in nature, is today one of the great research libraries of the world. With many additions and changes taking place over the centuries, the present two-story structure was completed in 1934. In 2000, the library contained over 6,000,000 books, rare documents and periodical volumes (excluding maps and sheet music), covering all the disciplines taught in the university.

"That's what I love about the beauty of this old building," Dr. Andrews continued. "From the outside, nothing has changed much since Sir Isaac walked up these very steps over 300 years ago. But on the inside, now that's quite a different story. There have been a few changes since you were here last."

"Well, why are we sitting here?" Professor Schroeder commented as he proceeded to unbuckle his seat beat and open the passenger side door. "Let's go in and see!" Professors Schroeder and Andrews promptly exited the car and walked directly up the steps leading to the front entrance of the library. Looking up, a massive twelve-story tower rose stately above the main entrance of the library. Once inside, the main entrance hall was a breath-taking site to behold. Its high cathedral ceiling and dark walnut-stained walls were adorned with large original paintings of former British statesmen and royalty, including a large portrait of Sir Isaac Newton himself. A guard stationed at the front information desk acknowledged Professor Andrews and his guest with a hand wave and a "Top of the morning" as they walked by.

With the noon hour quickly approaching, the professors both agreed that the first order of business was lunch. Even though the university was not in session for the summer, the Tea Room, a cafeteria locate on the library's north wing, was filled with hungry tourists visiting the world's most famous library. Once in the Tea Room, the two professors picked up their food trays and made their way to the end of the long cafeteria line. The buffet style menu included a variety of hot lunches and sandwiches, a salad bar, and of course, the main staples of the Tea Room, a table well stocked with delicious-looking pastries, scones, croissants and the drink of choice, tea.

With only the checkout counter remaining along the buffet line, Professor Andrews turned his attention to the sparsely filled tray of the person directly ahead of him. "Ezra, aren't you famished after such a long flight? All you have on your tray is a small tossed salad and a cup of tea!"

"Doctor's orders," Ezra Schroeder replied. "My cholesterol was up on my last check up and I promised Rachel that I would watch what I eat while I'm away."

"Ezra, I believe my Diane is making a pot roast tonight. It's not too late to call her and change tonight's menu to something more appropriate."

"I can't resist a good pot roast," Schroeder conceded. "If I eat a healthy lunch now, I don't believe Rachel would mind if I had some pot roast for supper."

"Ezra, I see someone we both know sitting all by herself over against that far wall," Professor Andrews observed as he stepped away from the cashier. "She's been relentlessly bugging me about your arrival. Why don't we join her?" With food trays in hand, the two professors made their way across the crowded Tea Room dining area over to a table occupied by a young woman, perhaps mid twenties, with short, reddish-brown hair pushed to the side. With her empty lunch tray pushed to the side, she leaned forward on the table, focusing her full attention on the pages of a thick novel.

"That must be a good book you're reading to keep you that glued to your seat!" stated a familiar voice.

"Professor Andrews!" exclaimed the young woman as she looked up from her book to see two men staring down at her.

"Dr. Schroeder, you remember Lydia Long?"

"Of course I remember Lydia," Schroeder acknowledged looking down at the awestruck woman. "You were such a tremendous help to me the last time I was here." Two years prior, Lydia had been a graduate student assigned to cataloging the Earl of Macclesfield's vast collection of Isaac Newton's mathematical and scientific papers. After her graduation from the University, she accepted a position at the library cataloging newly acquired rare documents.

. "Dr. Schroeder, tell me if this isn't dèjá vu?" Lydia blurted out. "I'm sitting here at this very moment reading your book!" Lydia paused briefly to gather her thoughts before continuing.

"Oh, Dr. Schroeder, do we ever need your help right now!" she exclaimed. "That bloody Newton is at it again, trying to confound us mortals with metaphors and riddles that are beyond our comprehension."

"Lydia, do you mind if we join you?" asked Professor Andrews.

"Professor Andrews, you, of all people know how much I have been going on about Professor Schroeder. If you didn't sit here with me, you know I would plop myself at your table."

"What did I tell you, Ezra?" Professor Andrews boasted as he and Schroeder took their respective places across from their new host.

Lydia Long had every right to be excited. She was sitting across the table from the only person who could possibly shed light on John Craig's mysterious documents. Finally, she could no longer contain her enthusiasm.

"Professor Schroeder, I hope you don't find it rude of me acting this way, but I am so excited about the Craig documents. I feel like I'm going to burst if I don't tell somebody about it!"

"Please, don't do that!" Dr. Schroeder chuckled. "So tell me, Lydia, what did you find out so far?"

"I'll show you as soon as you've downed your lunch," Lydia proudly declared. "We'll go straight down to the lab." Aware that time was of the essence, the professors wasted little time finishing their lunches. Once lunch was completed, the threesome exited the Tea Room together. Their final destination was the imaging lab, located on the North Wing's ground floor. Once inside the imaging room, Professor Schroeder was greeted by yet another familiar face.

"Professor Newman, we meet again," Schroeder announced.

"Ezra, forget the formalities," Sara Newman responded with a brief handshake. "Around here, just call me Sara. How was your flight across the pond?"

"The best," Schroeder replied. "I slept almost the entire way."

"Harry tells me you'll be here until Friday."

"Actually, Thursday will be my last day spent here in the lab. My flight back to Washington leaves early Friday."

"Well then, we have bloody little time to waste," Sara confirmed. "But before you actually sit down in front of a computer and get to work, Lydia has a bit of a surprise for you."

"Ok, Professor Schroeder," Lydia acknowledged. "If you would please follow us back out into the hall, there is something we would like you to see."

Lydia Long escorted the professors down the ground level hallway toward the projection room, an instructional classroom equipped with a ceiling mounted LCD projector used to display presentations on a large screen.

Walking closely behind the human researchers were two towering angelic giants garbed in dazzling white robes. Each wore a protective golden breast plate and had a golden sword securely attached to their glistening golden belts.

Muriel, the taller of the two angelic beings, had a stance over eight feet. Even in angel standards, Muriel was exceedingly handsome. He was cropped with curly brown hair, dark olive skin, velvet brown eyes, cupid shaped lips, and a strong chiseled chin.

In contrast, Ariel's stance was slightly over seven feet tall. He had free flowing light brown hair, bronze colored skin, and a beautiful pair of sky blue colored eyes.

"Ariel, it is time." Muriel announced.

"Muriel, I have a question." Ariel turned and asked, "I am curious. Of all the humans, why has God selected Schroeder to possess the Message?"

"Two reasons," Muriel replied with a smile. "Not only is Ezra Schroeder a true descendent of Abraham, but he is also a strong believer in the Truth. Secondly, as with the prophet Daniel, God predestined Ezra Schroeder for this present task. And like Daniel, this human is a man of true courage and faith. I was the angel who told Daniel to seal up the prophecy for such a time as this. Very soon now, as God's Spirit leads, I will transfer that same message into the heart and spirit of Ezra Schroeder. You will then be charged with protecting this human from all attacks of the enemy. The moment Schroeder announces to the world that he knows the secret of Daniel's Prophecy, Satan and all demons in hell will do everything in their power to stop him."

"Muriel, I have one further question," Ariel innocently asked. "Newton

was not a true child of Abraham. Why was he selected to understand the Prophetic Message?"

"Of all the humans who ever lived, God's Spirit found Isaac Newton to be a true seeker of the very essence of His Truth. God's Word says, 'If you will seek after the Lord your God, you will find Him if you search for Him with all your heart and with all your soul.' Scripture also says, 'Delight thyself in the Lord; and he shall give thee the desires of your heart." Newton's heart's desire was to find God's Truth concerning the mysteries of God's creation. God's Spirit answered Newton's request by revealing to this one man hidden clues to God's creative power."

"But didn't Newton eventually stray from the Truth?" Ariel asked. "He believed for a time the doctrine of demons that the Godhead was false and that Jesus, the second person of the Godhead, was not Divine, but a created being."

"What you say is true," Muriel replied. "For the later years of Newton's life, he chose to separate himself from the Truth. During that time, all Divine revelations had ceased, and Newton anguished for many years over his failed accomplishments. It wasn't until his final days that Newton truly repented of his misleading. With his relationship with God restored, God's Spirit revealed to Newton the ultimate revelation, the meaning behind the prophetic message passed down from Daniel."

Lydia Long entered the room first, taking her place in front of a demonstration desk equipped with a laptop computer. The three professors followed behind, selecting their seating along the front row aisle.

Muriel and Ariel remained standing directly in back of the professors.

"This looks exciting," Schroeder jested. "Are we going to see a movie?"

"A Lydia Long production!" Professor Andrews announced to a small round of applause from the three seated professors.

"Ezra, before you actually begin to work this afternoon," Professor Andrews interjected, "we asked Lydia to prepare a PowerPoint presentation showing you what we have gleaned so far from Craig's documents. This way we can all view the documents in detail and possibly answer any questions you might have."

"Excellent idea!" Schroeder cheerfully agreed. "But you shouldn't have gone through all this trouble just for me."

"Not at all!" Sara affirmed. "Once you have finished deciphering the last of the documents, we eventually plan to show a finished presentation to the entire university and the general public."

"Now, if everyone is ready," Professor Andrews interjected. "Lydia, the stage is all yours."

On cue, Lydia clicked the computer mouse and the first PowerPoint slide projected on the large screen directly above where she was seated.

Lydia began the presentation with a series of introductory slides showing Professor Andrews carefully removing and displaying the three newly discovered documents on the examining table. "As you will soon see, the first two documents are simply straightforward. They require no interpretation. Document one, published in 1699, is John Craig's *Theologiae Christianae Principia Mathematica,* accounting Craig's personal belief that there was a mathematical relationship between Christ's return and the diminishing belief over time in biblical Truth. What makes this document such a find is that this is Craig's original manuscript. We had an old copy on display, but now, we have the original! The entire manuscript was written in Latin, but once the final presentation is ready, we will have an audio translation spoken in English for the general public.

"Professor Schroeder, I'm sure you are very familiar with Craig's work," Professor Newman commented. "Do you have any specific questions or requests about it before we go on to the second document?"

"Yes, Lydia, could you turn to the beginning of chapter three. I would like to translate Craig's first sentence if you don't mind."

"Just give me a second, Professor Schroeder, and I'll find it… Found it! I'll have it up on the screen with the click of a mouse."

First, Schroeder read the entire opening sentence of Craig's chapter three in its original Latin. He then went on and translated it into eloquent English. "If God does not exist, the skeptic loses nothing by believing in him; but if he does exist, the skeptic gains eternal life by believing in him."

"Bravo, well said!" stated Muriel. Ariel smiled.

Professor Newman looked over at Professor Andrews and simply rolled her eyes. Unfortunately, Schroeder caught her petty act of disbelief.

"Any other requests, Dr Schroeder, before we go onto the second document?" Lydia asked.

Schroeder simply shook his head and said, "No. Please continue."

Clicking the mouse again, Lydia projected the next document onto the screen. "The next series of slides," she continued, "will show a short, one-page, handwritten letter. Professors Newman, Andrews and I are now in complete agreement that this letter was written by Catherine Barton Conduitt, Isaac Newton's niece. If you look carefully at the bottom of the letter, the signature is not hers. It is signed by her uncle, Isaac Newton."

"Harry, this is the famous retraction letter that you were telling me about!" Schroeder sighed in amazement. "Did you tell anybody yet?"

"If you mean did we tell the press, no, not yet," Professor Andrews replied. "The University's Chancellor and his staff are aware of it, but they decided it best to wait until all of the documents are fully understood before releasing the find to the public. Everyone agrees that this is too big to announce just yet. We must first make absolutely sure that we dot all of our 'I's' and cross all of our 'T's.'

"And that is where I come in," Schroeder followed.

"Precisely," Andrews affirmed. "We are all hoping that sometime between now and Friday, you will be able to tell us the meaning of Newton's message found in the third document."

"What about the journal?" Schroeder asked Lydia, referring to the remaining document. "Is it similar to the others we looked at two years ago?" Schroeder was referring to a box full of Newton's recently discovered alchemy notes.

"Let's take a look." Lydia announced into the microphone stationed on the desk.

The next series of slides showed views of the final document, a faded black leather bound notebook, the same type Newton used to record his notes for his alchemy experiments.

"To our surprise, for a three-hundred-year-old document, it was amazingly well preserved. The original is in an airtight vacuum bag stored on a shelf in a climate-controlled room with the rest of Newton's manuscripts and documents. In all, the journal consists of fourteen pages, all written in Newton's own handwriting. At first, we thought it was simply one of Newton's lost alchemy journals like the ones discovered in 1936, but upon further inspection, we believe it is something far greater. From what we can gather so far, Newton truly outdid himself on this work."

"How so?" Schroeder asked.

"Each bloody page is a coded enigma. It appears that old Sir Isaac decided to make this journal his final masterpiece of confusion, filling every page with twists and turns and metaphoric mazes. Not only is it filled with alchemy terms, the bloody devil uses Arabic number codes as well!"

"Ingenious. But why would he take such painstaking care in making this particular journal so difficult to interpret?" Schroeder asked.

"The title, for one, is written in Hebrew," Lydia informed their guest. "No other document of Newton's has any shred of Hebrew whatsoever."

After viewing the entire series of slides showing Newton's newly discovered journal, Dr. Schroeder sat motionless, just staring at the final slide projected on the screen. Professor Andrews turned to his right and noticed the dazed look on Professor Schroeder's face. "Ezra, what on earth do you suppose would prompt Newton to write an entire journal in ancient alchemy and a title written in Hebrew?"

"Because this is not a typical journal composed of simple alchemy recipes," Schroeder admitted. "The metaphors he used seem to be leading more toward places, dates, times, and events more than anything else. I may need more than three days to crack this puzzle!"

Thursday, August 31*st*
10:30 *a.m. GMT*
The Digital Research Lab
Lower Ground Floor of the Cambridge Library

Had Ezra Schroeder finally met his match? Throughout college, he was a confident, straight-A student. He had graduated near the top in his class at MIT where he taught mathematics for over ten years before accepting a position as a senior cryptologist at the National Security Agency in Maryland. No matter how difficult the code, Schroeder could always find an algorithm to solve it. Now at the age of 66, a semi-retired Ezra Schroeder was working for NSA as a part-time consultant in times of national emergencies.

But even in his senior years, he still prided himself as the master code breaker; that is, up until today. For three straight days, working in front of a computer monitor from morning until night with the best software available, Schroeder found himself in a position he had never experienced before, a state of complete frustration. Nothing made any sense. Newton's entire text appeared as a hodgepodge of Arabic numerology, ancient Roman and Greek mythology, and mystical Jewish Kabbalahism all placed in a blender.

In an act of desperation, Schroeder placed his head between his hands and cried out to the only one who could possibly help him.

"Lord, I come to you now with a big request. You are well aware that I have sat here in front of this computer for days now, attempting, to the best of my ability, to understand what Newton is trying to tell me, but I am no further along now than when I first started. I ask you, in the name of my Lord and Savior, Yeshua, to show me, in exact detail, what the message is that Newton has written in this journal. I sincerely repent for attempting to do this feat solely on my own power, and I ask for your Holy Spirit to now guide my thoughts and give me supernatural wisdom to solve this impossible puzzle.

Again, I ask this in the name above all names, Your Son and our Messiah, Yeshua."

"God's Spirit says it is now Schroeder's time," stated Muriel.

"Will you reveal the entire message to him?" Ariel asked.

"No," Muriel replied. "For now, only in part. Rulers and kingdoms will soon be in place, but now is not the time to reveal the entire prophecy."

With that said, the Archangel Muriel placed his mighty left hand upon Schroeder's head, raising his right hand toward heaven, and proclaimed in a thunderous voice.

"Who is worthy to open the book, and break its seals? Behold, only one, the Lion that is from the tribe of Judah, the Root of David, has overcome so as to open the Book and its seals. By the power granted to me, Muriel, Archangel of Him who lives forever and ever, I answer this human's request and now impart and unseal the prophecy given by the prophet Daniel so long ago for this end of time generation."

As if struck by a bolt of lightning, a single thought began to permeate every neuron in Schroeder's brain. *The title is the clue! The title is Hebrew for "Our Blessed Hope," an expression used by Paul in the book of Titus for the time of Yeshua's return!* Tears of thanks welled up in Schroeder's eyes. He knew beyond a doubt that God Himself had answered his prayer.

The title is written in Hebrew. Hebrew letters and numbers are synonymous. Praise God! That's it. All the Arabic numbers are Hebrew letters, all the Arabic letters are Hebrew numbers. The Greek and Roman alchemy metaphors must also be translated in Hebrew. Everything must be translated into Hebrew!

Immediately, Schroeder opened the PDF file where Lydia had placed the entire text of Newton's manuscript. Reaching into his brief case, he unzipped the center compartment and pulled out a flash drive that contained a program for converting multiple languages and numbers into Hebrew. For the next seven hours, Schroeder worked non-stop changing every word, symbol, letter, and number that Newton had written in his journal to Hebrew. At five o'clock, even though he had translated the entire text of Newton's journal into Hebrew, Schroeder wasn't finished; his task had just begun. It would be several more weeks before he could fully interpret the meaning of Newton's Riddle.

Even with our best intentions, time sometimes ends up being the ultimate winner. Dr. Schroeder's three-day visit to Cambridge ended before he could fully interpret Newton's mysterious journal, but he wasn't disappointed. He arrived in Cambridge on Tuesday not knowing what to expect, and left on Friday with the full knowledge that he was in possession of a treasure far more valuable than his wildest dreams could ever imagine.

Before leaving Cambridge, Schroeder assured Professor Andrews and Newman that he was confident he would be able to forward the university the full meaning of Newton's journal no later than the end of September. He was also acutely aware that for at least the next few weeks his daily schedule would be a whirlwind adventure filled with book signings and radio and television promotions for his best selling book, *Newton's Passion.* In spite of all the exciting challenges ahead, Schroeder could sense a peace and a presence of God more than any other time in his life. He knew beyond a doubt that God was totally in control and His will would be done.

Chapter Four

"The Son of man shall send forth his angels, and they shall gather out of his kingdom all things that offend, and them which do iniquity."

Matthew 13:41 KJV

Tuesday, September 12th, 8 a.m.
Providence, Rhode Island
Main Studio Headquarters
Gospel Broadcasting Network (GBN)

Ariel was amazed. The passing of three hundred years had brought about so many changes in the natural world that even for a supernatural being, the term "overwhelmed" was an understatement. Though not quite angel speed yet, human travel had vastly improved since the days of Sir Isaac Newton. As Schroeder's guardian angel, Ariel's days of standing mostly in one secluded spot were a distant memory. Two human weeks had now passed and during that time, Ariel experienced his first airplane flight, riding onboard a jumbo jet across the ocean to a land that he had never visited before. Accompanying his protectorate, Ariel got to travel by car, subway, train, and jet to all of Schroeder's appointed destinations across this new and beautiful land called the United States of America. The final destination on Schroeder's two week book tour blitz was a guest appearance on one of the most popular worldwide Christian broadcasts, known simply by the acronym "PTW."

"I would like to welcome our next very special guest on PTW. He's a retired MIT mathematics professor and a senior cryptologist, that's code breaker for you and me, for the United States National

Security Agency, Dr. Ezra Schroeder. Dr. Schroeder is also a best selling author whose latest book, *Newton's Passion,* is presently rated number one on the New York Time's non-fiction bestseller's list. Dr. Schroeder and his wife, Rachel, reside in Rockville, Maryland, and are long time members of Beth Messiah, a messianic congregation located in Silver Springs, Maryland." With a gracious introduction, Tom Reid, president and host of the popular national and international daily Christian broadcast, PTW, stood up from his chair and extended a firm welcoming handshake to the older gentleman seated to his left. "Dr. Schroeder, as president of Preach the Word Ministries, it is my honor to have you on today's show."

"The honor is all mine, Dr. Reid," responded his guest, a distinguish looking gentleman somewhere in his mid to upper sixties. "Needless to say, my wife, Rachel, and I have been watching PTW ever since your wonderful father Patrick, God rest his soul, introduced all of America to Christian television over forty years ago."

"You're going way back to the glory days when I was just a boy. Dad was a struggling pastor of a small Pentecostal congregation over on Bay Side Avenue. Back then, we didn't have much money and as the story goes, both Mom and Dad heard separately, on the same day, the voice of God telling them to sink every penny they had into buying a small UHF television station along the banks of the Narragansett Bay. If I remember correctly, the signal back then was only strong enough to reach the other side of the bay," Tom joked.

"Well, it was strong enough to reach all the way across the border into the city of Boston because my wife and I were watching back then and through PTW, we both heard for the very first time the truth about our Messiah, Jesus. Yeshua has been our Messiah ever since. My wife and I pray for this great ministry everyday, along with our children, and now, even our seven grandchildren.

"Praise God, everyone!" Tom Reid sat back in his tall winged-backed chair and clapped his hands together. "Believe me when I say, what you just heard ladies and gentlemen was totally unplanned. I had no idea, Dr. Schroeder, that it was through PTW that you and your family have found the Lord. What a phenomenal testimony!" The entire studio audience stood up and applauded. "Dr. Schroeder," Tom continued, "we have never met before today but I can truly feel a real bond forming between us. Do you feel that same thing?"

"Tom, in Hebrew we call that *Mishpochah*, which means family." You and I are now family, Jew and gentile bonded through Messiah Jesus into one new man with a Jewish heart."

No sooner did the words proceed from Schroeder's lips than the two former strangers got out of their seats and warmly embraced each other sealing their newly formed kinship on national television. Again, the entire audience broke out into applause. Turning again toward the television cameras and the audience, Tom Reid jokingly replied. "I don't know about all of you, but I'm getting a strong urge for some matzo ball soup right about now!

The audience returned with laughter and applause.

"Dr. Schroeder, I'm definitely going to have you come back on the show. I'm afraid we are going to run out of time even before we get started today so let's talk about your newest book, *Newton's Passion*." With a more serious look on his face, the show's host held up for all to see a copy of a book displaying on its cover Sir Isaac Newton holding a magnifying glass over an opened Bible. "To be perfectly honest with you, I thought this was going to be some dry biography, way above my head, but once I started reading it, I literally could not put it down. Tell us, Dr. Schroeder, what kind of man was Isaac Newton?"

"Well, to the world, Isaac Newton was the genius of geniuses; possibly the greatest intellect who ever lived. But the truth of the matter is, during most of his life he was a miserable soul.

"How so, Dr. Schroeder?" Tom Reid inquired.

"As a child, he grew up a love-starved, insecure little boy, abandoned by his mother at the age of two to be raised by his grandparents. I truly believe that it was this experience of loss and betrayal at such a tender age that permanently damaged Newton's capacity for trust and friendship later in life."

"That is so sad!" Tom sympathetically replied. "What effect did this have on Newton as an adult?"

"The lesson he learned from these painful experiences during those early years was the meaning of rejection and how not to trust people. As an adult, Newton was deeply introverted and extremely protective of his privacy. He remained insecure throughout life, and was given to fits of depression and outbursts of violent temper, which at times led to violent and vindictive attacks against friend and foe alike. There are those who adamantly believe that his overexposure to mercury from numerous chemistry experiments brought on his bizarre behaviors, but I personally believe Newton was haunted as an adult by a host of childhood demons."

"Literal demons?"

"Literal, who knows?" Dr. Schroeder answered. "But as you can see, Newton's life was anything but happy. With that said, the reason I wrote the book is that I found Isaac Newton and I had many things in common."

"How so?" asked Tom.

"Well, for one, we both are seekers of Truth, following basically the same path. Our compass needle is mathematics and our map, the Holy Scriptures. There is one undeniable fact present in my book that is totally ignored and passed over by the scientific community at large. Sir Isaac Newton was the number one proponent of intelligent design."

"Say that again, Dr. Schroeder," Tom Reid interjected. "I don't think America was listening."

Facing the cameras head on, Dr. Schroeder boldly proclaimed. "It is absolutely true. As a scientist, Sir Isaac Newton was the number one proponent of intelligent design. Isaac Newton was a formidable biblical scholar and believed that God created everything, including the Bible. Surprisingly, only 12% of Newton's vast library contained books on the subjects of mathematics, physics and astronomy, the disciplines on which his scientific fame rests. This may shock some people, but the vast majority of Isaac Newton's books were on the subject of theology. Isaac Newton believed that the Bible is literally true in every respect. Throughout his life, he continually tested biblical truth against the physical truths of experimental and theoretical science. He never observed a contradiction. In fact, he viewed his own scientific work as a method by which to reinforce belief in biblical truth. Newton looked at the entire universe and all that is in it as a cryptogram set by the Almighty. A riddle that could be read simply by applying pure thought to certain evidence and clues that God had hidden throughout the universe. Newton sincerely believed that all would be revealed to him if only he could persevere to the end, uninterrupted, all by himself, no one coming into the room, reading, testing, no criticism, voyaging through God's ocean of thought alone."

"Could that be the reason why Newton never married?" Tom asked.

"Perhaps," Schroeder said. "Outside of his research, he had very little time leftover for relationships. But Newton had one final obsession, solving Bible prophecy. Newton assumed that by the same powers of his introspective imagination, he could solve the riddles of past and future events that he believed God encoded in the Bible, specifically in the books of Daniel and Revelation. To Newton's mind, it was clear that some prophecies would not be understood until the end of history. Listen while I read what Newton wrote concerning the timing of when these prophesies would be revealed."

"Dr. Schroeder," again Tom interjected. "Forgive me for interrupting, but before you read the words of Isaac Newton, we are going to project Newton's statements up on the screen so the folks watching at home can also read along."

> *This prophecy is called the Revelation, with respect to the Scripture of Truth, which Daniel was commanded to shut up and seal, till the time of the end. But in the very end, the Prophecy should be so far interpreted so as to convince many. Many at that time shall run to and fro, and knowledge shall be increased. Tis therefore a part of this prophecy that it should not be understood before the last age of the world. But if the last age, the age of the opening of these things, be now approaching, then it is my strong belief that*

the Almighty has impressed on me as an Interpreter, to be encouraged more than ever to look into these things.

"To put it simply," Dr. Schroeder continued, "the greatest physicist who ever lived, who worked out the mechanics of the solar system and the universe, spent the greater part of his lifetime attempting to treat the Bible as a source of scientific data. He truly believed that before he died God would reveal to him the secrets of prophesy that were locked inside the Bible."

"According to your book," Mr. Reid again interjected, "isn't it true that Newton never found the mathematical model for revealing hidden biblical prophecies? You wrote that Newton died still searching."

"That was a true statement at the time when I completed writing *Newton's Passion*, but I am here today to tell both you and the world, it isn't true now."

"Hold on, Dr. Schroeder. Are you now saying that Sir Isaac Newton actually discovered God's hidden message of past and future events before he died?"

"Almost one month ago to this very day, two British researchers from Cambridge University discovered what I would call one of the greatest theological finds of our time, a possible answer to Newton's riddle. Since their discovery in July, I traveled to Cambridge, England, examined those same documents, written by Newton himself, and I am presently attempting to decipher all of its content."

PTW's theme music began to play in the background signaling that the final minute of the program was approaching.

"What an exciting show we had today," Tom Reid announced toward the audience and the studio cameras. "Dr. Schroeder, you must promise to come back again soon and share this exciting discovery with us! And to our worldwide viewers of PTW, always remember, we'll be back here once again tomorrow, same time and same channel, to preach the Word. God bless you everyone and please don't forget to tell someone today that Jesus Christ is the reason for your joy."

It was a long standard practice for Tom Reid to answer the audience's questions directly after the end of each show, but today, he simply waved to the audience and exited toward the back of the stage while his team of co-hosts were cued to carry on his duties.

"Dr. Schroeder, do you have a few minutes?" Reid asked as he quickly approached the former MIT professor who was exiting through the back entrance of the PTW studios.

"Tom, call me Ezra," Schroeder replied as he placed his hand on the televangelist's shoulder.

"Ezra. I don't have to tell you that you have struck a strong cord of my curiosity. Why didn't you tell me about this discovery last week? We could have given you more time on the show to go into detail."

Dr. Schroeder paused for a moment and looked deep into Reid's eyes. "Tom, could you find time in your busy schedule to meet with me at my Maryland home sometime in the next few weeks? Of course, your wife is also invited. While Cindy and Rachel get to know each other, I'll show you something astounding that I discovered that could literally change the entire destiny of humans on planet earth."

"Ezra, with a challenge like that, how could I possibly refuse?" Tom jokingly accepted. "Tell you what, I'm scheduled to meet with my brother John next Friday in Washington for a dinner meeting to discuss politics. Why don't you and Rachel join us at the restaurant? My brother would love it. Politics aside, he's a real big fan of history and I know he'll die for an opportunity to pick your brain about Newton!"

"Sorry, but my smart, yiddish mother told me never to discuss religion and politics at the same table. It is very bad for digestion!" Schroeder replied in a semi serious tone. "Of course, speaking on behalf of my wife, we would love to be there. And Saturday, after morning services, you and your wife are invited to our home for a luncheon. Afterwards, I will show you what I have decoded so far from Newton's greatest riddle. You will be the first person besides myself to see it!"

Chapter Five

"But the Spirit explicitly says that in later times some will fall away from the faith, paying attention to deceitful spirits and doctrines of demons."

1 *Timothy* 4:1 NASB

Friday, September 22nd, 5:30 p.m.
Washington, D.C.
Caesar's Kitchen, an upscale Italian restaurant

With an old love melody sung by crooner Dean Martin softly playing in the background, a lone busboy scurried about putting the finishing touches on a large circular table reserved for a party of six along the far back corner of the Caesar's Kitchen Italian Restaurant, just two blocks away from the U.S. Capitol Building. The first members of the party to arrive were a husband and wife. While his wife went to the ladies' room located along the back hallway that led to the kitchen, her husband selected the left two chairs along the back wall.

"Tom, please excuse us, but we were running a little late. Traffic was a horrendous mess from New York Avenue all the way back to the beltway."

"No apologies needed. And you must be Dr. Schroeder?" Dr. Schroeder stood staring at the person seated at the table in a state of confusion.

"Before you think you've totally lost your mind, let me introduce myself, Dr. Schroeder. John Reid, Tom's twin brother. My brother has told me all about you, but obviously, going by the surprised look on your face, he hasn't told you a lot about me."

"You're twins!" Dr. Schroeder announced out loud.

"Mirror image twins to be exact; I'm left on everything, Tom's right!" John Reid followed.

"I've never seen two adult men look so much alike. It's amazing. Even your mannerisms appear identical!" Schroeder confessed with an obvious surprised expression.

"I'm afraid, Dr. Schroeder, that is where all of our similarities end. In the case of Tom and myself, when I say I'm left and Tom's right, I mean that quite literally. To give you an analogy in terms that a scientist like yourself can appreciate, if you could place my brother and I on the electromagnetic spectrum, I would be somewhere on the left side of radio waves and Tom would be on the far right side of gamma rays. Tom's pro-life, I'm pro-choice, Tom's against gay marriages, I'm their biggest supporter, Tom remained at home and took over the family business. I chose instead to leave and become the prodigal. Are you getting the picture?"

A slight nudge on his right side brought Ezra Schroeder's mind back to reality. "Oh, excuse me, Mr. Reid. I'd like to introduce you to my wife, Rachel."

"Mrs. Schroeder, the pleasure is all mine." Before Rachel Schroeder could graciously respond, a familiar voice rang out in the background.

"Sorry that we're late. Traffic was a beast out there," Tom Reid proclaimed as he and his wife, Cindy, entered the reserved dining section in the back of the restaurant. "Did I miss all the introductions?"

"Just getting started," John declared as he turned to see a familiar person approaching from the rear of the restaurant. "Now here comes my lovely Miranda." Miranda, John's second wife of less than a year, was not only an attractive blonde beauty, but also a recent Harvard Law school graduate.

"I believe I can safely say the gang's all here, and not a moment too soon may I add," John Reid announced to the party of six. "I have been so looking forward to eating some good veal parmesan. And take my word for it, no one makes veal parmesan like Caesar's Kitchen." With John's declaration, each member of the party took turns introducing each other. Even the restaurant's owner, Carmen Gambino, made his introductions.

"As owner of Caesars's Kitchen, it is truly my honor to have all of you here with us today. Anthony, our head waiter, who happens also to be my oldest son, will make sure your experience at Caesar's is an eating experience you will never forget. And to back up my words, as first time visitors, your selection of drinks and appetizers are on the house!" Every member of the dinner party was very impressed and applauded the owner's generosity.

Immediately, Anthony made his rounds taking orders from the restaurant's impressive selection of imported wines, while another waiter graciously passed out tempting samples of cheese- or meat-filled tortellini, breaded mozzarella, and antipasto.

"Besides good looks, my brother and I also share a common love for Italian food," Tom joked. "I suggest that we say the blessing now before we get started."

"You go right ahead," John followed. "But please don't wait for me. I really have to go to the little boy's room." Without giving his brother's request a second thought, Tom asked the remaining members of the party to hold hands and bow their head as he went on to thank God for bringing the entire group together in fellowship, to bless the wonderful meal that was set before them, and to bless the owners and staff at Caesar's Kitchen for preparing such a wonderful feast. With the completion of Tom's beautiful prayer, the sampling began.

"The cheese tortellini is delicious!" exclaimed Cindy Reid, Tom's wife.

"So is the breaded ravioli," Miranda commented.

"I'm afraid I'm not going to have room for the main course," Rachel Schroeder confessed.

"Dr. Schroeder, I must confess," John Reid commented as he returned to his seat, "I'm about the only person in America who has not read your book, but I did see that program that PBS ran called 'Newton's Dark Secret.' Your man Newton turns out to be a regular

Harry Potter with all that hocus pocus talk about mixing together green dragons and the menstrual blood of the sordid whore!"

"John, that's disgusting!" Miranda protested.

"It's true, Miranda," Schroeder interjected. "The thought of Newton actually using such bizarre language conjures up images of black magic and sinister, dark robed sorcerers, but those are the precise metaphors that Newton chose."

"Now, apologize!" John jokingly replied.

"You must understand that back in the 17h century, chemistry as we know it was just in its formative stages," Schroeder continued. "Those who dabbled in it back then were called alchemists. They had no access to a periodic chart. In reality, alchemists like Newton, didn't have a clue what an atom looked like. All they had was a basic understanding of how certain elements combined and a coded language called alchemy composed of ancient metaphors. The best way to look at these metaphors is in the light of riddles. The 'menstrual blood of a sordid whore' is a code riddle. The 'menstrual blood' simply means the metallic form of element antimony extracted from the 'sordid whore,' which is antimony's ore."

"I was under the impression that the practice of alchemy back then was illegal out of fear that some alchemist could possibly discover the so-called philosopher's stone, a way of changing common elements into gold."

"I am truly impressed with your knowledge on this subject, Mr. Reid," Schroeder admitted.

"I told you he would pick your brains," Tom laughed.

"Tom, your brother is absolutely right." Schroeder continued. "Before Newton came along, the practice of alchemy was declared illegal in fear that someone would actually discover the philosopher's stone and ruin the gold standard. I've studied most of Newton's experimental notebooks and I have come to the conclusion that Isaac Newton was indeed trying to produce the philosopher's stone."

"With all of his fame and notoriety, why would Newton jeopardize his reputation attempting something considered illegal?" Miranda Reid inquired.

Dr. Schroeder was in his glory. Next to his Lord and family, he loved talking about his favorite subject, Sir Isaac Newton. He folded his hands behind his head, leaned back in his chair and continued. "What you have to understand is that, more than anything else, Newton loved to solve riddles. The thought of being the first alchemist to discover the mystical formula for changing a common substance into gold was a challenge that Newton couldn't resist. That is the reason he, and others like him, wrote the details of their experiments under the veil of a secret code."

"Well, Dr. Schroeder, how does old Isaac's coded message stack up to some of the high tech codes you receive over at NSA?" Cindy Reid inquired.

"Good question, honey!" Tom Reid proudly responded.

"Excellent question, Mrs. Reid," Dr. Schroeder admitted. "Believe it or not, in some ways, Newton's codes are harder to break. You must understand, Newton was not only a genius of mathematics and physics, he was also a genius when it came to languages. He was an expert interpreter of most ancient languages, including Greek, Chinese, Arabic, and Hebrew. His coded notes were written as gigantic puzzles composed of a hodge-podge of ancient languages, all wrapped up in a mystery, riddled with a number of misleading clues."

"And can you decipher all of that?" John Reid asked in amazement.

"Given time and the aid of some pretty sophisticated computer programs, the answer is mostly yes," Dr. Schroeder modestly admitted.

"Well, needless to say, I'm very impressed," John commented.

The discussion on Newton's alchemy came to an abrupt end when Anthony, accompanied by a team of three bus boys, began clearing the appetizer plates to make room for the selected main courses. In a matter of a few short minutes, Anthony and his team of servers transformed the large round table into a smorgasbord of Italian cuisines.

Sensing it was time for a change in topic for their causal conservation, Tom turned his chair toward the Schroeder's and asked, "Rachel and Ezra, I'm not sure if I told you what my brother John does for a living."

"Are you also involved in the ministry?" Rachel innocently asked to a chorus of a few chuckles. Feeling slightly embarrassed by the unexpected response, she asked, "Did I say something wrong?"

"That's an interesting concept, Mrs. Schroeder," John responded. "You may be on to something. I never thought of what I do in terms of a ministry before."

"Stop teasing her," Tom followed. "Rachel, my brother is involved in Washington politics. In fact, John is the campaign manager for Analise Devoe."

"Analise Devoe, the former Attorney General turned presidential candidate?" Schroeder exclaimed.

"The one and only. Do you remember me mentioning that I was meeting with my brother to talk politics? It is on her behalf that John arranged today's dinner date."

"How did you get to meet Analise Devoe?" Rachel inquired.

"It seems like I've known her forever. We graduated from Harvard together. I also worked with Analise in the justice department the entire time she served as Attorney General. Let me emphatically tell all of you, she is a true public servant with a servant's heart. Analise is pro-family and pro-middle class. Her jobs program is guaranteed to put millions of Americans back to work in high paying jobs. Mark my words, Analise Devoe is going to become one of the greatest presidents this country has ever known."

"Doesn't she need to be elected first?" Tom jokingly asked.

"Brother, there is absolutely no doubt in my mind that she will be elected. She has the answers to America's problems. The other two jokers running are clueless."

The two "other" presidential candidates that John Reid alluded to were the Republican nominee, popular moderate and former New York governor, Robert Berry. New to the political scene, but gaining in the polls, was the newly formed American Value's Party headed by Eliot Graham, well know in Christian circles as the founder of the national radio ministry based out of Dallas, Texas, American Family Values.

"Why don't we table this discussion until we're all finished with the main course? We can pick it up again after Anthony serves us coffee with some tiramisu dessert," Tom interjected. "As Ezra's wise Jewish mother once said, talking politics while eating Italian is not a good kosher idea, or something along that line. Right, Dr. Schroeder?"

"Close enough!" Schroeder chuckled.

"Please excuse me, everyone," John apologetically asked. "I do get rather carried away anytime the subject is brought up, but forgive me, I've never been so passionate about anything before."

Miranda appeared restless and uncomfortable as her husband of eleven months continued spewing rosy accolades about his current boss. Even John Reid's voice took on a serious tone as he continued, as if his entire persona had changed.

"Analise has this election all wrapped up! The Republican defectors to Graham's Christian right-wing party are just enough to keep Berry, at best, a distant second in the polls."

Standing directly in back of John Reid and Miranda were two tall imperceptible forms. The taller of the two, slightly pale yellow in color, had his claw-like hand buried deep within John's torso. Beelazad, the captain of demon spirits, spoke verbatim the same words that projected from John's mouth.

"The Republicans will have no chance in hell of touching our girl," John Reid proclaimed.

"John, that's enough!" Tom abruptly interjected. "That's the very reason Dad never involved the ministry in politics, and as long as God permits me to remain where I am, no politics will ever be mentioned on any broadcast of PTW, no matter how righteous the cause may be. We will preach the Word and allow God to minister, free of human control!"

"Mission almost accomplished," Beelazad whispered to Zorah, the familiar spirit assigned to both John Reid and his wife.

Following his failed attempt to overthrow his Creator, Satan, along with at least one third of the created angelic beings who rebelled with him were cast out of heaven to dwell on earth as demonic aberrations of their former selves. Because demonic beings were fewer in number than their angelic counterparts, those designated as familiar spirits sometimes are charged with more than one unsaved human in the same household. Demonic rankings on earth were based entirely upon their former heavenly status. Demonic princes, the highest order of demons, were Archangels in their former state. Except for their yellowish skin and their distinctly bright yellow eyes, demonic princes retained much of their former angelic appearance. On the other hand, midlevel demons, former warrior angels, were more reptilian in stature than angelic with a body covered with scaly yellowish skin and a grotesquely fashioned snakelike head. Familiar spirits, the former guardian angels, were one rank below the midlevel demons. Also referred to as chimeras because of their half human, half animal appearance, familiar spirits were given the deceptive ability to change into any form at will. At the bottom of the demonic hierarchy, the former ministering angelic spirits transformed into tiny, frog-like spirits that cause the majority of mankind's sicknesses and diseases.

"What a perfect scene, two mighty angels protecting their feeble humans from the likes of us. I'm really scared!" Beelazad sarcastically scoffed at the two angelic warriors, Ariel and Muriel, standing directly behind Schroeder. "Zorah, why don't you show the mighty Muriel and the Jew protector, Ariel, how really frightened we are of them."

"My pleasure, Lord Beelazad," Zorah replied as he transformed his human-appearing facade into that of beautiful young seductress. "Ariel, your Jew will soon be mine. I will send him where all Jews belong, the crematoriums of hell."

"And big, strong Muriel, Prince of Truth, when will you ever learn? Humans don't want truth; they want lies. Don't waste your time with that feeble human. He says he serves Jesus, but he is no different than his weak-minded twin. He too will be mine!"

"Beelazad, I'm a little disappointed in your choice of company these days," Muriel fired back. "Isn't it a little unbecoming for an important demon of your rank to be associated with such a low level entity? Shouldn't

you be out haunting some Hollywood celebrity or somebody of equal status instead of interrupting this benign gathering of humans?"

"Come, come now, mighty Muriel. You're the disappointment. We're all well aware of the message that the Jew now possesses. I know all about your plans to have Newton's sealed message announced to the world through this putrid, disgusting Jew. I will tell you emphatically that all the powers of hell are at my disposal to make sure this Jew never lives long enough to get the words of Newton's message out of his filthy, Hebrew mouth. Tell Ariel, the protectorate of old Jews, that this is one mission He is going to lose."

At last Ariel broke his silence. "I have a voice, Prince of lies. You and all of your lying cohorts have no authority or power over those under my charge. These humans have already been purchased from the pits of hell by the blood of the Lamb and I will never allow any of them to escape from my protective covering."

"Pretty words, protectorate of the Jew. You'll soon find out that these pretty words are all you have."

"Ezra, I'll be right back. I have to go to the ladies' room," Rachel whispered in her husband's ear.

"Is everything all right?" Ezra asked in a hushed but concerned voice.

"Don't be silly," Rachel affectionately whispered. "My body is simply telling me that I had too much to eat and drink and it's time to do something about it. If Anthony comes back before I return, just order me a cup of decaffeinated coffee. I'm afraid that tiramisu is a little too rich for me."

Only Beelazad took note that the smirk on Zorah's face grew even wider as Rachel Schroeder passed to their right on her way to the ladies' room. The unsuspecting victim was about to get caught in their fiendish trap.

Ezra Schroeder stared down at his watch with a look of concern. Five minutes had passed and his wife had not returned from the bathroom.

"Excuse me, but Mrs. Reid," Schroeder quietly signaled to Cindy Reid, seated to his far left, "could you do me a favor?"

"Absolutely, Dr. Schroeder," Cindy said with a smile.

"My wife's in the ladies' room. Could you be so kind as to check on her? She has been gone for some time now and I'm getting a little concerned."

"Don't even ask. I'll be right back."

Schroeder's brief conversation with Cindy Reid went unnoticed by the other humans at the table, but not from the watchful eyes of Ariel and Muriel. Both angels were well aware that Rachel Schroeder's presence was missed and that her husband was very concerned.

"Ariel, I'm going to follow Cindy Reid," Muriel stated. Ariel remained at his post guarding Ezra Schroeder as Muriel followed Cindy into the ladies' room located in the far back corner of the restaurant.

Cindy hurried out of the bathroom and turned immediately into the kitchen to her right. "Quick!" Cindy hand gestured one of the cooks busily preparing his next order. "A woman from our party has collapsed in the ladies' room! Call 911."

Immediately, the cook grabbed the wall phone and relayed the message to a DC 911 operator. Two other women in the kitchen stopped everything they were doing and followed Cindy back into the ladies' room.

Once in there, the three women found Rachel Schroeder lying on her side on the ceramic tile floor, appearing totally unconscious. "I know CPR!" stated the older of the two women. Immediately, she repositioned Rachel Schroeder, tilting back her neck and feeling for a pulse.

"She's breathing and she has a pulse," the woman announced with a sigh of relief. By this time, every one in the restaurant was aware that something was going on in the back ladies' room, especially the party at the back table.

"John, you and Tom stay here with Ezra. I'll be right back," Miranda ordered as she too headed toward the ladies' room."

"Something's definitely wrong!" Ezra thought out loud as he too got up and raced toward the bathroom.

Beelazad stared from directly across the dining room table at his arch-enemy and sarcastically chanted a mocking rhyme, "Pretty words are all you say. Your wasted plans, all gone today! The Jewish wife, lies on the floor, the luncheon tomorrow, all out the door."

Ariel was now acutely aware that the demons would use all of their skills and fiendish tricks to keep Schroeder's message from being revealed to the world. It was now time to call for additional help.

A team of paramedics had arrived and all other humans were ushered away from the ladies' room and into the main dining area. As the paramedics checked on Rachel's vital signs, Muriel noticed something very strange going on behind the unconscious woman's head.

A small, froglike demon was attached to the base of Rachel Schroeder's skull. His thin, spindly fingers appeared to penetrate into her head and pinch off a capillary feeding the blood supply on the left side of her brain.

Muriel immediately reached his arm under the ceramic floor and around the back of Rachel Schroeder's head, gripping the head and trunk of the tiny demon of infirmity, and squeezing its body until it popped into a cloud of reddish brown smoke.

"Her vitals are improving!" the examining paramedic declared. "Her pulse is back to normal, blood pressure is stabilized."

"We have the patient stabilized," the other paramedic announced via his headset to the attending doctor at the hospital. "We'll be in route to Washington Hospital Center ASAP! Let's move her now!"

"Sir, how is my wife?" Dr. Schroeder nervously inquired of the first paramedic exiting the ladies' room.

"Your wife's vitals are stable. We are just about ready to carry her out to the ambulance. Sir, you are more than welcome to ride along in the ambulance."

"Ezra, ride with your wife. Cindy and I will follow right in back, praying the entire time," Tom reassured. "They're taking Rachel to Washington Hospital Center, one of the best hospitals in the country. She's going to be all right."

"I must apologize, but our luncheon plans for tomorrow must be placed on hold," Ezra said softly, in a state of overwhelming shock.

"Only temporarily, Ezra," Tom said with a tone of authority. "I believe now, more than ever, that Satan is doing everything in his power to make sure our meeting does not take place. As soon as

Rachel has fully recovered, we will all get together again. Next time, the powers of hell cannot stop us!"

Chapter Six

"The god of this world has blinded the minds of the unbelievers, to keep them from seeing the light of the gospel of the glory of Christ."
2 Corinthians 4:4 NIV

Saturday, October 9th, 9 a.m.
Rockville, Maryland

Humans have an old saying that timing is everything. The slightest change of the smallest detail in the course of time and all future events can be affected. Spirit beings, both angelic and demonic, are also well aware of this truth and they use this tactic of altering time events in an attempt to gain an advantage over one another in their eternal struggle to either fulfill or destroy God's prophetic plan.

A convoy of four vehicles drove slowly through an upper-middle-class Rockville neighborhood comprised mostly of older two-story brick colonials surrounded by manicured lawns and large mature oak trees. Led by a late model black Lincoln Navigator, the procession of four turned left at the end of a cul-de-sac onto a driveway marked by an attractive brick mailbox with an address plate 229 Chevy Chase Court. Unbeknown to the human passengers, accompanying each of the four vehicles were two massive angelic beings sitting high atop each roof.

"Momma, they're here!" shouted seven-year-old Melissa MacDougal, who was patiently staring out of the family room window for the arrival of her daddy and fellow family members. Melissa and her mother, Leah MacDougal, arrived earlier in the day to prepare the welcome home celebration for their mother and grandmother, Rachel Schroeder. Melissa raced to the front door and ran out to the driveway to greet the driver of the large dark blue van parked directly in back of the lead Lincoln Navigator.

"Daddy, I helped mommy all morning decorate the entire house for Grandma and Grandpa!" Melissa exclaimed as she jumped into her daddy's awaiting arms.

"I am so proud of you!" Mark MacDougal lovingly responded back with an affectionate kiss on his daughter's forehead. "Now can you help Daddy get Grandma out of the van?"

The large Ford Econoline van was specially equipped with a hydraulic handicap lift for accessing a wheelchair in and out through the large panel side doors.

"Honey," Mark motioned to his daughter, "stand over here by Daddy while I open the big door for Grandma and Grandpa."

By this time, all four vehicles were parked in a row lining the long blacktopped driveway from front to back. All of the occupants from both the vehicles and the house, twelve in all, the three grown children and their spouses, plus six of the seven grandchildren of Ezra and Rachel Schroeder, were anxiously surrounding the van as Mark MacDougal opened the side doors. For over two weeks, Rachel Schroeder remained hospitalized in the intensive care unit at the Washington Hospital Center where she was initially diagnosed with a major stroke on the left side of her brain. She was later transferred to the Washington Adventist Hospital's rehabilitation center for victims of strokes located in Takoma Park, Maryland. During the entire ordeal, her husband of forty-seven years was never far from her side.

As the van door opened, a frail but smiling Rachel Schroeder, wrapped snuggly in a warm blanket, stared down at her loving family from her wheelchair. Holding her hand, sitting in the seat next to his wife, was her husband, Ezra.

"One- two-three! Everyone, altogether," shouted Gerry Schroeder, Ezra and Rachel's middle child. "Welcome home, Grandma!"

With twelve of his fellow warrior angels attentively watching in the background, Kiel, the demon slayer, turned to Ariel and commented,

"No other human that I can remember was so well protected. My

warrior angels have been assigned to protect the lives of Schroeder and his wife, his children, their spouses, and his seven grandchildren. Until Michael says otherwise, Schroeder and his family members will be the safest human beings on planet Earth!"

Initially, Rachel Schroeder's suspected stroke left her partially paralyzed on her right side and unable to speak. The very moment the ambulance left the restaurant in route to the hospital, Tom Reid contacted his offices in Providence by cell phone and immediately called PTW's worldwide prayer network into action. Also, within an hour of receiving the word, members of the Silver Spring's Beth Messiah Messianic Congregation started calling other members to form around the clock prayer teams to pray in agreement in the name of Jesus that Rachel Schroeder would be totally healed and restored to her former self. Except for a weakness on her right side and a slightly slurred voice, she was well on her way to recovery.

The Schroeder children decided to limit the family gathering only to an afternoon brunch. They didn't want to overstress Grandma on her first day back home. Besides, Mark volunteered to take care of both the new baby and Melissa overnight while his wife, Leah, and Rachel's youngest daughter, Rebecca, remained to take care of the needs of their parents. With all the many kisses and hugs now over and Grandma tucked into bed for an afternoon nap, Ezra and his two daughters decided to relax in the family room and share some quiet conversation.

"Papa, you've been with Mamma everyday now for the past few weeks and Rebecca and I both agree, you also need a break. While we're here, why don't you go downstairs and work on your computer."

"Papa, weren't you working on some really important paper before Mamma got sick?" Rebecca asked.

Both girls could see visible tears welling up in their father's eyes. Looking down toward the floor, Ezra responded to his daughter's question in a faint broken voice.

"Girls, I want the two of you to know that I blame myself for your mother's condition."

"Papa, don't even think that for one moment!" Rebecca commanded in a stern voice. "What happened to Mama was not yours or anybody's fault. Strokes happen!"

"Leah, Rebecca, listen. I have done a lot of soul searching over the past few weeks and I realize now I have been neglecting your mother. She means everything in the world to me and I have been selfishly placing my research and everything else I do in front of her. I have made up my mind: from now on, your mother comes first!"

Now both daughters had tears welling up. Leah snuggled over to the edge of the loveseat where her father sat and gave Ezra a big hug and kiss on his cheek while Rebecca positioned herself on the floor below looking up with loving concern.

"Papa, listen to me!" Rebecca softly demanded. "Mama wouldn't have it any other way. She has told all of us over and over again that she is so proud of you and your accomplishments. That's what makes her happy. You have never neglected her, not for one moment. Now, you march yourself right down to your study and finish that important document! Do I make myself clear?"

Ezra wiped the tears from his youngest daughter's face and shook his head in agreement. "God has truly blessed me with such a wonderful family."

Ezra knew in his heart that his daughters were right. For almost three weeks, he had not placed a finger on a computer keyboard. His email messages must be several pages long, but more importantly, he was well aware that he had neglected to contact Harrison Andrews and the Cambridge University staff as promised with the decoded Newton document.

Sitting back in his office chair, Ezra stared for a moment at his blackened computer monitor and prayed. "Lord, why me? I am irresponsible and I now have a sick wife to take care of. Please choose someone more responsible or who has fewer responsibilities for such an important task."

With that said, Ezra pressed the start-up button on his desktop computer and proceeded to unlock the top right drawer of his computer desk with a small key he kept hidden under his keyboard. Once unlocked, he removed what looked like a small storage device marked with a big red number 1. Within seconds, he plugged the device into the computer's front USB port, clicked the security icon label ES1, and typed in a secret pass code giving him access to his private NSA site. Once there, all Schroeder had to do was click on an icon labeled secured addresses, and instantly, an entire alphabetized page of email addresses appeared on his screen.

"There you are, Harry, handrews@lib.cam.ac.uk."

Two angelic beings stood patiently by in the background as Schroeder proceeded to type his long-awaited message. No sooner did Schroeder's fingers start clicking across the computer keyboard than a third angel appeared standing directly in back of Schroeder.

"Muriel," Ariel inquired "Is now the prescribed time for Schroeder to release the prophetic message?"

The Archangel turned and gave Schroeder's guardian a quick pat on the shoulder.

"For now, we'll give the humans just enough to satisfy their curiosities," Muriel replied. "The entirety of the prophetic message still remains hidden. We will reveal it to Schroeder at the proper time."

"Muriel, you are aware that there are more than just humans awaiting this message," Kiel commented with a voice of concern.

"Have patience, my mighty comrade, it's all part of the plan," Muriel replied with a smile.

Monday, October 11th
8:00 a.m. GMT
Cambridge University Library
Cambridge, England

"Sarah, I believe our package has finally arrived!"

Sarah knew exactly what Professor Andrews meant. She immediately got up from her desk and proceeded across the room to observe first hand the email message displayed on Harrison Andrews' screen.

"Oh, dear God, Rachel's had a bloody stroke!"

"Is she all right?" Sarah asked in a voice of concern.

"Ezra writes that she was in intensive care for a time and then transferred to a rehabilitation center somewhere in Maryland. He also says that she is now home recuperating and improving daily."

"Well, that bloody well explains why we didn't hear from Ezra until now."

"Can you even imagine, Ezra starts out here asking us to forgive him for being late!"

"Well, Harry, you email him right back and tell him how silly he is!"

"I'll do just that as soon as I finish reading Ezra's take on Sir Isaac's message"

"Telazard, get your ugly wench out of my way. I can't see the screen!" demanded Abrazar, a familiar spirit recently assigned to Harrison Andrews.

"There's nothing to see. The Jew is just rambling on about utter nonsense!"

I don't care if he's quoting Jesus Christ; get her out of my way, now!"

Even by chimeras standards, Telazard was as mean and nasty as any aberration of his ranking. The slightest distraction from his mission was catalyst enough to set him off in an explosive rage. Telazard immediately swung his lizard-shaped head around and snarled vehemently at his antagonist while displaying a mouth full of razor-edged teeth.

"Say one more word and I'll bite you in half!"

He then proceeded to plunge both of his reptilian clawed hands deep into Sara Andrews' torso and twist her stomach into a mass of undulating knots.

Immediately, Sara's face grimaced in pain. She held tight to her left side and turned toward the entrance door.

"Harry, please excuse me, but I need to dash out to the ladies' room for a bit."

"Sara, is every thing all right?"

Stopping briefly at the door, Sara regained her composure and replied. "I don't know what's come over me, but my stomach is feeling a bit unsettled right now. Harry, promise me that the moment you finish reading it you give out a shout. I've been waiting in suspense for almost two months now for the answer."

Completely unnoticed by both spirit and human, two angelic princes supernaturally observed the entire scene through a wall in an adjacent room. Archangel Yahriel, the prince of prophetic wisdom and worldly affairs, turned to his companion and smiled.

"It appears that everything is going just as planned."

"By the looks of those two, our friend Beelazad must be very desperate these days," Muriel replied

"I'd say he's scratching the very bottom of his cesspool to find the likes of these."

"I'll be satisfied just as long as they get their facts straight and report them back to Beelazad."

"Amen, Muriel. Amen!"

Once alone, Professor Andrews turned his full attention to the remainder of Schroeder's email message:

> *I am attaching the entire text of Newton's journal with this message. As you might recall, before I left England I had just finished deciphering the original text from its coded form into Hebrew. The attachment I am now sending contains the original text, its Hebrew translation, and most importantly, the translation back into English. Once you have thoroughly examined the pages of this document, I believe you and the entire Cambridge staff will come to the same conclusion as I did: that what we have in our possession could possibly be one of the greatest finds in the history of mankind!*
>
> *I am now going to give you a detailed account of my interpretation of what I believe to be Newton's final message. Once I was able to decipher the entire original text into Hebrew, I saw before me what appeared to be a tangled web of prophetic Scripture verses starting first with the book of Daniel. I then discovered that by putting the fol-*

lowing verses from the books of Daniel, Genesis, Psalms, Ezekiel, and Zechariah together in Newton's sequence produced a logical message: Daniel Chapter 12 *verses* 9*; Genesis Chapter* 12 *verses* 2 *and* 3*; Daniel Chapter* 12 *verses* 3,10, *and* 11 *; Daniel Chapter* 9 *verse* 25 *and* 26*; Psalms Chapter* 83 *verses* 2 *through* 4*; Ezekiel Chapter* 38 *verses* 2 *through* 8*; Daniel* 12 *verse* 7*; Zechariah Chapter* 12 *verses* 13 *and* 14*; and returning to Genesis Chapter* 12 *verses* 2 *and* 3.

Now for my interpretation:

Newton sincerely believed that God had rewarded his lifetime of unwavering faithfulness by selecting him to be one of the chosen few mentioned in Daniel Chapter 12 to receive God's prophetic insight. Newton started his message by quoting one of the most familiar verses found in Scriptures, Genesis Chapter 12 verse three. It is here that God swore a solemn oath to bless any people or nation who blesses Abraham's chosen descendants, the Jewish people, and to curse any people or nation who do harm or evil in anyway to the Jewish people.

He then returns to the book of Daniel where things get really interesting. Newton understood from reading Daniel that there would come a future time when the Jews would return from their worldwide dispersion to the land promised to them by the God of Abraham. He also accepted the argument that each of the prophetic weeks described in Daniel Chapter 9 were numerically equivalent to seven-year periods. But Newton vehemently disagreed with the scholars when it came to the interpretation of the two separate weeks quoted in Daniel Chapter 9 verse 25, "So you are to know and discern that from the issuing of a decree to restore and rebuild Jerusalem until Messiah the Prince there will be seven weeks and sixty-two weeks; Jerusalem will be built again, with a plaza and moat, even in times of distress." The vast majority of biblical scholars interpret this verse by simply adding the seven sevens and the sixty-two sevens to come up with 483 years, the timing of Christ's first coming. Sir Isaac differed completely with this logic. He concluded that the first seven weeks of years or the forty-nine years prophesied by Daniel were entirely separate from the remaining sixty-two weeks of years. Newton calculated that the prophetic time clock of Christ's second coming would take place the moment Jerusalem was once again in the hands of the Jews. Christ's return would take place forty-nine years after this future event. Newton also stressed that none of these events could ever take place by the hands of the Jews alone, but only through the assistance and protection of a friendly nation.

Next in Newton's timeline, the Archangel Michael arises to do battle against the enemies of God's chosen people. These enemies of Israel are all listed in both Psalm 83 and Ezekiel 38. Along with two evil northern empires named in Ezekiel 38 as Gog and Magog, the entire confederation conspires together to carry out an evil plan to utterly destroy Israel and the Jewish people. At that time, the Jewish nation will find herself totally alienated and hopeless. They will at last cry out in dire desperation to their one and only true Messiah, Jesus Christ, and at last they will see their redemption.

Harry, I consider you to be one of my dearest and most cherished friends. You and I both share a burning passion in quest for truth. You also know me to be a man of sound mind. In closing, I would like to share with you my personal thoughts concerning Newton's message. It is my firm conviction that God truly did reveal his end-times plan to Newton. I also believe that we are presently living in those predicted times. According to Newton's interpretation, the hands of God's prophetic clock started ticking the moment Israel's army recaptured the city of Jerusalem in June of 1967. If you add the forty-nine years predicted in Daniel Chapter 9 verse 25 to that date, then Christ's possible return to Earth will be on or before the year 2016.

I also believe that Newton's friendly nation called to support and protect Israel is none other than the United States; and, as long as this strategic relationship lasts, Israel will remain safe. I find it extremely interesting that Newton included direct quotes from Genesis 12 verse 3 twice in his message, once at the very beginning and once at the end. "And I will bless those who bless you, and the one who curses you I will curse." This was purposely inserted as a warning to any nation that they would suffer severe consequences if they were to abandon Israel in her time of need or attack her when she was vulnerable. In spite of this warning, the Scriptures make it perfectly clear that on some future date, all nations, including the United States, will desert Israel. When that day arrives, the devil himself will lead the final charge to totally destroy what God has called the 'apple of his eye.'

Harry, I will close now with what I call Newton's ultimate riddle. I have to confess, Newton ends his message with a line that even I have yet to solve. "Always remember to never forsake the words of this prophesy, for concealed within these very lines, the wise shall know the end of times."

After reading the entire text of Schroeder's message, Harrison Andrews sat back in his chair and thought to himself, *Poppycock. Pure poppycock!*

"I hope you got all of that?" Abrazar demanded.

"Got it and I'm on my way to Beelazad," Telazard replied with a broad, devilish smile. "With information like this, we should be richly rewarded!"

Yahriel turned to Muriel and let out a big sigh of relief.

"Mission accomplished!" Yahriel proclaimed.

"Let's just pray that Satan takes the bait!"

Chapter Seven

"Satan's neatest trick is convincing men that he does not really exist."

C.S. Lewis

Midnight November 6th
Eve of the Presidential Election Day
Washington, D.C.
John F. Kennedy Center of the Performing Arts

Since the beginning of time, Satan and his millions of demons have been acutely aware of the one major guiding force behind all of their motives and plans, their ultimate fate. Putting off the inevitable by attempting to alter the events of God's prophetic time clock has always been their game plan. Every demonic plan has only one motive in mind, "how does this plan further my cause of avoiding God's judgment in hell at the end of time?" As the seconds on God's prophetic clock tick off even louder, Satan and his evil cohorts plan a final scheme in a desperate attempt to ward off the inevitable.

Though it was standing room only in the Concert Hall at the Kennedy Center of the Performing Arts, the spectacle went totally unnoticed by human eyes. The last time a supernatural event of this magnitude was held was November 30, 1947. Over two thousand were in attendance that night at Westminster's Central Hall in London, the day after the United Nations General Assembly met at that location and declared the birth of the state of Israel giving Jews back their eternal homeland.

For this bizarre occasion, every seat in the Kennedy Center's 2,242 seating capacity Concert Hall was taken and all the aisles were filled. All present could sense a high degree of expectancy as the main speakers made their way to the front of the room. A large yellow banner draped across the stage displayed in bold red letters the theme of tonight's clandestine event, "A Frog in a Frying Pan!" The entire audience knew the subtle meaning behind the banner's message. If you place a frog in a cool frying pan, and slowly turn up the heat, the frog will not sense the temperature change and will cook to death. After his failed attempt at killing all Jews in Europe and placing Hitler and his Third Reich in as the world dominant power, Satan's newly conceived strategy was to utterly destroy God's final plan for establishing His thousand year Millennial kingdom on earth.

On the eve of what could possibly be America's most important Presidential election since the beginning of the Civil War, high-ranking demonic princes from all over the world gathered at this great secular arena built on the shores of the Potomac River. They had come to honor each other's devious achievements and to plan out the final demise of their two greatest foes, their "frogs in a frying pan," Israel and her sole protectorate, the United States of America. Bael, the demon prince of the East, and his entire command of sixty-six demon legions were positioned on the roof top and all along the entire perimeter of the building. Their mission was to make absolutely sure that not a single angelic being invaded their boundaries. With so many demons leaving their worldwide posts unattended, during this particular night the incidence of crime, wars, strife, and disease took an unexplained drop. It was now the hour, midnight Eastern Standard Time.

As tonight's demonic host walked out on the stage, an ominous hush permeated every square inch of a theater. Baal-berth was selected as host for one obvious reason: he was so grotesquely huge and ugly that every demon feared him. With sagging layers of reptilian-like scales covering his massive yellowish-black form, Baal-berth was without a doubt the most ominous-looking arch demon of all. Stopping just short of the edge of the front center stage, the arch demon host raised his clinched left fist and belted out a thunderous opening statement.

"I, Baal-berth, Master of rituals and pacts, call this meeting to order. I welcome all the princes from every corner of the earth who are represented

here tonight. Everyone stand and give homage to our lord and eternal king while his anthem is performed."

In Nazi-like fashion, every demon stood to his feet, and in a show of solidarity, saluted with clinched fists in the direction of an unseen figure seated alone in the left onstage balcony box seats. The entire assemblage remained locked in this position as the hideous music, sounding more like a hellish blend of heavy metal rock music, permeated outward from that same upper balcony direction. The moment the hideous anthem stopped, Baal-berth rapidly dropped his massive scaly arm to his side signaling for everyone to be seated. Baal-berth stood for a moment and gave a threatening glare at the entire audience. He then fixed his yellowish-orange eyes on a mischievous horde of midlevel demons who were hanging precariously over the upper left tier railing, and then, belted out this ominous warning.

"I will begin tonight's meeting with the severest of warnings to all of you midlevel demons invited here tonight. At the risk of immediate death, there will be absolutely no screaming or shouting out at anytime for any reason. Only clapping at the appropriate times will be tolerated! Do I make myself clear?"

With that said, Baal-berth's entire demeanor changed. His squinty eyes widened and a broad welcoming smile projected across his drooping scaly jowls.

"It brings me pleasure beyond measure to welcome all of you here tonight on the eve of what will be our greatest victory. I say "Our victory" because all of you gathered here have played a major role in making sure that operation 'Frog in a Frying Pan' would lead us to only one outcome, total and absolute victory. Before we hear tonight from our great king and leader, I am honored to be in the company of such a distinguished gathering of princes, rulers of Earth's great cities and nations who have come from their distant assignments to be with us tonight. I will now call on the commander of our great campaign to present special category awards to those demons under his leadership who have performed their assigned duties to the highest order of success. Our presenter for tonight's awards will be Arch Demon Amducious, known simply as 'the Destroyer.'"

Except for the pair of black, bat-like wings that jutted out from his massive back shoulders, Amducious appeared strikingly angelic. Standing over ten feet tall, his jet-black hair flowed freely over his muscular broad shoulders as he walked. His true identity was easily revealed by the combination of his distinctively yellowish-black skin, a high protruding brow, and a deep-set pair of piercingly yellow eyes.

As arch demon Amducious made his way onto the Kennedy Center stage, the entire upper left tier of the auditorium, completely disregarding Baal-berth's warnings, erupted in a wild outbreak of cheers and hollers that eventually spread across the large auditorium. The popular arch demon stood for a moment on the center stage just soaking up the attention. Being selected tonight's sole presenter was an honor Amducious didn't take lightly. Those demons under his command had diligently worked hard behind the scenes to destroy the envied moral perception that America once exhibited to the world. Along with his fellow demons, Amducious was proud of this great achievement and stood for a moment longer boasting and soaking up the glory.

"I hope you weren't just applauding me for this honor," Amducious boasted. "You need to be applauding yourselves. I wouldn't be standing here if it wasn't for the efforts of millions of hard working demons like those of you present here tonight, glory be to our great lord Satan! When we started out on our 'Frog in a Frying Pan' campaign back in the human year 1947, the task looked insurmountable. But our failures have taught us one big lesson, learn from them and never repeat them! In 1947, America was crowned by all the superpowers of the world. They had just defeated all of our plans to conquer both Europe and Asia. Americans were boasting of their lofty ideals of freedom based on responsibility and commitment. The American family was a strong and vibrant institution and American Judeo-Christian values were looked up to everywhere on Earth. Oh, how times have changed!"

Amducious paused momentarily as his fellow demons vented their agreement of his last comment with a short outburst of hoots and hollers.

"Before I announce the recipients for each category of our awards tonight, I want to acknowledge an almost totally forgotten group. Without this group's blind assistance, nothing we do could ever be possible."

The demons in the audience smiled broadly as they clearly sensed a sarcastic tone in Amducious' voice.

"Will you all stand now in a moment of silence while we play the funeral dirge in honor of all the billions of self-centered human disciples, past and present, who have unwitting pledged their eternal souls to the service of our lord and king Satan. We honor tonight the Satanists, the New Agers, the reincarnationists, the astrologers, the mediums, the atheists, and all the cultists and members of false religions throughout the Earth."

As the funeral dirge played, demons mockingly stood with their hands raised high honoring Satan. The moment the ominous music stopped, Amducious led the entire audience in a unifying shout, "Praise be to Satan!"

"I would now like to recognize the following leaders in our campaign to destroy America according to their special fields of expertise."

Amducious proudly announced the names of three of his most loyal demonic princes and called upon each to join him center stage to be recognized for their achievement. As the award recipients made their way up to receive their award, their commander Amducious declared their individual achievements.

First to be recognized in the category of lust and sensualism was Prince Asmodeous. Asmodeus walked out and was met at center stage by Amducious. With similar forms and facial features, demon princes differ only from their arch demon superiors in stature and height. As with most demon princes, Asmodeus stood a mere eight feet tall. Asmodeus bowed slightly as his proud commander draped a scarlet ribbon supporting a gaudy looking gold medal in the form of a frying pan around his neck.

Once again, the same horde of midlevel demons located in the auditorium's upper left section erupted into a deafening roar of cheers for one of their own. The cheering didn't last more then a minute when Baal-berth stormed out from left stage and shouted in his thunderous voice, "Shut up or you'll be obliterated to the pits of hell!"

Baal-berth's threat was heeded, at least for the time being. With order briefly restored, Amducious proceeded with his speech.

"When we first started our Frog in a Frying Pan campaign, the only

place you could find anything considered pornographic was down some back ally in a city ghetto. That's when Asmodeus came up with the ingenious plan of gradually desensitizing American humans to pornography while legally supporting these gradual changes under the cloak of free speech rights found in their own constitution."

Acting more like a TV evangelist, Amducious spent the next ten minutes preaching from the stage to his faithful following how Asmodeus and his millions of seducing spirits succeeded in saturating every aspect of the American life with pornography. Step by step, Amducious methodically demonstrated how his loyal prince used subtle means to desensitize America's perception of pornography. Holding up popular magazines of scantly clad cover girls, Amducious scoffed as to how these once-consider soft-porn images were now placed in plain view at every grocery store's check out counter. His audience cheered as vivid scenes flashed across the stage of innocent American public school children, some as young as ten years old, being exposed to graphic, sexually explicit content while being taught the proper methods of having 'safe sex.' For the grand finale, Amducious demonstrated how Asmodeus' ingenious use of the hottest new technologies now delivered hardcore pornography directly into every home by satellite cable television and even the Internet. Americans could even receive pornography on demand through their personal cell phones.

Before dismissing Asmodeus to return to his seat in the audience, Amducious placed his massive hand on his subordinate's shoulder, then turn toward the audience and proudly proclaimed, "Thanks to the concerted efforts of Asmodeus and his demons, America is no longer perceived as a society based on responsibility and commitment. America today is a sexually enlightened society, decadent, and void of any thoughts of decency or shame, driven by self-gratifying relationships. As a direct effect of their newly acquired taste for self-overindulgence, most Americans are completely disconnected from one another. For example, in 1947, the number of marriages ending in divorce was under ten percent. Today, the American divorce rate has increased to almost sixty percent! Better yet, the overwhelming number of failed marriages has helped foster a rejection of marriage altogether. In America today, cohabitation is in and marriage is out! Love them and leave them with a sexually transmitted disease is the common lot for these unfulfilled relationships. The vast majority of their children now grow up to be insecure, disconnected, dysfunctional adults. The final outcome of Asmodeus' mission has been the destruction of the once strong backbone of American society, its families."

"Prince Asmodeus," Amducious concluded with a raised right fist, "we salute you and the millions of demons under your leadership for a job well done!"

Asmodeus' exit resembled that of a heavy metal rocker walking off the stage with both arms raised high gesturing a victory sign with one hand and the sign of Satan with his other. The entire audience responded back in the same outrageous fashion displaying satanic hand gestures and shouting out obscenities. The wild response finally brought on another reappearance of Baal-berth to reinstate order. As the rowdy audience reluctantly submitted to Baal-berth's threatening presence, Amducious, the Destroyer, continued,

"It has been decided that due to the complex nature of our next category, tonight's final recognition will be a dual award," Amducious proudly proclaimed, "In order to bring America to the brink of destruction, we had to solicit the combined talents of two highly specialized princes. It is my pleasure to announce the names of the final recipients of tonight's 'Frog in a Frying Pan' award, Prince Pyro, chief demon of all lying spirits, and Zagam, the master prince of deceit and counterfeiting.

Baal-berth had already prepared for the anticipated outburst of rowdiness. On cue, as the deafening screams and hollers commenced, a massive demon assigned to stand guard near the front of the stage indiscriminately rammed his sword into the shoulder of a midlevel demon sitting in the second row aisle seat and lifted his twitching form high into the air for all to see. Instantly, shock and fear permeated the entire auditorium and dreaded silence prevailed. Without uttering a threatening word, Baal-berth again signaled the guard who responded by walking out of the auditorium with his victim still precariously suspended from the edge of his sword.

"I guess he got his point across!" Amducious joked, but to no avail. Not even a chuckle could be heard. By this time, the two award recipients were

standing side-by-side center stage. Holding the scarlet ribbon awards in his right hand, Amducious proceeded with his final speech of the night.

"Once again, it is my pleasure as commander in the campaign to destroy America to recognize two of my most trusted and valuable princes according to their combined specialties in the areas of lies and counterfeiting, Prince Pyro and Prince Zagam.

Both Princes Pyro and Zagam bowed low to the sound of silence as Amducious draped the awards around their necks. A faint, but distinct clapping could be heard coming from the left stage balcony area. Not even Baal-berth would interfere with the perpetrator of this sound, for he, as well as every demon present, was acutely aware of who was sitting in that left upper balcony seat. The clapping slowly spread throughout the large auditorium until every demon, including Baal-berth, joined in recognition of the newly awarded demon leaders. Amducious respectfully waited until all the clapping stopped before proceeding.

"Back in 1947, I asked Princes Pyro and Zagam to employ the same successful tactics they used to destroy the Roman Empire. Our plan was quite simple. Make Americans the richest and most prosperous people on earth. Refocusing Americans on the pursuit of wealth and material happiness caused them to forget all about their lofty ideals of self sacrifice, loyalty, respecting authority, rewarding diligence, and most importantly, trusting in God."

For the next half hour, Amducious detailed how Zagam and his army of lying demons were able to subtly replace the word need with greed in the minds of Americans. Amducious boasted how Zagam's brilliant plan was simply to introduce America to the temptation of easy credit.

"Before the 1950's, credit cards were virtually nonexistent in American society." Amducious declared. "Americans could purchase only the things they could afford, the necessities of life. Introducing them to easy credit was like placing a group of children into a room full of candy. Need turned instantly to greed. One television wasn't enough. Americans wanted one in every room. They were no longer satisfied with an old reliable car that got them around town. They wanted the same expensive gas-guzzler like the rich people drove down the street. It didn't take long before every American over the age of eighteen was the proud owner of a wallet full

of credit cards. The credit card gave Americans the false security that they could purchase things they could never afford. They are now addicted to spending more than they could ever afford to pay back. Their expensive high-mortgaged homes are now stacked full of things and gadgets that just collect dust. Thanks to Zagam's ingenuity, today's Americans have all the things their greedy hearts could ever desire, but dwell in constant misery because they are buried deep in mountains of debt. Praise be to Satan!" Amducious declared.

"Praise be to Satan!" thundered back over two thousand demon voices in unison.

"On a much larger scale," Amducious continued, "Zagam focused his main plan of attack on corporate America. American corporations back in the early 1950s started out needing the advanced skills of the American workers to make their products vastly superior compared to any produced around the world. During the 1960s and 70s America was the leading exporter of everything from cars to shoes. That all changed when their need turned to greed. Millions of Zagam's specialized demons rolled up their blue collar and white collar sleeves and went to work tempting union bosses to strike for higher salaries and corporate executives to dream of larger mansions, sportier cars, and long, expensive corporate vacations. The workers began demanding higher wages from their bosses to pay for all the things they owed on their credit cards and American corporate bosses demanded higher profit margins to pay for their expensive lifestyles. The end result was American companies pulled up their corporate stakes and migrated to those areas of the world where labor was cheap and profits were high. Without high-paying jobs, American workers were left with mountains of debt."

Amducious placed his hand on Zagam's shoulder and declared, "Good and faithful servant of Satan, I commend you. Job well done! Praise be to Satan!"

"Praise be to Satan!" the audience responded.

"I now turn your attention to the great Prince of lies." Amducious declared. "Pyro had a different plan of attack. He told me back when we first started our campaign that the easiest way to bring down a large oak tree was to poison its roots. I have to admit, he was absolutely right! Pyro's

plan was also quite simple. Change the way Americans think, and you'll change the way Americans act. The roots of America are its children and Pyro's plan of attack was to infiltrate and bring fundamental changes to the ways Americans think through both their public schools and the university systems.

"It's hard for even me to appreciate the speed of his plan. Before 1947, a large majority of America's universities, including Harvard, advocated conservative Christian principles as one of their basic tenets. For over 150 years, more than half of Harvard's graduates were Christian pastors. Up until 1963, open prayer and Bible readings were accepted practices in public schools all across America and the Ten Commandments were posted somewhere in every public school building. Children were also encouraged to believe that they were created in the image of God."

Those last few statements produced a spontaneous round of booing and hissing throughout the large auditorium.

"Pyro's first plan of attack was to replace the thoroughly established conservative minded college professors with a new breed of free thinking, liberal idealists. It wasn't long before the subversive attitudes of these 'open minded' professors filtered down to their students. These newly enlighten students went on to become the lawyers, judges, and politicians of America during the 60's, 70's and 80's. These enlighten governmental policy makers passed laws banning public prayer and Bible reading in every public school across America. The posting of the Ten Commandments was outlawed in public schools in 1980. Starting in the 1960s and every year since, public school children were taught through their science curriculums that evolution was a scientific fact and humans were not placed on Earth by a special act of God, but by some accidental occurrence through slime and time. Once we were able to make them accept that they were nothing more than mere animals, it wasn't hard to convince them that 'sinning' was nothing more than acting out their own basic animal instincts. The most amazing thing to me, they bought it all, hook, line and sinker. They would much rather believe the big lies we told than the absolute truth that God created them! What a stupid, gullible lot is man!"

The demons could no longer restrain themselves. Even Baal-berth, sitting along the edge of the stage, broke out into a thunderous applause.

Deep within their miserable spirits, they could sense that evil was finally gaining an upper hand for the eternal battle of man's soul. The entire auditorium was on the verge of total chaos with demons screaming out blasphemic obscenities toward God, hordes of midlevel demons running up and down aisles, some flipping and diving off the balcony walls. With his speech near completion, Amducious solicited the assistance of Baalberth in an attempt to regain order. Assistance wasn't needed. A blinding bluish pulse appearing at first to be lightning bolted out from the top left balcony, producing a penetrating crack that brought every demon to their knees. Amducious smiled and in an act of gratitude, lifted his hand high to praise his lord and king seated in the top left balcony. With order restored, Amducious completed his speech without interruption.

"And the final outcome is, Americans today don't really believe in anything. They think they do, but in reality, they don't! They have allowed themselves to be brainwashed into believing the big lie of multiculturalism, that there are no such things as a moral absolutes. The ethics of multiculturalism are the accepted practices in today's educational systems. Children are now taught in schools to be tolerant of the strange behaviors of others and not be judgmental. Children are even encouraged to read books about likable wizards where they are eventually drawn into the belief that dark magic and witchcraft are cool and acceptable practices. I personally consider this to be Pyro's greatest achievement." Amducious boasted. "Even the vast majority of so-called mainline denominational Christian churches have replaced their belief in God's absolutes with the big lie of moral tolerance. In churches today, seldom is heard a discouraging word like 'repentance and sin.'"

"Praise be to Satan!" a group of demons cried out in the background.

"Instead, you will hear today, Jesus is a God of love and tolerance," Amducious smiled as he sarcastically placed both hands across his chest. "He accepts all those who love him including our friends the fornicators, the adulterers, the homosexuals, and the sexual deviants."

"We love them all!" shouted a demon from the balcony.

I agree!" Amducious shouted back. "After all, they are all victims of human intolerance, and as their Creator, Jesus made them that way."

"Blame it on Jesus!" echoed another shout from the balcony above.

"In the name of tolerance," Amducious mockingly shouted out imitating the familiar stereotypic tone used by a fire and brimstone Pentecostal preacher, "mainline denominational churches have not only accepted these once considered scriptural abominations, they have even openly endorsed these practices as normal. With the church's silent approval, Hollywood is now free to produce movies that promote the acceptance of homosexual marriage, and best of all, blaspheme the very existence and Deity of God himself. I am so happy to say, most of today's Christian churches don't even practice what they once preached!"

Amducious paused momentarily to let out a big sigh of both satisfaction and relief. He knew in his self-absorbed spirit that his assignment was now over and his mission was a complete success. Once again, he lived up to his name, the Destroyer. With arrogant pride beaming from his face, he stood center stage and made his farewell statement.

"In closing, I want to thank each and every one of you present here tonight for a job well done. Because you remained unified to our cause, our mission was a success far beyond all of our expectations. America today is just a dim shadow of its former self. The world now views America as a decadent, lazy, self-indulgent society made up of irresponsible pleasure-crazed people who are less willing to work hard to achieve what they want. The country that once boasted of supplying most of the world wants. Because Americans have been so willing to trade their high moral ideals for the price of a season of pleasure, their sacred institutions of marriage and strong families lie crushed and in shambles.

"And finally, I stand here proud to say that because of all your concerted efforts, Americans today are no longer able to make any moral distinctions based on behavior. What was once called 'good' in America is now called 'evil' and what once was called 'evil' is now called 'good!'

"My role as commander of operation 'Frog in a Frying Pan' is officially over and I am now anxiously waiting along with all of you for our new assignments to be announced momentarily by our great lord and king. I will now turn the remainder of tonight's program back over to our Master of Ceremonies, Baal-berth."

The popular Arch Demon walked off the stage to a thunderous applause by his admiring troops. Before exiting, he raised a clinched left fist high above his head and shouted a final, "Praise be to Satan!"

Chapter Eight

"You had the seal of perfection, full of wisdom and perfect in beauty. You were in Eden, the garden of God; every precious stone was your covering: The ruby, the topaz and the diamond; the beryl, the onyx and the jasper; the lapis lazuli, the turquoise and the emerald; And the gold, the workmanship of your settings and sockets, was in you. On the day that you were created they were prepared. You were the anointed cherub who covers, and I placed you there. You were on the holy mountain of God; you walked in the midst of the stones of fire. You were blameless in your ways from the day you were created until unrighteousness was found in you. By the abundance of your trade you were internally filled with violence, and you sinned; therefore I have cast you as profane from the mountain of God. And I have destroyed you, O covering cherub, from the midst of the stones of fire. Your heart was lifted up because of your beauty; you corrupted your wisdom by reason of your splendor. I cast you to the ground; I put you before kings, that they may see you."

Ezekiel 28:12–17 NKJV

The Throne Room of God
Before the Creation of the Universe

If there is one name that portrays its owner's universal persona more than any other, that name is Satan. It is a name that comes with at least a dozen aliases, each one painting a descriptive layer of a personality so mysterious and so misunderstood that words alone have never truly been able to define it. The only way to describe Satan's true nature is to depict him in terms of the ultimate antonym of God. His name itself carries the meaning of "opponent" or "adversary." In every aspect of character where God is defined as everything holy and good, Satan is the embodiment of all evil, hatred, pride, and destruction. He is the enemy of God and man, the enemy of everything righteous and pure.

From the very beginning, Satan was the envy of all created beings. Christened Lucifer, the light of God, by his Creator, he was fashioned specifically by God to be one of two covering cherubs, a special category of angelic beings made perfect in all their ways, full of beauty and wisdom, having full access to the throne of God. In the presence of God, the two covering cherubs humbly bent low allowing their magnificent white-feathered wings to act as perfect coverings for the brilliant glory emanating from their Creator.

Lucifer's flawlessly sculptured body shone as polished gold and was covered by precious stones of beryl, diamonds, onyx, sapphires, rubies, and emeralds. His head was crowned with free-flowing golden hair and with a triune face to reflect the three-fold character of his creator, with each side possessing a stunning set of jewel colored eyes; ruby red on the left, sapphire blue in the front, and emerald green on the right. Beneath each set of eyes was a nose and mouth leading to a set of perfectly fashioned vocal chords capable of producing harmonious sounds of every pitch and octave imaginable. God specifically fashioned Lucifer in this manner for the dual purposes of serving as a covering cherub and for leading praise and worship in God's throne room

The Throne Room of God
Shortly After Creation of the Universe

It wasn't long after God created the universe that the unthinkable occurred. Something happened that was so cataclysmic that its effects rocked even the thresholds of God's own Throne Room. A major rebellion was discovered that involved over one third of the created angelic beings from every ranking, from seraphim and cherubim all the way down to the lowest cherub.

Treachery of this magnitude might have been too hard to accept, but God was expecting it. This was a risk that He was willing to take, the price of allowing His created beings free moral choice. They didn't have to serve Him. They didn't even have to obey Him. All God ever wanted, all He desired in return for creating them, was much more than their loyalty and devotion. More than anything else, the Creator of the universe wanted His creation's total, intimate love.

Even for an omniscient, all-knowing being, God was devastated to learn the identity of the rebellion's leader. It was his most trusted angelic being, Lucifer, the very one God fashioned into His own triune likeness. He was considered by both God and angels alike to be the pinnacle of holiness, the most trusted of all God's created beings. Lucifer was found guilty of committing the ultimate breach of trust, declaring in his heart that he alone should be worshipped, that he alone should be God.

Every skill that God had placed in His worship leader had now become perverted by the sin of pride. Craftiness replaced wisdom; his integrity was now deceit. By making evil appear good and good appear evil, Lucifer was able to deceive his fellow angels into believing that he alone should be worshiped as God.

His rebellion cost him everything. The first of all created beings, formed in the image and likeness of God, the covering cherub, the Throne Room's worship leader lost much more than his status and position in heaven. Lucifer had to forfeit his relationship with God. For committing such a heinous sin, Lucifer and over one third of his fellow angelic conspirators were evicted from the Kingdom of heaven.

Rather than cast them all into the Lake of Fire right then and there, God had other plans. God decided to banish the rebellious angels deep within the recesses of his newly created universe to a small, inconspicuous planet known as earth.

From the moment of their banishment, Lucifer was renamed Satan, and his millions of angelic accomplices were now called demons. They were instantly transformed from angels of light into grotesquely distorted aberrations of their former selves. Though fallen and his beauty removed, Satan was permitted by God to retain some of his former power. Within the boundaries set by God, Satan will remain the god of earth until a future date known only to God himself when Satan's evil realm on Earth will finally be crushed and he and his millions of fallen angels will be cast forever into the eternal Lake of Fire. Until that day comes, in their desperate attempts to destroy the lives and eternal souls of God's newly created beings, humans, Satan and his demonic hordes will use any and all devious means at their disposal to make sinning look attractive and appealing.

Tuesday, November 7th
Presidential Election Day
Washington, D.C.
John F. Kennedy Center of the Performing Arts

An eerie silence permeated the capacity filled concert hall. Even Baalberth stood in silent awe anticipating the next and final speaker. From the instant they were banished from heaven, each demon lived in dreaded fear of this moment. No other time in their earthly existences were they more acutely aware that their time was rapidly coming to an end. There was only one source of hope for warding off the inevitable. Thousands of yellowish eyes were fixed in the direction of the top left balcony directly above the stage. There they sat, all on edge, anxiously awaiting the appearance of the only one who could possibly postpone their destined appointment in the Lake of Fire.

Without notice, the lighting in the entire auditorium went black. Even for a room full of scary demons, this was really terrifying. Suddenly, the most horrendously detestable 3D images of human death and destruc-

tion flashed across the stage. This was real entertainment for a room full of demons. They all sat smugly back in their seats viewing in devilish delight hundreds of broken human bodies crushed under tons of twisted steel and concrete from buildings toppled over by a massive earthquakes. Flashing next across the stage was the spectacle of thousands of bloated corpses floating down debris-filled, hurricane-swollen rivers, followed by a series of monstrous tsunami waves smashing through densely populated coastal cities, totally obliterating everything in their path.

"Praise be to the god of this world!" shouted out a demonic voice from the blackened background. "I just love those 'acts of God!'" jubilantly shouted another.

The very moment the grotesque images were projected, a dramatic change took place in the audience. The timing of the carefully orchestrated special effects achieved their intended goal. The once blackened chamber that was temporarily immersed in doom and gloom, now was instantly transformed to a brightly lit auditorium filled with all typical demonic hoots, screams, and obnoxious hollers that one would expect from a room full of crazy demons. The stage was now set for the master of tonight's ceremony, the lord and king of the demons.

Once again, all eyes were fixed upward on what appeared to be a solitary figure standing with his chest pressed against the left onstage balcony railing. Except for a slightly yellowish skin tone, his height and appearance were almost human-like. Standing a mere seven feet tall, this figure was dressed more like a professional businessman, wearing dark sunglasses, a gray pinstriped suit and tie, and sporting a short, dark cropped hair style. With the click of his finger, the lights again dimmed and ghastly 3D images of the 9–11 jet airliners crashing into the World Trade Center's twin towers appeared on the stage.

"My fellow demons," Apollon, supreme commander of all demons announced in a slow pronounced voice, "this small display of heroic ingenuity was merely the prelude to our final victory, the first shots fired over the bow so to speak. In a brief moment, I will step aside and allow our Lord Satan to reveal to all of you our plans and preparations for Project G 123, our final solution to rid ourselves once and for all of our greatest

enemies, known to our Muslim friends as the Saturday people and the Sunday people."

Apollon was alluding to the Jews who attended their Sabbath on Saturday and the Christians who worshiped on Sunday.

"Lord Satan has given me the honor of personally coordinating the final plans of Project G 123," Apollon bragged. "I will be closely working with the great princes who rule over the former regions of ancient Persia and Assyria, all the nations belonging to our Muslim friends who presently occupy almost every square inch of the Middle East."

Apollo paused briefly and held out both hands in front of him demonstrating with his fingers the close spacing of one square inch.

"I stress almost, because when project G 123 is all said and done, every square inch of Middle Eastern land will be firmly in the grip of their great god Allah, and every single one of those despicable Jews who illegally occupy present-day Palestine will be cast fifty miles out into the Mediterranean Sea."

Apollon knew his demons well. His brief introductory statements were meant to fire up his troops by exploiting the one single passion that all demons cared about almost as much as they did for their own wretched existence, their unified hatred of Jews. Apollon's strategy succeeded as planned. The audience exploded in pandemonium. Not a single demon could be found sulking around any longer in self-pity. They returned once again to their typical, self-absorbed wild selves, running up and down the aisles screaming and hollering, cursing the Jews and blaspheming the very name of God.

Apollon knew his small role was completed. He had successfully set the stage for his leader. With another click of his finger, Apollon ended the mayhem as quickly as it started. The original yellow banner draped across the stage vanished and was instantly replaced by an even larger banner displaying in black letters G 123 printed across a bright red background. Without a spoken word, demons throughout the great hall immediately ceased their mischief and stood at straight attention with clinched right fists held high. Instinctively, they could sense a familiar beckoning calling out from behind the center stage. Each demon seated in the great hall knew that at any moment now their lord and master Satan would be making his appearance.

Inauguration Day
Thursday, January 20th
Noon
West Front Steps of the U.S. Capitol

Under the crisp, crystal blue Washington skies, with the eyes of the entire world watching, the president-elect, Analise Devoe was about to be sworn in as America's first ever woman president. Not only was this an historic first for America, the president-elect's winning percentage of only 36% was also the lowest winning percentage for any presidential election in American history. Her challengers finished an extremely close second and third with the Republican Governor Berry receiving 33% of the popular vote and the campaign spoiler, the third party candidate Eliot Graham, with a surprising 31%.

During her entire campaign, Analise Devoe vowed to bring sweeping changes to America and true to her word, her first major change shocked even her supporters. At the president-elect's personal request, all vestiges of traditional religious expression were banned from her inauguration. That included the presence of clergy on the presidential platform and the placing of the left hand upon a Bible while being sworn in.

With her proud husband, Ethan, beaming at her side, Analise Devoe, a tall, attractive forty-eight-year-old brunette, valedictorian of her high school class, the top graduate in her class at the Harvard Law School, turned confidently to face Chief Justice John O'Reilly. With her left hand firmly held against her side, the president-elect lifted her right hand and proudly repeated the words spoken by the Supreme Justice, "I do solemnly swear that I will faithfully execute the office of President of the United States, and will to the best of my ability, preserve, protect, and defend the Constitution of the United States."

The very moment Analise Devoe completed her oath of office,

everyone present in the stands above and the crowds below could sense something of importance was missing. Ever since the first inaugural oath was administered, presidents had completed their oaths of office by declaring the traditional phrase, "So help me God!" For the first time since George Washington was sworn in as America's first president, precedent was broken. Analise Devoe's omission of the closing phrase sent out chilling shockwaves that even raised the eyebrows of Washington's most liberal elite.

Standing proud and unapologetic, the newly sworn president turned and gave recognition to the governmental officials surrounding her on the VIP platform.

"Senator Hartman, Mr. Chief Justice, Mr. President Kovack, Vice President Nelson, Senator Greenberg, Speaker O'Dell, and my fellow American citizens, this peaceful transfer of authority is rare in history, yet common in our country. With a simple oath, we affirm past standards, and make new beginnings. As I begin, I want to thank President Kovach for his eight years of dedicated service to our nation. I also want to thank both Governor Berry and Mr. Graham for a contest conducted with spirit, and ending with grace.

"I am honored and humbled to stand here, where so many of America's leaders have come before me, and so many will follow. In the eyes of many observers, this four-year ceremony we accept as normal is a demonstration that we Americans are a united people pledged to maintaining a political system which guarantees individual liberty to a greater degree than any other. This transition of power is a strong exhibit to the world that the business of our nation will go forward.

"For the past decade, our great nation has been confronted with an economic affliction of greatest proportions. We have suffered through the longest and one of the most painful financial periods of our national history. It has distorted our economic decisions, penalized thrift, and crushed the struggling young and the fixed-income elderly alike. It threatens to shatter the lives of millions of our citizens. I, for one, could not stand by any longer and watch my beloved country and people suffer any longer. For the past year and a half, I have invested all of my time, my money, my heart and soul campaigning all across our nation sharing my vision on how we can make America great again. You have given me your vote of confidence and I promise all of you, before my term as president is over, America will be number one again! "

Suddenly, as if a Fourth of July skyrocket had just exploded right on the stage, the human masses in the stands and in the crowds below appeared to instantly disappear into a million vibrant colors. In turn, the surrounding blue skies and the entire Washington backdrop rapidly dissolved into an inky black nothingness. Awestruck by the spectacle, the demon audience sat back in their seats speechless, totally overwhelmed by what they had just witnessed. Instantly, the entire concert hall stage reappeared. There, standing all alone and smiling at the center stage podium was Analise Devoe, or so it appeared. As she proceeded to raise both of her arms upward, she quoted out loud the words of the human author Charles Dickens, "Are these the shadows of things that will be, or are they the shadows of the things that may be?"

Instantly, the person standing at the podium transformed from the figure of Analise Devoe into a towering three-headed aberration with two pairs of scaled covered wings protruding out from its muscular shoulders. The head on the left, topped with raven black hair and ruby red eyes, spoke out horrendous blasphemies in harmonic rhythms against both God and man. At same time, the head on the right, identical in every detail to head on the left but with emerald green eyes, sang out arrogant melodious praises to itself. The head in the center was the exception. Cropped with golden hair and sapphire blue eyes, the center head had retained all of its former beauty and splendor.

Satan was now standing center stage ready to deliver his fateful message. With both opposite heads now silent, the center head began to speak in a cold, harsh voice.

"I want to make this perfectly clear to every one of you present in this room. There is nothing I can say and there is nothing I can do that will buy any of you one more second of existence."

The center head paused momentarily to allow the heads on the left and right to admonish the audience with the same repetitious words. "Listen as the master speaks!"

"Our past victories are now history," Satan continued. "They're behind us and won't mean anything if we are not totally focused on this final victory. There is no more looking back. Every one of us has worked long and hard to get to where we are and I can tell all of you, victory is so close right now I can reach out and touch it. I can put it in my mouth and taste it! Victory is ours if only we work together!"

This time, the center head joined in with the other two heads and shouted out in unison, "Victory is ours. Victory is ours!"

"Take a good hard look at those black letters on the banner behind me," Satan shouted. "The G 123 is more then a simple acronym on a banner. It is our road map to victory. We all know the prophecies! When God's son returns, he plans on setting up his headquarters in Jerusalem. I am here to tell all of you, that is not going to happen! We are not going to let it happen. Not only will there be no Jerusalem left for His return, there won't be a single Jew left alive to greet his arrival!"

Satan again paused in order to allow his audience of restless demons a moment to vent their hyper suppressed energy before continuing. As soon as all the hoots and hollers ceased, Satan continued.

"The nicest thing about G 123 is that we didn't have to lift a finger to plan it. God was gracious enough to do it all for us. We didn't even realize that God was dumb enough to place it right in front of us the entire time! To think of all the time we wasted makes me sick!" Satan cried out.

The demons sat on the edge of their seats, both totally confused and at the same time, totally captivated by their master's words.

"G 123," Satan continued, "stands for that cursed verse that we're all too familiar with, Genesis Chapter 12 verse 3. God established this as protective hedge for those descendants of Abraham. Don't you remember that every single time we came up with a brilliant plan to utterly destroy the Jews, G 123 was right there to snatch victory out of our hands, every single plan, every single time!"

Satan paused once again raising a clinched fist high as the two opposite heads shouted out obscene blasphemes toward heaven.

"I've made my mistakes in the past and I have no intentions on ever

repeating them," Satan admitted. "If I've learned anything at all over all these millennia, it is this one important detail. You must first know your enemy. You must study him in every detail before you can defeat him."

As Satan continued to speak, the bloody image of Jesus hanging upside down on an inverted cross appeared in the background. The entire audience spontaneously reacted with a wild outburst of hisses and boos.

"Now, listen and take note," Satan commanded. "This is how we are going to use G123 to our advantage. I know my enemy. At one time I thought God was invincible, but I was wrong. God does have a weakness. He cannot go against His written word and we, my friends, are going to use this to our advantage. Now, I ask all of you, what is the only human nation on planet Earth that still protects the Jew?"

"America!" the demons hordes replied.

"What does Genesis 12:3 say God would do to any people or nations who comes against the Jew? Satan again asked.

"They will be cursed!" the demons screamed.

"What will happen if America turns her back on those Zionistic Jews who are now occupying Muslim Palestine?" Satan shouted.

"God will curse and destroy America!" the demons shouted back.

"Then that will be our charge," Satan replied in a smooth, confident voice. "We must do everything in our power to convince America to stop all support for Israel. After that, we can simply sit back and let God take care of the rest. With America out of the way, Israel will be all ours."

The entire audience stood to their feet and broke out into a deafening applause. All three of Satan's heads turned around in every direction with each displaying a devious, grinning smirk.

"If you are ready to destroy the Jew, once and for all, shout it again, even louder!" Satan's center head commanded.

Even though the screams and holler were now beyond deafening, Satan had one more request for his army of demons.

"Now," all three heads shouted in unison, "if you are ready to destroy, America, the protectorate of the Jew once and for all, then scream out, "Death to America!"

The demonic response to Satan's final command was so overwhelming that several humans assigned as night guards reported seeing the Kennedy

Center's walls vibrating back and forth like a tuning fork. Satan stood for a moment longer just gloating at center stage, puffed up with pride. Just as he had done so many years prior in Nazi Germany, he once again had his entire demonic army all fired up in one accord. Everything was ready. Project G 123 was about to commence.

Chapter Nine

"Today there are approximately 100 *million American church members who have very little to no understanding of Bible prophecy. These church members are from replacement theology churches that don't teach Bible prophecy and who look at prophetic scriptures as allegorical and not literal. Consequently, they do not understand the importance of Israel to the God of Israel or God's redemptive plan for Israel and the nations. These church members also have no understanding of the biblical significance of what is transpiring today in Israel, Russia, China, Iraq, Iran, Syria, Turkey, and in other Middle East nations. They are also not aware of the significance of the formation of the European Union, new ID technologies and much more."*

Bill Koenig, Koeign International News

In every war, regardless of the sides or positions, there is a foe. In every battlefield, there is a frontline. For thousands of years, the major foe in the eternal battle for the destiny of mankind on planet Earth has been a highly misunderstood word called "religion." In all of the centuries from past to present, the frontline of this eternal battlefield has never changed position. It runs along the same fateful route taken thousands of years ago by a man named Abraham, considered to be the founding father of mankind's three great monotheistic religions, Judaism, Christianity, and Islam. Over the centuries, billions of faithful have passionately lived out their lives and died fervently believing the same ancient claim—that God's promises made to Abraham pertained solely to "their" religion. Over the millennia, millions of faithful have willingly sacrificed their lives in holy wars and battles, passionately believing with all of their heart, soul, and might that their religion held an exclusive entitlement to God's promises.

As Satan's closing hours on Earth rapidly approach, he turns once again to one of the most successful weapons in his vast arsenal of lies and deceit used solely for the purpose of either delaying or possibly destroying once and for all God's prophetic plan. Using the time proven disguise of "religion," Satan's final attempt to thwart God's plan will be to draw each of the three rival religions into a climatic battle with a frontline in the exact place where the conflict all began thousands of years before, at a Judean hill called Mt. Moriah.

Wednesday, November 8th
Ramallah, West Bank

For well over a generation, the people living in the West Bank city of Ramallah, located only nine miles north of Jerusalem, have seen their share of good and bad times. Surrounding this beautiful Middle Eastern city, which in Arabic means "God's hill," are orchards of fig and olive trees, and grape vineyards as far as the eye can see. Once considered the most affluent and culturally diverse of all Palestinian cities, Ramallah was home to not only the largest Arab Christian and Muslim populations, but also, Palestinian poets, artists, and musician as well. Unfortunately, those days of prosperity are long gone. Two Palestinian uprisings or intifadas against the Israeli military occupation over the past twenty years has left the city's economy in shambles and caused an exodus of fully one third of the Ramallah's wealthiest natives to the United States. In their void, thousands of homeless, displaced Arabs poured into Am'ari, Qalandia, Qadourah, and Jalazon, the four refuge camps surrounding the outskirts of Ramallah leaving this one time jewel of the Middle East to squander in hopelessness and despair.

As a new day dawned and the first rays of sunlight over the eastern mountains began dissipating the cloak of darkness covering the city of Ramallah, so too, a new sense of hope began to rise up in this city's overlooked people. As the residences of the city made their way out into the streets and neighborhoods, hand waves and gestures of victory signs were openly visible on every corner and at every shop throughout the city. Smiles of hope replaced the frowns of despair that were evident on faces just twenty-four hours earlier. For the people of Ramallah, there were unspoken feelings that today was definitely going to be a good day, a very good day. The prospects of an American president being elected who would be supportive of their cause appeared this morning to be a very real possibility. Not since the days of their famed leader Yasser Arafat have the people of this city expressed so much hope for their future.

Wednesday, November 8th
8 a.m. Israeli Standard Time
Grand Park Hotel
Ramallah, West Bank

A white minibus with a seating capacity for eighteen passengers was parked outside the front entrance of the Ramallah Grand Park Hotel waiting to pick up and transport a group of seven American Episcopal Bishops for an 11 a.m. conference at their appointed destination 35 km south in Bethlehem. The bishops were part of a contingency of American clergy sent by their respective denominations to the West Bank on a duel mission; first, as part of a interfaith delegation to investigate alleged atrocities reportedly carried out by Israeli troops on Palestinians living in Ramallah's refugee camps, and secondly, to represent their respective denominations at the annual conference of the International Worldwide Council of Churches held this year in Bethlehem.

The first to arrive at the minibus was Anderson McShay, the bishop representing the Northeastern dioceses of the American Episcopal Church. Bishop McShay, affectionately named Bishop Andy by the people of his home state of Rhode Island, was rather tall and slightly on the rotund side. Crowned with a perfect bald spot, his appearance was more monk-like than clergy. Two hotel porters followed Bishop Andy with his luggage out to the awaiting minibus. There he was met by a strikingly handsome, taller than average, middle-aged Palestinian named Fahim Jahromi, the delegation's assigned tour guide for the remainder of their stay in Palestine. Fahim respectfully greeted his American guest with a warm smile and gracious handshake.

"Your Excellency, did you have a good night's sleep?"

"Well, Fahim," Bishop Andy responded with a nod and a smile, "if you consider three hours a good night's sleep, then I had an excellent sleep."

"Ah, your Excellency, you stayed up to watch the election results, didn't you?"

"Fahim, if there is one thing that drives me crazy it is a cliff-hanger and this election has been the mother of all cliffhangers."

"Have they declared a winner yet?"

"When I turned off CNN five minutes ago, Devoe had a slight lead, but they said it was still too close to call," Bishop Andy commented as he wheeled his large suitcase toward the front of the bus.

"No, no, your Excellency," Fahim interjected, "please, allow me to store your luggage here." Fahim proceeded to stoop down and open the latch to a special luggage compartment located along the bottom passenger side of the bus.

"Now that's a first," Bishop Andy admitted. "I've never seen a minibus with its own built in luggage compartment.

"It is a wonderful addition on all the new models, your Excellency"

After carefully positioning the large suit case to the back of the compartment, Fahim looked up from his kneeling position and innocently asked "If it is not too forward of me, your Excellency, could I ask, who did you vote for?"

"Analise Devoe," Bishop Andy proudly stated as he handed his tour guide a final small carrying case. "There was no other choice."
"I'm a little surprised, your Excellency."

"You thought that because I'm a Christian bishop I would vote for the American Value's candidate, Eliot Graham," Bishop Andy smugly replied. "Personally speaking, Eliot Graham is what we call in America a right-wing nut, the Christian equivalent to your Muslim extremist."

"I don't understand," Fahim looked up with a puzzled look. "I am aware that Christians come in a variety of sects like us Muslims, but I have never heard a Christian use those terms before in reference to a fellow Christian. I thought all Christians were called by Christ to get along and love one another."

"If it could only be that simple," Bishop Andy replied as he shrugged his shoulders and turned to greet an approaching familiar face.

"Andy, aren't you the early bird!" commented Benjamin Allen, bishop of the Chicago diocese and representing his Midwestern district. Bishop Allen could be described as tall, thin and extremely likeable. He wouldn't let a person pass without first introducing himself and extending a warm friendly handshake. He was also Chicago's first black Episcopal bishop.

Following right behind him was Manuel Gonzalez, Bishop Manny as he was called back in his Dallas/Ft. Worth diocese. Bishop Manny was the shortest of the three. Standing only five foot five, what this human dynamo lacked in stature he more than compensated in heart. Back in Dallas, Bishop Manny was known as the bishop who never slept, working night and day, seven days a week, making sure the needs of all the people in his diocese were met. For his tireless efforts, Bishop Manny was selected Dallas/Forth Worth's "Person of the Year" for two consecutive years.

With Fahim's assistance, Bishops Allen and Gonzalez, followed by four other high-ranking Episcopal clergy, loaded their personal items and luggage into the bus's special storage compartment, and finally, off they went, destination Bethlehem.

For over twenty-five years, Fahim Jahromi had been directing guided tours to the famous Holy Sites located in the Palestinian cities of Bethlehem, Hebron, and Ramallah. As a young Muslim boy growing up in the poorer outskirts of Bethlehem, Fahim would tag along with the visiting religious groups touring Bethlehem's most popular sites such as the Church of the Nativity and the Shepherd's Fields. Having a keen mind, he was able to absorb and put to memory every word spoken by the different tour guides. As a teenager, Fahim was literally consumed with reading every book he could find involving the history and archeology of the Middle East and the Holy Lands. It was this innate passion to learn and share all about the ancient history of his people that made Fahim Jahromi one of the most sought-after tour guides in Central Palestine, so much so that he was presently booked almost a year in advance. As the minibus carrying Fahim and his party of seven departed Ramallah traveling south through the barren Judean desert, Fahim's inquisitive American passengers immediately began riveting their astute Palestinian guide with a barrage of probing questions, starting first with Bishop Andy.

"So, Fahim, when we first started planning this trip early last year, we were told by the Palestinian minister of tourism that you were the person that we should talk to first."

"Praise be to Allah, your Excellency," Fahim proudly replied as he glanced back in his rearview mirror. "I am very much honored to be at your service."

"Have you always wanted to be a tour guide?" Bishop Allen followed.

"I have had a passion for our people's history as long as I can remember. Every day I wake up I am still amazed to think that my ancestors have lived continuously in this land for thousands of years. I am so blessed by Allah that I can go to work every morning and get paid well for simply telling the true stories of my culture and my people to anyone who will listen."

"Fahim," Bishop McShay asked, "how has the Israeli occupation affected you and your family?"

"Well, your Excellency," Fahim smiled as he glanced back at his passengers in the rear view mirror, "to earn a living for my family I have to commute daily between Bethlehem and Ramallah. My commute between Bethlehem to the north and Ramallah to the south is about 35 kilometers. Up until 1991, the natural road between Bethlehem and Ramallah passed through Jerusalem. Being a student of history, I can't tell you how much I enjoyed driving daily through parts of Jerusalem and viewing the walls of the old city. Even with the occasional traffic jams, it was a very convenient ride. I could usually reach my destination in 35 minutes. Unfortunately, that is all just a distant memory. Since 1991, thanks to the Jewish authorities, the opened door to Jerusalem was permanently closed in the face of all Palestinians."

"Fahim," Bishop Manny interjected, "I believe quite possibly you could be our answer to prayer."

"Me, your Excellency?"

"It is quite obvious that you possess a tremendous amount of insight into the present situation of your people," Bishop Allen followed.

"Your Excellency," Fahim humbly replied, "there are many of my countrymen who know more than I about the depth of our people's troubles."

"Perhaps," followed Bishop Manny, "but we're running out of time. We need some answers now. Our conference ends in two short days and before we leave the West Bank, we have some big decisions to make."

"Fahim," Bishop Andy again interjected. "We have all come a long way to find out for ourselves the truth about what is really taking place here in Central Palestine. I believe with your unique background, you could shed some real light for us on what is really going on with your people."

"Of course!" Fahim replied. "How can I be of help, your Excellency?"

"Just tell us from your prospective how you see the situation today between the Israelis and your people," the bishop said in a voice of compassion.

"Well, I will do my best," Fahim agreed. "Ever since the first intifada in 1991, to be able to travel through Jerusalem, the Jews require we Palestinians to go through a lengthy procedure of obtaining permits. The most tedious of all was to be able to provide a reasonable excuse. Praying at the Al-Aqsa Mosque or passing through to work was never accepted as good enough reasons. While the closure was enforced for "security reasons" during the gulf war, the war ended years ago but the closures have remained."

Fahim paused momentarily to look out at his side view mirror for oncoming traffic. He was about to exit Jappa Rd. and enter Highway no. 60, a modern four-lane expressway that was constructed along the same ancient system of roads that served for thousands of years as trade routes for commerce throughout the Middle East. Today, this north/south route acted as the backbone of transportation for the entire West Bank.

"Now," Fahim continued. "here is my present dilemma. If you look out your windows at that upcoming road sign, you will see we are now exiting the Jappa Road and about to enter onto Highway no. 60. Before the 1991 intifada, Highway 60 would take you directly from Ramallah to Bethlehem in less than 35 minutes, but today, there is one small problem."

"And what is that problem?" Bishop Allen inquired.

"That's simple," Fahim followed. "I am not a Jew! Only a Jew is permitted to travel along the entire length of Highway 60, which passes through the walled off region called Area C."

Fahim was about to give his American guests a brief lesson on how the international powerbrokers had divided up the West Bank. As part of the 2002 Oslo Agreement, Palestinian territories designated within the boundaries of Area "C" were to remain under complete Israeli military control. Under the agreement, the territory administered by the Palestinian Authority was divided into two sections; Area A, under full Palestinian control and Area B, in which Israel had control of security.

"We Palestinians are not permitted to travel on any roads found within Area C. We can only travel on the opened sections of the highway found in regions designated by the Jews as Areas A and B. Once we come near to a Palestinian city, we must exit the highway and take an alternative bypass road passing through areas A and B. So, out of necessity and to avoid the hassles of all the checkpoints in area C, I had to find an alternative road for my daily travels. For me, the infamous Hill Valley Road was my only option. It goes from Bethlehem to the east until you approach Jericho where it then turns north to Ramallah. A trip that once took me 35 minutes to travel from Bethlehem to Ramallah now takes me over 90 minutes on poorly asphalted, very steep mountain roads. I must admit, it had taken me some time before finding the courage to drive on this road."

"So the bypass roads have no checkpoints?" Bishop Allen interjected.

"Check points, there are a few, just not as many. The real hassle is with the Israeli police," Fahim said with a frown. "Even way out here in the Judean wilderness the Israeli police still enjoy hunting Palestinian cars for traffic tickets. We Palestinians are easily identified by a different color of our car's license plates."

"Don't you ever get depressed?" asked Bishop Waters, representing the greater Southwestern diocese.

"At first, but to avoid getting depressed, I've tried to find ways to enjoy my new route. Climbing the hills of the Judean deserts, going near the villages surrounding both Jerusalem and Ramallah, and becoming an excellent driver were most of the positive aspects of using this road. Being forced to see the rapid growth both in number and extent of Israeli settlements all through my travel was a sad indicator of how far we are from reaching a peaceful solution. But with time, I am now accustomed to my newly imposed reality."

"How do your people feel about these restrictions?" Bishop McShay followed.

"Hate!" Fahim emphatically stated. "How can you not hate someone who has broken into your home, stolen all of your possessions, and stripped you of all of your dignity?"

"Fahim, yesterday in Ramallah we heard both sides of the story," Bishop Manny commented. "We were able to interview the IDF [Israeli Defense Forces] soldiers and the Palestine officials, as well as the refugees in Jalazon refugee camp. Can you give us something more specific?"

"Specifics you want?" Fahim briefly turned around to face his passengers with a solemn expression. "Specifics I will show you! Look carefully out your windows to your left at all the twisted heaps of wood and rubble along the side of the road."

With that said, the seven bishops all moved to the left side of the bus and gazed out of their windows in amazement. They saw what appeared to be twisted and splintered wooden timbers deposited in huge piles along the entire length of the road, about 100 feet away from the highway's shoulder and spaced about an equal distance apart.

"It is impossible to tell now, but those heaps of discarded wood were the roots, trunks, and branches of trees making up fig and olive tree orchards owned by the local Palestinian farmers. Last year, the Israeli bulldozers came at night, backed by Israeli tanks and machine guns, and began uprooting the Palestinian farmer's livelihood, orchards that have been in their family's possession for thousands of years, and transforming them into this beautiful wasteland as far as the eye can see."

"Why would they do such a horrible thing?" Bishop Manny asked in a tone of shock and disbelief.

"Why? Why do they do anything?" Fahim snapped back. "They have control, they have all the tanks and all the weapons and nobody complains but us Palestinians. If the Jews wanted to widen the road and put up a wall, do they ask our permission to come in and flatten our homes, our trees and our crops, our livelihoods? The fig and olive trees gave us food. They provided our people with jobs. Now they are fit only for the fire. We believe the Jews want to deprive us of our livelihood, drive us off our land and make common laborers of us, so we have to go to the cities and work for Israelis. No! They just do it and nobody says a thing."

"Fahim, how can you stand for this?" Bishop McShay sharply interjected. "I'm as mad as hell and I don't even live here. The Jews are treating you and your people like second-class citizens. To me, this system you're living under is intolerable, it's nothing less than an apartheid."

"Your Excellencies, please understand." Fahim said emphatically. "I do get mad. I get very mad, but my anger is not kindled against all the Jews. I've worked with Jews and I lived around Jews my entire life. Like my own people, I know many Jews who are decent, caring people. What makes me mad is the system. I get mad at the system that exists on both sides of the wall, both the Israeli system on the west side of the wall and the Palestinian system on the east."

The wall Fahim alluded to was a 659 km long, 100 meter wide network of fences, anti-vehicle trenches, and concrete walls authorized by the Israeli government and constructed by the Israel army as "a defensive measure," designed to block the passage of terrorists, weapons and explosives into the State of Israel. Called a "security fence" by its supporters and a "wall of oppression" by its opponents, this controversial barrier ran north to south passing just inside of western edges of the West Bank and around the city of Jerusalem.

Area C, the land located between the wall and Israel's preoccupation 1967 borders was designated as a special military area. Although all Israelis and Jews, regardless of nationality, could enter this region freely, Palestinians could enter only with special permits even if they were residents of the dozen or so Arab villages totally within its borders. Many who tried to obtain permits were refused them. For those living on the eastern side of Area C, the wall served only to sever the ties of thousands of Palestinians from their homes, schools, families, towns, farms, and water, dividing them into ghettos, permanent prisoners and refugees in their own land.

"I would like to be an idealist," Fahim continued "and believe that one day Jews and Arabs can all live together in peace, but I cannot see that ever happening."

"Why not, Fahim?" Bishop Allen asked. "Why can't they just live in peace?"

The last question apparently struck a chord of discontent. Not only did Fahim pause briefly before responding, his calm demeanor took on a much more serious tone.

"There is one simple reason that all of you from the western world fail to understand. Our people's hatred for one another runs too long and too deep!" he abruptly replied. "It goes all the way back to our father Abraham! We Muslims believe Allah's promises to our father Abraham were passed on through the line of Ishmael, Abraham's first-born son by the Egyptian woman Hagar. According to our blessed Koran, the first-born child, and all of his descendents after him, will inherit everything that the Father possesses, including all of his property and all of his land. On the other hand, the Jew's believe Allah's promises are traced through Isaac, Abraham's second born son through his wife Sari. As long as there have been Arabs and Jews living on this land, there has never been peace and there will never be peace. Until Allah decides differently, that is how it is and that is how it will remain."

For the first time since they departed from the Grand Park Hotel, the party of seven bishops sat in total silence pondering the rather bleak perspectives presented by their guide.

Realizing now was a good time for a change in conversation, Bishop Manny casually blurted, "Hey, Fahim, so how long do you think it will take us to get to Bethlehem from here?"

Looking back in his rear view mirror, Fahim responded to Bishop Manny's subtle hint with a smile and a wink, "With Allah's help and no hassles from the Israeli police, I expect a little over an hour. We should be pulling up to the front entrance of Bethlehem's Jacir Palace Intercontinental Hotel no later than 9:30 a.m., giving all of you plenty of time to find your rooms and freshen up before your 11 a.m. conference."

The intense discussions over Middle Eastern hostilities settled down to a relaxed atmosphere of sharing thoughts and ideas about problems within each of the bishop's local dioceses.

In the natural, at least for the time being, all was calm in the front sections of the bus, but in the supernatural, all hell was about to break loose in the back of the bus.

"Will you look at that!" declared Jaelar.

"Look at all those pompous idiots just sitting along that stupid wall," commented Pylazad, Bishop McShay's assigned familiar spirit.

"Who the hell do they think they are waving at?" shrieked Baelar, the spirit assigned to Jake Patterson, the Bishop representing The Pacific Northwest.

"Let me give them all the finger!" Haebar followed thrusting all four of his greenish yellow appendages through the side of the bus and projecting out from each a scaly clawed middle digit.

Up until now, these four ugly chimeras inside the bus were too busy amusing themselves by stirring up hatred and strife amongst their human hosts. They didn't notice the legions of warrior angelic beings positioned up and down the length of the barrier wall just outside their windows. But now, the sight of scores of their angelic nemeses taunting them from atop the great wall was more than they could bare. Momentarily abandoning their human sport, each of these grotesque demons thrust their scaly reptilian heads through the side of the bus, twisting their faces into the most bizarre contortions while at the same time spewing out the grossest of obscenities toward God, the Jews, and the angels alike.

The demons inside the bus had absolutely no clue that all the angelic waving and taunting was not directed totally at them. For unbeknownst to them and the human passengers inside, two others had been accompanying the minibus ever since their departure from Ramallah. Sitting quite comfortably high on top of the bus were two mighty angelic warriors, Ambriel and Pethel, both on special assignment by orders of their great angelic general, Michael. Their presence was not only for the protection and safety of their human cargo. Their main mission was directed toward just one single passenger, to make sure that this human was given his appointed rendezvous with destiny.

Wednesday, November 8*th*
9:15 *a.m. Israeli Standard Time*
Beit Sahour, 5 *kms East of Bethlehem,*
West Bank

"Fahim, stop the bus!"

Without saying a word, Fahim immediately responded to the urgent call and pulled the bus off to the side of the road and placed it in park. He then turned around to face his passengers and asked with a voice of concern. "Bishop McShay, is everything all right?"

"Fahim, I am really sorry for being so impetuous and blurting out like that," Bishop McShay apologetically followed, "but right out of the blue, while I was marveling at the beautiful countryside, I think I spotted someone I know. Unless my eyes have deceived me, I think it is someone from my hometown."

Bishop McShay's eyes were not deceiving him. About one hundred yards behind their bus were five parked vehicles along the shoulder of the road, three cars, a truck, and large white van with a microwave dish mounted on its top and a familiar set of large blue letters printed along its side, GBN-Gospel Broadcasting Network.

"Fahim, I promise I'll be right back," Bishop McShay stated as he promptly exited the bus and hastily walked toward the direction of the vehicles parked along the side of the road. As he neared the vehicles, he could see what appeared to be a crew of about a dozen individuals moving about in an organized fashion unloading and setting up video equipment for some sort of on-sight television program. Off to the side, away from the busy technical crew, sat a group of four individuals huddled together in a circle, reading and discussing the details of their project. A very attractive black woman, looking up her lines, was the first to spot the stranger in their midst.

"Sir, can I help you?" she asked the stranger out of concern.

"No," replied Andy McShay with a smile, "but I believe this gentleman sitting in front of you can."

Upon hearing the gentleman's voice, other group members abruptly stopped their discussion and turned to look up at the sight of a rather tall, heavyset man dressed in priestly garbs smiling down at them.

"Andy McShay?" joyfully announced the group's leader, a middle-aged man wearing a Boston Red Sock's cap.

"Tom Reid?"

"This isn't Providence," Tom joking commented as he stood to his feet and locked hands with the person he knew since his childhood. Both Tom and Andy grew up in the same neighborhood and attended thirteen years of public school together. Their paths separated briefly in college, but amazingly enough, both had entered the ministry about the same. Since then, they continued to keep in relatively close contact with each other. "Andy, what are you doing all the way out here in the middle of nowhere?"

"The Lord's work, of course!" Bishop Andy jubilantly replied.

"Me too!" Tom replied, "But actually, we're just getting ready to shoot our Christmas special to be aired next month. You have to admit, you can't find a better backdrop than this with the town of Bethlehem in the background and actual shepherds out in the fields tending their sheep!"

"Who's running the show when you're out of town?"

"Did you ever hear of co-hosts?" Tom smiled. "But really, what brings the Bishop of Rhode Island to the outskirts of Bethlehem?"

"Do you see that bus down the road?" Bishop Andy asked as he placed his hand on his friend's shoulder and pointed in the direction of the minibus. "I'm part of a contingency of Episcopal bishops sent here to represent our church at the annual conference of the World Wide Council of Churches."

"I heard about it," Tom replied. "I believe they said it's going to be an historic meeting, the largest church gathering ever in Bethlehem."

"That's what I was told." With that comment, Bishop McShay's entire character instantly changed from cheerful and lighthearted to serious and direct. Before he could say a word, a thought flashed through his mind.

"Arrange a meeting with Tom Reid while you are both here in Bethlehem. Impress upon him how important it is to expose to the Christian world the way the horrific Jewish oppression you witnessed is affecting the poor Palestinian people living in the West Bank."

"Tom, how long are you planning on staying in Bethlehem. I really have something very important to discuss with you?"

"Well, Andy, our schedule here is really tight. We have three more shoots to make in and around Bethlehem We're planning on having everything wrapped up sometime tomorrow afternoon. After that, our flight back to Providence leaves from Jerusalem 9 a.m. sharp Friday morning. How's about we schedule a meeting someday next week when we're all back home and things are a little less hectic?"

"Tell him you 'must' meet with him before tomorrow evening!"

"Tom, you mentioned before that this makes a perfect backdrop for your Christmas special." Looking out toward the grass covered terrain dotted with Palestinian shepherds herding their flocks of sheep, Bishop McShay continued, "This is also a perfect backdrop for what I have to ask you."

The serious tone of Bishop McShay's voice stirred Tom Reid's curiosity. What could possibly be so important that it wouldn't wait until they were back home next week? But for him, curiosity alone was not a deciding factor. Tom had learned from past experiences to seek God first in all of his decisions, large or small. *Lord, what would you have me do?* he silently prayed.

"You are to meet with him tomorrow evening. Take him to this very place and I will tell you what to say."

"Ok, Andy," Tom obediently replied to the voice of the Holy Spirit. "Let's meet tomorrow evening. Tell me where you are staying and I'll pick you up around six o'clock."

Instantly, Bishop Andy's jovial demeanor returned. He shook Tom's hand, said his goodbyes to the GBN's staff and crew, and hastily returned to his awaiting bus.

"You did very good!" Ambriel sarcastically complimented the ugly chimera held tightly in his angelic grip. In general, angels were under strict orders, regardless of how tempting it would be, never to destroy a human's familiar spirit. Only a human could rid himself or herself of a familiar spirit by fully repenting of their sins and turning their lives over to Jesus to be made whole. Only under the directives of a superior archangel, in this case Michael, could a warrior angel intervene directly between a human and his assigned familiar spirit. In this case, both Ambriel and Pethel were given directives from Michael to do what ever was necessary in order to arrange a meeting between Tom Reid and Andy McShay.

Moments before McShay noticed Tom Reid and the crew from GBN along the side of the road, both Ambriel and Pethel made their presence known inside the bus by making a surprise attack on the demons in the back of the bus. With his mighty sword drawn, Pethel kept the four demons at bay in the back of the bus while Ambriel positioned himself along side of Bishop Mc Shay and spoke directly into him thoughts, "Look at the person standing along the side of the road."

Back on the bus, all was quiet. While the humans patiently awaited the return of Bishop McShay, they occupied their time discussing their upcoming conference. On the other hand, the three demons in the back of the bus also found themselves totally occupied by the edge of Pethel's sword.

"I kept my end of the bargain, now release me!" demanded Pylazad as he and his captor made their return.

"The pleasure is all mine!" Ambriel commented as he released his tight grasp on the scaly arms of Bishop McShay's familiar spirit."

As they parted company, the curious little demon shouted out to the great warrior, "Tell me, mighty warrior, why would a filthy Jewish scum protector be interested in arranging a meeting to expose the plans of the Israeli pigs to the world?"

"To tell you the truth, I really don't know," Ambriel honestly replied. "I guess we'll both have to remain patient and wait to find out for ourselves!"

Chapter Ten

"Ye shall know the truth and the truth will make you free."

John 8:32 KJV

According to Albert Einstein, insanity was defined as doing the same thing over and over again and expecting different results. If Einstein was correct, then Satan is truly the most insane creature ever in existence. From the very beginning, he has been the author and chief architect of anti-Semitism. Using religion as his platform and a poisonous mixture of human ignorance, prejudice, and greed as its supports, Satan and his myriad of demonic forces have persistently employed the same main goal: to utterly destroy God's prophetic plan by totally eliminating the Jews, the true recipients of God's promised covenant with Abraham. Covering a time period of over three thousand years, Satan has colluded with the world's most influential leaders, both secular and religious, in a succession of failed attempts to eliminate the Jewish people and the Jewish nation Israel from the face of earth.

Never being able to achieve his ultimate goal, Satan attempted to do the next best thing: keep the Jews as far as possible away from their promised homeland by scattering them to the four corners of the earth. This was first successfully accomplished in the year 70 AD, when the Roman army under General Titus destroyed the city of Jerusalem, massacred over a million Jews, and sent millions of survivors into permanent exile. From that time on, the exiled Jewish people found no resting place for the soles of their feet. For the next two thousand years, the scattered Jews living in the Gentile nations had to endure a long, long tale of Satanically inspired persecutions, suffering, tears, blood, and torture, all done in the name of Jesus.

Labeled "Christ killers" by the church in 1096, Jews were systematically hunted down and slaughtered throughout Europe and the Holy Lands by the advancing crusaders. The persecutions accelerated in the thirteenth century when Jews found themselves banished from countries they now called their homes; in 1290, all Jews were expelled from England, in 1306 from France, 1492 from Spain, and in 1497 from Portugal. By 1555, Jews were considered social outcasts and confined only to designated ghettos found scattered throughout Europe and Russia.

Beginning in the late 19th century, Russian Jews experienced numerous programs or anti-Semitic acts of violence. Thousands of Jewish homes were destroyed, Jewish women were sexually assaulted, and families were reduced to living in extreme poverty. Just as Haman and the Persian Empire were used by Satan back in the 6th century BC as an attempt to destroy the Jews, Adolf Hitler and Nazi Germany became another timely Satanic plot to annihilate the true descendants of Abraham in the 20th century. When Adolf Hitler became Chancellor of Germany in 1933, he set out on a concentrated program to intensify his nation's hatred of the Jews. Hitler mounted a powerful propaganda campaign designed and implemented by Joseph Goebbels, who blamed the Jews for Germany's many economic problems, as well as the worldwide threat of Communism. At the same time, fearful of Nazi inroads into the Arab world, the British government issued the infamous 'White Papers' limiting Jewish immigration to Palestine, thus virtually locking Jews into a Europe that was being overrun by Hitler. This hatred of the Jews ultimately led to what was known as the "Final Solution," the physical annihilation of almost six million Jews in Nazi death camps reducing their number in Europe to a mere fraction of their original population.

Vowing "never again" to allow themselves to be trapped into another Holocaust, Jews the world over rallied to the Zionist cause of returning to their homeland. Though faced with violent opposition from Palestinian Arabs and others, Jews persisted in their quest for freedom and autonomy in the land given to them by God. Finally in 1947, the United Nations partitioned Palestine into Arab and Jewish states. The Jewish state, Israel, declared its independence on May 14, 1948. After almost 2000 years of separation, the Jews were once again back in their promised land, but not without cost. Even before the ink on the U.N charter declaring Israel an independent nation had dried, the tiny, newly formed Jewish state was attacked from all sides by the invading armies of six Arab nations: Eygpt, Syria, Transjordan, Lebanon, Iraq and Saudi Arabia. In addition, local Palestinian forces joined in to fight a country so new, they didn't even have time to organize an army. From 1948 until the present day, each time Israel was invaded, terrorized, or threatened by its Arab neighbors, the outcome of Satan's relentless attacks has always been the same; with the supernatural help of her protectorate, Michael and his multitudes of angelic warriors, Israel has crushed the invading military forces and seized large amounts of land from their foes. With his time on earth running out, Satan once again resorts to "religion," his favorite anti-Semitic tool of choice to remove the Jews once-and-for-all from the land deeded to them thousands of years ago by God.

Thursday, November 9th
10 *a.m. Israeli Standard Time*
Ad-Dar Cultural & Conference Center
Bethlehem, West Bank

From all over the globe they've come. Men and women from every culture and walk of life have descended upon this historic city for what they expect will be an equally historic event. Dressed in the traditional religious garbs of their homeland, delegates representing over 300 churches worldwide exit taxis, limousines, and buses lined up along Pope Paul VI Street in the Old city of Bethlehem, all walking toward the same destination, Bethlehem's newly constructed ad-Dar Cultural and Conference Center. Located in the heart of the old city of Bethlehem, this up-to-date facility built specifically for sponsoring local, national and international concerts, theatre, and large conferences, will, for the second consecutive day, host the annual two day meeting of the World Council of Churches.

As the delegates arrived for their final meeting, they were greeted once again by a large white banner with blue lettering draped across the building's front entrance stating "Bethlehem Welcomes Delegates from the World Council of Churches." Anticipation mounted as the seconds ticked off toward the ten o'clock hour. With every seat in the four hundred person capacity Addar Hall auditorium filled, each and every delegate in attendance sat well aware of the historic implications of the final agenda set before them. At exactly ten o'clock, the first speaker made his way up on the stage to the front podium.

From its conception in 1948, when representatives from 147 churches from both mainline Protestant and Christian Orthodox backgrounds assembled in Amsterdam, the organization has grown today to include over 340 member denominations representing over 550 million Christians worldwide. With the end of World War II as a backdrop, the World Council of Churches or WCC held its first meeting with one noble purpose in mind, to bring Christian unity to a fractured worldwide church. From that day forward, the WCC set as its main goal to achieve something that had never been attempted or accomplished before in the two thousand year history of the church, "ecumenism" or the "unity of the churches."

As years passed, the WCC put aside its original goal of achieving church unity and set its sights on achieving a much bolder vision. The organization that started with the noble aim of unifying the body of Christ, unwittingly adopted the doctrine of demons, seeking instead to be man pleasers instead of God pleasers, the WCC refocused its energies on more worldly goals, such as achieving unity amongst all the world's religions and attaining world peace. As the conference began, the WCC's general secretary, Dr. Columbo Kolapeebo, the tall, very popular outspoken Bishop of Kenyan's African Methodist Episcopalian Church, stepped up to the podium and once again welcomed the over four hundred delegates seated before him. With a deep, rich African accent, the WCC's General Secretary began his speech:

"My fellow brothers and sisters in Christ, it is my great pleasure and honor to welcome the distinguished members of the delegation of the Church to this great Ecumenical Centre once again. At this time, I would like to personally thank all the staff members of ad-Dar Cultural and Conference Center, a Lutheran-based, ecumenically-oriented institution serving the whole Palestinian community for hosting us over the past two days."

Dr. Kolapeebo paused momentarily to give recognition to the conference's fifteen hosts all seated to the right of the stage, a staff of mostly Palestinian women headed by the Lutheran minister Rev. Dr. Mitri Raheb. WCC's general secretary folded his hands and bowed in sincere gratitude before continuing.

"Today, you serve as a 'common house' for all member churches of the World Council—Anglican, Old Catholic, Orthodox, Protestant—that have committed themselves to join in a 'fellowship of churches.' We, the members of the World Council of Churches, thank all of you from the bottom of our hearts for your gracious and wonderful hospitality."

After a brief, appreciative applause, the general secretary turned once again toward the audience and continued his speech.

"On this historic occasion, we welcome with great joy and gratitude the spiritual heads of all the churches present with us today. We will open today's meeting with a prayer and a favorite hymn, selected just for this special occasion.

"Directly following today's hymn," Dr. Kolapeebo paused. A visible look of concern was apparent on the general secretary's dark, wrinkled face. Taking in a deep breath, he continued, "we will introduce our new, all gender-inclusive doxology voted on just yesterday by an overwhelming majority of represented delegates. I will now ask Reverend Elizabeth Worthington, president of council of United Methodist churches, to begin today's meeting with prayer. We will then all stand and sing one of my favorite classic hymns 'O

Little Town of Bethlehem,' followed immediately by the singing our newly revised doxology."

The general secretary exaggerated slightly when he mentioned an overwhelming majority voted for the doxology change resolution. It was more like a simple majority of 53%, mostly the extreme liberal denominations which pushed hard for years, and finally succeeded, in having three little words changed on the classical Christian standard of faith that, up until this day, was attached to the end of Christian hymns to expressed the true triune nature of their Creator. Using the accepted mantra that today's church must be more sensitive and more inclusive for the feelings of others, the resolution passed using the divisive wording that the church should seek fresh ways to speak of the mystery and wonder of a triune God.

After a brief prayer asking God's guidance and blessing on today's all important meeting, Reverend Worthington asked delegates to stand with her and sing the famous hymn responsible for etching the name of this small, obscure Palestinian town into the minds of perhaps more than half the world's population. All stood to their feet and sung with their deepest Christian convictions the words to all the verses of 'O little town of Bethlehem' presented on the large stage screen, but the moment the newly worded doxology was projected,

"Praise God, from Whom all blessings flow; Praise Him, all creatures here below; Praise Him above, ye heavenly host; Praise Creator, Child, and Spirit of Love" at least one third of the delegates, including Bishops Allen and Gonzalez of the Episcopal delegation, sat down in silent protest.

Throughout the prayer and singing of the hymn, a contingent of over fifty demons from every ranking stood in the background booing and hissing at the very mention of the name of Christ. But during the singing of the doxology, each demon proudly raised their right fist high and shouted praises to their lord, Satan.

"To tell you the truth, Master, I never though I would see the day!" stated Beelazad with a look of awe on his yellowish face. "To think that

these religious leaders would go as far as changing the very foundation statements of their faith."

"O' Ye of little faith," Apollon seethed as he turned to the captain of his demon spirits. "After all of this time, haven't you learned anything at all about these stupid, wretched creatures?"

Wearing the same gray pinstriped business suit he had worn just days before at the Kennedy Center, Apollon, Satan's second in command, turned and looked outward toward the human audience. "Religious or not, a human is a human. They are weak-minded, self-centered little fish. Can't you get it into your thick heads yet? What have I preached to all of you over these thousands of millennia? Are you all deaf? If you use the right bait, humans will hook themselves, every single time!"

"What about Mother Theresa?" scoffed a low-level chimera standing in the background.

"Mother Theresa wasn't human, you idiot!" Apollon snapped sharply. "She was an angelic plant."

All the other demons stared at each other in amazement at Apollon's last statement. Was it possible that some of the humans-those who were the most difficult to tempt -were actually angels in disguise, or was their commander simply lying? No one would dare question.

"Now shut up and watch in amazement as all these stupid little human fish swallow whole that big chunk of delicious tasting bait we have been feeding them all these years."

With all delegates seated, the General Secretary Kolapeebo again steps up to the podium, this time joined by an Arab interpreter hired to translate his important speech from English to Arabic.

"Again, I welcome all of you here to the very place where it all began. According to biblical scholars, that blessed event, the birth of the Prince of Peace, took place here over two thousand years ago in a cave, not far from where we sit today. From that one blessed so long ago in the town of Bethlehem, God has now beaconed his children back home, those of you seated here today, the representatives of Christ's body, to fulfill a destiny that was set in motion so long ago in this very place. Christ was born in very poor, humbling conditions. May I add, not much better than the living standards we find most people living here today. At the time of Christ's birth, this city and this land knew no peace. The people living in Palestine two thousand years ago were suppressed by the cruel and viscous occupation of the state of Rome. I must confess to all of you something I have wrestled with my entire Christian life."

Again, Dr. Kolapeebo paused momentarily and stared out toward the audience before continuing.

"I have always had trouble understanding how we can call Christ the Prince of Peace. When he was born, the Romans were in charge. And when he died, Bethlehem was still under Roman occupation. Now two thousand years later, Bethlehem still has no peace. This city and this land is still occupied. I have prayed and gone sleepless many nights seeking God for the answer to this dilemma and I believe he showed me. Recall, if you can, the first three lines and the last line found in verse two of the song we just sang. 'For Christ was born of Mary, and gathered all above. While mortals sleep, the angels keep, and peace to men on earth.'"

Dr. Kolapeebo again paused before stressing his point.

"I believe within these few simple verses, sung by millions, both young and old alike, lies the answer to not only my dilemma, but perhaps, the answer for some of you as well. 'While mortals sleep,'" he again paused briefly.

"My dear brothers and sisters in Christ, we are the mortals, we who make up the Church. When Christ came to earth, we were the ones asleep. For the past two thousand years up until this very day, there has been no peace on earth for we, the body of Christ, have remained asleep. Let me stress with all of you. It is by no accident that we are here today. Listen to the words of Christ himself, 'Would that even today you knew the things that make for peace! But now they are hid from your eyes.' I tell you brothers and sisters in Christ, God has looked through his portal of time. He has destined us to be here for such a time as this—working together, as the most powerful religious body of believers this world has ever seen, we can stop the oppression that has kept the people of Palestine prisoners in their own land for thousands of years. Today, we the mortal representatives of Christ on earth, have an opportunity to change history.

"Upon the screen, and also found in the packets you received this morning, are details on resolution 1246. For simplicity's sake, we will refer to its acronym, IDP for the Israeli Divestment Plan—a process of phased in selective divestments from multinational corporations involved in and supporting the occupation of Palestine. I assure all of you, our peace committee has researched this resolution thoroughly and unanimously recommends that this action is commendable in both method and manner. It uses criteria rooted in faith and calls members to do the 'things that make for peace' as spoken of in Luke 19:42. We encourage all of our member Churches to give serious consideration to applying these economic measures, very similar to those successfully employed in South Africa that ended their horrible apartheid. We must pressure the Israeli government to release its strangle hold on Palestine, and give back all of the land including East Jerusalem to their rightful owners, the Palestinian Arabs."

Tat-ha-tat-tat-tat-tat. Without warning, the deafening sounds of nearby automatic weapons and gunfire sent everybody in the large auditorium running for cover, behind chairs or simply diving onto the floor to make themselves as small a target as possible.

Immediately, the doors of the auditorium burst open. Standing at the front entrance of the auditorium stood a man armed with what appeared to be an automatic weapon. With a broad smile across his face, he looked out at the empty isles and jubilantly proclaimed, "She has won! Your new president is a woman, Analise Devoe—friend to the Palestinian. She has been declared the new President of the United States! Praise be to Allah!" he shouted. "Allah is great Allah is great!"

"Do you hear what they're saying about me, boys?" Apollon boasted. "Take note. That idiot is calling me great, and I humbly must agree. This means Project G 123 has now officially begun. Mark my words, by this time next year, Allah will be celebrated and called great not just here in Bethlehem, but also in every city throughout Palestine, including all of

Jerusalem and that Jewish cesspool along the Mediterranean called Tel Aviv."

Thursday, November 9th
6 p.m. Israeli Standard Time
Bethlehem's Jacir Palace Intercontinental Hotel
Bethlehem, West Bank

As the dim light of the evening's twilight faded into darkness, there still remained one location that shone brightly over central Palestine. Illuminated by a brilliant array of outdoor lighting, the Bethlehem's Jacir Palace Intercontinental Hotel, a magnificent 100-year old palace turned five star hotel, beckons its beauty in the night sky in all directions, as far as Jerusalem to the north and the village of Beit Sahour to the east. With the ugly remnants of bullet scars that riddled its carved stone façade repaired, the final reminders of the many gun battles that took place here between the IDF soldiers and Palestinian militants during the 2001 Al-Aqsa intifida, the magnificent hotel has now been completely restored and opened for business. As an added amenity, for the protection of its guests and staff, the only access to the hotel and its extensive gardens and pools was through the hotel's gated main entrance, staffed by armed security.

It was a few minutes shy of the six o'clock hour when a late model Volvo pulled up in front of the Jacir Palace Intercontinental Hotel's security gate. The driver inside the car showed the security guard his credentials and the guard promptly contacted the hotel lobby's main desk to notify one of their guests that his ride has just arrived and was waiting outside. In a matter of moments, a man, with jacket in hand, walked out of the hotel's main lobby and proceeded over to the awaiting car at the main gate.

"Six o'clock, right on the money!" commented the rather tall gentleman as he opened the passenger door and proceeded to sit down."

"It's an old habit of mine," jokingly replied the driver. "When you have to do live television everyday, you have no other choice but to be on time."

With that said, the passenger closed his door and off they went, traveling south down Manger Street and then eastward toward the village of Bet Sahour.

"Andy," the driver commented, "as I was getting ready to come over here, I heard what I thought was a funny story on a local news channel."

"Tell it to me," the passenger emphatically requested. "I need to hear something funny after everything I went through today."

"Well," replied the driver, "from what I gathered from the reporter on the news, some local Palestinian militant was so ecstatic and blown away with what he had just heard, he just had to share this good news with somebody, so—he decided to burst into your meeting, automatic weapon in hand, and announce his good fortune to all who were present at the meeting of the World Council of Churches."

"Excuse me if I don't share in your humor," the passenger responded with a scowled look, "but you wouldn't be so amused right now if you were the one hearing the deafening rounds of automatic gunfire going off and then some crazy person burst into the room you were in waving his automatic weapon. That nut scared the hell out of me!"

For Tom Reid, attempting to keep a straight face while driving was now nearly impossible. Turning toward his childhood friend sitting in the passenger seat beside him, Tom couldn't hold back any longer. He instantly broke out into uncontrolled laughter.

"Now, what's so funny!" demanded Andy McShay.

"Oh, Andy, you should have seen your face when you said he scared the hell out of you! You looked like a little boy crying out to his mommy!" Tom replied with tears streaming from in his eyes. "I'm sorry, it must be my sick sense of humor. I just picture, here you all are, peacefully debating how you can help bring peace and stability to these people and one of the locals burst in to thank you for your concern by shooting up the place, waving a gun in your face, and scaring the hell out of you! Oh-yah-yah-hah-hah-oh my. I've got to stop laughing before I run off the road and kill the two of us!"

"Now that's really a scary thought!" Andy commented as he turned toward his friend of over forty years and started chuckling. "Right now, I only wish it was you sitting there in the auditorium instead of me. Then we would see who would be laughing so hard!"

"You're absolutely right!" Tom half-heartedly admitted as he once again broke out into laughter.

"You know, Tom, the more I think about it, the less I see the humor in the whole thing!" Andy again chuckled and shook his head. He than sank back in his seat and continued in a more reflective tone

"Tom, did you ever stop and think about this. Who would have ever thought that two young boys growing up along the shores of Narragansett Bay would be sitting here right now laughing at the craziness of a world gone nuts."

"God did," Tom confidently replied as he turned toward his friend and smiled. "I believe He looked down the road of time and saw the two of us sitting here right now, an important Bishop of the Episcopal Church and a silly Pentecostal televangelist, both caught up in crazy events that only He knows the final outcome."

The lifetime friends arrived at the base of a darkened hillside just outside the village of Bet Sahour. Tom made mention that this was the same location of their surprise reunion the previous morning, directly across from the Shepherd's Field. About 100 meters further up the road, the headlight illuminated a small road sign with an arrow pointing to the left and lettering too small to read at that distance but clearly written in Arabic, Hebrew, and English. Tom proceeded to exit the main road at that point, turning left onto a smooth gravel road that meandered up through a darkened hillside. Finally, after cutting through a thick darkness lined by olive trees, the headlights fixed on a small, stone-cut structure near the top of the hill.

As Tom pulled up along the side of the building and parked the rental car, his confused passenger turned and commented, "I think all tours have ended for today."

"Not all tours," Tom replied. "Andy, I think you'll need your jacket. It's pretty chilly out here at night this time of the year," Tom commented with a sly smile as he removed the keys from the ignition and proceeded to get out of the car.

As they both walked around toward the brightly lit front entrance of the structure, they were met there by a man dressed in a monk-like brown hooded wool robe, tied at the center with a brown sash.

"Welcome, Dr. Reid and your Excellency, to the Franciscan's Shepherd's Field Chapel, where every day is Christmas day."

"You two know each other?" Andy turned toward Tom and asked.

"We friars at the Bethlehem Franciscan order are all big fans of Dr. Reid's television ministry," the robed man interjected. "There is hardly a day that goes by that we do not watch PTW on Middle East television using our satellite dish."

"Andy McShay, it is my pleasure to introduce you to Father Michel Sabbah," Tom Reid proudly announced. "Father Sabbah is the head of the Franciscan Order here in Central Palestine, which is appointed by the Roman Catholic Church as *'Custodia Terrae Sanctae,'* custodians of the sacred ground. Father Michel is also the first Palestinian to become the senior Roman Catholic official in the Holy Lands."

"Father Sabbah, it is truly an honor meeting you," Bishop McShay responded by extending the friar a firm handshake

"I met Father Sabbah yesterday shortly after you got back on the bus and left for your meeting. Father Sabbah graciously accepted my crazy request to open the Franciscan Chapel for our meeting here tonight."

"No, Dr. Reid, yours is not a crazy request," Father Sabbah responded. "I am very honored to have the two of you meet here tonight."

Turning to Andy McShay, Father Sabbah began briefing the Episcopal Bishop on the past history of the stone structure. "As I told Dr. Reid yesterday, this present sanctuary, which was erected in 1953–54, stands over a cave in which the shepherds are supposed to have lived, perhaps the very shepherds where the angels announced the birth of Christ. The sanctuary was built in the shape of a tent, a polygon with five straight and five projecting sides. The light that floods the interior reminds one of the strong light present when the angels announced the divine birth."

Looking out toward the surrounding darkness, Father Sabbah passionately stated, "Bishop McShay, you and your family must visit us here during Christmas. My words cannot begin to describe the magnificent sight when these darkened fields are crowded with thousands of pilgrims holding thousands of glowing candle lights and singing Christmas carols in every language to celebrate the most joyous event in all of the history of mankind."

Father Sabbah graciously gave both of his guests a personal tour of the sanctuary's interior describing in detail the history behind the beautiful murals and artifacts found there. When he had finished, he accompanied his guests outside and around to the back of the sanctuary where a series of stone steps led to the entrance of the cave below. After giving them a brief tour and explanation of how the local shepherds had utilized the cave in times past, their gracious host parted company, leaving Tom Reid and Andy McShay alone for their meeting.

No sooner did the Friar leave the cave than Andy McShay turned toward Tom and stated his case. "Tom before you say anything, I need you to hear me out. I left Rhode Island this past weekend with an opened mind. Without bias and media influence, believe me when I say, I wanted to find out for myself what was really happening over here."

"Have you found your answers, Andy?" Tom sincerely asked.

"I believe I have. These poor people have been robbed of all their dignity."

"What do you mean by robbed?" Tom calmly asked.

"This has been their land since time immortal; they've lived here, they've died here, they've farmed the land, raised their families here, and through no fault of their own, the Palestinian people have had one oppressor after another come in here only to deny them of their lawful and moral rights."

"I believe this is what you are going to ask me," Tom followed. "You want me to use PTW to expose the plight of the Palestinian people to the world?"

"Tom, exactly!" Andy beamed. "Look at the unbelievable influence your broadcast has. Look, you even have monks living in a remote area like this watching your program every single day. Even when all the members of our council return home this Sunday to their own congregations, nothing they can say or do will carry the power to influence that your program carries."

"Andy, I only have one thing to ask," Tom followed. "What does God say about this entire situation?"

By the expression on Andy's gleaming face, Tom knew immediate that he needed to rephrase the question. "Brother Tom, I am so glad you asked! In Matthew Chapter 5:9 Jesus says 'blessed are the peacemakers; for they shall be called the children of God.'"

Tom smiled and then said, "Let me rephrase what I want to ask. Who does God say are the rightful owners of this land?"

Andy paused momentarily to gather his thoughts. He knew exactly where Tom was leading and needed to come back with a solid answer that would defend his case against Israel's claim to the Palestinian territories.

"God demands peace in that land. Things have gone on too long. The children of Abraham must reconcile their differences now. Tom, just as God made Jesus intermediary between Himself and man, I believe God wants the church to be the intermediary between the Jews and the Palestinians, to bring peace to the Holy Lands once and for all."

"Andy, you purposely evaded the question because you are well aware of the answer," Tom calmly replied. "God made an everlasting covenant with Abraham that Abraham's descendants through his wife Sarah, not Haggar, would inherit this promised land. Regardless of what you see happening over here to the Palestinian people, they are not the descendants of the promise that God made Abraham. They are the descendants of Ishmael and Haggar, the Egyptian. God did not promise them one single grain of sand. According to God's word written in Genesis 15:18 'In the same day the LORD made a covenant with Abram, saying, Unto thy seed have I given this land, from the river of Egypt unto the great river, the river Euphrates.'

Tom paused and smiled before continuing "You see, Andy, according to God's word, the geopolitical borders of modern-day Israel are all wrong. Israel's borders don't end with a manmade concrete wall or some imaginary green line. They begin on the eastern border at the Nile River and continue all the way to the middle of present-day Iraq, right along the Tigris and Euphrates Rivers."

"But, Tom," Andy interjected, "the Jews living in Israel today are as godless as they come. Haven't you read the statistics in papers lately that Tel Aviv leads the world in abortions and that Jerusalem recently hosted the biggest homosexual parade in recorded history?"

"Again, let's take a look at what the Bible says about this." Tom followed as he opened his Bible to Jeremiah 18: 12. "God says this about Israel or any nation that thumbs it's nose at His mercy. 'But they replied, "That is hopeless! So we will walk according to our own plans, and we will everyone obey the dictates of his evil heart." In other words," Tom paraphrased, "the people are saying don't waste your breath on us, God. We will continue to live as we want to, following our own evil desires. We are surely a big nation, bigger in our own eyes, perhaps, than in reality. We will walk after our own devices; after all, who's to stop us? If we want homosexuality made lawful, who's to stop us? If we want to abort babies, who's to stop us? If we want to declare sex outside of marriage perfectly OK, who's to stop us? If our ministers, pastors, deacons, bishops, and others want to ordain wickedness, then who's to stop them? So far, so good should be our adage.

"Andy, one thing the Bible has shown us time and time again, once a nation gets to this point, when all fear and respect of God's authority has ceased and sin runs rampant, so will God's mercy come to an end and God's judgment will swiftly follow. In Psalms 9 verses

7–10, David says that 'the LORD shall endure forever: he hath prepared his throne for judgment. And he shall judge the world in righteousness; he shall minister judgment to the people in uprightness.' The Bible declares that Israel will someday go through horrible trials for their sins and unbelief, but God will never desert them. God says in Jeremiah 30:11, 'For I am with you and I will save you, says the LORD. I will completely destroy the nations where I have scattered you, but I will not destroy you. But I must discipline you; I cannot let you go unpunished.' Finally, to paraphrase a rock solid promise God made to the nation Israel, in Jeremiah 31: 36 God emphatically states, 'I am as likely to reject my people Israel as I am to do away with the laws of nature!'"

In his heart, Tom knew he had said enough. Out of love, he placed his hand on Andy's shoulder and said, "So, my good friend, as you can see, I could never go against the word of God on any broadcast."

Tom's last statement set off in Andy's psyche a mixed bag of emotions, including anger and betrayal. *Why did Tom want to meet at all if he already knew before hand what I was going to ask? Why did he go through such elaborate arrangement to have such a futile meeting?* Before Andy's heart could harden any further, the Holy Spirit instantly gave Tom discernment on what to say next. "Andy, look at me," Tom boldly requested as he made eye-to-eye contact with his friend. Filled with the compassion and love of God's Holy Spirit, Tom boldly proclaimed, "Andy, God wants you to know that He loves you with the deepest love possible. He also wants you to know that He is a jealous God and He will not share you with the world. There is no room for a man pleaser in His Kingdom. He told me to tell you that you are to stop trying to appease those who seek after the things of this world and come back to him."

Andy McShay stood in a state of shock. The words of God's spirit spoken through his friend had penetrated a place in his heart that existed there many years before, but had been covered up by thick layers of lies and self-deception.

"Andy," Tom continued, "I want you to sing the words of this hymn with me, right here and right now. Sing them just as we sung them so long ago as we sat in the back of my Father's church. Andy, sing it and mean it with all of your heart. I'll start you off."

"With tears streaming down his face, Tom Reid started singing the first verse of the classical hymn sung by millions. *"My hope is built- on nothing less- than Jesus blood and righteousness. I dare not trust the sweetest frame, but wholly in Jesus' Name."*

As silent as a dead man, Andy McShay sat there on the same hard stone floor where 2000 years prior shepherds sat dumbfounded by the angelic announcement that the Creator of the Universe wanted them to be the sole witnesses to the birth of His Son.

"Come on, Andy, sing with me now!"

With sincere tears of repentance, Andy McShay right then and there recommitted his life to the King of Kings and Lord of Lords and joined in to sing the chorus of this old familiar song, *"On Christ the solid Rock I stand, All other ground is sinking sand; All other ground is sinking sand."*

As Andy McShay began to sing the anointed words of this blessed hymn, his familiar spirit, Pylazad, started hissing and shrieking while his scaly yellowish reptilian form began twitching and convulsing uncontrollably.

At that split moment, Michael appeared standing directly in back of the ugly little chimera. With a smile on his face, Michael reached for his flashing sword and with one blinding swipe, the Archangel sliced through the trembling spirit, and in a puff of dark brown smoke, Pylazad vanished forever. Holding his drawn sword high over his head, Michael was joined by thousands of his fellow angels praising God in unison for the salvation of one single human sinner. That night, all the angels of heaven joined in with the two small humans in singing the same chorus, "On Christ the solid Rock I stand, All other ground is sinking sand; All other ground is sinking sand."

The unexplainable peace and joy that Tom and Andy were experiencing as they left Shepherd's cave and walked in loving Christian fellowship up the stone stairs toward the car came to an abrupt end with the ringing tone of a cell phone.

"Sorry, brother," Tom laughed. "Can't escape from the world forever."

"Hello. John!" Tom shouted out. "It's my twin!"

"Tell him congratulations from me." Andy replied. "He must be on top of the world right now."

"Little brother," John shouted back from thousands of miles away. "I just wanted my better half to be the first to know before it's announced to the entire world. Your identical twin brother has been selected to be the next Presidential spokesman."

"John, you are the man!" Tom shouted. "I am so proud of you and I know that Dad would have felt the same way, too."

"Thanks Tom, I truly appreciate your vote of confidence. Hey, listen, I've got to run. By the way, where are you?"

"Brother, you wouldn't believe. You would not believe!"

Chapter Eleven

"America is great because she is good. If America ceases to be good, America will cease to be great."

Alexis de Tocqueville

Monday, January 24th
6:30 *a.m. Eastern Standard Time*
Washington, D.C.
Cabinet Room
West Wing of the White House

The weekend craziness was over, the endless parties, the ballroom celebrations. America awoke this morning to the dawn of a new day. Burdened by years of rising inflation, high energy and fuel costs, and an ever shrinking domestic job market, Americans voted for change and that is exactly what they got. Americans had elected their first woman president who campaigned on the promise to make the American economy number one once again. For Washington, D.C., the weekend's festivities were a brief respite from the hectic wheeling and dealing pace of the nation's capital.

It may have been the first official day of work for the new Devoe administration, but unseen vestiges of past administrations remained on duty. Strategically positioned along the fenced perimeter of the White House grounds, an entire legion of sword drawn warrior angels remained stationed at the exact post assigned to them after the British army sacked the White House during the War of 1812. From that time until the present, the guardian warriors of the White House were charged not only with the protection of the president and the human inhabitants within, but more importantly to deny access to unwelcome spiritual intruders, namely demonic spirits. On any given day, until their human host exited through the heavily guarded White House gate, scores of familiar spirits assigned to the White House staff and other invited human inhabitants had to wait patiently outside the fence just as any member of the uninvited human public.

It was early Monday morning. In the White House's Cabinet Room, five women and twelve men sat around a long cherry wood table anxiously awaiting the arrival of their Commander-in-Chief. Located just doors away from the president's oval office, all of the newly appointed cabinet members, seventeen in all, including the Vice President, Neil O'Sullivan, were assembled for the very first time in a room used exclusively by presidents to plan with their closest advisors the strategies they deemed vital for America's future. At exactly 6:30 a.m., all members stood to their feet and clapped as the president made her entrance into the room.

"Thank you, thank you, everyone," President Devoe graciously commented as she entered the long narrow room with four large arched French doors leading to the outside Rose Garden along its back wall, and Presidential portraits of Washington, Andrew Jackson, and Teddy Roosevelt hanging on the near wall.

"I don't know about all of you, but my feet are still killing me," the president jokingly complained as she positioned herself behind a vacant leather backed chair strategically position along the back center of the table between a flag with the Presidential emblem and an American flag. "I don't think I've danced as much in my entire life as I did this weekend!"

"My feet feel the same way, Madame President," commented James Metloff, the Secretary of State standing directly across the table from the president.

Standing briefly behind her chair, the president acknowledged each of the cabinet members flanking her on the right and left with a smile and a gracious nod. She then proceeded to announce her first official order to her cabinet. "Ladies and gentlemen, you may all be seated."

Once seated, the president continued with her opening comments. "Before we begin, I first and foremost want to thank all of you from the bottom of my heart for accepting your positions as members of my cabinet. I also want all of you to know that you were selected to head up my cabinet on just one premise: that like myself, everyone seated here has a deep-seeded passion to see the American economy back on top once again, free from debt, strong and vibrant, second to none. I know each of you has placed your personal lives and your successful careers on hold for the purpose of achieving this greater good, and on behalf of the America people, I once again say thank you!"

With that said, the president's voice took on a more serious tone. "And I want to make this perfectly clear: with all of your help, I plan to deliver to the American people exactly what I promised, nothing less, starting right now!"

Every person in the room sensed the deep conviction behind the president's words. What she had achieved in a few short minutes took some past Presidential administrations years to accomplish: complete solidarity among her cabinet members. Each cabinet member sat in awe of the reality that they now possessed the reins of power to guide their beloved nation out of decades of apathy and despair.

"Now, are we ready to get started with our plan to put America back on top once again?" the president asked.

"We are more than ready to get started, Madame President," answered her Secretary of Energy, Tyler Chandler, seated to her immediate left.

"Good, Ty," the president replied with a smiled. "You'll be the first one I'll call on this morning."

With both hands folded and her elbow pressed firmly against the table, the president stared intently at her cabinet members seated on both sides of the elongated oval-shaped table.

"Folks, I only wish we had more time to work out all of the

details," the president confessed, "but with the State of the Union address scheduled for this Friday, we have no more time to waste. Before we leave this room today, we must be absolutely sure that we have dotted all of our 'I's and crossed all of our 'T's. We are about to make public the greatest economic reforms that this country has seen since Roosevelt's New Deal."

Friday, January 28th
8 p.m. Eastern Standard Time
Capital House Chambers
Washington, D.C.

"Mr. Speaker, the President of the United States," announced the U.S. House Sergeant at Arms. This was the signal for all invited guests and visiting Heads of State seated in the galleries above, for every elected representative from both sides of the aisle of the United States Congress seated below, the nine Supreme Court Justices, the members of the military's Joint Chiefs of Staff, and all those present in the House chambers for tonight's State of the Union address, to stand to their feet and give a thunderous ovation to tonight's person of the hour, America's first elected woman president, Analise Devoe.

With the entire world watching, the president entered the House chambers, taking several minutes to greet and shake hands of the members of Congress as she made her way down the aisle toward the podium at the front and center of the House chambers. Upon her arrival at the platform, the president turned and handed the copies of her address to the Vice President, Neil O'Sullivan, and the Speaker of the House, California congresswoman Barbara Ann Raushback, both of whom would sit behind the president for the duration of her speech.

Once the entire chamber settled down and the attendees took their seats, Speaker Raushback stood to her feet, tapped her gavel loudly on her desk and announced, "Members of Congress, I have the high privilege and distinct honor of presenting to you the

President of the United States." Another standing ovation followed lasting a record four minutes before the president finally began her address to the nation.

"Speaker Raushback, Vice President O'Sullivan, members of Congress, distinguished citizens and fellow citizens, and may I present for the first time in our nation's history, my Mr. First Gentleman, Ethan Devoe."

Instantly, everyone in the House chambers broke out in laughter and applause, including the usually reserved members of the Supreme Court. Momentarily, all the attention was focused off the president and directed to the top balcony area where the president's husband, Ethan Devoe, stood waving to the crowds below and taking several bows.

This decision to interject humor at the very beginning of the speech was a strategy conceived by both the president and her press secretary, John Reid, in hopes of buffering any pessimism that might result from hearing the shocking data on the present state of the American economy. Signaling her approval to her husband with two thumbs up, Ethan Devoe took his wife's cue and sat back down in his seat allowing the boisterous applause to quietly subside. Now, literally beaming with confidence from the center podium, the president was ready to continue with her prepared speech.

"Every year, by law and by custom, we meet in this great chamber to consider the state of the union. This year, we gather once more deeply aware of decisive days that lie ahead."

Looking up from the words of her digital text projected through the clear surface of the podium's built-in teleprompter, the president paused momentarily and attempted to make eye contact with both the multitudes of people and cameras facing her. Always the risk taker, the president decided then and there to do something totally unprecedented, to forget the prepared speech and do what she did best, speak boldly and passionately from her heart.

"Ah oh!" whispered John Reid to his wife, Miranda, sitting beside him in the top balcony section of the House chamber.

"John, what's wrong?"

"I can see it on her face from here. She's not going to use the speech. She's going to wing it!"

"Can she do that?" Miranda questioned.

"Oh, yes!" John replied. "Believe me, Analise can do that!"

John Reid's intuition was correct. With the exception of the time she felt ill at a campaign stop in Pittsburgh, every speech that Analise DeVoe had ever made, either as Attorney General or on the campaign trail, was spontaneous and highly effective.

"At this point," the president commented while scanning her audience, "some past presidents have stood where I am standing today and made the comment that our country 'now stands at a crossroads.' Unfortunately, the American economy was at such a place four years ago. Even though all of the warnings were shouting out at us, no one heeded their call. It is now with a heavy heart, that I stand here today before all of you gathered in this great hall to say that America is no longer at a crossroads. Opportunities to solve and resolve the economic problems plaguing our great country during the past administration have been, for the most part, totally ignored and now we must face the following grim realities."

Most political leaders would not have had the courage to stand face-to-face with their constituents and expose the shocking truth, but Analise Devoe was not a typical politician. She knew that the acceptance of her economic recovery plan rested solely on her ability to convince both the Congress and the American people that the present economy was so bad there was no other way out. For the next five minutes, the president stood firmly at the center podium and stated her case to the general public as honestly and thoroughly as possible. The stark silence in the House chamber that followed did not deter her from continuing.

"Before I made my decision to run for this office," she continued, "I would find myself sitting home with my husband watching the evening news and asking the same questions that I believe most Americans were asking themselves. How could America allow itself to get in such a mess? My fellow Americans, you elected me on the promise that my plan would bring high paying jobs back to the American workers, jobs with security and real benefits that will be there for the next generation of Americans and for generations to come. I stand here before you with no hidden agenda. I have no affiliation with any special interest group. America is my special interest and now I plan to deliver!"

Silence no more! Except for the members of the Supreme Court seated in the front row, everyone seated on both sides of the House floor and the balcony area above were on their feet giving the president a thunderous applause.

The moment that Analise Devoe had dreamt of over the past six years had arrived! With the entire world as her stage, the President of the United States was ready to disclose the details on how her administration planned to save America's economy. Energized by the crowd's ovation, the president pressed forward against her podium and continued her speech.

"There must be something wrong when the most innovative, resourceful country this world has ever known has allowed itself to become so negligent and so dependent on foreign goods and oil that it has placed it's entire national security at risk!

"There must be something wrong when more than 75 percent of the price of regular gas that is sold at our pumps goes into the pockets of foreign producers who have absolutely no vested interest in America whatsoever!"

Applause.

"There must be something really wrong with our system when Brazilians can fill their cars' tanks with homegrown ethanol produced from sugar cane for half the price we Americans pay for a gallon of regular gasoline. According to the latest figures from the World Bank, at current prices, Brazil can make ethanol from locally grown sugar cane for about $1 a gallon. That compares with the international price of gasoline of over $1.80 a gallon. Even though ethanol gets less mileage than gasoline, in Brazil, ethanol is still far cheaper to drive per mile"

The president's bold comments fired up the members of House

chamber to such a feverous pitch that she had to resort to raising her arms in an attempt to quiet their applause in order to be heard.

"Finally," she shouted out "there is something wrong when country music legend Willy Nelson can drive his Mercedes up to any Wendy's or McDonald's and fill up his tank with peanut oil. Now, they say the only drawback is that the exhaust from Willie's car smells just like French fries."

Laughter now filled the chamber.

"But all joking aside," the president continued, "peanut oil is just one of the many biofuels that can power our cars and trucks, and folks, there's absolutely no drilling involved. There are no foreign middlemen taking the hard-earned money out of the pockets of our American workers. Biofuels are clean. There is no polluting the atmosphere with excess greenhouse gases because biofuels are considered to be 'CO_2 neutral'; that is, not adding to the carbon dioxide level in the atmosphere. Biodiesel and other biofuels such as ethanol can be made from any number of crops and can be run in either normal diesel engines or slightly modified combustion engines. They can be also used to power small-scale farm and workshop machinery and electric generators as well as boats and other recreational vehicles. These renewable, domestically grow-your-own fuels can be grown on-site in villages and towns throughout the country, profiting both our citizens and farmers and most importantly, as I will demonstrate in a few minutes, domestically grown biofuels will open up entirely new job markets for our American workers."

Another standing ovation.

"For years we heard it preached by politicians and economists alike that it is markets, not governments that will decide which jobs and technologies are chosen in the future. That theory may have worked in the distant past, but as I have just painstaking presented to all of you, today's economy needs a shot of immediate governmental intervention if it has any chance of improving. We in government must take the lead in giving clear, credible, long-term signals to the market that will enable companies to develop cleaner and more energy efficient technologies."

Pausing for a moment, the president turned her attention to the top balcony area.

"Will Mr. Henry Jarvis, Mr. Raymond Wilson, and Mr. Larry Brown please stand up?"

All eyes were now focused on three gentlemen standing to the left of Ethan Devoe in the top balcony.

"I want to thank these three gentlemen for setting aside their busy schedules to be here with us tonight. Allow me now to introduce them. On the far left is Mr. Henry Jarvis, CEO of Chevron Texaco; to his immediate right is Mr. Raymond Wilson, CEO of Shell Oil; and finally on the far right, I would like to introduce Mr. Lawrence E. Brown, CEO of Exxon/Mobile. Among these three gentlemen, their companies supply gasoline and diesel fuel to our nation's nearly 200,000 gas stations. That compares to less than one quarter of the stations nationwide carrying ethanol and only a pathetic 650 stations carrying any form of biodiesel. I am proud to announce that after meeting with these fine gentlemen in early December, all three have agreed to set a target date of the end of next year to produce enough alternative domestic fuels to supply all of our nation's fuel stations." Another overwhelming standing ovation followed this announcement.

"Folks, I am just getting started," the president proudly proclaimed. "In order for these three gentlemen to reach next year's biofuel quotas, they needed a little help. That help came to us in the package of a lady from the 'show me' state of Missouri. Will my Secretary of Agriculture, Ms. Sydni Baker, please standup?"

Sydni Baker was all the president could hope for in a Secretary of Agriculture. As former president of the American Farmers Association, she had been the farmer's voice for educating the populous on the importance of converting excess food crops such as our nation's yearly surplus of corn and soybeans, plus all of the animal waste produced by cows, pigs, and chickens, into enough biofuels to supply the entire country.

The president next introduced Secretary of the Interior, Jonathan Blake, and his plan to blanket the millions of acres of non-productive public lands with enough electricity generating windmills to supply endless amounts of low-cost power to most, if not all, Midwestern and Western towns and cities. One after another, the president called on individuals seated along the top balcony row to stand and have their contributions to her economic plan be recognized. The most innovative idea came from Rosalie Jablonski, the Secretary of Housing and Urban Development, whose plan was to promote and equip local city dwellers to utilize vacant lots and open fields found scattered throughout America's large metropolitan areas to do city farming of biofuel crops.

The president had one surprise remaining. The final three gentlemen asked to stand and be recognized were the CEOs of Detroit's top three automakers. With beaming pride, the president stood at the podium and made an announcement that no one was expecting.

"I have saved the best for last!" the president boasted, "America's top three automakers have all agreed to a four-year plan that would place a biofuel burning engine into every new model car, truck, and SUV made in America!"

The ovation from this phenomenal announcement transcended even the House chambers. People could be heard cheering from their living rooms in every home tuned into the president's speech, from sea to shining sea.

"America, if all goes as planned," the president summarized, "our nation will be totally energy independent in as little as four years from now. The new jobs created by such an enormous undertaking would cover every facet of our society, both locally and regionally, from north to south, east to west, from high tech to blue collar, from the service industries to factories, from the farm belt to the rustbelt, I promise all of you, all parts of the American society will benefit!"

Applause.

"My fellow Americans, before I close, I must be totally honest with all of you."

The president paused one last time and stared directly into the television cameras with a look of sincere compassion.

"In order to achieve our four year goal of total energy independence, we at the federal level must make some hard choices over the next year. Major shifts of funding must go into areas like agriculture, energy, and commerce and away from those areas that are now considered least cost effective. If we have learned anything at all from our tragic past mistakes, we have learned that America can no longer afford to squander hundreds of billions of dollars and waste thousands upon thousands of precious American lives fighting for causes that both alienates our country and results in increased tensions and hatred against America and American interests throughout the world.

"In closing, I ask all Americans to support our goal to restore our economy so that the present and future generations of 21st century Americans can live out their lives with the peace and security of knowing that their families, their jobs and their energy needs are secure and protected from all outside influences. We are a people that have continued to rise through every age against every challenge, a people of great works and greater possibilities, who have always found the wisdom and strength to come together as one nation.

"Thank you, America, for your confidence and support."

Friday, January 28*th*
9:15 *p.m. Eastern Standard Time*
229 *Chevy Chase Court*
Rockville, Maryland

"Wow! What a speech!" exclaimed Rachel Schroeder as she reached over for the remote resting on the couch cushion and turned off the television.

Her husband, Ezra, just sat staring at the darkened television screen, oblivious to his wife's comments.

"Ezra, you were not impressed?" Rachel asked with a voice of concern.

"Impressed?" her husband replied in a raised voice. "If she were the devil, I might be impressed!"

"Ezra, she is the president. What did she say that upset you so?"

"Rachel, it's not what she said, it's what she didn't say!"

"You're upset that she didn't end her speech with the traditional 'God Bless America'?" Rachel followed. "Ezra, she's not a believer, what did you expect?"

"No," Ezra shook his head and grumbled. "That much I expected."

Looking up at the concerned expression on his wife's face, Ezra confessed what was troubling him so. "She didn't say where the money would come from to fund all of her big ideas."

"You think she is going to cut the military budget, don't you?"

"She all but said it!" Ezra admitted. "Rachel, I have a very bad feeling about all this. Ever since this woman was elected, I haven't stopped thinking about what might happen this time if Israel were attacked as they were back in 2006. Would America come to her rescue?"

"America would never desert Israel," Rachel responded with a reassuring smile.

"That may have been true in the past, but I am not sure if that still holds true today."

"Could Schroeder be correct?" Ariel asked the angel standing to his right. "Will America abandon Israel?"

"It is entirely possible." Muriel replied. "It appears that America could blindly be following this president into Satan's trap."

"If this is true," Ariel smiled, "we must be very close to revealing the final part of Newton's riddle to Schroeder."

Saturday, January 29th
4:45 a.m.
Qom, Iran

Halfway around the world in the most holy Shiite city of Oom, five men sat silently in a semicircle in a dimly lit room, reflecting on the speech just delivered by the American president thousands of miles away. All eyes in the room were fixed on a white-bearded man seated directly in front of a large blank television monitor. No one dared to say a word until this man, garbed with a black headdress and a full-length black robe, opened his eyes and spoke.

Also present in the same room were six demonic spirits, two high-ranking princes and four chimeras. Each chimera either knelt or stood directly behind their assigned human host, but the two demonic princes focused their full attention on the bearded man sitting on the chair.

"It is finished!" stated Allahzad, the Demonic Prince of Persia, as he leaned forward to withdraw his massive clawed hand from the skull of the bearded human sitting in a trance-like state before him.

"Let's wake him and hear what he has to say," commented Allahad's commander, Apollon, as he too leaned over the bearded human and blew a puff of reddish smoke into the human's nostrils.

"Look, the Ayatollah's eyes are opening," whispered one of the men seated to the far left.

"Praise be to Allah!" announced Ayatollah Ali Khamenei, the Iranian Islamic Revolution Leader, in such a clear resonating voice that its penetrating sound sent electrifying shivers literally down the spines of everyone in the room.

"Allah has given me a vision!" the Ayatollah commented as he turned with eyes wide opened and faced his equally amazed Shiite companions.

"Ayatollah, what did you see in your vision?" demanded President Mahmoud Ahmadinjead, second in command in all of Iran.

"I saw a Jewish household, all decorated for celebrating the Passover. The dining room table was covered not with a typical tablecloth, but an Israeli flag with a large blue Star of David in the center. The mother and children sat patiently at the table as the father stood and was about to begin the Seder. At first, the father had his back turned toward me so I couldn't see his face. Just as the father was about to speak, another woman appeared in the room standing directly in back of him. As clearly as I see all of you, I saw the face of this woman. She was Analise Devoe, the President of the United States! Standing directly in back of the father, she held up a long bladed knife gripping its handle colored in red, white, and blue. I then watched as she plunged the knife blade deep into the father's back. I looked down in amazement as I stared at the face of the man lying dead on the floor. It was the face of the Israeli Prime Minister."

The Ayatollah smiled and placed both hands on the shoulders of the Iranian President.

"Call a meeting with all of our brothers immediately," the Ayatollah requested with an evil grin. "The little Satan Israel is about to celebrate its last Passover!"

Chapter Twelve

"O God, do not remain quiet; Do not be silent and, O God, do not be still. For behold, Your enemies make an uproar, and those who hate You have exalted themselves. They make shrewd plans against Your people, and conspire together against Your treasured ones. They have said, "Come, and let us wipe them out as a nation, that the name of Israel will be remembered no more."

Psalm 83:1–4 NKJV

Thursday, February 20*th*
8:15 *a.m. GTM*
South Midlands in north Tipperary, Ireland

A thick cover of morning mist greeted Eddie Fogarty and Tommy Shand as they pulled up in their bulldozer and backhoe to their new job site at the edge of the Faddan More bog. Both Eddie and Tommy were employed as heavy equipment operators by local contractors and the bogs owners, brothers Kevin and Patrick Leonard, of the Irish townland of Faddan More. Eddie and Tommy had just completed a job burying fiber optic cables along the roads passing throughout the lush green hills of north Tipperary. This new assignment was entirely different. Their task would be to dig and remove the rich layers of ancient peat that covered the surface of the Faddan More bog. Tommy's job was to dig and remove three-foot sections of the bog's top surface layers with the backhoe while Eddie used his bulldozer's wide shovel to transport these freshly cut layers of peat into neatly stacked piles beside the gravel road, later to be removed, bagged and sold as commercial garden soil.

With the first official day of spring still nearly a month away, the temperate North Atlantic breezes had allowed the rich Irish soil to thaw just enough to make Eddie and Tommy's job that much easier. Both men stood momentarily along the edge of the mist-covered meadow that appeared to go on as far as the eye could see.

"Where do you suggest we start?" Tommy turned and asked his partner.

"Right here is as good a place as any, I expect," Eddie replied as he rested his arm on the shoulder of his childhood friend. "Tommy, I almost forgot! Patrick asked that we might do one more thing while we're out here diggin in the bog."

"And what is it that Mr. Leonard might have us do, Mr. Fogarty?" Tommy followed with a smile.

"Keep an eye out for anything strange that might pop up as we dig. He said the bog is known to hold some ancient things that once belonged to an old monastery that use to be around here."

"Well, I'm afraid until this fog clears," Tommy commented, "we're not going to see anything at all, not even the dirt on the ground."

"Well, Tommy boy, let's get hopping. The day's a wasting and there's a lot of dirt around here to be dug!" With that said, Eddie patted his friend on the back, then turned and stepped up into back of his bulldozer.

"The human is correct," commented one of two observing angelic beings standing only a short distance away. "They will never be able to see anything through all this fog!"

"That won't be a problem," responded Jofiel, a rather tall, muscular, bronze-skinned angel standing to the right of his fair featured angelic companion, Coriel.

No sooner did the angel finish his statement then the fog instantly vanished and the entire green meadow came into clear view.

"Have you ever seen the likes of that!" Eddie shouted over to his friend operating the backhoe.

Tommy responded back with an equally confused look.

"Tommy, I'm getting the strangest feeling we're not alone out here!" Eddie shouted with a wide grin.

"There you go again, trying to scare me into believing in the UFOs!"

"You're looking mighty scared there, Tommy boy!"

"Blarney!" Tommy replied back. "Just shut up and get on with the job!"

"After all this time, do you think it is still there?" Coriel asked.

"Why wouldn't it be," replied Jofiel. "This land has not been touched since the Vikings invaded and sacked the monastery over 1,200 human years ago."

"Just the same; after all this time, isn't it possible that some human could have stumbled by here and found it?"

"Well, we are about to find out." Jofiel turned with a smile. "The human operating the backhoe is about to drop his shovel over the exact spot where it was buried. It is about time to get the attention of the man on the bulldozer before the object of our mission is destroyed by the shovel."

Both Coriel and Jofiel were messenger angels. Their present assignment was to make sure a small, leather-bound book, buried in the same bog over a thousand years earlier by Christian monks fleeing for their lives from the pillaging Viking invaders, would be now located and placed into the proper human hands.

The very instant Jofiel said the word "destroyed," his companion Coriel reappeared on the bulldozer, standing directly in back of its human operator.

Coriel then proceeded to crouch down behind the human and whisper into his thoughts. "Tell Tommy to stop digging and look down at the ground in front of the shovel!"

"Tommy, stop!" Eddie shouted out over the deafening roars of the two diesel motors.

"Have you gone mad!" Tommy fired back with a look of confusion at the sight of his friend waving his right arm all about and pointing down at something on the ground with his left hand. Locking his backhoe securely into place, Tommy immediately jumped off and walked over to inspect a mound of freshly exposed peat where the backhoe's bucket had just penetrated.

"Do you see it?" Eddie again shouted as he in turn shut off his bulldozer.

"Ya," Tommy replied as he stood staring in awe down at the small mud-covered object protruding out from a clump of freshly dug peat.

"What do you make of that?" Tommy asked his friend, now standing along side shaking his head in disbelief.

"Looks like somebody's lost wallet," Eddie replied.

"It isn't a wallet." Tommy commented as he bent down to get a closer look. "It looks like some sort of book. I can see writing on the front of it! No tellin how long it's been buried here!"

"Well, I've got to call Patrick," Eddie interjected. "He said if we spot anything, call him immediately!"

"Here, you can use my cell phone," Tommy stated as he removed his phone from its belt holster. "We better not dig any more until he gets out here!"

"Mission accomplished!" stated Coriel.

"Next stop, Dublin!" replied his angelic companion.

Monday, February 24th
10:00 a.m. GTM
National Museum of Ireland
Dublin, Ireland

Several large television communication vans with satellite dishes mounted to their sides began pulling up to the front entrance of Dublin, Ireland's premiere museum located on Kildare Street. All of the major cable news networks were present, busily setting up and positioning cameras on the sidewalk below in anticipation of a big announcement to be made by the museum staff exactly at the noon hour. Not since its 1890 opening at it's present location on Kildare Street had the museum, known for its famous collection of Bronze

Age prehistoric ornaments and early medieval Irish metalwork, seen so much excitement and fanfare.

Inside the museum, things were just as hectic. Museum staffers were busily scurrying about making final arrangements before they presented to the world what some were saying would be Ireland's equivalent to discovering the Dead Sea Scrolls. The center of all the excitement was a small, mud covered book presently stored in a museum refrigerator with sole access given only to Dr. Ian Wallace, the director of Ireland's National Museum.

No one wanted more than Dr. Wallace to tell the world about his museum's discovery. It wasn't everyday that the Dublin museum could compete toe-to-toe with her English rival, Cambridge University, for a news worthy story big enough to attract the likes of such international news networks as the BBC, CNN, MSNBC, and CBS. That was one of the reasons Ian Wallace had contacted his old acquaintance from Cambridge University to be present when his big announcement was made.

Sitting outside of the museum director's office was a tall, thin man wearing a brown tweed suit and a matching tweed cap. This gentleman had been patiently waiting and watching for over twenty minutes as a constant flow of museum personnel entered and exited the office door. Finally, the director's secretary looked up and announced, "I apologize for the long wait, Professor Andrews. It's been like this all morning. Dr. Wallace can see you now."

No sooner did the secretary make her announcement than a short, rather plump man with grayish-red hair was standing at the office door.

"Harry Andrews," Dr. Wallace announced with a broad smile and extended hand in friendship. Ever since their first meeting over thirty-two years ago at an antiquities conference held in London, there was always a bit of a professional rivalry going on between them. "I hope I didn't keep you waiting too long, old chap. Harry, you of all people know how hectic things get when CNN comes to town."

"Indeed," Professor Andrews smiled.

"Please, have a seat for a second," Wallace offered as he closed the door behind him. "I told my secretary to give us at least fifteen minutes alone to get all caught up on things."

Professor Andrews knew exactly what Wallace meant by "catching up on things." The only reason Ian Wallace asked Harrison Andrews to come all this way was to brag about his big find. But petty rivalries aside, Harry Andrews had his own motives for leaving the comforts of his office at the world's most prestigious educational university to cross the Irish Sea. He could not pass up this golden opportunity to view first hand such a rare find in the field of antiquities.

"It isn't everyday that I can have the famous Harrison Andrews standing in the background while I get my chance to announce to the world such a big discovery!" Wallace gloated as he plopped himself down on his big leather chair.

"Wallace, you wicked old dog," Professor Andrews fired back. "You had me come all this way so you could rub your discovery in my face!"

"There may be some truth in that statement," Wallace confessed as he stood to his feet. "But, Harry, in all seriousness, would you care to take a look at our museum's newest prized specimen?"

"Lead the way!"

Dr. Wallace led Professor Andrews through a labyrinth of small narrow passages and rooms filled with inconspicuous artifacts until they finally arrived at the door to the museum's main lab.

Looking oddly in both directions to see if anyone else was watching, Dr. Wallace proceeded to remove a key attached to a necklace that was concealed under his collar.

"One can never be too cautious these days," Dr. Wallace commented as he placed the key in the door lock. "You know, terrorists and all!"

Professor Andrews just shook his head and chuckled to himself.

"Here we are, Professor Andrews, our museum's humble laboratory room."

Professor Andrews stood at the door astonished. "I see you have your very own clean room!" the professor declared.

"Not only a clean room!" Wallace boasted as he pointed to the opposite side of the room. "Over in this section, we can radiocarbon-date the slightest sample down to the very hour it was made."

"Go on!" Professor Andrews said as he once again shook his head.

"Well, we don't have much time to waste," Wallace declared as he looked at his watch. "I have fifteen minutes before I meet with the president."

"Of Ireland?" Professor Andrews exclaimed.

"None other," Wallace proudly stated. "So if you want to see it, we'll have to suit up!"

"It's in the clean room?"

"It's not only locked up in the clean room, it's also locked in a refrigerator. As I said, one cannot take too many chances these days."

Dr. Wallace proceeded to use a retinal scan to gain access to the clean room's suiting chamber. Once inside the main room, Dr. Wallace unlocked the large stainless steel refrigerator and carefully removed from the center shelf an object protected by a clear, transparent vinyl bag.

"Well, here it is, Harry!" Dr. Wallace proudly proclaimed. "I can now understand how Indiana Jones felt when he discovered the Lost Ark!"

"Come now, Ian, the lost Ark? This might be a great discovery but it is a far cry from the Ark of the Covenant!"

"Nevertheless, Harry, this small mud-covered book is my lost ark! It is a miracle beyond miracles. Can you even imagine what the odds are that something this fragile could survive buried in a bog at all, and then for it to be unearthed and spotted before it was destroyed! Harry, it is so incalculably amazing. Something I've always dreamed that I would find!"

"Go on, Ian, you have my full attention."

While Professor Andrews listened intently, Dr. Wallace went

on to detail how he had been searching the South Midland bogs for years in hopes of discovering a buried treasure from the past. From his studies of the region, he knew that bogs were often used by Irish monks as hiding places for valuables in the face of Viking raids. He felt that due to their low oxygen levels, the bogs would provide unusual preservative conditions. In addition to low oxygen levels, sphagman moss, of which the peat bog was composed, causes organic material to undergo chemical changes itself that make it impervious to rot.

"Last year," Wallace continued, "I sent out a notice to all bog owners in north Tipperary that I was offering a handsome sum if they were to locate any buried artifacts. Never in my wildest dreams did I ever believe something like this would turn up."

"Get on with it, man. What did they find!"

"It was discovered by bulldozer driver Eddie Fogarty. A co-worker extracting peat with a backhoe dug it up and, don't ask me how, but Eddie saw it there on the ground, sticking out of the peat. Thank goodness Eddie had enough sense to cover it back up in mud again or the air would have dried it out and destroyed it!"

"So, Ian, what is it?"

"Well, it appears to be a section of an early Christian Psalter written on vellum," Wallace replied.

"Prayer book?" Professor Andrews interjected.

"Exactly." Wallace followed. "A 1,200-year-old prayer book to be precise! Come on. Let's take a closer look."

Wallace placed the small wallet-sized book in the center of a long stainless steel observation table, almost the exact size and dimension as the one found in Professor Andrews' lab back at Cambridge. Dr. Wallace then positioned a large magnifying lens over the book for closer inspection.

"Look Harry!" Wallace requested as he repositioned the lens directly over the bottom right corner of the exposed page. "The first thing we did when it was brought in on Saturday was to take a small inconspicuous clipping from the corner here and date it. Each time, the numbers came out the same, about 800 AD give or take a year or two. We then did a spectral analysis of the material and found it to be animal skin, perhaps pig. The pages appear to be those from a somewhat larger book with a wraparound leather cover from which this smaller section had slipped out. It is impossible to say how it ended up in the bog. It may have been lost in transit or dumped by monks after a Viking raid, but it testifies to the incredible richness of our Early Irish Christian heritage. Just trying to determine the safest way to pry open the rest of the pages without damaging or destroying them could take us months!"

"I noticed the words are written in Latin," Professor Andrews commented as he continued to inspect the front page.

"Correct," Wallace concurred. "We spent all weekend studying that one page in detail. There are about forty-five letters written per line and forty lines all together. It so happens to be one of the Psalms."

"Psalms?" Professor Andrews asked with an amazed look.

"You know, book of Psalms from the Bible," Wallace replied. "The 83rd Psalm to be exact! That's the one in which God hears the complaints by the Jews of how certain groups of ancient people conspire together to wipe Israel off the face of the earth."

Professor Andrews just stood for a moment staring down in awe at the small brown book resting on the table.

I must be dreaming! This is the exact same passage Schroeder deciphered from Newton's journal, he thought to himself. *What are the odds of something like this ever happening? Two ancient documents saying the same exact thing! Perhaps Schroeder was right about Newton's prediction.*

Wallace also took note of the puzzled look on Professor Andrews' face.

"Harry, you have a strange look about you," Wallace said with a voice of concern. "It looks as if you've seen a ghost from the past!"

Ghosts from the past? Professor Andrew silently thought. *I believe this time both Wallace and Schroeder could be right!*

Chapter Thirteen

"The Arabs can fight, and lose, and return to fight another day. Israel can only lose once."

Golda Meir

Mention the word "predator" and images of feared creatures such as poisonous snakes, great white sharks, ferocious lions, or even scary monsters from Jurassic Park might come to mind. These animal predators come already hardwired from birth with the basic instincts to search out and kill nature's weak and vulnerable. This is their lot in life. The animal predator possesses neither malice nor hatred toward their prey. They only kill to survive. They live out their lives by serving the vital natural function of helping to maintain an ecological balance between predator and prey.

Unfortunately, predation is not limited to the animal kingdom. Over the millennia, Satan, the author of human death and destruction, has finally fashioned for himself the makings of a true killer driven not by instinct, but cultivated from birth in an environment of hate. Now at the beginning of the 21st century, Satan's ultimate predators hide behind the veiled masks of radical Islam. Birthed in the Muslim Middle East with no core country to call their own, these freelance killers with names like Al Qaida, Hezbollah, Hamas, and the Islamic Jihad have struck as much fear into the hearts of people worldwide as any dreaded predatory animal. Unlike their animal counterparts, these human predators fear not even death. They have been brainwashed into believing the satanic lie that the reward for martyrdom is an instant pass to paradise.

By manipulating the powerful influences of the worldwide media, these cold-blood killers are now able to broadcast their message of hate and fear into every household. Horrific scenes of jet airliners filled with innocent passengers crashing and exploding into skyscrapers or the graphic images of the mutilated bodies of innocent hostages are forever etched into the memories of millions. But the most insidious method used for instilling maximum fear has been the random suicide bombings. In the name of Allah, hundreds of deceived young men and women, mostly of Arab descent, have willingly offered up their bodies to become human bombs. They have subtly infiltrated the safe areas of our lives; our subway and railway stations, our buses and cars, our marketplaces, our innocent men, women, and children.

Like an unstoppable malignancy, Satan's predatory army of radial Islam will continue to spread fear, death, and destruction across the globe until they have achieved their ultimate goal, the complete annihilation of the Judeo/Christian Western Civilization. Only when the infidels, all the Christians and the Jews, have either been killed or conquered, when the role of women around the world has been reduced to second-class status, when the entire civilized world is totally under the submission of Allah, only then will Satan's 7th century religion of submissive intolerance and hate become the so-called "religion of peace."

10:15 *a.m. GTM*
Abu Kamal
Along the Syrian Border with Iraq

Everyone stood to their feet and clapped as if a hero had just stepped into their midst. The room was filled to overflowing with a who's who from every Middle Eastern Islamic terrorist group in the region. So important was this meeting that even the hatred that existed between the sectarian leaders of the Shiites and the Sunnis tribes had been put aside momentarily in order to present a totally unified Muslim front. Everyone remained standing and clapping vigorously as the black bearded man, garbed in the typical black robe and a headdress worn by a Shiite Holy man, made his way to the front of the room. To an Islamic terrorist, Sheik Hassan Nasrallah was truly a hero, a modern-day David who stood toe-to-toe with the Goliath, Israel, and won.

Sheik Nasrallah became the leader of Hezbollah after Israel assassinated the movement's leader, Abbas al Musawi, in 1992. Under Nasrallah's leadership, Hezbollah became a serious opponent of the Israeli Defense Forces in Southern Lebanon. Through his Iranian contacts, he successfully improved the organization's military capabilities by smuggling advance weapons such as anti-tank and surface to air missiles, and long range katuchia rockets across Lebanon's border with Syria. Nasrallah personally planned military campaigns against the IDF troops stationed in Southern Lebanon increasing the killing rate to approximately two dozen Israeli soldiers per year. Hezbollah's relentless attacks were believed to be one of the main factors that led to the Israeli decision to withdraw from Southern Lebanon in 2000, thus ending eighteen years of occupation.

But as far as Sheik Hassan Nasrallah and the rest of the Arab world were concerned, his greatest achievement came in the form of a cease-fire at the end of the month-long Israeli-Lebanon war during the summer of 2006. The war was triggered when Hezbollah guerrillas successfully launched a raid into Northern Israel resulting in the murder of eight IDF troops and the capturing of two IDF soldiers. During the month that followed, Hezbollah's Southern Lebanese rag-tag guerrilla army had to endure the entire wrath of the IDF's superior air and ground forces.

After a month-long war, Israeli forces limped home as Hezbollah, Syria, and Iran all claimed victory against the Jewish state. For the very first time, the Israel Defense Forces did not accomplish a single one of its war objectives. Squeezed by diplomatic pressure from all sides, the Israeli government caved in and accepted a substandard U.N.-imposed cease-fire, leaving Hezbollah largely intact and their leader Hassan Nasrallah, now a cultish hero. Israel failed to eliminate Hezbollah's arsenal of rockets. Worst of all, Israel came home without the two hostages kidnapped by Hezbollah that prompted the war in the first place.

With the strong presence of Israeli blood in the air, the clandestine meeting of the new century was now about to commence. Not to the surprise of anyone present, the first speaker to address the room full of Islamic terrorists was Sheik Hassan Nasrallah.

"To my Arab brothers from the great Saudi Arabian Peninsula, Libya on the African coast, Egypt, Iraq, Syria, Jordan, Palestine, Gaza, and our Persian brothers living in Iran, I bring you greetings in the name of Allah from all our brave Lebanese brothers."

Beaming with arrogant pride, Sheik Nasrallah paused and looked around the room at the loosely knit confederacy of like-minded killers.

"I consider it truly an honor to stand here this morning as a representative of the great Ayatollah Ali Khamenei. It was the Ayatollah himself who called for this meeting after Allah gave him a vision showing him what we are to do. More than anything, the Ayatollah truly wanted to be with us this morning, but he knew that leaving Iran at this time would draw the world's attention. So in his place, I have been asked to be the first of our brothers to address this historic meeting."

The Sheik paused briefly for an applause before continuing.

"My brothers, until now, I have only dreamt of this day when we would all come together in one place united under Allah for achieving one common goal, the total destruction of our mortal enemy, the little Satan, Israel. Allah has shown the great Ayatollah that now is the time for his people to unite under the banner of Islam and liberate once and for all, the entire land of Palestine!"

Everyone in the room stood to their feet and applauded.

"It is also the firm belief of the Ayatollah, the Iranian President, Mahmoud Ahmadinejad, and myself that once the Jews are finally defeated, the "Mahdi," our long-awaited Messiah, will finally appear and lead us to final victory against the heathen infidels living in the land of the great Satan, the United States of America."

The humans in the room were totally oblivious of the physical changes taking place all around them. Instantly, the lighting in the room began to dim and a reddish brown haze filled the air. Standing along side their human hosts appeared ugly yellow skinned demon aberrations joyfully laughing and shouting out praises to their lord and master Satan. In addition to the room full of chimeras, five high ranking demonic princes stood along the side wall also celebrating the moment with handshakes and pats on the back.

"All appears to be going as planned." bragged Allahzad, the demon prince of Persia.

"Just make sure that it does!" Apollon chided his immediate subordinate. "Lord Satan wants this to be flawless. Make sure that there are absolutely no slip-ups, is that understood? Everything must be perfectly in order for the Jew's final Passover."

"Lord Apollon, you have my word, the Jews will have a Passover that they will never forget!"

The entire scene started to instantly dissipate as a familiar penetrating voice became louder and louder.

"Ezra, wake up!" demanded Rachel Schroeder as she gently patted her sleeping husband on the shoulder. "You're only having a bad dream!"

"Dream?" Ezra shouted out loud as he sat up in bed. "No, it wasn't just a dream! Rachel, it was too real to be a dream! I could see everything going on. They're going to attack Israel on Passover!"

"Ezra, look at me," demanded his concerned wife. "You were only dreaming. You were having a very bad dream!"

"Thank God, Rachel," Ezra Schroeder proclaimed. "I have never had a dream like that in my life. Everything was so real. I mean, I can actually sit here and tell you everything I saw, detail by detail, as if I was there myself."

"Well then, tell me about it," Rachel said as she reached over to the side of the bed and turned on the light. "I want you to tell me what you saw in your dream."

"OK," Ezra began. "I was standing in this large room somewhere out in a desert region in the Middle East, Syria perhaps. One by one, I watched as known Muslim terrorists from all parts of the Middle East started entering the room until there were no seats left and there was standing room only. The final terrorist to enter was none other than the head of Hezbollah himself, Hassan Nasrallah.

"He said that their religious leader, Ayatollah Khamenei, stated that now was the time to destroy Israel, and once Israel was completely annihilated, they planned next to go after America."

"Ezra, while you were sleeping, you kept saying that the terrorists are planning to attack Israel on Passover," Rachel commented.

"No," Ezra followed, "the terrorists didn't say that, the demons did!"

"Demons?" Rachel asked with a look of skepticism. "Ezra, did I hear you say demons?"

"I'm sorry, my dear." Ezra conceded as he looked over at the alarm clock sitting on the night table. "You're right, I had a bad dream. It's only 5: 25 a.m. Let's go back to sleep!"

"Muriel, why did we go through all the trouble of showing him the meeting if Schroeder thinks it was only a dream?" Ariel asked.

"It's all part of Michael's plan for Schroeder," Muriel followed. "Before we reveal the entire riddle, Schroeder has to believe beyond a shadow of a doubt that it is real. Be patient, my friend. Today was only the first step. Tomorrow we will show him step two."

Monday, February 11*th*
8:00 *a.m. Eastern Standard Time*
NSA Headquarters
Jessup, Maryland

Overnight, a strong nor'easter blanketed the entire Mid-Atlantic region with over a foot and a half of fresh snow, bringing everything, including much of the federal government to a complete standstill. In an area noted for its snarled traffic jams and congestion, on this particular morning the metropolitan area's vast network of snow-covered roads and highways were mostly deserted. For the majority of people living in the Washington/Baltimore corridor, a snowstorm meant a day off from work or school to either relax in the comforts of their homes or go outside and enjoy the snow. But for the employees whose jobs provided critical services—the police, emergency workers, or those working in vital governmental agencies—staying at home this morning was not an option. For these unfortunate workers, a snowstorm simply meant that getting to work today would be more of a challenge.

But such was not the case this morning for a group of seven NSA employees who worked in the agency's top-secret SIGINT division. These seven men were all members of an elite team of cryptologists responsible for decoding foreign signals intelligence using the most technologically advanced digital tools on the planet. No force on earth, not even a crippling snowstorm, was going to keep them from carrying out their duties, especially today. So vital was their presence this morning, that an army humvee from nearby Fort Meade was dispatched to pick each man up at their doorsteps and transport them safely to their jobsite at the Jessup, Maryland's NSA headquarters. As their humvee passed under the main gate's first security checkpoint, the large lettering on the overhead banner was snow covered, but still legible:

> *The ability to understand the secret communications of our foreign adversaries while protecting our communications—a capability in which the United States leads the world.*

Under normal circumstances, the presence of all seven experts at one time was not needed, but today was not normal. As if a silent alarm had gone off, the NSA computers housed in NSA's OPS 2B Building began recording a literal explosion of Middle Eastern communiqués over the weekend. Commonly called chatter, the mostly digital transmissions indicated that something big had just taken place. As the seven departed their transport and slowly trudged along a snow-cleared path leading to Building 2B, their boss, Dr. Gerald Gans, met them at the building's front entrance.

"Can you believe this?" Dr. Gans asked as he held open the entrance door for his shivering peers. "Of all mornings for a snowstorm to hit!"

"I hope this is not an ominous sign of things to come!" commented Lester Morgan, the first man through the door.

"Right now, I'm only dreaming of some hot coffee," commented Mike Fisher as he removed his gloves and stuffed them into the pocket of his thick winter jacket.

"I just put on a fresh pot," replied Dr. Gans, "and there's a tray filled with hot Danish, scrambled eggs, bagels and toast awaiting all of you in the conference room."

For seven cold, hungry men, the lure of a fresh pot of hot coffee and a hot breakfast was all that was needed.

"I'll show the way," quickly replied Joe Oliver as he led the group to the conference room down the hall. As the men quickly filed past their boss, one man remained behind.

"Ezra, I can't tell you how much it means to me that you came in today of all days!" Dr. Gans sincerely commented as he extended a warm handshake of gratitude. Though officially retired for almost two years, Ezra Schroeder worked from time to time as a consultant for the agency. "I knew I could always count on you for the big ones."

"Well, I must confess," Ezra replied, "from what you told me on the phone on Saturday, I wouldn't have missed this for the world!"

"By the way, Ezra, how's Rachel doing?" Dr. Gans inquired.

"Praise God, Gerry, she's fine." Ezra thankfully declared. "Even Rachel's speech has returned to normal. She'll be staying with my youngest daughter Rebecca and her family until I return home on Wednesday."

"Ezra, about how long have we known each other?" Dr. Gans asked.

"Well, you were probably one of the first persons I met when I started at the agency back in '94," Ezra replied.

"Then you've known me long enough to know that I am not an alarmist."

"Tenacious, yes, alarmist, no," Ezra commented with a smile. "You, my friend, are the number one stickler when it comes to checking and rechecking. I've seen you check every bit of data at least a dozen or more times before even coming up with a decision, and even then, you check it again before passing up to the next level."

Ezra paused, stared directly into his bosses' eyes and asked, "Gerry, do you have something you want to tell me?"

"Ezra," Dr. Gans replied, "as you already know, I've been here since early Saturday morning. I've taken a look at almost everything that all of you will be seeing. I believe that something big, very big, is about to take place over there!"

"In the Middle East?"

"That's affirmative!" Dr. Gans said with look of confidence. "From what I've seen, they were all there."

"Who are 'they'?" asked Schroeder.

"Al Qaida, Hezbollah, Hamas, Islamic Jihad, every radial Muslim fundamentalist who lives for the day when they see Israel cast 100 kilometers out into the Mediterranean Sea," Gans replied.

Ezra Schroeder stood in silent awe. *This sounds strangely familiar!* he thought.

"There's more," Gans continued. "I don't believe they're hiding their intentions."

"What do you mean?"

"I believe they want us to know exactly what they are doing right down to the last detail."

"Gerry, I have to ask you one question," Ezra commented in a serious tone. "Were the communiqués coming from any specific location?"

"Well, for the most part, they're scattered," Dr. Gans replied. "Quite a few were from Saudi Arabia and Iran. Some were from the West Bank, the Gaza, Jordan and Lebanon. But, I'd say the vast majority of chatter was coming from Abu Kamal, a Syrian border town out in the middle of nowhere!"

"Abu Kamal," Schroeder repeated with a distant look on his face.

"Ezra, is there something wrong?"

Shaking his head, Ezra smiled and asked, "Gerry, did you ever have a bad dream come true?"

"Off hand, not lately," Dr. Gans admitted. "But perhaps you might want to tell me about your dream."

"If I told you, you might think I'm crazy." Ezra again smiled.

"Then, perhaps your dream was simply a case of de-ja-vu. It's happened to me on more than one occasion."

"I believe it's more than de-ja-vu," Ezra quickly replied. "What would you say if I told you that in my dream, I saw everything you just mentioned, right down to the exact location?"

"Ezra, let's look at the facts," Dr. Gans replied. "You are a creative author. You also work at a spy agency that decodes communications coming in from Middle Eastern bad guys. Combine that with a vivid imagination and what do you get? Bad dreams!" Patting his old friend and colleague on the shoulder, Dr. Gans made one more suggestion. "Ezra, try to be more like me. If you tap into your left-brain logic, you won't let your creative right brain get the better of you. And also, until we all have a chance to sit and discuss our findings, let's keep all this between ourselves."

After breakfast, the elite team of NSA cryptologists got right down to business attempting to decode a huge array of cell phone and email messages plus other digital transmissions gathered over the weekend from known and suspected Middle Eastern terrorists. Working in groups of two in a small circular room they had dubbed "Cryptocity," each specialist began opening and scanning through top-secret digital files available to their eyes only on the most advanced computers on earth. Each team was assigned a specific task related to their specialty. While Mike Fisher and Frank Jakobe sat side-by-side analyzing suspected terrorist's microwave cell phone transmissions, Alex Virtello and Al Levin poured over hundreds of emails and scanned thousands of text messages posted on popular radical Islamic web sites and chat rooms. The team of Joe Oliver and Ezra Schroeder, experts in every known Middle Eastern language and dialect, oversaw the translation of all analog and digital audio communiqués in English.

But by far, NSA's most advanced means for obtaining digital intelligence on whereabouts of known terrorists was assigned to the team of Lester Morgan and Gerald Gans. Using special EMF (Electromagnetic Force) equipped SIGINT satellites, these top NSA cryptologists were able to both track and remotely glean the actual brainwave thoughts emitted by anyone on earth. Once a terrorist's individual EMF was identified, the SIGINT EMF scanning network along with the NSA's supercomputers could then pinpoint and track that person 24 hours-a-day.

Monday, February 11th
7:40 p.m. Eastern Standard Time
Comfort Inn,
Jessup, Maryland

As evening approached and the cold blue skies over the Washington, D.C. metropolitan area began fading into darkness, local road crews were still out working overtime to clear the last remnants of snow from the local interstates and major highways before tackling the secondary and neighborhood roads. It was also time to call it a day for the NSA cryptologists. For almost eight straight hours, they sat fixed in front of their computers, stopping only briefly to down a sandwich for lunch and several cups of strong coffee before returning to their tasks. At the end of the day, they had made much headway in deciphering the huge data bank of digital chatter, but at least one more day was needed to finish their job. By now, all of the sidewalks and roads within the nation's largest spy agency had been cleared and an awaiting humvee was parked outside of Building 2B ready to drive the team of eight to their nighttime lodging two miles up the highway, the Jessup Comfort Inn. After a relaxing dinner at a restaurant adjacent to their motel, the cryptologists agreed to meet each other at the same restaurant in the morning at 6:30 a.m. for an early breakfast. They then retired to their individual rooms.

The first thing Ezra Schroeder did when he entered his motel room was to locate the phone and call his daughter's home to check up on his wife. Little did he realize as he sat on the edge of the bed that the response on the other side of the line was about to change the rest of his life.

As the phone rang, a female voice answered and immediately asked, "Daddy, is that you?"

"Rebecca, what's wrong?" Ezra quickly responded.

"Daddy, nothing's wrong!" Rebecca quickly replied. "Everyone here is fine and Mom is doing great! Daddy, find the television in your room and turn on the news. Something wonderful has happened!"

No sooner had Ezra located and picked up the television remote on the bed stand than there was a knocking at the door. He quickly clicked the "on" button on the television remote and walked over to answer the door.

"Good, you've already heard the news!" announced Joe Oliver, the person standing at the door.

"What news?" asked a totally confused Ezra Schroeder. "Can somebody tell me what is going on around here?"

"Then you really don't know?" Joe asked as even more co-workers arrived at the door.

"Ezra, turn on a news channel," Mike Fisher requested.

"Which channel?"

"It doesn't matter," Mike replied as he sat down on the side of the bed. "It's the number one story. It's all over the news."

Ezra Schroeder couldn't change the channels fast enough. He finally stopped scanning when he spotted a very familiar person addressing a large group of reporters assembled in the White House's Press Briefing Room. By this time, every member of the NSA team was either standing or sitting on the edge of the room's twin beds, all eyes fixed on the television.

"Mr. Press Secretary," asked a female reporter on the television. "Who are the major players in this agreement?"

"From what we can tell, all current members of the Arab League were involved," replied John Reid, the Presidential Press Secretary.

"What about the Iranians, and their sponsored terrorists groups, Hezbollah and Hamas?" asked the same reporter.

"As far as I know, the Iranians are onboard," John Reid replied.

"As for Hezbollah and Hamas, our sources say that both groups are offering Israel a guaranteed ten-year ceasefire in exchange for the land deal.

"What does the president have to say about all this?" asked a Washington Times journalist.

"All this has happened so fast," John Reid admitted. "I really haven't had a chance to sit down and discuss it with the president. But as we speak, the president is down the hall meeting in an emergency session with all of her staff."

"Has there been any word from the Israelis?" another reporter asked.

"Not that I've heard," John Reid again replied. "I'm sure the Israeli Prime Minister has a lot on his plate right now.

"Mr. Press Secretary, what do you personally have to say about all that has happened?"

Before answering the reporter's question, John Reid paused briefly and displayed a firm smile as he looked out over the large assemblage of reporters representing every form of media on the planet. Not knowing the president's thoughts on this all important question, John Reid had the rare opportunity to make a definitive statement that could very well reflect America's policy on the future of the Middle East. With confidence, he continued, "I believe the answer now rests with Israel. But let me say this. For the first time in recorded history, all of her surrounding Arab neighbors—Syria, Lebanon, Turkey, Saudi Arabia, Jordan, and Egypt—are offering Israel peace."

"But Mr. Press Secretary," a reporter from a conservative news agency stood up and commented, "as far as the Israeli government is concerned, aren't we talking about a conditional peace with a giant price tag attached. From what I understand, the Arabs are only giving Israel a one-month deadline to accept their demands for Israel to totally withdraw from the entire West Bank, return all of the Golan Heights up to the northern end of the Sea of Galilee, and surrender most of East Jerusalem, including the entire Temple Mount."

"That's right," John Reid conceded, "that's what we're also hearing. But that is the sacrifice that Israel must be willing to make if they truly desire a permanent and lasting peace with their Arab neighbors."

Ezra stood speechless just staring at the television screen, while everyone else in the room either sat or stood in silent awe, initially unable to take it all in. Finally, Mike Fisher broke the silence and made a lighthearted comment to his sitting boss. "Well, Gerry, I guess this means our job is over for now."

"We still have all day tomorrow to finish up and send in our findings," Gerry Gans replied as he shook his head in disbelief. Standing to his feet, NSA's chief cryptologist turned to his group of seven and soberly reflected, "Well, gentlemen, I believe I've had enough excitement for one evening. I think I'm going to go back to my room and turn in for the night. I am absolutely confident that they'll be talking all about this tomorrow morning and for all the days to come. I'll see everybody bright and early at the restaurant for breakfast."

With that said, each member of the NSA team followed their boss's lead and bid their goodnight, leaving only Ezra Schroeder and Joe Oliver remaining in the room.

"Ezra, you haven't said one word since I walked in," Joe commented. "I'd like to know what's going through your mind."

"This isn't good!" Ezra declared as he shook his head from side to side.

"I'm curious, Ezra," Joe asked, "why don't you see this as a good thing?

"Joe, this offer has 'trap' written all over it!" Ezra declared. "Everyone's placing Israel between a rock and a hard place, and that includes our own government!"

Schroeder proceeded to raise his hands high and in an act of frustration shouted, "Am I the only one who sees this? The Israelis are damned if they accept the Arabs' terms to give back all of their strategic land and they are damned with a possible all out war if they reject it!"

"Ezra, you are absolutely right!" Joe quickly followed. "I can't see how any rational person could say otherwise."

"Believe me, my friend," Ezra commented as he placed a hand of reassurance on his partner's shoulder, "when it comes to anything involving Israel, rational thoughts aren't considered."

"Ezra, is it all right if we change the subject for a moment?" Joe requested as he stood and turned off the television. "I have something I need to show you."

"By all means," Ezra graciously replied. "Please, have a seat."

Both men now sat on the ends of the adjacent double beds, facing each other. From the excited look on Joe's face, Ezra knew that Joe had something big to share with him.

"You might think I'm crazy, Ezra," Joe continued, "but last year, some guy at our church told me about a secret code written in Hebrew that was found hidden throughout the Old Testament. He said it was discovered by an Israeli mathematician named Eli Rips. Have you ever heard about it?"

"A little, but I must tell you, I am highly skeptical," Ezra admitted without divulging the fact that he had personally met with the world-renowned mathematician years earlier in Jerusalem during the time when he himself was researching whether or not Sir Isaac Newton had actually discovered the hidden Bible codes before he died.

"Well, Ezra, at first, I too was skeptical!" Joe admitted. "But, being in the business that we are in, my curiosity got the better of me, so I had no other choice but to check it out for myself."

What Joe didn't know was that when Ezra Schroeder made up his mind on something, he usually refused to revisit it, especially on a subject that he considered himself to be an expert. Not wanting to quench his partner's enthusiasm, Ezra decided it was best to just sit there and let him talk.

"The first thing I did was to read everything I could find on Bible Codes, all the pros and cons. You might find this hard to believe, but I read that Isaac Newton spent the greater part of his life searching for the codes himself. Too bad old Isaac didn't have a computer back then! He could have changed the whole world as we know it today!"

Schroeder chuckled to himself, but it wasn't for anything that Joe had said. It was for the fact that Joe didn't have a clue that Schroeder had written a number one bestselling book on that very subject!

"The whole idea that there may be special codes hidden throughout the text of the Bible just blew my mind!" Joe exclaimed as Schroeder just sat on the edge of the bed and patiently listened.

"That's when I decided to run my own experiment, something similar to Rips'. Dr. Rips believed that he had succeeded where Isaac Newton failed. It would have taken Newton more years than he had to process all of the numbers and then read the code. What Dr. Rips had in fact done was to write a randomization analysis program similar the very ones we write here at the agency. Rips' program both searches out equidistant letter sequences and eliminates all of the spaces between the words of the Bible, thus turning the book into 304,805 letters. By doing this, Rips had restored the Torah to what legend says was the way that Moses originally received the Bible from God, 'continuous and without break of words.' The way the code works is very similar to that of a word search puzzle. Encoded messages are recorded backward, forward, vertically, horizontally, and diagonally. In the end, Rips had confirmed what Newton had suspected all along, the Bible was encoded."

Leaning forward, Joe looked his partner directly in the eyes and said, "Ezra, I can't explain it, but I truly felt the presence of God on all this. First of all, I didn't have to learn Hebrew. I already knew it!" Joe exclaimed. "The next thing I did was to write my own algorithms and come up with a program similar to that used by Rips. My program not only crunches each book of the Old Testament into a continuous sequence of Hebrew characters with no punctuation marks, but like Rips', it also searches out and locates any equal distant messages and creates its own matrix!"

Joe's enthusiasm was slowly chipping away at Schroeder's skepticism. The onetime Bible Code skeptic was about to find out for himself if these hidden messages from God really did exist. Grabbing his partner's hand, Joe looked Schroeder directly in the eyes and proclaimed, "Ezra, it's there! It's really, really there!"

"Joe, I really want to believe this!" Ezra sincerely replied. "I want you to prove it to me beyond a shadow of a doubt so I can believe it too!"

"Then you wait right here!" Joe hastily replied. "I have the entire program on my laptop in my room. I'll be right back!"

No sooner did Joe exit the room and close the door behind him than Ezra noticed the phone resting off its hook on the nightstand.

Rebecca! he thought, *I must be losing my mind! I totally forgot that I was talking to her when Joe knocked on the door. Could she possibly still be on the line?* Thinking that it might by a waste of time, Schroeder picked up the phone and casually said "Hello."

"Daddy?"

"Sweetheart?" a shocked Schroeder replied, "I can't believe you waited the entire time!"

"Daddy, I had no other choice." Rebecca followed. "I didn't have a clue what motel you were in, so I just started praying that you would finally spot the phone off the hook and pick it up!"

"Rebecca, I am so sorry," declared her embarrassed father. "Right after you called, Joe Oliver knocked at the door, then before I knew it, everyone else I work with was also standing here in my room."

"Daddy, I just wanted to tell you what we saw on the news today."

"Honey, I already know," Ezra interjected. "That's what all the boys came in to tell me!"

"Isn't it great, Daddy!" Rebecca cheerful announced.

"Rebecca, I hate to differ with you, but I can't see how an Arab ultimatum toward Israel is anything to be happy about!"

Rebecca paused momentarily, apparently caught off guard by her father's unexpected rebuke. "Daddy, I didn't hear anything about the Arabs and Israel!" Rebecca admitted in a confused tone of voice. "We were all sitting in the family room watching the news when we spotted your English friend, Harry Andrews, standing along side of some man who runs an Irish museum. The man then announced that they had just discovered some great find buried for thousands of years in an Irish bog. According to what we heard, what they found buried and perfectly preserved was a section of the book of Psalms. Daddy, here's the most exciting part of all: the exposed front page of book was totally legible and written in Latin. Daddy, it was Psalm 83!"

Ezra immediately stood to his feet and stared at the phone in his hand. *This is not a coincidence and this is not my imagination,* Ezra Schroeder silently declared.

Placing the phone back up to his ear, Schroeder commented in a calm clear voice, "Rebecca honey, I have to go. Kiss your mom for me and tell her that I will see all of you on Wednesday afternoon."

That was all that Ezra said before hanging up the phone. Just as he placed the phone back on its receiver, the motel door opened and Joe Oliver entered the room, this time holding his laptop computer under his arm. Joe instantly noticed the troubled look on his partner's face and assumed that something was wrong.

"Ezra, are you all right?" Joe asked with a concerned look.

"Something is happening." Ezra mumbled to himself.

"Ezra, what do you mean something is happening?" Joe asked again, "Are you experiencing chest pains?"

"No, don't worry," Ezra replied "I'm physically fine."

"Then what's wrong?" Joe repeated. "You look as if you've seen a ghost!"

Three tall angelic beings stood at the far end of the room carefully observing and listening to every word that was being said. "Job well done, Periel!" Muriel commented as he turned and gave his nodding approval in the direction of the angel standing to his right.

"All praises go to the Lord for his plans are always perfect," Periel, Joe Oliver's guardian angel, humbly responded.

"Amen to that," Muriel followed, "but nevertheless, you did well!"

Turning his attention now to the angel on his left, Muriel simply said, "It is time."

Ariel knew exactly what his superior meant. The meeting between the two humans was no accident. All the arrangements and details for them to meet at this very moment and at this very place had already been worked out eons ago. Now Ariel's long awaited moment had finally come. The reward for his unwavering loyalty to his mission and his God was to be the angel selected to reveal the next part of Newton's riddle. Leaning over his human charge, the huge angelic warrior simply whispered, "Ask Joe Oliver to run a matrix on Psalm 83."

"Joe," Schroeder quickly interjected, "you said you have your Bible Code program already loaded in your laptop."

"That's right!" Joe replied. "It's already loaded and ready to go!"

"Good. I want you to do something really important for me," Ezra asked.

"Anything, just name it!" Joe smiled.

"I want you to run a matrix on Psalm 83," Ezra followed.

"Absolutely, but may I ask why that particular Psalm?" Joe asked with a puzzled look.

"Because God had King David write it over 3000 years ago!" Ezra proclaimed. "It's one of the few unfulfilled prophecies remaining in the Bible. I believe it was written specifically for our generation to proclaim its words in order to frustrate an Arab conspiracy to destroy Israel."

Joe proceeded to type the Hebrew words and equivalent numbers for Psalm 83. With the click of his mouse, instantly, a matrix of Hebrew characters appeared on the computer's screen. Looking up at his wide-eyed partner, Joe Oliver then asked, "Give me any key words that you can think of."

Ariel again leaned over and whispered the following words as Schroeder continued to speak as Joe Oliver typed. "Type in Israel- Attack - Date–Bomb- City." Instantly, vertical, horizontal, and diagonal circled messages in Hebrew began appearing all over the screen. Both Schroeder and Oliver sat in a complete state of awe just staring at the computer screen in amazement.

"I see it, but I don't believe it!" Joe Oliver uttered in a state of shock.

Even before Schroeder could state his response, Ariel once again whis-

pered into his assigned human's thoughts, "Remember what Newton wrote at the end of his journal."

Instantly, Schroeder recalled the words written in the last sentence of Newton's journal. "For concealed within these very lines, the wise shall know the end of times." *That's it!* Schroeder thought to himself. *Newton was trying the tell me how to find his hidden message, but I was too pigheaded to see it!*

Joe Oliver then turned to his colleague and asked "Ezra, tell me, what do we do with this?"

"Before we do anything else," Ezra replied, "we have to pray and ask God what we need to do next! Until then, we will say nothing about this to anyone. Agreed?"

Ezra then extended out his right hand in agreement. "Agreed!" Joe Oliver replied as he locked his right hand with Schroeder's and sealed a pact that that would change their destinies forever.

Long after his colleagues had returned to their own rooms, Schroeder remained awake. He was too overwhelmed by the day's events to contemplate sleep. As he sat back in his bed, the same thoughts kept racing through his excited mind.

I don't know how he did it, but he did it! How could Newton have cracked the Bible Code without a computer? It had to have been God that showed him! A human couldn't possibly come up with this on his own! The moment I get home, I'm going to run Newton's entire journal through Joe's program! I've got to see for myself what God showed Newton!

"The first part of your mission is now accomplished!" Muriel commented as both he and Ariel stood watch over Schroeder. "The most important part now begins. Guard him well!"

Ariel smiled as he placed his massive hand on Schroeder's forehead and released an aura of peace over the restless human, sending him fast to sleep.

Chapter Fourteen

"For happily the government of the United States, which gives bigotry no sanction, to persecution no assistance, requires only that they who live under its protection should demean themselves as good citizens, giving it on all occasions their effectual support...May the children of the Stock of Abraham, who dwell in this land, continue to merit and enjoy of their other inhabitants, while everyone shall sit in safety under his own vine and fig-tree, and there shall be none to make him afraid."

From George Washington's famous letter to the Jews of Newport

"God Bless America" is a song considered by some to be America's unofficial anthem. It was written by a young Jewish immigrant named Irving Berlin who left his home in Siberia with his mother and father for a better life in America when he was only five years old. Like the Berlins, people from every corner of the world have forsaken and risked everything to come to its shores for a chance to share in America's ideals of freedom, prosperity, and most importantly, its blessings. Some may deny its source, but few will deny the fact that America is blessed. Unfortunately, fewer yet will ever accept the biblical truth recorded in Genesis 12:3 that America's ongoing blessings are the direct result of how our country has treated the Jews, the true descendants of God's covenant with Abraham.

With only the sad exception of President Franklin D. Roosevelt's inexcusable abandonment of millions of European Jews trying to escape the Nazi Holocaust, every American presidential administration since George Washington has been a strong supporter of Jewish rights and freedom. In his famous letter to the members of the Touro Synagogue, George Washington warmly welcomed Jewish civic participation and condemned bigotry in the strongest terms. John Adams wrote to Mordecai Noah, a Jewish leader in America: "I wish for your nation to be admitted to all the privileges of citizenship in every country of the world." Thomas Jefferson, America's third elected president wrote concerning the Jews, "I am happy in the restoration of the Jews, particularly, to their social rights, and hopes they will be seen taking their seats on the branches of science as preparatory to their doing the same at the board of government."

For the first time since their dispersal from their homeland some 1800 years prior, the scattered people of Israel saw in America a beacon of true hope. Every day since the founding of this newly formed country, thousands of persecuted Jews worldwide arrived at its shores and took full advantage of their new found American freedoms. Many have since been elected as governors, senators, congressmen, speakers of state legislatures, and appointed chief justice of the supreme courts. Using their innate, God-given talents, Jewish Americans over the past two centuries have benefited every aspect of America society by taking on leadership roles in science, law, education, medicine, entertainment, and business.

It is by no coincidence that America's phenomenal rise to superpower status after World War II corresponded to the formation and establishment of the tiny state of Israel on May 14, 1948. Since that famous date, foretold thousands of years earlier by the prophet Isaiah, America has remained Israel's staunchest ally and loyal supporter both financially and militarily. During this same time, God has continued to honor the promise He made so long ago, to bless those who bless the descendents of Abraham. As long as America maintains her supportive role as Israel's protectorate, her blessings will continue. The moment America chooses to follow a different course and end her relationship with Israel, God will have no other choice, but to end his relationship with America.

Tuesday, February 12th
8 a.m. EST
United Nations Headquarters
New York City

All across the world, people were awaking to the same breaking news story, "Peace in the Middle East?" Overnight, traveling at the speed of light via satellite, cable, and the Internet, the news of a possible peace deal in the Middle East reached every corner of the globe. The amazing headlines not only captured the attention of every reader or viewer, it seemed to spark a sense of euphoric wonder. Awestruck people worldwide either stood or sat fixated to their computer screens, televisions or newspapers asking themselves the same questions, "Could the unthinkable be true? Is it possible that peace between Arabs and Jews could now be a reality? Has true peace finally come to the Middle East?"

Wall Street thought so. At the opening bell, stocks had skyrocketed, surpassing their all time highs. Church bells rang out in harmonic unison announcing a message of peace from hundreds of villages, hamlets and cities all around the globe. Phone circuits quickly became jammed as onslaughts of millions of exuberant people began calling friends and family to share the good news.

But nowhere were spirits lifted any higher by the phenomenal morning news than for the diplomats and personnel who worked at the United Nations headquarter in New York City. For these people, the concept of achieving peace anywhere on earth was more than a lofty ideal; it was their passion in life. Unfortunately, the very organization they dedicated their lives to had let them down, time and time again. A long history of internal corruption amongst its 192 member countries not only dampened the UN worker's spirits, it prevented their vision of eliminating wars and maintaining world peace from ever becoming a reality, at least, not perhaps until this day.

Something was noticeably different this morning in the halls of the UN headquarters. Smiles were everywhere. Not only were smiles evident, the entire atmosphere within the large building was charged with excitement. Not since the fall of the Berlin Wall had there been such a reason to cheer at the UN. For the UN workers, the very thought of peace in an area of the world that had never known peace was more than a dream come true. Nothing like this had ever happened before. Last night's announcement came as a complete shock even to the diplomats representing the Middle Eastern countries involved. Such an important unilateral decision involving so many countries usually takes months or even years of negotiations in order to achieve an agreement.

Not everyone at the UN was caught off guard by the news. Just down the hallway behind the closed doors of the UN Security Council's chambers a high level meeting of sorts was just about to conclude. The members of this meeting were well aware of what was taking place in the Middle East. They were the very ones who painstakingly planned it out in every minute detail. Like a team of master chess players, Satan and his demonic princes have strategically worked behind the scenes of human history moving and removing, positioning and repositioning nations and people groups all across the globe for the sole purpose of achieving their goal, the destruction of the tiny state of Israel. As far as Satan was concerned, all the pieces in his grand plan were now in place with only one more move left before his final checkmate,- the removal of Israel's protectorate, the United States of America.

After a long night of finalizing plans, tension now filled the room full of demons. Even the elite group of princes who sat up front in a semicircle around the final speaker were visibly on edge for they could sense time was running out. In less than an hour, the human Security Council was scheduled to convene in the same room. With only moments left in closing, the final speaker, Arch Demon Amducious, turned to address his superiors seated directly behind him.

"In closing, I stand here honored before my Lords Satan and Apollon and before the great assembly of princes in this room. I pledge to all of you that you will not be disappointed in your decision to place me in charge of Project G 123. With the trust you've given to both me and my army, I will conclude with this solemn vow; before our comrades in the East com-

mence at the end of next month with their Passover surprise for the Israeli pigs, America the Great will be no more."

Amducious then raised a clinched fist high above his head and led the entire group in a closing declaration, "Praise be to Satan!"

Tuesday, February 12*th*
10:15 *Israeli Standard Time*
Plenary Hall, the Knesset
Jerusalem, Israel

No matter where you looked in the large chamber, the expression of doom and gloom was clearly visible on each face. Never in its sixty year history has the Knesset, Israel's democratically elected legislative body, been so hopelessly divided on such a critical issue and never has it seen such a degree of unabated vicious attacks by its members.

"Peace!" rang out a shout from amongst the standing room only crowd gathered in the balcony above the Knesset floor. "Vote for peace!"

"We will never have another opportunity like this again!" echoed a member of the Labor party from the Knesset floor below.

"You're fooling yourselves if you see this offer as peace!" followed Chaim Ebban, the Speaker of the Israeli parliament "It's suicide! If we accept these terms, it's the end of us all!"

"Has anybody thought of what will happen to our water supplies to the north if we give back the Golan?" questioned Rabbi Yosef Ben Michael of the Shas Party, representing Israel's Sephardic Jewish population. "Do you think the Syrians will give us one drop of water after they suck Lake Kinneret as dry as a bone?"

"Are you all deaf and blind!" interjected Kadima's Shimon Herzog "Have you no eyes to see and no ears to hear? This morning's *Post* says that even the Americans are throwing their full support for the peace plan. We have no other alternative but to go along!"

"I'm sure if Hitler were alive, he would support it too!" scoffed Yitzhak Halpern, head of the Nation Religious Party.

"Hitler would stand up and cheer!" shouted out another person from the balcony above.

"Anyone one of you who votes to sacrifice even a square inch of East Jerusalem to the Arabs is not a Jew; he is a devil and he should die!" shouted still another as the Knesset police stormed the top balcony area in an attempt to silence the crowd of hostile onlookers.

No one expected this to happen. The Israeli intelligence was supposed to be the best in the world, but once again, the Israeli government was caught totally off guard. What should have been a typical legislative day of only minor nonessential issues attended only by the Speaker of the parliament and a few dozen Knesset members turned out instead to be a firestorm of raw emotions filling the entire 120-seat Knesset chamber to standing room only. The entire Israeli government was broadsided by yesterday's Arab announcement leaving all of Israel's political parties, especially its ruling majority Likud-led coalition with precious little time to sit down and strategize with its members.

Satan was well aware that military attacks against Israel in the past had proven to be fruitless. The Israelis, regardless of their political party or religious background, had always been unified in matters of war, survival, and national security. They had also been protected by the ever watchful eyes of Michael and his angelic army.

But now, Satan and his crafty princes had possibly discovered a true weakness in Israel's once thought impenetrable resolve. This internal flaw could prove to be so divisive to the Israeli psyche that if exploited correctly, Satan could destroy Israel. From the beginning of their tiny nation in 1948, the Israeli people had never agreed on a unified approach to the biggest problem facing them, peace with their Arab neighbors. By offering Israel the façade of a peace deal with a time limit attached, Satan now gambled that he could destroy tiny Israel with the simple biblical principal, "A house divided against itself cannot stand!"

After almost five full minutes of name calling and mean spiritedness, the prime minister, Yacov Ben Yizri, seated among the members of his own Likud party to the left of the speaker, stood to his feet. Known and admired by his allies and political opponents alike as a man of patience, he had taken all he could take of the endless bickering. Unprecedented, he abruptly left his assigned area of the Knesset floor and walked to the front of the rostrum to confront the Speaker directly. After a brief exchange, the Speaker of the Parliament sat down, allowing the prime minister to take his place at the podium to address the entire Knesset.

"My fellow countrymen," the prime minister solemnly stated, "I first want to thank Speaker Ebban for allowing me to break with protocol and take his place at the podium. I stand here now before all of you because my conscience would not allow me to sit by any longer and watch my beloved country destroy itself from within!"

With tears streaming down his cheeks, the prime minister paused momentarily to wipe his face with his right hand before making a desperate plea to his fellow Knesset members, "Can't you all see what's happening here? We are playing right into the Arab's hands. This is exactly what they want! Without the Arabs firing a single shot, we have allowed ourselves to sink into anarchy! I'm afraid what we have here is a hopeless impasse and arguing back and forth won't get us anywhere."

Once again, the Israeli Prime Minister paused, but this time he stood firm at the rostrum and gathered his resolve before continuing.

"So the Arabs have given us one month to decide. I say let the people of Israel decide their own future!" the prime minister declared. "A decision of this magnitude must be left up to our people, not the politicians. I call for a referendum to be drawn up immediately covering all the points of the Arab's demands. I am asking the Knesset to declare a national vote to be made two weeks from today. This should be sufficient time to setup the voting booths and more importantly, to give the world our answer. Israel belongs to all of us, and all of us together; every Israeli man and woman must decide once and for all our own destiny!"

Wednesday, February 13*th*
6:30 *a.m. Eastern Standard Time*

Washington, D.C.
The Cabinet Room
West Wing of the White House

Once again, the five women and twelve men who made up the president's cabinet along with the vice president found themselves sitting around the Cabinet Room's long cherry wood table awaiting the arrival of their boss. For the second time in less than a month, the entire presidential cabinet was summoned by the president to meet in the West Wing, but this time, domestic matters were not part of the agenda. At exactly 6:30 a.m., all members stood to their feet and clapped as the president made her entrance into the room.

"Good morning, everyone," President Devoe graciously announced as she entered the long narrow room and promptly proceeded to a chair left vacant in the center of the long table. The president smiled as she turned to face the entire group and commented, "I want to thank all of you for coming on such short notice. You may all be seated."

There were intentional changes made to secretarial seating order for this meeting. Both the energy and treasury secretaries who flanked the president in the first meeting were moved to opposite ends of the table and replaced by Vice President, Neil O'Sullivan to the president's left and the Secretary of the State, James Metloff, to her right. Also, Secretary of Defense, Leslie Shaeffer was now seated directly across the table from the president.

"What a difference a day can make," the president sighed as she opened the meeting. Everyone smiled and nodded in agreement for the secretaries knew that the president was alluding to the Arab/Israel peace offer. "The reason I have called all of you together this morning is that I need all of you present once again to be my sounding board before I address the nation in a televised broadcast tonight. I can't tell you how much all of your input helped me prepare for last month's State of the Union address."

By the relaxed tone of her voice, everyone in the room could sense that the president appeared exceptionally at ease this morning, as if a great burden was lifted off her shoulders.

"Folks, these are truly amazing days that we are living in," the president continued with an elated expression of joy. "Who would ever have dreamt just two short days ago that we would be talking seriously about peace in the Middle East?"

"I for one didn't have a clue," chuckled Secretary of State, James Metloff. "Nor did anyone else working at the State Department, and we are the ones who are suppose to know these things,"

"Well, I promise all of you, we are not going to let this opportunity slip through our hands," the president affirmed. "With every fiber of my being, I am committed to making sure this happens! By this time next month, there will be a peace deal in the Middle East."

"Madame President," said the Education Secretary, Susan Harding, "what do you foresee as America's role in making sure this happens?"

"For one thing, I promise we will not duplicate the mistakes of the past," the president responded in a firm, controlled voice. "We will not pander to one side or the other, nor will we dictate the outcome. We've tried that route in the past and what did we get? Every September 11th, Americans will be reminded of how our past imperialistic ways helped bring the wrath of the Muslim world down upon us. Today, we grievously mourn along side of the thousands of American moms and dads over the wasted sacrifice of their children's lives in still another military quagmire of our own doing."

The president paused briefly and stared at each of member of her cabinet.

"I say never again. From now on out, America must be perceived by the Arab world as an impartial partner, ready always to assist, but never again to impose our will in their business."

"Madame President," said Secretary of Labor Diana Peters, "am I correct in sensing from your comments that America is preparing a major policy shift in our support for Israel?"

"My short answer to your question, Diana, is a strong, unequivocal, 'No,'" the president emphatically stated, "Our support for Israel as America's friend and democratic ally in the Middle East will never change."

The president paused briefly in order to carefully gather her thoughts before making her next comment. "We will support and give assistance to the Israeli government in anyway we can, but only in respect to the transition time made necessary for their returning to their original pre-1967 borders."

With that said, the president abruptly ended her comments and turned the remainder of the meeting over to Secretary of State James Metloff.

"Thank you, Madame President," the Secretary of State acknowledged. "Tomorrow, I am scheduled to leave for a weeklong trip which stops first in Israel, then I move onto to Syria, Egypt, Saudi Arabia, Iran, and finally back to Israel. The president is proposing that the Israelis agree to the strictest terms of the UN Security Council Resolution 242, the complete return of all lands occupied since 1967, including East Jerusalem. In return, the Arabs must agree to recognize Israel's right to exist as a free and independent nation and also, to unanimously rescind their demand of right of return to lands and properties within the pre-1967 borders of Israel. If all parties agree, then the peace agreement can be signed within a month, hopefully just prior to Passover."

"Mr. Secretary, forgive my bluntness," the Secretary of Labor interjected, "but what you are proposing is impossible. How can we expect the Israeli government to move thousands, perhaps millions of people in less than a month?"

"You are absolutely right. I whole heartedly agree; it is impossible," Secretary Metloff admitted. "The signing of the peace agreement is simply phase one of a three-part deal. Once we have an agreement on paper, the Israeli government will be given six months to totally withdraw all of their citizens and troops from the occupied territories to areas securely within Israel's own borders. The final phase of the transfer will begin on the first day of the Muslim Holy month of Ramadan. At that time, a final treaty will be signed reestablishing all lands to their prior owners, and recognizing for the first time in recorded history the nation of Palestine, with East Jerusalem as its eternal Capitol."

"Secretary Metloff, what will be America's role in all this as far as our financial and military commitment?" asked the Commerce Secretary, Almanzo Gomaz.

"Good question. As far as financial support, we are going to ask Congress to fund what we believe will be a generous and equitable amount for both sides. Right now, we're thinking in the range of thirty billion dollars. We are also asking the Russians, the Chinese, and the European Union to either match or surpass our amount."

"Folks," the president interjected, "what we are talking about here has never been attempted. It will involve moving, relocating, and resettling over a million people. This will give all parties involved the funds necessary to make the transition work. As far as our military involvement, I'll let Secretary Schaefer answer that question."

"Thank you, Madame President. We will be positioning our aircraft carrier, the USS Theodore Roosevelt just off the coast of Cyprus. From that vantage point, we will be carefully monitoring the entire situation from start to finish. As far as our providing any ground assistance using U.S. military personnel, the answer is 'No.' There should be ample ground assistance from the UN troops already positioned along Israel's borders with Egypt, Syria, Lebanon, and Jordan, plus the Israelis have their own military to assist them. We would only be in the way."

"Then I have one final question," Secretary Peters once again interjected. "What happens to all of these elaborate plans if the Israelis decide not to accept the Arabs' terms. Aren't they leaving the decision up to a voter referendum?"

"I can guarantee all of you, that will not happen!" the president abruptly replied. "From our latest, most reliable sources, we're finding that almost the entire world is behind the Arab proposal: the Vatican, the EU, the Russians, the Chinese, the Council of American-Muslim Relations, and the United Council of Churches."

"Madame President, with all due respect," the Labor Secretary boldly responded, "there are also other large and very influential groups who are emphatically against Israel compromising any of their land for a peace deal."

"Secretary Peters," the president herself interjected, "I believe you are referring only to a small minority of right-wing religious groups like the Baptists and the Pentecostals."

"To mention a few, Madame President," Secretary Peters quickly followed. "There are also over forty-five conservative Jewish organizations who are also adamantly opposed to this plan."

"Secretary Peters," Secretary Metloff responded, "I'm sure you will agree that we will never come up with a perfect plan that will satisfy everyone, but this is an historic opportunity to bring real peace to a region of the world that has never known peace."

"Well said," the president again interjected in a firm, direct voice. "And with that, I call this meeting to an end."

In the minutes following the adjournment of the meeting, after the final human had left the room, two large angelic warriors remained behind, standing side-by-side staring out through the large glass panes of French doors leading to the Rose Garden.

"It's hard to believe that after all this time, the day has finally come," the Archangel Muriel commented to his commander, the Archangel Michael. "If only America would have stayed true to its commitment."

"We both knew this day would come," Michael replied as he continued to stare out through the glass door. "God's word is infallible. Prophecy must be fulfilled."

"I only pray that there was some other way," Muriel sorrowfully admitted with a heavy heart. "I can't stand the thought of allowing Satan to have his way with America!"

"It is too late now," Michael sighed as he turned and placed his hand on his comrade's shoulder. "The Lord is in control and He says it is time. Give the order to all of your princes guarding the great American cities and to all of the warrior angels assigned to guarding America's borders that it is time to remove their hedge of protection. America has committed a grievous sin. She has turned her back on the Apple of God's Eye and now she must suffer the curse."

Chapter Fifteen

"There hath no temptation (testing) taken you but such as is common to man: but God is faithful, who will not suffer you to be tempted above that ye are able; but will with the temptation (testing) also make a way to escape, that ye may be able to bear it."

1 *Corinthians* 10:13 KJV

Thursday, February 14*th*
6:30 *a.m. EST*
National Naval Medical Center
Bethesda, MD

With the exception of a lone admission around 4 a.m. with a possible case of appendicitis, the doctors and nurses at the Bethesda Naval Hospital emergency ward were just about ready to wrap up a rather routine, uneventful night. For once, a rarity in the stressful field of emergency trauma care, no traumas! With only a handful of minor cuts and scraps to tend, the nightshift staff found themselves with plenty of extra free time to spare. While some of the nurses and physician's assistances decided to decorate the bland walls and halls of the emergency ward with some colorful red Valentine's Day hearts and cupids, others simply took the needed time to just relax and discuss the hottest issue of the day, last night's televised presidential address concerning the Middle East's peace plan. It was the topic on everyone's mind. No matter who you talked to, everybody was abuzz about it, and besides, what better time to discuss the concept of world peace then on Valentine's Day?

It was now 6:30 a.m., time for the crossover shifts to meet briefly in order exchange medical records before parting company. While the night and morning shift nurses met behind the desk of the triage nurse, Captain Michael Roberts, the ER's head nightshift doctor and his morning shift counterpart, Captain Steven Byers, sat down by themselves on a quiet bench located just a few feet away from the ambulance entrance doors.

"Easy night?" Captain Byres asked as he leaned forward to take a sip from his cup of coffee.

"Steve, it was one of those nights you only dream about," replied Captain Roberts as he sat back on the bench displaying a big relaxed smile. "No traumas, no beltway accidents, no drive by shootings, just a young boy requiring a couple sutures and some guy with a very bad belly ache."

"Well, I'm hoping to be just as lucky!" Captain Byers commented as he took another sip of coffee. "If my memory serves me correctly, not much ever happens around here on Valentine's Day."

"Steve, to change the subject, did you catch the president's address last night?"

Before answering, Captain Byers broke out into an equally wide grin. Holding his coffee cup in one hand, he too sat back on the bench, crossed his legs and placed his free hand behind his head. "Who didn't!" he replied. "That's all Julie and I talked about last night. Ever since the mention of Middle Eastern peace, I've been watching my portfolio literally explode. Mark my words, Mike, if this peace deal pans out, I'm seriously thinking about retiring this summer and buying that ranch I've been talking about in Montana."

"I'm afraid I'm not as confident as you are, my friend," Captain Roberts followed with a less optimistic look. "As far as I can see it, this deal is tenuous at best. What if the Israelis thumb their noses at the deal? Then all of your skyrocketing stocks will head south faster than a flock of geese."

"Well, I for one can't see why the Israelis won't go for it," Captain

Byers commented as he stood to his feet and started slowly walking back toward the triage desk. "This is what they've always wanted, living in their own homeland, safe and secure."

"I hope you're right." Captain Roberts followed as he too stood and turned to make his final departure out through a back exit door. "Only time will tell."

No sooner did Captain Roberts make that final comment when flashing red and blue lights on the wall in front of him caught his attention. An incoming ambulance had just arrived!

"Incoming!" shouted Captain Roberts in the direction of the gathered nurses.

"Well, there goes my peaceful morning," Captain Byers commented as he shook his head and bent down to deposit his half finished paper coffee cup into a nearby trash can. Both Captains Byers and Roberts stood to the side as the automatic doors opened and two paramedics quickly wheeled out what appeared to be a young teenage boy.

"Joe, what do we have?" Captain Byers asked the lead paramedic as his partner proceeded to push the patient in the direction of the nursing station.

"We have a young male, fifteen years old, high fever, complaining of difficultly breathing."

The paramedic paused for a moment and looked both doctors in the eyes.

"You two are not going to believe this!" Joe commented with a serious look, "This kid's entire family is on their way."

"That's all right, we'll talk to them when they get here," interjected Captain Byers.

"Doctors, that's not what I meant," the paramedic interjected. "They aren't driving. They're all in route here in separate ambulances, mom and dad, two younger brothers and an older sister."

"The entire family?" blurted out a surprised Captain Byers.

"That's not all!" Joe replied.

"There's more?" Captain Roberts followed.

"The father is Senator Hawkins!"

"The head of the Senate?" both shocked doctors responded in unison.

"The same," Joe quickly followed.

"My God, wake me if I'm dreaming!" commented an overwhelmed Captain Roberts.

"I only wish I was," Dr. Byers hastily replied as he quickly turned and made his way down the long corridor toward the emergency room's nurses' station. Serving two tours of active duty as a trauma doctor in both Iraq and Afghanistan, he had long been conditioned for moments like this, to expect the unexpected. Immediately, Captain Byers took complete charge of the situation. In a commanding voice, he stopped briefly at the desk of the head triage nurse and gave his first order. "Nancy. I want the boy taken around the back to room twelve, STAT! I want him isolated and the five other rooms in the back prepped and manned immediately!"

"It will be taken care of immediately, Dr. Byers!" the triage nurse affirmed.

Turning his attention now to the group of over a dozen shocked nurses and assistants standing near by, Captain Byers ordered. "Sorry, folks, as of right now all night shift personnel are here by ordered to remain on duty until further notice. I want everybody here suited up and ready to go. We have five more incoming patients with the same symptoms and I want them all isolated."

"Mike?"

"Say no more, Steve!" replied his nighttime counterpart following along side. "I'll catch some sleep later. Just tell me what you want me to do."

"Until we know what were dealing with, I want this situation completely isolated. I want all of my nurses in the back with me and all of your staff manning out front, out of harm's way."

Stopping, Captain Byers placed his hand on Dr. Robert's shoulder and made one final request before parting company. "One more thing, Mike. I believe Deputy Commander Malanoski is presently on duty. I need you to contact him immediately and make him and the other hospital staff aware of our present situation down here."

"I'll get right on it!"

With that said, Captain Roberts had just enough time to turn and locate the phone on the triage nurse's desk before another ambulance pulled up to the emergency room's back entrance. This time, as the automatic doors opened, the paramedics appeared to be wheeling in a young teenage girl down the corridor leading toward the emergency room.

"Doctors," echoed a shout from the lead female paramedic. "We have a young female, age seventeen complaining of difficulty breathing and presently experiencing a high fever of 104F."

Within a matter of moments, the new patient was wheeled up to the desk of the triage nurse. "We've been expecting her," Captain Byers replied. Turning now to his personal assistance, Captain Byers ordered, "Linda, take 'Senator Hawkins' daughter down the hall to room 13 across from her brother."

"Doctor, this girl is not Senator Hawkins' daughter," the paramedic interjected. "Her name is Angela Kirshner, and her father Martin works at the Pentagon. When we left her house, another crew of EMTs had just arrived. It seems the rest of the family has similar symptoms."

Both Doctor Byers and Roberts stood in a state of shock. Never in all of their years of service at the Naval Medical Center or on active duty had they experienced anything quite like this.

"What the hell is going on, Steve?"

"You tell me, Mike! This isn't a dream, it's a freaking nightmare and somebody needs to wake me up, now!"

Captain Byers was much closer to the truth than he realized. This was just the beginnings of a nightmare so unimaginable, that even horror writer Stephen King could not even fathom it. It all started the very moment Michael gave the order to remove the angelic hedge that securely protected America's spiritual borders. Without the ever vigilant oversight and protection of her millions of assigned angelic warriors, America now stood totally defenseless against the onslaught of Satan's demonic attacks.

Upon Satan's command, millions upon millions of tiny froglike aberrations from the pits of hell were unleashed exactly at daybreak with the specific orders to invade at random every unprotected human dwelling found within America's borders with a whole host of disease causing infirmities. As the morning progressed, emergency rooms all across America became overwhelmed by a massive flood of new arrivals all complaining of the same sever symptoms. By afternoon, hundreds of deaths of otherwise healthy people were being reported all across America from California to Maine. Not since experiencing the nerve numbing events on the infamous date of 9–11–2001 had America felt the deep impact of such instantaneous panic and fear. At long last, phase one of Satan's Project G 123 had commenced and soon, all of America would be at his mercy.

Thursday, February 14*th*
1:15 *p.m. Eastern Standard Time*
Washington, D.C.
Oval Office, White House

"Madame President, Dr. Janet Rothberg, the Director of the CDC, is on the line."

"Thank you, Alex," President Devoe acknowledged to her personal secretary with a nod and an affirming smile. "I'll turn on the speaker phone so all of us can listen."

The president, the vice president, her chief of staff, and both secretaries of defense and health and human service were all gathered in the Oval Office. The president had been notified shortly after 7 a.m. that a possible pandemic with sever flu-like symptoms was occurring in every corner of the nation without any advanced warning signs or possible causes. Even several members of the president's own staff had reportedly called in sick early this morning with flu-like symptoms, including the Secretary of State, James Metloff.

"Good morning, Dr. Rothberg," greeted the president in a cordial, but serious tone. "I am sitting here with several members of my staff including a friend of yours, Secretary of Health, Dan Walters. Could you kindly tell us, Dr. Rothberg, what the hell is going on?"

"Madame President, as you are well aware, this entire situation is totally unprecedented and it has caught all of us off guard," admitted the Director of the Center of Disease Control located in Atlanta, Georgia. "In the entire sixty year history of the CDC, we have never seen anything like this! I will assure you and your staff, we are currently in the process of ruling out all the possibilities. Unfortunately, as of noon today, the Atlanta area alone has had over fifteen confirmed deaths reported, and we are having fresh tissue samples from suspected victims coming in even as I speak."

"Dr. Rothberg, could this possibly be an outbreak of the bird flu?" asked Dan Walters

"That's the first thing I thought of this morning, but it was quickly ruled out. The symptoms don't seem to match up with those caused by the H5N1 virus."

"What about some form of biological attack?" interjected Defense Secretary Schaeffer.

"At this point, I would say that's a real possibility." affirmed Dr. Rothberg. "I'm seeing possible signs of anthrax or something just as deadly."

"But from whom?" the president spoke out "We are presently at peace! Who the hell would want to harm us?"

"Please, don't get me wrong!" followed Dr. Rothberg. "I'm not saying biological weapons were involved here. I'm just saying that it could be a possibility. Until we've narrowed down the cause, Madame President, I believe it would be prudent to close not only America's borders, but for the interim, until we get a definite handle on this, I suggest that you order a temporary quarantine to be imposed on the entire country."

"I can't believe I am hearing this!" the president admitted as she sank back into her chair. "Dr. Rothberg, do you have the slightest idea what you are asking me to do?"

"Madame President," Dr. Rothberg grimly replied. "Until we at the CDC have identified the cause, I don't see that you have any other choice!"

Thursday, February 14th
2 p.m. Eastern Standard Time

229 Chevy Chase Court
Rockville, Maryland

For well over an hour, the old man sat motionless in a dazed-like trance just staring at what appeared to be a hodgepodge of Hebraic letters scatter across his computer screen. Finally, after a series of four or five loud knocks at his office door, Ezra Schroeder came back to reality.

"Ezra, are you all right?" shouted the familiar voice of his wife from behind the locked door.

"Daddy, please unlock the door!" demanded Leah, Schroeder's youngest daughter, "we need to know if you're all right!"

"Dad, please open the door!" echoed his oldest daughter Rebecca.

"I'm all right!" Ezra announced as he unlocked and opened his office door to the concerned looks from his wife and two daughters.

"Why aren't the two of you at home with your families?" a confused Schroeder asked his daughters. "Aren't the kids coming home from school soon?"

"Daddy, Mamma's been watching the television and she's really scared." confessed Leah. "She said you went into your office about eight o'clock this morning and you haven't been out since. She tried calling you through the door, but you didn't answer!"

"That's when she called us and we came right over," followed Rebecca.

Only now had Schroeder realized how much time had passed since he had last talked to his wife. "Forgive me, my dear," he pleaded in a trembling voice. "Rachel, I can't explain it! My mind just went blank! "

For Rachel Schroeder, her husband's brief explanation did not suffice. Visibly shaken, she stared directly into his grayish blue eyes and angrily vented, "Ezra Schroeder, don't you ever lock your office door again, do you understand me? You scared the hell out of me!"

"I don't understand," he asked with outstretched hands, "What is going on around here? Why is everyone so upset?"

"Daddy, you really don't know?" Leah emphatically asked after observing the confused look on her father's face.

"Know what?" Schroeder once again asked.

"The president just came on television," Rebecca responded. "She has just ordered the entire National Guard in every state to active duty."

"Daddy," Leah immediately followed. "As of nine o'clock tonight, America is being quarantined. No one is to leave their house, not even for an emergency! The National Guard is then going to go door to door distributing face masks, gloves and disinfectants."

"That's insane! Why? For what possible reason?" Schroeder demanded. "What did the president say?"

"Daddy, a really bad flu bug has hit all over the country and people of all ages are dying!" Rebecca answered.

"Oh, no! God, no!" Schroeder cried out. "Oh Lord, it's happening!"

"Daddy, what do you mean, 'it's happening'?" Rebecca demanded. "You say that as if you really know what it is!"

"Unfortunately, I believe I do!" Schroeder admitted as he turned toward his daughters with a fatherly look of concern. "Oh Lord, are the children all right?"

"They're all safe at home," Leah replied. "They're all fine! The schools sent them all home before noon."

"Daddy, tell me again," demanded Rebecca "What did you mean when you said 'you know'?"

"Girls, I don't want to scare you any more than you already are," Ezra replied.

"Please, Daddy," Leah now asked, "if you know something about what's going on, we want to know, too! Please tell us!"

Schroeder was torn. In all of his years of working at the agency, he had never once compromised on anything considered secure information. During that time, there had always been an unspoken family understanding that no one was to ever ask him about his work at the agency. It was considered classified, top-secret information, and that was that! But this time, things were different. Schroeder's secret could possibly involve the lives of his entire family. *Lord, what should I do?* he silently asked.

"Show them what you know!" Ariel spoke into Schroeder's thoughts.

"All right, girls. Follow me," he relented. "But before I show you anything, you must all promise me, you are to tell no one, not even your husbands!"

All three women, mother and daughters, nodded in agreement. Standing at the opened door to Schroeder's office, they proceeded to raise their right hands and swore an oath before God not to tell anything concerning what their father was about to show them.

Even though Rebecca and Leah spent most of their teenage years growing up in their parent's Silver Springs home, there was one room in the house that was etched permanently into their memories as "off limits." Even now, as grown women with their own families, this room held a strange aura of childhood mystery. As they entered, to their surprise, there was nothing in sight to match the vivid imaginations of two teenage girls. There were no James Bond weapons hanging from the wall and no autographed pictures of their father shaking hands with past presidents. The only pictures adorning their father's office walls and desk were those of their mother, themselves, and their own children. There was one exception. Directly in back of Schroeder's high back leather chair was a unique painting of Jesus holding the stone tablets of the Ten Commandment in one hand and His blood-soaked cross in the other.

"I need all of you to stand on this side of my desk and look up at the computer monitor," Ezra requested.

As computer monitors go, Schroeder's was exceptional. Almost the size of a small LCD television, its 27-inch rectangular screen covered almost the entire top of his desk. With the click of his mouse, the large darkened screen instantly brightened, displaying an image appearing strangely like a massive word search puzzle, only with Hebrew letters instead of English. The Hebrew lettering instantly caught both girls' attention. Being raised not only in a Jewish home, but also with a world-renowned expert in ancient languages, both girls were able to speak and write Hebrew fluently. Leah and Rebecca immediately were drawn to the different colored Hebrew letters that crisscrossed the entire screen in diagonal, horizontal, and vertical patterns.

"Daddy, what is this?" Leah asked.

"It's what we call in the world of code breaking a matrix," Ezra proudly proclaimed. "What you see on the screen is a matrix composed of equidistant Hebrew letters taken from Genesis, Chapter 12. All the spacing between the words has been removed and all that is left are letters."

"I remember this!" Rebecca quickly responded. "It's called the Bible Codes. Daddy, didn't you meet with the man along time ago who claimed to have discovered possible hidden codes throughout the Bible?"

"That right!" Leah interjected. "I saw an entire program all about it last year on the History Channel!"

"But Daddy," Rebecca stated with a confused look "I thought you didn't believe in hidden Bible Codes!"

"You girls haven't changed one bit!" their proud father declared. "You two are both just as sharp and as inquisitive as ever!"

Schroeder now directed everyone's attention back to the highlighted letters that crisscrossed the screen. "What you see here," he pointed out with his finger, "is a matrix revealing a hidden Bible Code message."

"I have something I need to tell all of you," Schroeder confessed as he looked up at his wife and two daughters. "In light of some very recent, compelling evidence, I am now a firm believer in the Bible Codes!" Turning back toward the screen, he sadly declared, "I only wish that the matrix on the screen wasn't true!"

Now both daughters were really curious. If their skeptical father was now thoroughly convinced that Bible Codes were real, then what did the message on the screen have to say? Each girl took her turn leaning forward and reading aloud the highlighted Hebraic words displayed on the screen.

"America - Cursed- Forsake–my people–will be destroyed."

"Daddy! "Rebecca cried out. "Does this mean that God has now forsaken America because our government is supporting this new Middle Eastern Peace initiative?"

"I'm afraid you might be absolutely correct!" Ezra sadly confirmed.

"Daddy," Leah inquired, "how did you find out about all of this?"

"I might as well tell you," he replied as he sat back in his chair and put up his hands in surrender. "Now, you're really going to think I've lost it, but I was told the answer by none other than Sir Isaac Newton."

Ezra paused for a second to study the looks on his daughters' and wife's faces. Surprisingly, they didn't appear at all shocked by his strange confession.

"Let me clarify myself. I am not going crazy, and I didn't have a visitation from the ghost of Isaac Newton." He paused and smiled. "Sometime before Newton died in 1727, he concealed all of his secret research into Bible *prophesy*, a journal that wasn't discovered until recently. When I visited Cambridge last summer, Harry Andrews asked if I could decipher the contents of a certain journal written in some strange form of coded alchemy by Isaac Newton. At first, I couldn't make heads or tails out of it. Then, when I was just about ready to throw up my hands and give up, out of the blue, a thought popped into my head to translate the entire notebook into Hebrew. I completed the entire task before leaving England. What Newton had done was to literally bury over a dozen prophetic verses found scattered throughout the Old Testament into a hodgepodge blend of unrelated alchemy terms, most borrowed from the Arabs, Hindus, Chinese, and Greeks. Every single verse in the journal dealt specifically with Israel and her relationship with her surrounding hostile Arab neighbors, not to mention some other end-time related events. I thought it was simply just some fascinating tidbits of historical information until last week."

"What happened last week?" an excited Rebecca asked.

"Rebecca," Ezra turned toward his eldest daughter and asked, "do you remember last week when you called me at my motel room to tell me about the discovery of the Irish Book of Psalms?"

"I remember!" Rebecca quickly followed. "Daddy, this is so exciting!"

All three women, including Rachel, could hardly contain themselves. They were clinching and rubbing their hands as little children would do in anticipation of a surprise Christmas present.

"Well, after we hung up, Joe Fisher returned to my room with his laptop computer trying to sell me on the Bible Codes. He had no clue that I had already made up my mind that they didn't exist. I was trying my best to be polite and not discourage a fellow Christian, when once again, out of the blue, I got this compelling thought, "Ask Joe to run a matrix on Psalm 83."

"Wasn't it Psalm 83 that was discovered on the front cover of the ancient Psalm book they unearthed last week in Ireland?" Leah interjected.

"And Ezra," Rachel followed. "Didn't I hear you say that it is Psalm 83 where King David petitions God to defeat all nations who plan to destroy Israel?"

"Exactly! My girls are so smart!" Ezra proudly proclaimed as he continued with his story.

"Now, this is the really exciting part!" he exclaimed. "Once the matrix of Psalm 83 appeared on Joe's screen, I heard a clear, distinct voice in my head telling me to type in the words "Israel- Attack - Date–Bomb- City." To our utter amazement, the entire screen immediately lit up with encoded Hebrew letters and words criss-crossing each other in every direction. It only took us seconds to put the message together."

He paused as large tears welled up in his eyes.

"Ezra, what did it say?" Rachel demanded.

"It said that both the Israeli cities of Tel Aviv and Haifa would be attacked and possibly destroyed by nuclear missiles launched from submarines on the eve of next month's Passover."

"Daddy, that can't be!" Leah announced with her own tears streaming down her face. "God won't let that happen!"

At that moment, all four humans embraced each other in the security of a circle of love.

"Ezra, what are we going to do?" Rachel looked up and asked.

"I believe God has already shown me, my dear," Schroeder replied in firm, confident voice. "Before I act, I believe He wants us all to go to the Synagogue and pray for the protection of Israel, America, and our families."

"I'll be right back," Leah announced. "I hear the phone ringing out in the family room."

Within a minute or two, Leah returned to her father's office.

"That was Ruthy from Beth Messiah," Leah announced. "They're calling everyone in the entire congregation to let us know that the Shabbat service has been changed to tonight from five until seven instead of this weekend."

"Ezra," Rachel commented with a look of concern. "Considering all that is going on, do you think it wise to go out tonight, especially with the children?"

Ezra responded with a comforting smile and a reassuring voice of confidence.

"Rachel, you know better than anyone that the Lord is always watching over and protecting all of us. Besides, with all that is going on, I don't believe we can afford not to go."

Rachel shook her head in agreement. Now was not the time to show fear. Her family needed her strength.

Once again, the phone rang in the family room, but this time Rebecca left her father's office to see who it was. Everyone in the office decided it was also time to follow.

"Daddy!" Rebecca shouted out from the family room, "It's your English friend, Harry Andrews. You're not going to believe this, but he said that his scheduled meeting this afternoon at the Smithsonian, his reservations at his motel, and his return flight back to England tomorrow have all been canceled. He wants to know if we could possibly pick him up at his motel and if he could possibly stay with us until everything returns back to normal."

"Is he still on the phone?" Ezra called out as he and his youngest daughter and wife proceeded in the direction of the family room.

"Yes," Rebecca affirmed to her approaching father. "He is right now standing in the lobby of the New Carrollton Sheridan Inn. None of the employees there reported for work after hearing the news. The management had no other choice but to shut down."

Ezra answered with a smile. "You tell my old English friend that we wouldn't have it any other way. We would be honored to have him stay with us and we'll be there within a half hour to pick him up. We can all go to Beth Messiah together."

"Ezra," Rachel innocently whispered. "Didn't you say that Harry was an atheist?"

"Rachel," Ezra smiled. "I truly believe that the Lord is behind all this. He has arranged all this before hand in order for Harry to have an appointment to finally meet his Messiah. All praise be to Yeshua!"

"Amen!" Ariel declared.

Chapter Sixteen

"Now when Jesus came into the district of Caesarea Philippi, he asked his disciples, "Who do men say that the Son of man is?" Simon Peter answered, "You are the Christ (the Messiah), the Son of the living God."

Mat 16:13–16 NIV

What is Messianic Judaism? Most people you ask have absolutely no clue. They either say that they have never heard of the term or have never met anyone claiming to be a Messianic Jew. Others, including most of today's contemporary Jews, are somewhat familiar with Messianic Judaism. They view it as the classic oxymoron. They simply reason that a Jew cannot be Jewish while at the same time accepting Jesus of Nazareth as the prophesied Jewish Messiah. To them, it doesn't make any sense! How can a Jew be both Jewish and Christian at the same time? That would be unthinkable! They would be considered completely insane and labeled "meshugoyim."

For over the past two millennia, Satan, the god of this world, assisted by millions of lying demonic spirits, has managed to pull off one of mankind's greatest cover ups. By blinding the eyes of the Jewish people to the true identity of their promised Messiah, Satan has successfully deceived hundreds of generations of Jews, past and present, into blindly believing his big lie: that Jesus was merely a good man, perhaps a prophet, and that being Jewish is nothing more than maintaining a superficial adherence to a rigid set of religious traditions.

Even though the Torah clearly and explicitly defines their purpose and identity, still, millions of deceived Jews have lived out their lives never knowing for one single moment what it truly meant to be

Jewish. Sadly, most Jews have died and have never heard the truth that God selected them above all people, the chosen descendents of Abraham, to know Him through praise. To this very day, they have remain blinded to the fact that the word Jew, derived from the Hebrew word Judah, simply means to praise Yahweh or God. To praise Yahweh is to be a Jew. The reason God called King David "a man after his own heart" was not due to David's strict adherence to religious law. David, a confessed murderer and adulterer, found God's favor simply by honoring God with a humble heart filled with praise. Who can forget the story of how David, Israel's greatest King, unashamedly danced and praised God practically naked before all his people as the Ark of Covenant was being led through the streets of ancient Jerusalem.

In Romans Chapter 2, Paul of Tarsus, a former strict adherent to Jewish law declared, "a man is a Jew if he is one inwardly; and has a circumcision of the heart, by the Spirit, not by the written code. Such a man's praise (his Jewishness) is not from men, but from God!"

Paul also declared in the book of Romans, Chapter 12, that on some future day, Satan's deceptive blinders will be removed from the eyes of Jews worldwide and all of Israel will see their Messiah. In the Book of Zechariah, Chapter 12, God declares "And I will pour out on the house of David and the inhabitants of Jerusalem a spirit of grace and supplication. They will look upon me, the one they have pierced, and they will mourn for him as one mourns for an only child, and they will grieve bitterly for him as one grieves for a firstborn son."

At that very moment, Satan's blinders will drop from their eyes and every Jew will clearly see and fully comprehend the inherent Jewishness of Yeshua of Nazareth. Only then will Jews worldwide accept the fact that Yeshua was born a Jew in the prophesied town of Bethlehem, that he lived as a Torah-observant Jew, died with a legal proclamation above his head stating "King of the Jews." They will then clearly understand that this Jew named Yeshua completely fulfilled every single Jewish prophesy found written in the

Old Testament (Tanakh). He was resurrected a Jew of the linage of David. He ascended to heaven a Jew and is now seated in heaven at the right hand of his Father God a Jew of the tribe of Judah. He will one day return to earth as the King of the Jews. This is the "blessed hope" of the Judeo-Christian faith; that the Messiah (Ha Mashiach) has come, the Messiah has died, the Messiah has risen, and the Messiah is coming again. At that moment, all the natural Jews alive on planet earth will declare themselves Messianic believers in Yeshua Ha Mashiach, Jesus the Christ, the Messiah of the world!

Thursday, February 14*th*
5:00 *p.m.*
Beth Messiah Synagogue
Silver Springs, Maryland

On a typical Thursday evening, the parking lot outside of the Beth Messiah's synagogue would have been totally dark and void of cars, but this was not a typical Thursday. Not only was the parking lot brightly lit and filled to capacity, an overflow of cars were forced to park up and down New Hampshire Ave. While the remainder of the quarter of a million residents of this very affluent Maryland region scurried about shopping and gathering important last minute items before the imposed curfew was to take effect, the members of the area's largest Messianic congregation decided instead that it was more important to attend tonight's services.

With only a small window of time to get out the word, Rabbi Burt Rosenberg, his wife, and his staff of twelve went into immediate action. The daunting task facing them was monumental. They had to contact over five hundred of Beth Messiah's members, over two hundred households, to inform them that both the Friday night's and Saturday morning's Shabbat services had been canceled, replaced instead with an emergency Thursday night service that would be starting at five p.m. and ending promptly at seven. Amazingly, using every means of modern technology at their disposal—home phones, cell phones, answering machines, and the Internet—by 3:15 p.m., every member and household of the Beth Messiah congregation had been contacted.

Running a few minutes late, a black Lincoln Navigator with five passengers on board pulled up to a reserved handicap spot located directly in front of the synagogue's main entrance. As the side passenger doors opened, the sound of a little girl's voice shouting "Mommy, Mommy," could be heard coming from inside the synagogue's front entrance door.

"Melissa," commanded her father in the firm voice, "wait right here inside with Daddy and your brother until Mommy and Grandma and Grandpa arrive!"

"I take it that the little girl standing beside the man with a stroller belongs to all of you," commented one of the passengers, a tall gentleman dressed in a light brown tweed jacket and a matching tweed cap.

"That's our Melissa with her daddy, Mark, and her six-month-old baby brother, Ezra" proudly boasted her grandfather, Ezra Schroeder as his English friend, Harrison Andrews, looked on.

As the other members of the party of five made their way across the parking lot toward the main entrance doors, Professor Andrews remained behind just staring in amazement at the number of vehicles that were surrounding him.

"Ezra, I must truly admit that I am somewhat taken back," commented Professor Andrews. "You yanks are far more different than we Brits!"

"In what way?" Ezra curiously asked.

"Well, considering the seriousness of our present situation," Andrews admitted, "I would never have imagined that this many people would leave the safety of there homes to come out for a religious service."

"Well, my friend," Ezra responded with a smile, "as you will soon find out, this is no ordinary synagogue and this will be no ordinary religious service!"

Ezra Schroeder's comment was certainly correct; Beth Messiah was no ordinary synagogue. From its humble beginnings in the fall of 1978, with a simple sanctuary set up in the living room of its present Rabbi, Burt Rosenberg, Beth Messiah started out as this one man's vision to allow God the freedom to fashion together a group of local Jewish and gentile believers according to the verse found in Ephesians 2:14–22, "For He Himself is our peace, who has made both Jew and Gentile one, and has broken down the middle wall of separation...to create in Himself one new man...in whom you also are being built together for a dwelling place of God in the Spirit."

The tiny congregation, comprised at first of only four Jewish families, quickly learned to appreciate the expression "when God moves, get ready!" It wasn't long before the living room sanctuary was replaced by the cafeteria of a local elementary school. In less than a year, the Messianic congregation had completely outgrown the school's cafeteria and, in spring of 1980, construction began at its present site along New Hampshire Ave. A little more than two years after inviting some local Messianic Jewish friends to be part of a service he was starting in his living room, Rabbi Rosenberg's vision of a "One New Man" Messianic congregation had come to pass. With a seating capacity of over five hundred, Beth Messiah was dedicated as the greater Washington, D.C. area's largest Messianic congregation. From that day until the present, a large white and blue banner adorned with Israeli flags on each side greets everyone, guests and members alike, entering the synagogue's foyer with this bold proclamation:

> *Welcome to Beth Messiah, where Jews and Gentiles have been made echad (one) in their embrace of Yeshua as G-d's atoning Messiah, who will one day reign on David's throne as King of Kings and Lord of Lords.*
> *Amen!*

From the moment he entered the front lobby, Harrison Andrews had a strange feeling that something was different, something that his analytical mind couldn't explain. There was an indescribable aura of warmth inside this building, but not in the literal sense. As the entrance door closed behind him, the doom and gloom of the outside world seemed to instantly disappear as if he had entered some kind of new "spiritual" realm. With heightened senses, he could also detect the pleasant rhythms and sounds of vibrant music that grew even more pronounced as his American hosts led him down the hallway toward the sanctuary's white double doors. Before entering, Andrews paused briefly at the doors, as if to muster the courage needed to enter a foreign domain. Once the doors had opened, Harrison Andrews' eyes opened wide to a scene every bit as strange as he had envisioned.

This couldn't possibly be a religious service he thought to himself. *It appears more like a circus!*

A rock band, or so it appeared to Andrews, complete with singers, electric guitars and drums, performed on the front center stage a strange concoction of somewhat loud unconventional pop songs. Andrews watched in amazement as a large group of both men and women held hands, dancing in a circle to the left of the band, while several other women ran up and down the aisles waving all sorts of flags and banners. Never in his fifty-eight years had he witnessed anything quite like it. A religious man by no means, he had attended enough church services in some of England's greatest cathedrals to realize that this had absolutely no relationship whatsoever with any kind of religious ceremony that he had ever witnessed.

Where is the reverence? Andrews thought to himself. *It appears that Ezra belongs to some kind of religious cult!*

As he continued to follow his host family down the sanctuary's center aisle, Professor Andrews witnessed even more bizarre sights including people, both young and old, singing with their arms raised high, some crying with tears streaming down their faces while others appeared quietly mumbling to themselves in some kind of unintelligible chant.

This is definitely a cult!

Unbeknownst to their assigned human host, two small chimeras, one a lying spirit named Danis, and the other a religious spirit named Baylod, lay totally concealed deep within the lining of Harrison Andrews' tweed jacket. The ugly little chimeras had good reason to remain quiet and completely hidden from view. If detected, they knew their fate would be instantly sealed.

In addition to having sword drawn angelic warriors strategically positioned at the main entrance and all exit doors, a sizable contingency of guardian angels kept a constant visual from both the back and front of the large sanctuary on every man, woman, child, and infant in the room.

Every time Professor Andrews witnessed another human doing something strange like banging on a tambourine or shouting out, "Praise Jesus," the religious spirit Baylod would whisper, "This is a definitely a cult!" and, "These people are religious fanatics!" while the lying spirit Danis whispered, "Don't be deceived. These people are all crazy."

The most bizarre spectacle occurred just as Andrews was about to take his seat in a left front row section reserved for the Schroeder family. He watched intently as a man standing on the edge of the stage appeared to be praying for a man kneeling in front of him. Without warning, the kneeling man threw up both hands and started shouting out loud in some crazy form of unintelligible gibberish.

"Your ears are not deceiving you," whispered Danis, *these people surrounding you are really crazy devil worshipers!"*

Fortunately for Harrison Andrews, Ezra Schroeder had carefully studied the expressions on his English friend's face from the very moment he entered the sanctuary. Schroeder knew well from his own past experiences what a person might be thinking who was not accustomed to the goings on inside a spirit-filled Messianic service.

For Schroeder to simply explain away his friend's apprehensions was useless. He had no way of knowing that this situation was now beyond human explanation. Harrison Andrews' mind was being manipulated by an unseen supernatural presence.

"Get the hell out of here before they brainwash you, too!" whispered Danis, the lying spirit. "If you stay in here any longer, your reputation will be destroyed!"

"Do you want to end up as Ezra Schroeder, a crazy, religious fanatic!" followed Baylod, the religious spirit.

With streams of perspiration running down his brow, Professor Andrews turned to Schroeder, and with a fear-stricken look, adamantly demanded, "Ezra, forgive me, but we need to leave here, right now!"

This is not the reaction that Schroeder had expected from a man he considered to be completely rational and solidly composed.

"Harry, forgive me if this is upsetting you," Schroeder interjected. "I should have prepared you before hand for what goes on in a spirit-filled service.

"Schroeder lies! Just get up and leave, now!" Danis shouted. "Oops!"

Too late. The overly anxious little demon knew instantly that he had just made a fatal mistake. God created His guardian angels with a keen sense of hearing, especially attuned for detecting the entire auditory range of demons. That little shout was all that was needed to catch the ever-observant eyes and ears of nearby Ariel.

With the wink of an eye and twitch on his right index finger, Ariel signaled Woriel and Dafiel, two warrior angels assigned to stand guard over the MacDougal family, to quietly position themselves one on the right and the other to the left directly in front of Harrison Andrews. While the other angels in the room intently looked on, Ariel proceeded to slowly withdraw his brilliant gold sword from its sheath and position himself directly in back of the professor's seat. Once everyone was positioned, Ariel bent low to carefully inspected a couple of inconspicuous bulges appearing directly below Professor Andrews jacket collar. He then held up two fingers on his left hand indicating they were dealing with two demons instead of one.

Woriel and Dafiel pressed in even closer, just in case the little chimeras tried escaping out the front of Andrews' jacket. With the accuracy of a skilled surgeon, Ariel quickly jabbed his sword blade at the precise angle as to pierce both bulges right through their fleshy midriffs. That was all that was needed. The very moment Ariel pulled back on his sword, a spindly lizard-like claw protruded out from the top of the jacket lining and momentarily held fast to the outside of Harrison Andrews' jacket collar.

In another second, the clawed hand and the two protruding budges disappeared into a puff of reddish brown sulfurous smoke.

Before Ezra could say another word, Andrews wrinkled his nose and asked, "Do you smell something like burnt matches?"

"Yes, come to think of it, I do," Schroeder affirmed. "But Harry, if you really feel that uncomfortable staying here, we'll leave."

"Leave? Who said anything about leaving?" Andrews leaned over and whispered.

Ezra sat there completely mystified. The person sitting to his immediate left couldn't possibly be the same person sitting there just one minute earlier.

Where did the perspiration go? Schroeder wondered. *Just a minute ago he was sweating profusely and now it has completely vanished!*

There was no more time for words. Rabbi Rosenberg walked up to the stage microphone and asked, "Will everyone please stand and sing aloud this next worship song dedicated to our Lord and Savior Yeshua."

Ezra's eyes now opened as wide as saucers. *This has to be a miracle!* he mumbled out loud, for not only standing beside him, but also singing the words of the song projected on the large overhead screen was none other than his always reserved, ever proper, God-denying English friend, Harrison Andrews.

"Ezra, why do you keep staring at me like that?" Andrews turned and asked his dumfounded friend.

"Harry, I can't believe what I'm seeing!" Schroeder confessed. "You, of all people, standing and singing a Christian worship song?"

"I never heard this one before," Harry replied with a smile. "I must admit, I find the melody is somewhat soothing and peaceful."

Ezra just shook his head in amazement and continued to praise the Lord!

After the completion of two more worship songs, Rabbi Rosenberg requested that everyone be seated. He then proceeded to pray a blessing in Hebrew over the entire congregation. While all eyes were closed and all heads were bowed, an audible chuckle could be heard coming from the direction of the left front row where the Schroeder family was seated. The chuckle was even loud enough to momentarily distract the attention of the praying Rabbi. "Ezra, I see we have a guest in our midst." Rabbi Rosenberg graciously noted at the completion of his blessing. "Would you be kind enough to introduce your guest to all of us? Perhaps he might like to share with us a little of his background?"

As one of the onstage singers approached the front row with a wireless microphone, it was now Ezra Schroeder who wanted to get up and leave.

What in the world is going on with Harry? Schroeder questioned. *First he demands to leave! Next he wants to stay! Now he has embarrassed me in front of the entire congregation because of his bizarre behavior*!

"Your Excellency," Harrison Andrews interjected as he stood up and accepted the microphone.

"Rabbi Rosenberg is fine."

With a totally confused Schroeder looking on, Andrews turned and addressed the entire congregation.

"Rabbi Rosenberg and fellow members of this wonderful congregation, please forgive me for my unconscionably rude behavior. I simply don't know what has come over me. For those who know me, they will tell you, this is not my typical behavior. I can't explain it. From the moment I sat down, a sense of peace has come over me and all I can say is, I'm presently feeling as giddy as a school boy."

"Praise God, brother Andrews," Rabbi Rosenberg followed with a clap. "I believe the Lord has just touched you with His shalom."

Everyone in the congregation responded with an applause.

"My name is Harrison Andrews," the professor boldly continued, "and by my accent, you can tell where I am from. I am a research professor of ancient British antiquities at Cambridge University. I was scheduled to speak this afternoon at the Smithsonian, but due to circumstances beyond my control, all of my plans were canceled, including my motel room and my flight back to England. My dear friend, Ezra Schroeder, and his wonderful family have all graciously offered to host me in their home until the flights back to England resume again. But let me add, my rudeness was not directed in any way toward what you were saying, Rabbi. As you started to pray, my attention wandered briefly to that large picture hanging over to the right. After reading it, I couldn't stop myself from laughing."

All eyes were now focused on a large, rather inconspicuous picture hanging on the right sanctuary wall depicting a stone tablet with the engraved inscription, "Traditions are doubt set in stone."

"Forgive me, Rabbi, for being so open, but I always thought of the Jewish religion as the words of that motto, 'traditions set in stone.'"

"Unfortunately, Professor Andrews, your astute observations are correct," Rabbi Rosenberg agreed, "but the Jews aren't alone. The same can be said for the majority of organized religion. We here at Beth Messiah have cast off the shackles of tradition and believe God's Word at face value. Professor Andrews, look around you. Do you see any sick amongst this entire congregation, anyone coughing or sneezing? In the book of Isaiah, the word of God says, 'By Yeshua's stripes, we are healed.' That is what God promises us and as long you stand on His Word and don't listen to the lies of the devil, you will be healed!"

The entire congregation stood to their feet and gave a thunderous applause.

"Professor Andrews, the Word of God says in Hebrews 11:6 that without faith, you cannot please God. We at Beth Messiah believe the key to God's continued blessings is to stand firm in faith on His Word. If the Word says it, we believe it will come to pass. No matter where you look in our sanctuary, you will see banners containing God's promised verses hanging on our walls. To your left, you will read the words from the prophet Isaiah promising that, 'No weapons formed against you shall prosper!' My personal favorite amongst God's promises is hanging on the wall directly in back of me, 'For He shall give His angels charge over thee, to keep thee in all thy ways,' Psalms 91:11."

The Rabbi paused briefly and looked out over his large congregation.

"How many of you here believe that God has placed his mighty angels within our midst here today? Well, I for one do," Rabbi Rosenberg admitted, "and there happens to be a very large angel standing with his sword drawn right here beside me."

"Did you tell him?" Ariel jokingly asked Boriel, Rabbi Rosenberg's guardian angel.

"Lucky guess!" Boriel replied with a smile as he stood with his large golden sword held close to his chest at his assigned position along side of Rabbi Rosenberg.

"Folks, due to the circumstances, we are going to dismiss tonight at 6:30," the Rabbi commented as he paused briefly to look down at his wristwatch. "That gives me a little over half an hour to talk to you."

The Rabbi smiled as he looked out at his congregation. God had truly blessed him. There wasn't an empty seat in the entire sanctuary. "I truly thank God for all of your faithfulness," he continued. "You could have chosen like the rest of the world to shut your doors in fear, but you decided instead to trust in the Lord with all of your heart and come out here tonight to seek His blessings instead of the world's curses. This will be my message tonight, and I promise, I will be brief!"

With all the confidence of a skilled trial lawyer, Rabbi Rosenberg stood before his congregation ready to state his case backed by prophetic verses detailing God's past warnings to America not to pressure Israel into dividing up her land.

"There is a little known verse found in the overlooked little book of Obadiah that we are going to use as our scripture reference today," the rabbi began. "Obadiah Chapter 1:15 says, 'The day is near when I, the Lord, will judge the godless nations! As you have done to Israel, so it will be done to you. All your evil deeds will fall back on your own heads.'"

In sadness, the rabbi paused momentarily to look out at his large congregation before continuing.

"My friends, what I'm about to say I do so with a very heavy heart. I fear the day of the Lord's judgment is now upon us. When America agreed this past week to willfully withdraw its support from the land of Israel, God had no other choice but to remove His protective support from America. The cataclysmic events we are all witnessing right now are more than warnings. God has sent us many warnings in the past and we didn't heed them."

The rabbi spent the next twenty-five minutes methodically detailing every single natural and manmade disaster to strike America since the fateful day of October 30, 1991, when American policy toward Israel changed from one of total support to a policy of divisive compromise. On that day, President George Bush Sr. opened the Madrid Peace Conference by presenting his new plan for offering up God's land, "Israel," as a sacrifice on the auction block for world peace. It was he who came up with the hellish idea of "land for peace." The moment the president stepped up to the microphone, the "Perfect Storm" developed in the North Atlantic, creating the largest waves ever recorded. Without scientific reason, the storm reversed course and retrograded over 1,000 miles from east to west. It then slammed into the New England coastline sending 35-foot waves crashing right through the living room of President Bush Sr.'s Kennebunkport, Maine, summer home.

The very moment the land for peace talks resumed in Washington, D.C. on August 23, 1992, Hurricane Andrew, one the worst natural disasters to ever to hit America, slammed into southern Florida's Dade County producing an estimated $30 billion in damage and leaving 108,000 homeless.

The rabbi continued for several more minutes listing specific unheeded warnings to America in the form of crushing earthquakes in her western cities, devastating hurricanes and tornadoes striking her vulnerable coastlines and inland cities, and horrendous acts of terrorism against innocent American citizens. (A detailed account of each of God's warnings to America is found in the reference section at the end of this book.)

"What America has done to Israel, God has done to America," Rabbi Rosenberg emphatically declared in summary. "Every single time, at the exact moment that America pressured Israel into dividing their God given land, disaster has struck America. Just as God sent prophet after prophet and judgment after judgment to warn ancient Israel to return to him and forsake the world, America has been warned and now, I believe, the warnings are over."

With tears streaming down his face, Rabbi Rosenberg raised both hands over his head and cried out, "Abba, God, I beg you, open the eyes of our president and America's leaders to the great sin they have committed. Let them clearly see that the land that you birthed is not theirs to divide. It is your Holy land and you have deeded that land to the Jewish descendants of Abraham until the time of Yeshua's return. Just as the blood of the Passover lambs were placed on the thresholds and doorposts to protect our people in ancient Egypt, as we depart tonight and return to our homes, I pray the blood of Yeshua and a continued hedge of protection around every member of this congregation. I also bind the spirit of fear and ask God's Holy Spirit , the Ruach Hakadosh, to watch over each of you and give you peace until we meet again. Father, I ask all this in the name above all names, I ask this in the name of Yeshua ha Mashiach. Amen."

Thursday, February 14th
8:45 p.m.
15 Potowomut Estates
Providence, Rhode Island

Something was wrong. It was early evening on one of the most celebrated nights of the year, but all up and down the waterfront of Narragansett Bay was unusually dark and quiet. Reservations made months in advance at Providence's most exclusive waterfront restaurant in anticipation of spending a romantic Valentine's Day evening dining out were all canceled. Except for the an occasional police cruiser or a passing National Guard humvee, the streets throughout the city and suburbs of greater Providence Rhode Island were totally deserted. Even the local convenient stores that remained opened on both Christmas Day and Thanksgiving were closed. This same scene was being played out all up and down the East Coast from Maine to Florida. For the first time, as the minutes ticked away toward the nine o'clock hour, millions of American citizens now prepared to spend their Valentines Day evening locked in fear within the confines of their homes.

"Honey, the phone's ringing and I can't get to it right now," shouted a female voice from behind the hall bathroom door. "Can you see who it is?"

"No problem, I'll get it," responded her husband. Picking up the receiver, he first noticed that the call was from out of state. *The caller ID says Maryland. I bet its John calling to check up on us!*

"John, I'm sorry I didn't call earlier. Are you and Miranda all right?"

"Tom, this is Ezra Schroeder."

There was a slight pause. "Ezra, I'm sorry," Tom Reid answered. "When I saw Maryland on the caller ID, I assumed it was my brother John calling."

"Tom, John is the reason I'm calling you," Ezra replied. "I need you to contact your brother immediately."

"Ezra, what's wrong?"

"Tom, I mean this with all sincerity," Schroeder firmly stated, "I need you to do me the biggest favorite that I could possibly ever ask!"

"Ezra, what can I do for you?"

Now Tom Reid was really curious. From the brief time he spent with Ezra Schroeder back in September, he remembered him as sincere man of deep faith. *What kind of favor could he possibly want from me?*

"Tom, I want you to ask your brother to set up a meeting between me and the president."

Tom paused momentarily to collect his thoughts. He could hardly believe what he had just heard.

"Ezra," Tom continued. "Do you have any idea how hard that would be, especially now, with everything else going on? Couldn't this wait until another time?"

"Tom, God wants me to meet with the president, now!"

A short pause followed.

"Ezra," Tom responded in almost a whisper. "If anyone else would have asked, I would have thought it was some kind of sick joke, but you're really serious, aren't you?"

"Tom, I know this all sounds crazy, but you've got to trust me on this," Schroeder implored. "The entire fate of America rests upon me meeting with the president. I need to talk face to face with Analise Devoe as soon as possible!"

"Ezra, I can't promise that she'll meet with you, but I can promise that I'll call John immediately and ask."

Thank you, Lord! Schroeder quietly prayed. "Tom, I can't thank you enough!"

"Ezra," Tom followed, "if what you are saying is truly from God, then I have complete faith that He will do the rest!"

Chapter Seventeen

"The Lord will also bring on you every kind of sickness and disaster until you are destroyed. You who were as numerous as the stars in the sky will be left but few in number, because you did not obey the Lord your God."

Deuteronomy 28: 61–62

Tuesday, February 20*th*
8:45 *a.m. EST*
James Brady White House Press Briefing Room
Washington, D.C.

It wasn't uncommon for every seat in the tiny West Wing briefing room to be filled with reporters representing every form of media on the planet. What made this scene so unusual was that the facial identities of every one of the 48 reporters present for the morning off camera briefing were concealed behind a white facemask. Not only were facemasks mandatory for everyone entering the White House grounds, special non-allergenic gloves had to be worn as well. At exactly 9 a.m., the man who everyone was waiting for entered the Press Briefing Room through the left front entrance.

"Good morning, everyone," greeted the masked White House Press Secretary as he stepped up to the front podium, "Or should I say, stick-um up!"

Everyone in the room laughed.

"From my vantage point, it's really hard to tell if we have any new faces with us this morning. Unfortunately, I've already been informed that some of our colleagues could not be with us this morning," commented John Reid in a solemn voice.

For the next few minutes, the press secretary took time to welcome over a dozen substitute reporters sent by their respective new agencies to replace White House reporters who were either too ill themselves or had to remain at home to attend to the needs of sick family members. With the introductions over, John Reid began the briefing with an unpopular request.

"Before I begin, I have a tremendous favor to ask on behalf of the president."

John Reid knew what he was up against. A presidential appeal just before an important briefing was not what a room full of weary reporters wanted to hear.

"The president has asked that until we meet for this afternoon's televised broadcast, she wants everything discussed this morning to be off the record."

The press secretary paused briefly to allow reporters time to vent their frustrations. Some began shaking heads while others closed their notepads and sat back in disgust.

"John, for God's sake, this is America!" voiced Reuter's reporter Max Hamel. "Good or bad, it's our job to report the news!"

"People are literally dying out there to find out what the hell's going on!" commented another frustrated reporter.

"Folks, believe me, the president and I couldn't agree more," John Reid passionately stated, "but right now, President Devoe feels what the American public needs more than anything is some good news and until the CDC releases its findings this afternoon, she's asking all of you to wait."

That last comment ignited an immediate response of hands. With too many to choose, the press Secretary pointed to a reporter sitting in the fourth row wearing the only blue facemask in the room.

"Sheila, I believe that's you hiding behind that blue mask."

"Aren't you the psychic!" jokingly replied Sheila Jones of Fox News. "John, why don't you tell us how bad things really are, and then let us be the judge as to how we should report it?"

Reid reluctantly agreed to the reporter's request. He began by quoting the latest CDC figures just faxed into the White House.

"Folks, all I can say is these latest numbers from the CDC are mind boggling. In a matter of just six days, there have been over 27,000 confirmed deaths and at least 10 million suspected cases reported in every single state, including Hawaii and Alaska. Keep in mind, these numbers are changing as I speak!"

"What about Canada and Mexico?" asked a reporter from the back of the room.

"Both countries are reporting normal numbers for this time of year," Reid replied. "Their health agencies see no evidence of an outbreak."

"John, how is that possible?" demanded Maggie Rowe from the *New York Times*. "Explain to me how a plague can stay confined within a country's borders without affecting its neighbors?"

"I believe we can attribute that to the fast action on our part," Reid replied. "The moment we realized we had a serious problem, the president immediately closed our borders."

"Then if what you are saying is true," continued the outspoken *Times* reporter, "how do you account for the fact that we're seeing similar outbreaks in both Alaska and Hawaii and nowhere else?"

For once, the press secretary stood silent. He couldn't answer the question because there was no answer. It defied human explanation. Regardless of governmental efforts, it only stood to reason that a rapidly spreading infectious disease could not be confined within the geographical borders of any one country.

"I admit, we don't have all the answers," Reid conceded, "but I'm sure the CDC's findings will help shed some light."

"John, how long can we expect this nationwide lockdown to remain in effect?" asked MSNBC reporter Mike Hunter.

"Again, Mike, that totally depends on the results from the CDC. The president is hopeful that some parts can be lifted maybe as early as tomorrow. I can tell you that schools will remain closed indefinitely until this crisis is completely over. That includes all colleges and universities; anywhere large groups of people would come together."

"John, the people I've interviewed are getting really tired of eating army rations delivered to their doors." commented Sal Broxton of the Boston Globe. "Can you tell us how the government plans to feed over three hundred million people once the travel restrictions are lifted?"

"Now that's a great question!" Reid answered. "Our local National Guard, working together with each region's local food suppliers have been busily stocking shelves in grocery stores all across America with non-perishable food items and frozen meats. We have also assigned each local area neighborhood as a designated zone, such as A through D. Once the quarantine is partially lifted, people living in these designated areas will be given a four hour period of time to leave their homes and return, thus limiting the nightmare of traffic jams and confusion.

"How are people going to pay for these supplies?" asked Mitchell Connor of the Baltimore Sun. "The banks have been closed for almost a week and many of our fixed income elderly haven't received their checks yet."

"Until this crisis in over, Uncle Sam pays all the bills," John Reid affirmed, "and that also includes making sure our power grid is up and running."

"John, I know this may seem an inappropriate question right now in light of all the suffering going on," commented Maggie Rowe, "but I can't stop thinking about how this crisis is affecting our overall economy."

It was obvious that Maggie Rowe's last comment struck a common chord with her fellow reporters. Every hand was down and silence filled the room as the reporters awaited the press secretary's response.

"That," Reid admitted, "is the million dollar question. For the past five days, all we've had time to think about were life and death situations. With everything else happening around here, we really haven't had time to stop and discuss the economy. I agree with Maggie, with everything shut down for a week, things can't be good.

Even after the quarantines are lifted, I'm sure many folks will still be afraid to venture out to the malls."

"John, in respect to the economy again," Maggie Rowe again interjected, "I'm sure the president is aware that both China and Japan are considering dumping the dollar for a more stable currency like the Euro. What do you have to say about that?"

"That's not going to happen!" Reid emphatically stated. "I don't believe any nation on this earth would stoop so low as to rub salt into the wounds of a fellow nation in times of dire crisis."

Reid knew the present health of the economy was an issue he wasn't prepared to discuss. Not wanting to open what could become America's next 'Pandora's Box,' he desperately looked around the room for a reporter he knew would stay on the present issue at hand. "Next question goes to the gentleman sitting on the end of the fifth row."

"Mr. Reid, my name is Marvin Epstein from Worldwatch.com "I'm replacing my boss, Sid Grossman, who is sick at home."

Worldwatch.com was known for its conservative stance on most political issues. It was one of a dozen Internet sites represented in the Press Briefing Room.

"Welcome, Mr. Epstein," acknowledged Reid, "Best regards to Sid. What is your question, sir?"

"There are those in the Religious Right who are saying that this 'plague' was America's own doing for abandoning Israel? How do you and the president respond to these accusations?"

"I can personally affirm that the president is tired of hearing how America is abandoning Israel," Reid firmly voiced. "Our position on this matter is clear. We fully support Israel's right to exist within the borders designated by the UN resolution 242. The president has instructed our UN ambassador to vote on that same resolution at next week's UN Security Council meeting to be held in The Hague. Those on the Religious Right have always been into voodoo politics. At every turn, they're always ready to demonize those of us seeking a lasting peace in the Middle East. These are just scare tactics by a small, desperate group of fanatics. I believe the American public is sick of it, may I add, it cost them the last election!"

"Mr. Reid, think about what you just said," Mr. Epstein boldly interjected in an equally firm voice. "You said quote, 'the American public is "sick" of it!' I believe you have inadvertently confirmed that the Religious Right may be right after all!"

Tuesday, February 20th
8:45 a.m. EST
Centers for Disease Control
Restricted Level 4: Pandemic Diseases
1600 Clifton Road, N.E.
Atlanta, Georgia

Every deadly disease pathogen known to man such as Ebola, hemorrhagic fever, smallpox, and avian influenza eventually finds its way down into the heavily guarded subterranean recesses of the CDC's Emerging Infectious Disease Laboratory. It is here that the world's leading epidemiologists are called to suit up daily from head to toe in an attempt to identify the specific cause of disease outbreaks anywhere on earth. Ever since the first tissue samples arrived at the Atlanta facility early on Thursday the 14th, teams of our nation's top disease experts, led by Dr. James McDevitt, have worked exhaustively around the clock in a desperate attempt to discover the present cause of the deadliest disease outbreak to ever strike America's shores.

With her 9 a.m. deadline looming, Dr. Janet Rothberg suited up and entered the airlock leading to the CDC's most restricted room, mankind's most deadly area known simply as Level 4. As the airlock door opened, the Director of the CDC stepped out into a brightly lit room full of high tech equipment and fellow health researchers busily scurrying about in their protective light blue body suits.

"Good morning, Janet," announced the familiar voice of her Director of Epidemiology.

"Jim, I hope you have some good news for me," commented Dr. Rothberg. "I have an army C-5 scheduled to fly me to Andrews in less than two hours to meet with the president for a televised press conference. I pray that you have some better news for me this morning."

"I'm not sure if I would use the word 'better,'" Dr. McDevitt confessed with an equally solemn look. "At this moment all I can tell you is what we don't have."

"I'm not exactly sure if that's what the president expects to hear right now.

Is there any good news I can tell her?"

McDevitt shook his head and smiled.

"Well, there is one thing we are able to definitely rule out. You can tell the president that it's not a virulent strain of the flu as we once thought."

"Jim, if it's not the flu, then what the hell is it?" Dr. Rothberg petitioned.

"We're still not sure," McDevitt again confessed. "Come over to the Big Gun. There's something there I need to show you."

McDevitt led his boss over to the world's most powerful research electron microscope. Nicknamed the "Big Gun," it was used specifically to pinpoint objects as small as molecules. Stopping in front the microscope's keyboard, McDevitt directed Dr. Rothberg's attention to a large display monitor located directly in front of them.

"I want you to carefully examine the following slides all taken from tissue samples from six deceased members of the same family."

"The entire family?" Dr. Rothberg exclaimed.

"Everyone," McDevitt replied as he touched the keyboard to bring up the first slide, "Mom, dad, and all four children; two girls and two boys ranging in ages from four to thirteen. Three died from bacterial infections, the others were viral."

"Is this typical of what we're seeing?" asked a shocked Dr. Rothberg.

"I'm afraid more often than not."

McDevitt proceeded to direct Dr. Rothberg's attention to an area on the monitor that appeared to be an indistinguishable tangle of bloody human tissue.

"The first sample we're looking at is from victim number one. We believe this may have started out as a common bacterial infection of the left frontal sinus cavity."

"I'm confused," Dr. Rothberg admitted. "This couldn't possibly be an image taken of a sinus cavity!"

"Twenty four hours earlier it was a sinus cavity." Dr. McDevitt confirmed. "What we are looking at here is a combination of grossly decomposed bone and brain tissue. The infection was so virulent that it ate right through the victim's skull!"

"Was she placed on antibiotics?" asked Dr. Rothberg.

"Immediately!" McDevitt followed. "According the records we received, the attending doctors administered the strongest doses with absolutely no effect what-so-ever!"

Dr. McDevitt proceeded to the second slide.

"This specimen comes from victim number two." McDevitt pointed out. "It looks identical to that of victim one, but this sample is from an area located inside the inner ear. What possibly started out as a minor childhood inner ear infection literally exploded into something that resembles the effects of Ebola!"

"My God, Jim, what's going on here?" asked a visibly shaken Dr. Rothberg.

"Victim three died from a massive bacterial infection that started in her bladder and spread eventually to all the major organs including the heart and liver."

McDevitt briefly paused and turned his attention toward Dr. Rothberg.

"Janet, I need you to pay particular attention to the following slides," McDevitt stressed with a noticeable tone of excitement in his voice.

"From what we can surmise from medical records and tissue samples taken from victims three through six, each started out at first with the common symptoms of the flu; chills, muscle aches, sore throat, vomiting and slight fever. In a matter of a few short hours, all three were comatose and died the next morning. The samples shown on the screen are all infected tissue taken from each victim's lung. The next slide shows the culprit, HIB (Haemophilus influenzae type B) or simply called influenza B."

"So that's it!" Dr. Rothberg excitedly declared. "HIB is known as the most important cause of bacterial infections in young children. It's also known to cause sever sinus and ear infections, meningitis, and bloodstream infections."

"That is exactly what we thought at first," McDevitt affirmed, "but I'm afraid there's one big problem with that conclusion. Records from the family physician show that every family member had a flu shot only three months prior containing the antibodies against HIB.

"Then perhaps this strain of HIB has mutated," followed Dr. Rothberg.

Dr. McDevitt turned and smiled. "Janet, we're both on the same wavelength, but take a look at the next slide."

The next image on the monitor appeared to be two identical samples.

"The virus on the left is our own HIB sample stored here in level 2," McDevitt pointed out. "The slide on the right is a sample of a virus taken from one of the victims."

"They look identical in everyway," Dr. Rothberg commented as she closely observed the monitor.

Pausing for a moment to gather her thoughts, she then turned to her colleague and declared. "Then the only other logical explanation is that something is causing an immuno-compromised response in the affected victims!"

"Exactly!" confirmed Dr. McDevitt with a smile. "Look very carefully again at an enhanced magnification of that last tissue sample. Do you see anything missing?"

"My God, yes!" Dr. Rothberg shouted. "There isn't a single T-cell present anywhere! That sample should been teaming with them!"

"My thoughts exactly!" McDevitt followed. "Unlike the AIDS virus that attacks and destroys T-cells, we believe there is something preventing the body's response from recognizing there is an invader present."

"So what you are saying is that something is possibly blocking the body's antigen response to foreign invaders"

"Exactly!" replied McDevitt.

Both researchers were now in agreement. Regardless of the source, something was preventing the victim's immune system from responding to a foreign attack. Looking face to face through their transparent plastic shields, Dr. Rothberg asked her chief researcher the question on the minds of over 300,000,000 Americans.

"So, Jim, what is it?"

"That's the million dollar question! Unfortunately, at the present moment, we don't have an answer."

"So what do I tell the president?" pressed Dr. Rothberg.

"The truth," McDevitt replied. "Tell her that we've identified the problem, but we are still left with a big challenge, to identify the cause. Tell her from me that we are doing everything humanly possible to find it!"

Chapter Eighteen

"They will lend money to you, not you to them. They will be the head, and you will be the tail! If you refuse to listen to the Lord your God and to obey the commands and laws he has given you, all these curses will pursue and overtake you until you are destroyed."

Deuteronomy 28: 44–45 NKJV

Most adults can remember playing as children a board game called monopoly. By the role of the dice, participants strategically moved their tokens or game pieces along the perimeter of a small board, buying or selling, wheeling and dealing, until only one player ended up with all the properties and money. With all other players in financial ruin, the game was over; monopoly achieved!

During the early part of the twentieth century, when the game of worldwide monopoly was just getting started, a series of economic disasters in the form of two World Wars and a global economic depression brought international trading almost to a complete halt. With the crushing defeat in 1945 of both Nazi-fascism in Europe and Japanese Imperialism in Asia, a literal explosion of new ideas and technologies started shaping the post-World War II economic landscape. Unfortunately, the new era of global peace was short lived. The freedom-crushing bondage of godless communism was soon given free reign to swallow up much of war torn Eastern Europe as well as the vast majority of the Asian continent including the Soviet Union and China.

For the remainder of the free Western world, an entire host of new economic players and their respective currencies began dominating the global markets. In order to achieve market supremacy, nations had to understand the one basic tenet governing all global economics: trade determined everything. Whichever country was selling or exporting more items than its neighbors was rewarded the dominant currency. As the balance of trade shifted from month to month and year to year, so did a country's currency. The value of the French frank could depend on the quality of their country's grape harvest and the amount of wine France exported, or the British pound might rise with sale of more wool sweaters to France.

Not long after the end of World War II, one Western economy literally exploded onto the world scene, becoming the world's leading producer and exporter of automobiles, aircraft, textiles, food crops, canned goods, raw and refined building materials such as steel. From the years 1950 through 1980, the United States of America held the title of the world's number one economic superstar and its currency, the dollar, held the title as king of the world's currency. While other Western currencies continued to fluctuate against each other based on trade and commerce, the dollar assumed a role as the world currency that never seemed to fluctuate. All across the globe, from Africa to Asia, when financial transactions took place, dollars were exchanged.

Most Americans living today have never lived in a world in which the dollar wasn't king. They have gone about their daily lives never giving thought to the fact that during the past three decades, American demands for inexpensive, cheaply produced foreign products, especially from China, Japan, and Southeast Asia, have far outpaced the ability of the American companies to produce and sell products to the rest of the world. To remain competitive, American companies began sending well-paying manufacturing and service jobs to countries with few, if any, protections for their workers or the environment. One by one, the once thought rock-solid American companies started vanishing, all victims of America's insatiable appetite for inexpensive foreign products. The first American jobs to go were the textile and clothing industries, the backbone of the New England economy. Next were the Midwest's once booming steel mills, followed by the auto plants, the life-blood of Detroit, and thousands of other auto-related industries. With the advent of the worldwide web, thousands of America's top technical jobs were being outsourced to third-world counties to cut labor costs all in the name of corporate saving. The final outcome, millions of well-paying American jobs with great benefits were lost, never to return.

The vast majority of Americans remain totally oblivious to the reason why. Why did America sit back for three decades and allow all of its major job industries to vanish from its landscape? Why, as America's trade deficit with the rest of the world has skyrocketed, hasn't the dollar plunged in value? If this same problem happened to any other country, the value of that nation's currency would have plummeted and the cost of its imports, including oil, would have risen through the roof.

Though the answer can simply be explained in terms of basic economics, the truth remains hidden just beyond our natural senses. America's phenomenal rise to economic stardom has fallen victim to Satan's original "Frog in a frying pan" strategy: human greed will replace the ideals of human need. During the late 1970's, Satan set out on a worldwide campaign to find a highly industrialized country willing to insure that its products would be attractive to America consumers at low affordable prices. By 1980, he had found such a country. Using as bait the unique capacity of the U.S. economy to absorb foreign imports, Japan began to develop their entire industrialization strategy around selling high-quality cars and electronics only to the United States market. In order to insure their trade monopoly with the American consumer, the Bank of Japan has done everything in its power to keep its currency, the Yen, weak and the U.S. dollar artificially strong. In doing so, Japan has successfully created millions of jobs based on the ability of the America consumer to buy their products only.

Satan's plan in weakening the Yen and strengthening the dollar was brilliant! As bait for his trap to destroy the American economy, he convinced the Bank of Japan to do the opposite of what Americans expected them to do as cautious investors. The larger the

U.S. trade deficits became, the more dollars the Bank of Japan would purchase, including buying billions in U.S. treasury bonds. Satan's strategy paid off. In a matter of three short decades, America had gone from being the world's largest creditor nation to the world's largest debtor nation, but Satan's plan wasn't finished.

Using the Japanese economy as his model, Satan seduced all the surrounding nations—South Korea, Thailand, Taiwan, Malaysia and especially, the giant of all Asian countries, China—to join his clandestine plan. As recent as 1980, China had virtually no trade with America. At present, China will sell the United States over $190 billion of Chinese products and purchase only $30 billion in America goods. Modeling after Japan, the Bank of China is now buying massive amounts of American dollars in the form of U.S. treasury bonds and other secure American assets. In turn, the U.S. Treasury uses these investments from China and other foreign counties to finance America's huge federal deficit of almost nine trillion dollars.

With enormous sums of dollars just sitting in Chinese, Korean, and Japanese banks, as well as other countries around the world, foreigners now own about eleven trillion dollars in U.S. assets while America owns about $7 trillion in foreign assets. America's foreign debt of about 4 trillion dollars is about 8 times higher then it was just a decade ago and is growing higher by over two billion dollars every single day. In absolute terms that is at least one hundred times bigger than the net foreign debt of any country in the history of the world! No country can sustain this much continuous debt and survive. Satan's trap for America is now set and the trigger supporting the bait tray is about to spring. All that is needed is a reason for Japan and China's central banks to stop buying more American dollars in the form of U.S. Treasury bonds, and instead, diversify into purchasing other currencies such as Euros, Canadian dollars and British pounds. Very soon now, the era of the dollar's long monopoly as the world's financial currency of choice will come to an end taking the American stock market and economy along with it. At that moment, America will be bankrupt and its financial status in the game of global monopoly will be over!

Tuesday, February 20th
10:45 a.m. EST
White House Oval Office
Washington, D.C.

Two humans patiently sat in the office of the president's personal secretary, anxiously awaiting their turn to be called through the unusual doorway fashioned to accommodate the oval shape of the adjoining president's office. As the secretary sat at her desk totally absorbed in her work, two massive angelic beings stood along the opposite wall, closely observing the two seated humans.

"Does Schroeder look a little nervous to you?" Yahriel, the prince of prophetic wisdom and worldly affairs, asked his Archangel counterpart, Muriel.

"I can understand why," Muriel replied. "It isn't everyday that a human is given the opportunity to change the mind of the President of the United States."

"Who is Schroeder's human companion?" Yahriel inquired.

"That would be Harrison Andrews, a brand new entry into the Kingdom. Standing behind him is his assigned protectorate, Nahiel."

"I'm curious, Muriel, how difficult was it to convince John Reid to arrange this meeting?"

"Let's just say that we had a little help from John Reid's chimera." Muriel smiled.

"Zorah?" Yahiel turned with a surprised look.

"You two have met?" asked Muriel.

"Briefly," Yahiel replied, "but I'm curious, why would a chimera offer assistance to an angel of the Lord?"

"Let's just say that the edge of a angel's sword speaks much louder than Zorah's devotion to Satan," Muriel replied with a smile.

The angelic conversation was placed on hold as two other humans entered the room.

"Dr. Schroeder, hello again," welcomed John Reid with an outstretched hand.

Dr. Schroeder in turn stood and locked hands with the man who made this meeting possible.

"John, I want to thank you so much for arranging all this!" Schroeder replied.

"No problem at all, Dr. Schroeder," John graciously followed, "I'm very sorry I couldn't meet you when you arrived, but things are a little hectic around here to say the least."

Turning his attention now to the gentleman in the brown tweed suit standing to Schroeder's left, Reid continued. "And this must be your English friend, the famous Professor Harrison Andrews of Cambridge University."

"I can't tell you how much of an honor this is for me to be here," Andrews gleefully responded. "Thank you so much for doing this!"

"You are more than welcome, Professor Andrews."

John Reid turned his attention now to the tall brunette standing to his left.

"Doctors Schroeder and Andrews," Reid announced, "I would like to introduce my personal secretary, Julia Morgan. Julia is going to remain with the two of you and explain exactly what you can expect before your scheduled meeting with President Devoe."

"Welcome to the White House, Dr. Schroeder and Professor Andrews," cordially greeted Ms. Morgan. "I've heard a lot of good things about the two of you."

"Folks, I'm sorry I have to rush," John Reid apologized, "but I have to make arrangements for a very important upcoming press conference this afternoon. I'm leaving the two of you in very good hands."

Before parting, Schroeder reached out and firmly grabbed John Reid by his right hand, preventing him from leaving. Looking eye to eye, Schroeder made a comment that John Reid would never forget, "John, I want to thank you again for doing this! You may not realize the implications of what you have done here, but I pray that one day the Lord will reveal to you that arranging this meeting was one of the most important decisions that you have ever made."

Without knowing it, Schroeder's words had penetrated a place in

John Reid's heart that had remained buried in his distant past. John Reid instantly recalled making a heartfelt promise to God as a young boy sitting in his father's church that he would do something great that would make both his earthly father and his Heavenly Father proud of him. As Schroeder release his hand, John acknowledged Schroeder's comments with a nod and a brief smile before turning and walking away.

"Well, Doctors, I know you're both excited!" Ms. Morgan interjected. "It's just about time for one of the most important meetings the two of you will probably ever have!"

Without realizing the true implications of her last statement, Julia Morgan went on to detail all the protocol involved with meeting the President of the United States in the Oval Office.

"I will be going into the room with you just long enough to introduce you to the president and then leave. Because of the president's tight schedule this morning, you will only be given a maximum time of ten minutes. Do you have any questions?"

There was no time left for questions. The president's secretary, Martina Sanchez, stood and announced, "Ms. Morgan, the president is ready to see you and your guests." Ms Sanchez then proceeded to get up from her desk and walk over to open the curved door leading to the Oval office.

For Ezra Schroeder, that opened door represented more than a meeting with the leader of the free world. It marked the start of an adventure beyond his wildest dreams. He also knew beyond a shadow of a doubt that it was God who had orchestrated this meeting. With total confidence, Schroeder walked boldly through the opened door knowing that the Ruach HaKodesh, the Holy Spirit of God, was in complete control of the situation.

"Madame President," announced Julia Morgan, "it is my great pleasure to introduce to you Dr. Ezra Schroeder and Dr. Harrison Andrews."

Immediately following Ms. Morgan's brief introductions, President Devoe got up from her desk and walked over to greet her guests. She then cordially welcomed both professors with a warm handshake and some kind words.

"Doctors Schroeder and Andrews, it's my great pleasure to welcome the two of you to the White House."

Glancing briefly at the nametags displayed on their jackets, the president turned her attention first to Harrison Andrews.

"Dr. Andrews, I'm not sure if you are aware of the fact, but I am a great fan of early English antiquities. I hear you are just the person to see the next time I visit England."

"Madame President," Andrews proudly proclaimed, "I would be honored to give you and your husband a personal tour of our entire antiquities collection at Cambridge."

"Then, we have a date," the president affirmed with a handshake. She next extended a welcoming hand to the gentleman standing to the left of Andrews.

"And Dr. Schroeder, I understand that you work as a senior cryptographer at NSA. I want to personally thank you for your dedicated service to our country."

"Thank you, Madame President, for your kind words and for seeing us on such short notice," Schroeder humbly responded.

"Please gentlemen, have a seat." The president directed the two professors to a stately antique couch. She then proceeded to sit on a matching winged back chair opposite her guests. The moment she sat down, she leaned forward and made eye contact with Schroeder.

"Dr. Schroeder, forgive me if I seem to be rushing, but because we're pressed for time, I want to get right to the point. From what John has told me, you believe you might have some information that can explain the mystery behind this horrible crisis we are now facing."

"Madame President," Schroeder in turn responded, "I truly appreciate you taking the time to meet with us, and I too will get right to the point."

With only three feet separating him from the most powerful human being on the planet, Schroeder looked the president directly in the eyes and boldly announced.

"John Reid was correct. I know exactly what has caused America's present crisis and I know exactly how you as the president can end it!"

The president sat back in her chair and stared at Ezra Schroeder intently. *How can he say such a thing? she thought. This man is either a lunatic or a crazy terrorist.*

"Dr. Schroeder, those are some bold statements you have just made. I hope you can explain yourself."

"Madame President, I asked my good friend Professor Andrews to accompany me to verify what I am about to tell you. As you are aware, Professor Andrews is respected as the world's greatest expert in English antiquities. But you may not be aware that he is also an expert in the writings of Sir Isaac Newton."

"Yes, I have been made aware of that fact, but to be perfectly frank with you, Dr Schroeder, I can't see how a long dead English scientist can help solve our present problems."

"Madame President," Schroeder followed, "beyond formulating the laws that govern the universe, Newton strongly felt that God had ordained him for the major purpose of deciphering the hidden mysteries locked in the prophetic books of the Bible, especially those found in the Old Testament."

"Dr. Schroeder, I must stop you right there," the president interjected. "You may not be aware of this fact, but let me enlighten you. I do not believe either in God or in the words of the Bible."

"Madame President, I am aware of your stance on these matters, but please hear me out," pleaded Schroeder.

"Then proceed," the president granted.

"Most people are not aware of this fact, but Newton dedicated over thirty years of his life to diligently studying the prophetic books of the Bible. He was looking for a hidden code that he believed God had placed there specifically for him to discover. Without the luxury of using a modern computer, Newton found a hidden code written in Hebrew that details the exact events that we see happening today."

Once again, the president sat back in her chair and stared at the two professors with a look of frustration. This didn't stop Schroeder.

"Madame President, last year Professor Andrews invited me to come to Cambridge University to decipher a newly discovered journal written by Newton. Using a software program similar to those we use at NSA, I was able to decipher all of the journal's contents and I will quickly summarize for you what it says: 'If America turns her back on Israel and the Jewish people, if she pressures Israel in any way to surrender the land given to her through God's everlasting covenant with Abraham, then America's blessings will be removed and America will be cursed.'"

"What exactly are you asking me to do, Dr. Schroeder?" the president smiled.

"Madame President, do not give in to the pressure of terrorists! Support Israel's right to possess all the land that God has given her. I swear to you, Madame President, God will instantly remove this curse."

Turning now to the gentleman who, up until now, was quietly sitting beside Schroeder, the reluctant president asked, "Dr. Andrews, do you go along with what Dr. Schroeder is saying?"

"Madame President, one week ago I would have been thinking as I believe you are right now, that this man is totally insane and needs to be committed. But today, I emphatically place my entire reputation behind every word he is saying."

Without saying a word, the president smiled and got up from her chair. Both professors stood up in response, confused by her actions.

Extending her hand toward Schroeder indicating the end of the meeting, the president closed with this comment, "Dr. Schroeder, you wouldn't happen to be Charlton Heston in disguise, would you?"

"Why do you ask, Madame President?" Schroeder inquired.

"Because I get the strange feeling that this meeting comes right out of the script from the movie the *Ten Commandments!*"

Schroeder smiled as he shook the president's hand in parting.

As Professors Schroeder and Andrew left the Oval Office with their angelic guardians, Ariel and Nahiel, the Archangels Muriel and Yahriel remained behind studying the president.

"Do you think Schroeder's words made any impression? Muriel asked.

"Well, the good news was she didn't throw him out!" Yahriel smiled.

"I sort of enjoyed the Moses/Pharaoh analogy," Muriel followed.

"Well, she's picking up the phone," Yahriel observed. "I believe we will shortly find out the answer to your question."

"Marty," the president curtly addressed her secretary, "have John Reid report to my office immediately!"

"Isn't it funny how human expressions speak louder than human words!" Muriel jokingly commented.

Soon there was a knock on the side entrance door to the Oval Office.

"Come in!"

"Madame President, Marty said you needed to see me right away."

Firmly entrenched behind her desk, the president looked up at her press secretary and disdainfully declared, "John, I am going to make this policy explicit to you, my chief of staff, and anyone else who requests a meeting in this room. In the future, as long as I remain in this office, no rightwing religious nut will ever step one foot past that threshold, do I make myself clear!"

"Yes Madame President, I promise that will never happen again."

"Did you get your answer?" Yahriel turned and smiled.

"Unfortunately for both her and America," Muriel replied with a serious look, "this president is about to get her response from the Lord."

"John, as you leave," the president requested in a more civil tone, "tell Marty I want her to get UN Ambassador Thenton on the phone."

"I'll get right on it, Madame President!" the embarrassed press secretary affirmed. Furious at his brother for placing him in a situation that could jeopardize his position as White House Press Secretary, John Reid existed the Oval Office, stopping only to pass the president's request to the her secretary before storming down the West Wing hallway.

In a very brief matter of time, the phone on the president's desk rang.

"Ambassador Thenton?" the president announced as she pushed the button for the speaker phone.

"Yes. Madame President."

"How are things in the Netherlands?"

"For those living here in the Hague, a lot better than things back home!" the American UN Ambassador replied.

"I just wanted to touch base with you concerning next week's vote."

"Any changes, Madame President?" asked Ambassador Thenton.

"Absolutely not," the president resolutely replied. "UN Resolution 242 will unanimously pass."

"I am so glad to hear that, Madame President!" answered the U.S. Ambassador. "America will finally cast her vote on the side of peace!"

No sooner did the president hang up the phone with the UN Ambassador, then there came an abrupt knocking at her door.

"Madame President," Marty opened the door and announced, "Sorry for the interruption, but Secretary Holmes and Federal Reserve Chairman Allan Brinkman are here to see you. They said it's an emergency!"

"All right, Marty. Send them in."

"Madame President, we have a serious crisis on our hands!" bluntly announced Treasury Secretary Holmes.

"Come out with it, Les," the president demanded. "What can be any bigger then a damn plague!"

"As we speak, the Chinese are dumping all of our treasury bonds."

"What are you talking about, Les!" the president shouted out in frustration. "You're the one who stood here just two days ago and said that would be impossible. You emphatically told me to my face that the Chinese would be committing financial suicide by dumping the dollar!"

"Madame President, I admit it, I was wrong!" Les Holms reluctantly confessed. "All the Chinese can see now are boat loads of their products just sitting in their ports going nowhere."

"Madame President, I am afraid that's not all," commented the Federal Reserve Chairman Allan Brinkman in a very subdued voice. "China is not the only country dropping the dollar. It looks like the domino effect is taking place all over the Asian Pacific; South Korea, Thailand, Taiwan, Malaysia are following suite, and I'm afraid Japan is right behind them."

"God help us!" the president cried out in desperation. "I can't believe this is all happening!"

"Do you seriously believe she meant to say that?" Muriel turned and asked his angelic companion.

"Perhaps," Yahriel replied, "or perhaps it was just a slip of the tongue. In any case, I truly believe we are starting to get her attention."

The moment they exited the Oval Office, Professors Andrews and Schroeder were met once again by their secret service escort assigned to direct them back to the visitor's entrance. During their short walk to the entrance, Ezra remained unusually quiet while Professor Andrews did all the talking.

"Ezra, I can't believe I just invited the President of the United States to Cambridge and she accepted. Wait until Diane hears about this. I can't thank you enough."

"Don't thank me, my friend," Ezra commented as he continued to walk. "Thank the Lord. He's the one who made all this possible."

The moment Schroeder made mention of 'the Lord,' Andrews immediately stopped and turned toward his friend.

"My God, Ezra," Andrews said with a look of dismay, "you forgot to tell the president about the Passover prophesy."

"I didn't forget," Schroeder quietly announced.

"Then if you didn't forget, why didn't you tell her?" asked his thoroughly confused English friend. "I thought that was our purpose for coming!"

With the secret service agent patiently looking on, Schroeder leaned over and quietly whispered, "Harry, every time I was about to tell her that Israel was going to be attacked on Passover, I clearly heard the word 'wait!' Even as we were about to leave the Oval Office, I heard it again, but this time I heard, 'wait until next time.'"

"Ezra, I don't understand," Andrews commented. "You were right there, talking face to face with the President of the United States! Why didn't you say something then?"

"I can't explain it," Schroeder replied. "I only know in my heart that it was not the time. Sometime in the near future when the time is right, Analise Devoe and I will meet again."

"Ariel, I watched as you whispered in Schroeder's ear to wait," Nahiel commented. "Do you know when Schroeder will meet again with the president?"

"I only know what Muriel has told me. Only when the United States repents of her great sin and comes to Israel's aid will God intervene and save her."

"Tell me," Nahiel asked. "What happens if America doesn't repent?'

"Then there will be no more visits to the White House."

Chapter Nineteen

"Thus says the Lord GOD: 'Behold, I am against you, O Gog, the prince of Rosh, Meshech, and Tubal. A long time from now you will be called into action. In the distant future you will swoop down on the land of Israel, which will be lying in peace after the return of her people from many lands. You and all your allies-a vast and awesome horde-will roll down on them like a storm and cover the land like a cloud.'"

Ezekiel 38:3,9 KJV

Presently, there are about 15 million Jews in the world and they are a majority in only one country: Israel. The last time a satanically inspired world leader threatened to exterminate the Jews, only a generation ago, he annihilated 75% of the Jewish people. Yet, with the shadow of the holocaust rapidly fading from the world's memory, the Jews living in Israel are once again openly threatened. Its Arab neighbors have repeatedly attacked their tiny nation. All of Islam has now declared a jihad, a holy war against Israel in order to reclaim the land that Muslims vehemently believe is their birthright; the land, according to the Qur'an, that was passed down to the descendants of Ishmael through God's promise to his father, Abraham.

Israelis today are deceived into believing that it is their superior military capabilities in the region that have kept the inevitable from happening. Little do they realize that there are only two things holding Satan back from unleashing all of his forces from hell and destroying the tiny Jewish nation once and for all: the support given to Israel by her staunchest ally, the United States of America, and the constant protection provided by Israel's ever-watchful guardians, the Archangel Michael and his legions angelic warriors.

Sadly, the vast majority of Jews living in Israel have long since abandoned their faith in the God of their fathers for the secular pleasures that this world has to offer. But God has not forgotten the promise He made so long ago to their Father Abraham. Very soon now, God will allow one or both of Israel's protective supports to be painfully removed, leaving the tiny Jewish nation outnumbered and completely surrounded by its enemies. At that moment, may the people living in the land of Israel cling once again to the words recorded thousands of years ago in the Old Testament Book of Joshua, "As for me and my household, we will serve the Lord."

Wednesday, March 7th
10 *a.m. Central European Standard Time*
The Peace Palace
The Hague, Netherlands

The temporary closing of America's borders was not going to stop the determined fifteen members of the UN Security Council from voting on one of the most important resolutions in their organization's history. All that was needed now was an alternative site, and where better to hold a vote for world peace than the UN's very own Peace Palace located in The Hague. A palace in every sense of the word, the beautiful Neo-Renaissance structure is used to house both the UN International Court of Justice and The Hague Academy of International Law.

Location aside, the most important reason for holding the vote at The Hague was timing. The following day, the Israeli citizens were scheduled to cast their votes on whether or not to accept the Arab's demands for a total withdrawal to their pre-1967 borders in exchange for a guarantee of regional peace. For the first time since Resolution 242 was drafted on November 22, 1967, all fifteen UN Security Council members, including the only lone holdout, the

United States, would send the Israelis a unified message to "withdraw" or face the consequences of total worldwide isolation.

One by one, the UN ambassadors representing their respective countries entered the large chambers used specifically to rule on global issues ranging from international treaty disputes to crimes against humanity. In order to portray today's historic vote as a world event, a large contingent of media was invited and strategically positioned in front of the raised platform where the fifteen ambassadors would be seated. Cameras flashed as each ambassador took his or her assigned position with the five permanent council members; China, France, the Russian Federation, the United Kingdom and the United States seated directly in center. All that was needed to pass a resolution was an affirmative vote from nine of the fifteen members including the concurring votes from all five permanent members. In only a matter of five short minutes, their historic votes would be cast.

Regardless of how the humans were to vote, there now were plans underway to make sure that in less than a month's time, Israel and its population of over five million Jews would be no more. With the humans totally preoccupied with the events going on in the front of the chamber, an informal meeting of sorts between Apollon, Satan's second in command, and his chief princes was about to adjourn in chamber's far back corner just in time to watch the historic human vote.

"Well, comrades, everything appears to be going as planned," commented Apollon. Dressed for today's special occasion in a floor-length black robe, the demonic prince remained seated on the edge of the back row bench as his three generals stood before him.

"The moment the humans vote to ratify Resolution 242, our official countdown to Operation Passover will commence. Before we end our business here and move to the front, I want each of you to briefly repeat your specific assignments to me one more time."

Except for their yellowish facial features, the physical identities of each of the standing princes were totally concealed within their floor-length hooded robes. Apollon turned first to the tallest of the three princes stand-

ing to his left with visible locks of jet-black hair resting on his high-browed forehead.

"Amducious, get right to the point and state your mission!" Apollon demanded.

"My pleasure, Commander," Amducious replied with an evil smirk. "On the morning of the next full moon, my demons are instructed to unleash on America devastation so unimaginable that all memories in the minds of Americans of the events of Hurricanes Katrina and 9–11 will be instantly erased."

"Excellent," Apollon grinned in approval. "Before I move on, Lord Satan and I want to congratulate you and all of your demons for a job well done. As of this morning, over five million Americans have died and millions more are still too sick to get out of bed. For those who will survive, the price of all their imported goods such as gasoline, electronics, and clothing have all skyrocketed beyond what most can presently afford. One more disaster should do it! The Americans will be too overwhelmed with their own problems to worry about what is happening on the other side of the world to poor little Israel!"

"My demons and I are honored to do our part, Lord Apollon," Amducious commented with false humility as he bowed his head low and raised his left hand high in honor of Satan.

Apollon now turned his attention to the dark-skinned demonic prince standing in center.

"Allahzad, state your mission!"

Known by his superiors and fellow demons as the Prince of Persia, Allahzad had served his assigned mission longer than any other. His earthly kingdoms were well known in the annuals of human history: the Babylonians, the Edomites, the Philistines, the Assyrians, and the Persians to name a few. Throughout human time, it has been his charge to do whatever it takes to destroy God's chosen people.

It was also he who appeared before Muhammad in the cave on Mt. Hera pretending to be the Archangel Gabriel. Day after day, Muhammad returned to the same cave believing the entire time that he was receiving revelation about Allah from the angel Gabriel. In truth, it was Allahzad, posing as an angel of light, who deceived Muhammad into memorizing all of his visions and teaching his Muslim followers to submit to a pagan deity that Satan himself had named after the Arabian moon god, Allah.

Calm and methodical, Allahzad stated his mission.

"Regardless of tomorrow's Israeli vote, I have instructed my demons to raise up a unified cry throughout the Muslim world against the Jews. There will be nonstop marches and rallies calling for complete elimination of Israel from their holy Muslim soil. On the morning of the next new moon, my legion of Hezbollah demons within Lebanon and Syria will again unleash a punishing rocket attacks against Israel's Northern borders. This time, the Israelis will have no other choice but to launch an all-out attack against Syria.

"The surrounding Arab nations will view this Israeli attack on Syria as a violation of article 2 of the Arab League Defense Treaty, which states that an attack on one member state is considered an attack on all. This will, in turn, bring down upon those miserable Jews the wrath of the entire Arab world, over three hundred million strong. With America preoccupied with its own problems and the UN unwilling to get involved, the Jews will find themselves in final checkmate."

It was Satan's decision to save the best for last. Known simply as the Prince of the North, Gog had been patiently waiting in the background, ever preparing for this special day. Apollon called on his final prince. "Gog!" Just the mention of the name transformed Apollon's sinister grin into a glare of pure evil. "After all of these many millennia, your day has finally come. You know the prophecies better than any. You of all my princes know that God will do everything in His power to prevent you from fulfilling your destiny. How do you propose to outsmart God?"

"Outsmarting is a big task," Gog admitted with a slight smirk. "It has been attempted many times, but unfortunately, the outcome is always the same." Gog paused momentarily and walked slowly away from his fellow princes. He then turned and boldly declared, "I praise Lord Satan for allowing me the advantage of sitting back and observing the many mistakes of my fellow comrades. I swear to both you, Lord Apollon, and to Lord Satan, I will not repeat their same stupid mistakes."

Only Apollon was amused by Gog's brashness. Amducious and

Allahzad both sneered at their demonic counterpart, knowing well that Gog was referring directly to them.

"The one mistake I will not make is being overconfident!" Gog boldly proclaimed. "Just because you two think America will be preoccupied with its own problems, doesn't mean that the forces of God won't have their own plan B! Don't be deceived into believing our plans are foolproof! Michael knows exactly what we're doing."

Before closing, Gog turned toward his fellow princes and declared "I have my own plan B and no one, not even Lord Satan, will ever know about it unless your plans fail!"

Apollon now stood to his feet and smugly announced, "That is why Lord Satan has selected you for this mission. He has definitely saved the best for last. I see the humans are about to vote. Let's go over and cheer them on!"

Thursday, March 8th
6 p.m. Israeli Standard Time
Jerusalem, Israel

Lines still remained long, some extending more than a block away from the polling location. With the voting polls scheduled to close in an hour, a record number of Israeli citizens turned out to cast their ballots to determine not only the future boundaries of their tiny nation, but on the future of their very identity as Jews.

This was unlike any voting referendum this nation, or any nation for that matter, had even seen. Emotions ran raw as people in line slowly made their way toward the voting box. Literal tears of agony could be seen streaming down their faces as they were about to make the hardest decision of their lives. A "yes" vote meant that beginning on Sunday, the first day of the new week, all lands and property once considered sacred and eternal would be handed over to the people the Jews considered their mortal enemies in exchange for a promise of peaceful coexistence. A "no" vote would mean an open invitation for all-out war.

As the entire human world agonizingly sat back and awaited Israel's decision, God's angelic army calmly prepared for war.

"Michael, I know the outcome will be the same, but how do you think people will vote?" asked Pethel.

"It's hard to tell," admitted Michael. "These people are hard to read. They say one thing with their mouths, but their hearts say something else. I must admit I, too, am curious to see the outcome."

"What happens if the Israelis vote 'yes'?" Pethel asked. "Do we move all of our warriors back to the positions we held before 1967?"

"We have no other choice," Michael replied. "Unless the Lord himself says so, we cannot intervene. Rebellious man must suffer the consequences of his bad choices. "

"Michael," once again asked Pethel, "I know we've discussed this a thousand times before, but why is it that Jews always make the wrong choices? Don't they realize that they are covered by the covenant? They have God's eternal promises. They also have you and legions of angelic warriors to constantly watch over and protect them." Pethel briefly paused and looked directly into his commander's crystal blue eyes. "I know exactly what you are going to tell me. They are humans and humans are rebellious!"

Michael smiled. He fully understood his comrade's frustration with the weak human spirit, but Michael also knew that in spite of the human's shortcomings, their Creator still loved them.

"My friend, regardless of how the Jews vote," Michael reassured, "have confidence that God's prophetic plans will be fulfilled. Our warriors will be ready for anything Satan has in store."

Friday, March 9th
2 a.m. Standard Time
The 9,000 foot Summit of the Jabal Ash Shanin Ridge
Central Syria

The weather conditions couldn't be better, completely overcast with a fine light snow falling. Under the cloak of darkness, an unmarked armored truck arrived at its destination at the top Syria's Jabal Ash

Shanin ridge, the site of one of the most guarded secrets in the entire Middle East. The road ended at what appeared to be a small wooden structure built less than a hundred meters from the mountain's summit. As the vehicle came to a complete stop, a man fully concealed within a thick, fur-lined coat exited the structure's side door and approached the driver.

"Any trouble?" the man asked the driver.

"Did you expect any?" answered the driver as he stepped out of the truck onto the snow-covered rocky surface.

"Not with our officers positioned every ten kilometers along the entire 300 km route from the port of Tartus," smiled the man from the wooden structure as he embraced the driver with a big hug and some welcoming pats on the back.

"Nevertheless, Misha, we cannot be too careful," commented the driver as he warmly responded in turn with some hearty pats of his own. "The Israeli Mossad are well aware that we are up here and their spies are everywhere."

"Sergey, it's too cold to discuss these matters out here," Misha commented as he proceeded to slip on pair of thick, insulated gloves. "Help me unload our packages and then we can go inside to celebrate your successful journey over some Russian vodka and fresh caviar."

"Misha, are you serious?" Sergey asked. "We can't unload them all by ourselves! Each crate must weigh over a thousand kilos!"

Misha smiled as he removed what appeared to be a small remote-controlled device from his coat pocket. "I almost forgot." Misha again smiled. "This is your first visit to Jabal Ash Shanin. Stand back, my comrade, and be amazed."

With the click of a button, the structure's wooden double doors opened and what appeared to be a large forklift accompanied by at least a dozen Russian soldiers exited and proceeded to move toward the truck.

"Perhaps they can help lend us assistance." Misha laughed as he turned toward his friend.

"I think they can handle it all by themselves!" Sergey replied an equally hearty laugh. "Let's go inside and have some of that vodka you were telling me about."

Once he unlocked the truck's back cargo door, Sergey Petrov's three-hour mission was over. As a spy working for Russia's Foreign Intelligence Service, his assignment was simple. All he was required to do was transport a top-secret cargo along a deserted road linking the port of Tartus to a location high atop Syria's second highest mountain range. Little did Sergey realize that the mission he had just completed was his most important to date. He had safely delivered two four-by-eight-foot lead line crates, each containing a single, fully armed tactical nuclear warhead with enough power to destroy a large populated city.

Leaving the team of soldiers to remove the truck's clandestine cargo, the two Russian spies were met at the structure's entrance by Colonel Vladimir Ivanovich, the Russian commander in charge of the mountain's top-secret operations.

"Sergey, you are right on time, just as Misha said you would!" the colonel announced accompanied by a traditional Russian hug. "Come, let us show you where your precious cargo will go."

Sergey's eyes opened wide as he passed through the wooden doors into one of the most incredible of sights. The structure he had just entered was simply a wooden façade covering for what appeared to be a manmade cavern hewn out from the surrounding mountainside. Inside was a large, brightly lit cavity large enough to store several bulldozers and other highly sophisticated heavy-duty rock removing equipment.

"This is just our small foyer," M*i*sha jokingly commented. "Now you will visit our living room."

Sergey remained speechless as Misha and the colonel directed him to what appeared to be the stainless steel double doors of an elevator shaft. "This is just the beginning," Misha proudly stated as the three Russians stepped into the elevator. "This shaft goes down over thirty stories."

"How could we have done this without the Americans realizing it?" Sergey asked.

"The Americans know we are here," the colonel casually replied. "They can watch our every move by their spy satellites. Fortunately, they've been too preoccupied in Iraq to stop us. Their State Department protested a little, and that was that!"

"It is your special delivery tonight that the Americans have no clue about," Misha proudly stated. "All of their microwave transmissions were reflected off snow, making you totally invisible to their tracking satellites. And the thick lead lining of the crates prevented the radiation from your cargo from being detected."

As the elevator doors opened, Sergey once again stood speechless at the incredible sight before him. This was not the underground military facility that he had envisioned. It had the appearance of a small shopping mall, complete with flowing fountains surrounded by park-like benches.

"I told you wouldn't believe it," Misha bragged as he stepped out of the elevator and turned toward his friend. "Come, take a look!"

Sergey did just that. He proceeded to follow Misha and the colonel out into the underground courtyard filled with passing Russian military personnel of various ranks.

"Who would have the money to fund such a thing?" Sergey asked his Russian comrades.

"Sergey, you forget who we are dealing with!" Misha replied.

"Our friends have very deep pockets lined with oil," smiled the colonel.

Sergey responded to the colonel's comment with an equally big smile. He knew the Russian military could never afford to build such an extravagant facility on its own. Somewhere nearby was a wealthy Middle Eastern benefactor who also shared Russia's vision of a world without Israel.

"Comrade Petrov," asked Colonel Ivanovich, "follow us to the right and I will show you the final destination for your precious cargo."

"Commander, you are smiling like the human called Misha," commented Gog as he and Apollon followed closely behind their human escorts.

"Perhaps," replied his demon commander, "but I smile for an entirely different reason. The human is simply in awe of the natural sights that are pricking his senses. I, on the other hand, am eager to see the fulfillment of my dreams."

The group of three humans and two demons had to stop momentarily for a security check in front of a large set of stainless steel double doors. They were now about to enter the most restricted area of the entire underground complex. To gain entry, each human was required to have both their retinas and fingerprints scanned at the same time. As the large steel entrance doors opened, the combined party of humans and demons stood in speechless awe at the sight before them. Rising over sixteen meters above the solid rock floor below was the Russian version of the Iranian SHEHAB-4 medium range missile with a range of over 3500 kilometers.

"Comrade Petrov," Colonel Ivanovich smugly pointed toward the top of the ominous object, "Do you notice something missing from this missile?"

"Yes, Colonel Ivanovich," Sergey replied as he turned toward the colonel. "I believe it is missing its warhead."

"Correct, Comrade Petrov!" stated Colonel Ivanovich. "Come tomorrow, one of the two packages you just delivered will find its place on top of this missile. The other will be attached to its sister missile resting peacefully in another missile silo just a few meters from where we now stand."

Misha gestured a thumbs up to his comrade Sergey for a job well done.

The two demonic princes continued to stand in awe marveling at the massive missile.

"I take it that this impressive creation of yours is also part of our plan A?" Apollon asked.

"Your intuition serves you well, my commander," Gog responded without the slightest detection in his voice of pride or emotion. "Early in the morning of the next new moon, this missile, along with its twin sister in the next silo, will eliminate once and for all Israel's luxury of having a first strike capability. In as little as eight short minutes, the Israeli cit-

ies of Haifa and Tel Aviv along with Israel's hidden arsenal of nuclear weapons will be no more."

"What about Israel's protective shield of arrow defense missiles?" Apollon questioned. "Won't they be able to intercept and destroy these missiles before they arrive?"

The SHEHBA-4 was built specifically to fly fast enough and out of the range of any missiles in Israel's defensive arsenal," Gog replied, "but just in case, I have Plan B."

For the first time, the normally emotionless demonic prince of the north displayed a slight tinge of a smile.

"While we are all alone, would you mind sharing your Plan B with me?" Apollo requested.

"Only when the time comes, my Lord," Gog responded, not willing to divulge any hint of his secret.

As the humans were about to leave the missile silo, Sergey made mention of the large blue Arabic letters written vertically along the side of the missile.

"Colonel, what is that message written in Arabic along the side of the missile?"

"Death to Israel!" the Russian colonel and the demonic princes all replied in unison.

Friday, March 9th
2:45 a.m. Standard Time
The Russian Naval Base
Tartus, Syria

With the exception of the watchful eyes of the free-world's intelligence gatherers, the rapid expansion of Russia's naval presence in the Syrian coastal port of Tartus has been totally ignored by the Western media. Beginning with the dredging Tartus' harbor in the year 2000, Russia has done nothing to hide its ambitions of making Syria's second most important Mediterranean port a permanent naval base for its Black Sea Fleet of warships. It was also during this time that the Russians installed in the Syrian port a highly sophisticated defense system for the dual purpose of protecting their Tartus Naval Base and also for the launching of Iran mass produced SHEHAB-3 missiles made for the purpose of intercepting incoming ballistic missiles. At present, the entire naval base is totally operated by the Russian military with absolutely no Syrian involvement.

Throughout the long, lonely night, two Russian soldiers armed with AK- 47 Assault Rifles stood guard at their assigned post along the brightly lit docks of the Tartus Russian Naval Base. To amuse themselves, soldiers entertained thoughts that the long black objects they were guarding were perhaps some form of evil sea serpents. Little did they realize that the objects they were assigned to protect didn't even belong to Russia. They were in fact two special ordered Russian-made Kilo class submarines recently purchased by Iran and soon to be manned by Iranian naval personnel.

The soldier's thoughts of evil sea serpents were much closer to the truth than they even realized. Unbeknownst to these human guards, an entire host of demons had also been assigned to safeguard each submarine's precious contents. Secretly concealed within each of the Iranian vessels were two of modern naval warfare's deadliest weapons, the first being the Russian Klub-3M54 missile. What made this submarine-based missile so deadly was that each Klub-3M54 was tipped with a single tactical nuclear warhead capable of destroying an entire city within a range of 300 kilometers.

Even more ominous were a pair of 6,000-pound Russian-made Shkyal rocket torpedoes totally hidden within the depths of the twin submarines' torpedo rooms. These killer torpedoes were designed to literally fly through the water at more than 230 miles an hour, too fast to be detected by sonar. It was their stealth design that made these ingenious weapons so terrifying; for attached to each torpedo was also a tactical nuclear warhead capable of being launched at close range at an unsuspecting land-based harbor without ever being detected.

All the hellish ingredients for Gog's Plan B were now in place. All that was needed now was a human crew charged with the task of guiding each of these nightmarish instruments of death and destruction to their prophesied destinations: the Israeli seaports of Haifa and Tel Aviv.

Chapter Twenty

"The last hour will not come before the Muslims fight the Jews and the Muslims kill them, so that Jews will hide behind stones and trees and the stone and the trees will say, O Muslim, O servant of God! There is a Jew behind me; come and kill him."

Surah 9:30

When Muhammad died on June 8, 632, he left no document appointed a successor. Arguments soon broke out among his followers as to whether the successor to the great prophet should be elected or chosen through heredity. Some thought his heir should come from one of the original converts who had taught with Muhammad while others suggested from a powerful political family in the area. Still others felt that 'Ali, the cousin and son-in-law of Muhammad, had been divinely designated as his successor. The eventual outcome of the Muslim power struggle over choosing Muhammad's successor produced the two main denominations of Islam known today as the Sunnis (followers of the prophet's way) and the Shi'a (Shiites).

The Sunni school of Islam does not require as rigid a structure in its religious leadership. Sunnis, the majority of Muslims in the world (possibly 90 percent of Islam's adherents), consider themselves the "orthodox" faithful of Islam. In Sunni practice, leadership is a temporal issue, not a divine ordinance. They believe that succession from the Prophet Mohammed is a political matter to be determined by consensus or election rather than by inheritance through the line of family and tribal successors of the Prophet Mohammed.

In contrast, the Shi'a place a greater emphasis on the need for a spiritual leader and authoritative powers. Shiite leaders promote a fundamental interpretation of the Qur'an and strict adherence to its teachings. Consequently, Shiite religious leaders exercise great authority in guiding religious practice and interpreting doctrine and dogma. Shiites also follow a line of religious leadership, the imams, descended from Ali, cousin of Muhammad. They believe that Ali's succession itself resulted from specific appointment by Muhammad, who acted under divine guidance, and that twelve successive imams came to the appointment through divine intervention.

The most orthodox among Shiites believe that due to the mysterious disappearance of the last imam in the ninth century at the age of nine, only twelve imams have succeeded Muhammad. All subsequent leaders called mullahs or ayatollahs have since been divinely appointed by Allah to interpret Islamic law and doctrine under the inspiration of this Hidden 12th Imam or Madhi as he is commonly called. The entire credibility of the establishment Shiite systems as with Iran's mullah-run theocracy rests on the concept that the ayatollahs function as deputies of the Twelfth Imam on earth in his absence.

For Shiite Muslims, it is believed that the long-awaited return of Mohammed's successor, the Hidden 12th Imam, will bring about total world peace with the Islamic forces of good defeating the heathen forces of evil. When the Madhi returns at the end of the time, he will teach and lead all humanity to Allah's truth.

Wednesday, March 14th
4 p.m. Standard Time
Jamkaran, Iran

Even before the rising of the sun, a convoy of tour buses illuminated the only desert road leading to one of Islam's most beautiful, totally refurbished holy shrines, appearing on the darkened horizon as a blazing golden gem. Located only a few kilometers to the east of the Shiite holy city of Qom, this once dusty brown village was home for over a thousand years to the tiny, run-down Jamkaran Mosque.

After centuries of neglect, Islam's most overlooked holy site has now been transformed into one of the most breathtaking of shrines, built solely to honor the soon returning Madhi.

Shiite legend holds that this was the exact spot where the Madhi, the Hidden 12th Imam, took up residence in a subterranean well after his disappearance in the ninth century. The Mahdi was to remain in seclusion within the well until some future day when Allah calls him out of hiding to reign over a world in which Islam is universally embraced.

All morning long, with the newly constructed Jamkaran Mosque as a backdrop, tens of thousands of Shiite faithful have been gathering in front of a large, newly constructed stage surrounded by huge amplified speakers and an enormous video display. At first glance, today's massive gathering had all the earmarks of a peaceful outdoor religious concert. There were those who had visible tears streaming down their faces, while others either sat or stood listening intently to the words being sung by a group of singers performing on the large raised stage; but this was no music concert. Nor were the words being sung by the maddahs (veiled female and male religious singers) peaceful in nature. They were apocalyptic verses beseeching Allah for the immediate return of the Hidden 12th Imam, Muhammad al-Mahdi, the Shiite equivalent of the Christian messiah. At the close of their performance, the lead singer stood at the microphone and chanted a closing prayer.

"O mighty Lord Allah, we pray to you to hasten the emergence of your last repository, the Promised One, that perfect and pure human being, the one that will fill this world with justice and peace."

Those pacifying words stood in stark contrast to an ominous message written in red letters on a large black banner suspended high above the stage for all to see. Reminiscent of the Nazi hate messages of the 1930s, the first line read "Picture a world without Zionism!" followed by "Wipe Israel off the face of the Earth!"

Once the maddahs had exited the stage, a hush settled over the expectant multitudes. All eyes were now fixed on a thin-framed man, sitting with legs crossed all alone on the stage above. Wearing a casual disco-styled light blue suit and open-necked white shirt, his relaxed appearance stood in stark contrast to his reputation as being the most dangerous man on earth since Adolf Hitler.

Checking the time on his wristwatch, he smiled to himself. "It is time!" an audible voice inside his head affirmed.

Standing to his feet, the Iranian president confidently walked up and positioned himself to the left of his country's national flag. The moment he placed his right hand up to his heart, an entire chorus of children seated to the right of the stage stood to their feet and began singing the verses of the anthem of Islamic Republic of Iran.

"Entrance upwards on the horizon rises the Eastern Sun,

The sight of the true Religion, Bahman- the brilliant of our Faith.

Your message, O Imam, of independence and freedom is imprinted on our souls.

O Martyrs! The time of your cries of pain rings in our ears. Enduring, continuing, eternal, The Islamic Republic of Iran."

The voices of the Iranian children were soon joined by the voices of thousands of their countrymen. With the aid of the giant video display and several strategically placed amplified speakers, even the late arrivals seated at the far reaches of the newly paved parking lot turned outdoor arena could see and hear everything clearly.

It was now 4 p.m. The late winter sunshine that provided warmth all morning and into the afternoon for the tens of thousand of Shiite pilgrims had now vanished behind a thick overcast of dark foreboding clouds. Standing alone at a podium positioned near the edge of the stage was a man of vast contradictions. He was considered by some to be a peaceful family man who sometimes drove his 30-year-old Peugeot to work. To others, he was viewed as a brilliant intellect, a college educated PhD who lectured from time to time at the University of Tehran. But to his critics, both inside and outside of Iran, he was feared as the single most dangerous individual to the stability of the world. Recent Western headlines had painted him as a man crazy enough to nuke Israel and wipe out the Jews, even if it meant igniting a nuclear war that ended all civilization.

Today was the day that man standing alone at the podium, Iranian

President Mahmoud Ahmadinejad, the former mayor of Tehran, the elected president of the Republic of Iran, had long awaited, the day he planned to fulfill his promise to his followers. As the most powerful member of the semi-clandestine apolitical Iranian organization Hojjatieh, this soft-spoken son of a blacksmith had sworn to his followers to provoke chaos on a global scale in order to hasten the arrival of the messianic 12th Imam.

Before saying a word, the president looked toward heaven and silently prayed, "Lord Allah, I stand here before you and your people as your humble servant, a willing vessel here to do your bidding. Now is the time to bring an end to your enemies, the godless infidel and the hated Jew. I beseech you now, release the Madhi from his safekeeping."

Everyone in the crowd below gasped as a beam of intense light radiated down from a break in the clouds above, brightly illuminating the entire stage, but no more. Allahzad smiled broadly, for his moment on the world stage had finally come. With his claw-like hands buried deep within the Iranian president's torso, the demon Prince of Persia began to speak through his human host the same kind of mesmerizing message spoken less than a century earlier through a human vessel named Adolf Hitler.

For only the second time in his presidency, Mahmoud Ahmadinejad was about to experience the exhilarating empowerment of a supernatural presence while delivering a major speech. His first encounter with the supernatural occurred while addressing the UN General Assembly in September of 2005. Then, as now, an aura of bright light completely surrounded him at the podium as world leaders in the audience sat unblinkingly focused upon him.

With the unusual light remaining in place, President Mahmoud Ahmadinejad looked down at the awestruck multitudes seated before him and began repeating the exact words that Allahzad spoke, "My faithful followers, I am honored to be with you today of all days, the day we honor our beloved Madhi's birth. Today, I come with exceedingly good news. Our beloved Madhi has ended his seclusion."

Each man stood to his feet and stared at each other in awe of what they had just heard. *The Madhi has been released!* they thought to themselves. *Praise Allah, where is he located?*

"As I speak," the president continued, "the Madhi is here among us and he wants you to know that now is the time he calls all of his faithful servants to fulfill the words of our great prophet Muhammad."

The president's voice instantly deepened, taking on a more pronounced tone.

"The last hour has now come. We, the defenders of the faith, are called to hunt down every last Jew and kill them. Allah cries out to all of you, O Muslims, O servants of God, if the Jews will hide behind stones, the stone will say, 'There is a Jew behind me; come and kill him.'"

As the video cameras zoomed in on Ahmadinejad's face, the crowds viewing the huge video display marveled as their president's calm demeanor transformed before their eyes to a commanding presence the likes of which they have never seen.

"If you do not believe me, O blind ones of little faith," Allahzard thundered with such force as to stretch his human host's vocal chords almost beyond their breaking point, "then who do you think performed the mighty miracles we have all been witness to over the past month? The power of the Madhi has brought the Great Satan, America, the protectorate of the Jews, to its knees. Israel is now ripe for the taking!"

Allahzad paused momentarily, allowing a brief respite for his human's voice to recover.

A broad foreboding smile appeared on the president's face as he glared down at his mesmerized audience.

Standing to the president's immediate right, Allahzad also gloated at the expression fear and awe on the faces of the humans below.

"They are ready!" Allahzah softly spoke into his human's ear. "Now get ready for the grand finale."

An expression of pure evil emanated out from the demon spirit as he repositioned himself in back of the Iranian president. It was now time for the Prince of Persia to showcase the power of the Madhi, Allahzad's greatest act of deception. By thrusting his clawed hands deep into Ahmadinejad's chest, the ancient demon once again gained control of his human host's senses. Allahzad was now able to speak his carefully crafted lies to the brainwashed Shiite masses below.

"I swear before Allah, and all of my Muslim brothers, that before the sun sets tonight, the great Madhi will perform a miracle so frightful that all the world will tremble in fear and declare that Allah alone is god of the earth!"

Wednesday, March 14*th*
7 a.m. Eastern Standard Time
New Madrid, Missouri

Not much ever happens in New Madrid, Missouri. For the majority of the town's three thousand residents, sunrise only means another day of getting up and going downtown to check the job postings on courthouse wall. Nearly all of the good paying manufacturing jobs that once sustained New Madrid's small population are long gone, the victims of cheap foreign imports. But unlike so many of the small, impoverished river towns that dot the banks along the Mississippi, New Madrid does have one infamous claim to fame. It was ground zero to of one the greatest natural disasters ever to strike the North American continent.

Nine days before Christmas on December 16, 1811, this wilderness town, located downstream from where the Ohio and Missouri rivers meet the Mississippi, was struck without warning by an earthquake of unimaginable proportions. At exactly 2 a.m., a violent shaking and a roaring sound so deafening as to literally shatter eardrums abruptly awakened the terrified residents in New Madrid. Rising mounds of fractured earth instantly swallowed up the entire countryside surrounding the town of 400 residents. Forests were flattened, islands disappeared, and the Mississippi River shifted its course by over three miles. Survivors reported that the ground they stood on actually rolled, rising and falling like ocean waves. Damage was reported as far away as Charleston, South Carolina, and Washington, D.C.

with brick chimneys reportedly collapsing in Maine. So intense was the shaking that President James Madison was awakened from a deep sleep thinking intruders were in the White House. It has been estimated that the New Madrid Earthquake of 1811 affected more than 1 million square miles. Except for the 9.2 magnitude Good Friday Earthquake that struck Anchorage Alaska in 1964, no other North American natural disaster compares to that legendary event.

Time has since erased most of the earthquake's visible scars, but the cause of this great natural disaster, a 150-mile-long subterranean line of weakness known as the New Madrid Fault remains forever hidden beneath the tons of sediment deposited by the Mississippi River from America's heartland. Unlike the more elastic faults that underlie California and Japan, the ground above the New Madrid Fault is brittle. When it moves, there is no elasticity. The vibrations produced are so devastating and widespread that the ground has been known to actually liquefy causing surface features such as building and bridges to sink as if in quicksand.

An earthquake of equal intensity today would hit the cities of Memphis and St. Louis head-on. The loss of life would be on a scale never before imagined. Bridges, levees, sewage and water treatment plants up and down the river would be destroyed. Enormous destruction with property damage in the hundreds of billions of dollars would also be found in Kentucky, Ohio, Illinois, Arkansas, Indiana and Mississippi. From Californian to Maine, every region of American would be directly affected because almost every major natural gas and oil pipeline transverses the affected areas.

The frightening question still remains, when will the next great New Madrid earthquake strike America's heartland? Where once lived only rugged settlers and native Americans, today we find millions of Americans residing on top of a seismic time bomb that can explode at any moment.

Wednesday, March 14th
8 a.m. Eastern Standard Time
Providence, Rhode Island

Main Studio
Gospel Broadcasting Network (GBN)

Something was missing. With only minutes to go before the start of today's show, the auditorium was still empty. Noticeably absent were the enthusiastic claps and cheers from the live audience, all victims of the government-imposed travel restrictions. Also gone were the pleasant introductory scenes of happy families interacting at home, school, and church, replaced by the somber images of a nation gripped by tragedy.

"Ready on the set," PTW's director, Charlie Bennett alerts both his stage and control room technicians. "Cameras roll on five, - 4- 3–2- 1 . . ."

With the show's theme song playing in the background, the stage cameras panned in on PTW's host seated beside the day's special guest. With the flick of a finger, Charlie signaled his boss, televangelist Tom Reid, that he was now on live to over a million households all across America.

"Good morning, dear friends," Tom began the morning's broadcast with his ever-present, reassuring smile.

As Reid opened the show, a collage of images depicting sadness and misery from all across America was projected on the stage wall in back of him. "It was one month ago today that these horrific scenes you are now viewing became a hellish reality all across America and the question still remains on everyone's mind: 'Why?'"

Turning toward the camera to his right, Reid proceeded to list a series of hard-hitting questions.

"Why is it that only America is experiencing this nightmare?

"Why are only Americans getting sick and dying?

"Why hasn't there been a cure or vaccine by now?

"Why is our economy being dismantled right before our very eyes?

"And the number one question that remains in everyone's mind is 'Why hasn't God intervened by now?'"

The teleprompter positioned on the front of the stage began

flashing red, advising Reid it was time for him to warn parents that upcoming scenes may be too graphic for children to view. With that said, PTW's host continued.

"This past month, we at PTW have dedicated every single program to giving our viewers sound biblical reasons as to 'why' God may have permitted the unprecedented tragedies to strike only our country."

Reid went on to described the first of four reasons why God may have brought severe judgments on America. "We started by taking an in-depth look into the abortion issue and its effects on American society," Reid declared as an unbelievably clear 3D-image of a baby moving in the womb was projected in the background. "I can't even begin to imagine how God's heart must grieve over the deaths of each one of these precious little creations. To date, since the passing of Roe v. Wade on that infamous day on January 22, 1973, over 50 million innocent unborn American babies have been legally slaughtered in our country."

Like a hard-hitting trial lawyer stating his case before the jury, Reid clearly articulated every possible cause for America's present dilemma. Tapping in PWT's vast archives of video images to back up his claims, he one-by-one demonstrated how America's blatant refusal to recognize God's sovereignty over America has led to her gradual downfall. Issues ranging from the court system's judicial dismantling of America's once cherished Judeo-Christian foundations, the removal of God's Ten Commandments from public view, and the assault on the institution of marriage and it affects on the American family were discussed in detail.

"To summarize," Reid turned and sadly faced the cameras, "our society today is comprised of empty people desperately searching to fill their self-induced voids with sinful, lust-filled, self-gratifying lifestyles...To this end," Reid firmly stated before his viewers, "America has no hope!"

It only took Tom Reid a little over fifteen minutes to recap an entire month's worth of programs. It was now time to introduce today's guest, a man who could supply another answer as to why

God has possibly allowed America to enter His judgment. As the cameras panned out, Reid turned and introduced his guest.

"For today's show, I have asked a former guest to PTW to come back and present to our viewers another answer as to why our nation is presently experiencing these tragic dilemmas. Once again, I would like to welcome as my guest to PTW a former MIT mathematics professor, a NSA code breaker, a best-selling author, a Messianic Jew, and very good friend of mine, Dr. Ezra Schroeder."

Tom stood to his feet and graciously extended a hand welcoming his guest and friend. "I have invited Dr. Schroeder back on the show to share with us how he believes that America's present crisis is related to prophesied events foretold in the Bible, specifically how America's strained relationship with Israel may have contributed to our present dilemma."

As Reid continued to speak a picture of Sir Isaac Newton is displayed in the background. "Dr. Schroeder," Reid continued, "last year when you first appeared on the show, you brought to our attention a little-known fact about the world-renowned scientist Sir Isaac Newton. If my memory serves me correctly, your research has led you to believe that Newton had a life-long obsession that God had chosen him above all others to discover a hidden code placed purposely by God within the prophetic books of the Bible revealing the times and events related to Christ's Second Coming."

"Exactly," Schroeder replied. "Not only was Newton thoroughly convinced that this code existed, but he truly believed that before he died, God would reveal to him its coded message."

"You specifically commented at the end of last year's show that Newton died without that revelation being fulfilled," Reid interjected. "Has your view changed since then?"

"180 degrees, Dr. Reid!" Schroeder exclaimed.

"Please explain," Reid asked.

"A few weeks before I appeared on last year's show, an old leather-bound journal was donated to England's Cambridge University by a gentleman who claimed it had belonged to Sir Isaac Newton. The journal supposedly had been in his family's possession for over 300 years. Professor Harrison Andrews, the head secretary of Cambridge University's Royal Society of rare bibliographies contacted me and asked if I could come to England and assist in translating its contents."

"I understand from our conversations that Newton wrote in sort of a hidden code himself," Reid inquired.

"Unfortunate, but true," Schroeder concurred. "Complexity was one of Newton's trademarks. As I explained the last time I was here, Newton dabbled in the field of alchemy, a 17th century concoction of ancient chemistry and mysticism. He purposely wrote all of his works using the mystic symbols and metaphors of an alchemist."

"Where you able to interpret Newton's words?" probed Reid.

"Yes," Schroeder replied, "but again, with some difficultly. I did a lot of thinking as to why Newton made reading his works so difficult and I believe I now have the answer."

As Schroeder continued, excerpts from Newton's journal were shown to the home viewers.

"Well, I thought at first that Newton was a trickster, attempting to use confusing abstract clues to mislead me away from his message, but I was wrong," Schroeder confessed with a smile. "I believe I now know why he left certain clues behind. Isaac Newton intended his clues to act as keys to be used at a specific future date when advanced technology could make it possible to unlock the sealed prophesies of the Bible."

Reid was beside himself. Looking into the camera, he excitedly proclaimed, "I don't know what you folks are thinking at home right now, but I'm finding this absolutely fascinating! Please, go on, Dr. Schroeder."

"In the 12th Chapter of the book of Daniel, verse 4 says, and I quote, "But as for you, Daniel, conceal these words and seal up the book until the end of time; many will go to and fro, and knowledge will increase."

Schroeder looked directly into Tom Reid's eyes.

"Dr. Reid, isn't that exactly what we are witnessing right before our eyes?" he asked. "As we speak, aren't people in America running to and fro asking why is this happening? The key to opening God's sealed prophetic words is our present-day technology. As smart as Newton was, he couldn't do it! Computers and sophisticate software wouldn't be invented for another 300 years!"

"Let me stop you here , Dr. Schroeder, and recap what I think I'm hearing you say," Reid interjected. "You're saying that taking the clues that Newton left behind and applying them to our present high-speed computers, you have been able to unseal Daniel's prophecies?"

"Not only Daniel's, Dr. Reid, but all of God's prophesies!"

"Dr. Schroeder, this is the most astounding thing I have ever heard!" Reid admitted. "I can't believe I'm sitting here right now hearing you say this."

Reid paused before asking the next question. "What do the prophecies say?"

Wednesday, March 14*th*
8:14 *a.m. Eastern Standard Time*
3880 *Connecticut Ave NW, Apt* 58*A*
Washington, D.C.

In a high-rise apartment building with a breathtaking view overlooking Washington, D.C.'s Rock Creek Park, two humans sat in their living room completely absorbed by a conversation going on between two men on their large flat paneled television. *The humans were not the only beings in the room fixated on the television program. A two pair of yellow eyes was also watching the television intently from behind the humans.*

"Honey, my brother has finally lost his mind," scoffed an angry John Reid. "I can't believe he put Schroeder back on the show again!"

Miranda just sat propped by pillows at the end of their couch, slightly shaking her head, still too ill to speak. This was Miranda Reid's first day out of bed since being released from the hospital on

Monday with a severe kidney and bladder infection. Reid had been home since Monday, nursing his wife back to health.

"To think, I almost lost my job over that kook," Reid commented with his bosses' stinging reprimand still fresh on his mind. "I swear, when it comes to special favors, I'll never listen to my brother again!"

"Lord Beelazad, Schroeder must be stopped!" declared Zorah, the Reid's assigned spirit. "He is about to tell the entire world of our plans."

"He better say it fast," turned and smiled Beelazad, looking up at the ticking hands on the wall clock. "He only has fifteen more seconds!"

Wednesday, March 14*th*
7:15 *a.m. Central Standard Time*
Four Miles South of New Madrid, Missouri

"Lord Satan," Amducious announced as he bowed low before his master.

"I've waited a very long time to see this moment," Satan's middle head spoke while the adjacent heads just sneered and chuckled.

"I, too, my Lord," Amducious affirmed as he stood and placed his left fist against his chest.

"I will hold you accountable if this doesn't work, Amducious," the center head retorted. "I want this done right, just like we practiced. No miscalculations or excuses, do I make myself clear?"

"Yes, my Lord Satan," Amducious replied with a confident smirk. Thousands of his demons were now strategically positioned all along the 150-mile-long subterranean fracture in the earth's crust. "The fault's pressure is even greater now than it was when I first demonstrated its power to you back in the human year 1811. Just give the order and America will be no more!"

"Very well," Satan agreed. "On my order, Commander, you are to count slowly to ten and then commence. I want to be right at the surface to witness this beautiful event for myself!"

Wednesday, March 14*th*

8:15 *a.m. Eastern Standard Time*
Providence, Rhode Island
Main Studio
Gospel Broadcasting Network (GBN)

Ariel looked sad. He was aware that PTW's daily ratings had skyrocketed ever since the pandemic was first declared, quarantining millions of Americans to their homes. New viewers had tuned in daily to hear God's tangible answers to their seemingly unanswerable questions. Knowing that millions of people would be watching today's show, Ariel wanted desperately for today to be the day that Schroeder announced God's prophetic plan to the entire world. He also knew that his plans were not God's plans and that Schroeder's announcement would have to wait until another time, predestined before the beginning of the world.

"Dr. Reid," Schroeder acknowledged with a nod of respect as he turned to face the cameras, "and my fellow Americans. What I am about to say, I say with the utmost of humility. God has honored me with the unfathomable privilege to sit here before millions of viewers and reveal, not only why America is going through these horrendous trials, but more importantly, how to stop them before the next one occurs."

"Then Dr. Schroeder, you truly believe that more judgments are to come?" asked Dr. Reid.

"There is no doubt about that in my mind, Dr. Reid," Schroeder replied. "Over this past month, Dr. Reid has come on this show daily, openly exposing a list of grievous sins that America has committed against a Holy God. God has sent us many warnings in the past, beseeching all of us to repent and return to honoring Him as America's sole benefactor. I'm afraid that the time for God's warnings is over. America has committed a sin so grievous that God has lifted His hedge of blessings and protection on America and now judgment has been handed down."

As Schroeder continued, a very familiar Bible verse was projected on the screen.

"Genesis Chapter 12 verse 3 says that God will bless those who bless Abraham's descendants, the Jews, and curse those who do harm to the Jews. America has finally crossed the line. America has turned her back on Israel, the Apple of God's Eye."

"Dr. Schroeder," Dr. Reid interjected, "this is really an important point. In your opinion, how has America turned its back on Israel?" "Excellent question, Dr. Reid," Schroeder agreed. "I beg Americans, from the president on down, to listen carefully and understand this all-important truth. It was God himself who deeded the land of Israel to the Jews. The Bible clearly states in Joel Chapter 3 that God promises to bring heavy judgment against any people or nations who divide the covenant land given to Abraham's descendants through his son Isaac."

"And you, Dr. Schroeder, firmly believe that America is presently under God's judgment for pressuring Israel to relinquish God's covenant land, which includes the Golan Heights, the entire West Bank, and East Jerusalem, in exchange for a peace agreement with its Arab neighbors that is tenuous at best?"

With tears streaming down his face, Schroeder conceded with a smile. "Yes, Dr. Reid, but I have good news to share with you. We can still sway the hand of God's judgment, but we must act right now before it is too late. The devil has a plan to destroy Israel and we can stop . . ."

Before Schroeder could finish his sentence, his chair was thrust forward, then backward. The lights in studio flickered for a few seconds before returning to normal brightness. Both Schroeder and Reid stared at each other, shocked and unable to speak.

"Are we still on the air?" the director rushed over to the control room and asked his equally shocked crew of technicians.

"I don't know!" replied Bill Pierce, the head control room tech. "Did we just have an earthquake?

"That was either an earthquake or a nearby explosion!" the camera man replied.

"There's been a major earthquake." shouted a frantic female voice from the back entrance to the studio. It was Janet Filbert, the show's producer who had just stepped out briefly to locate a forgotten item in her car.

"An earthquake in Providence?" a confused Charlie Bennett asked.

"No, those were just shock waves," she replied as she ran toward the control booth. "The reporter on my car radio says that the epicenter was somewhere close to Memphis, Tennessee, or perhaps St. Louis."

"My God, that's over a thousand miles from here!" Charlie responded. "I never heard of shockwaves traveling such a distance."

"Everybody, come hear," beaconed Bill Pierce. "I have a live satellite feed from someone named Max stationed near St. Louis. I'm going to download it directly into our lines."

Everyone in the studio, over a dozen members of PTW staff, including the show's host Tom Reid and his guest Ezra Schroeder, gathered around the large onstage television monitor to witness the unbelievable scenes being broadcast over a thousand miles away. A man standing in front of what appeared to be a totally demolished shopping center was about to speak.

"This is Max Gilman for our FOX affiliate in St. Louis KMOZ reporting in front of a Wal-Mart parking lot, approximately fifteen miles from downtown St Louis. As you can see as my cameraman pans around, there is devastation all around me. The only words I can use to describe what I am seeing are scenes from 'hell.'"

The reporter paused listening intently to a message being broadcast on his remote headset. "Let me repeat what I just heard," Gilman continued. "According to the U.S. Geologic Survey, at approximately 7:15 a.m. central time this morning, a catastrophic earthquake registering an unprecedented 9.4 on the Richter has struck America's heartland. When it struck, my cameraman and I were parked only about twenty feet from where I am now standing. We were attempting to set our equipment for a story about the local St. Patty's day race that was scheduled to begin here a 8 a.m. At approximately 7:16, my camera man and I looked up to witness one of the most incredible sights imaginable. I can only describe it as a giant tsunami made up of a combination of land, buildings, and concrete coming right toward us out of the southeast. This monster wave literally picked up our entire van and lifted us, van and all, I can only guess, over twenty feet in the air before depositing us down at our present location."

Once again, the reporter paused briefly to gather more information on this rapidly unfolding story. "I'm right now receiving unbelievable reports coming from helicopters flying over the downtown area," Gilman reported. "They are saying there is no way into or out of the city of St. Louis. Most of the downtown area along the waterfront including St. Louis' famous Gateway Arch has completely vanished, swallowed up by earth. That includes all roads, bridges, and overpasses."

Trembling and visibly pale, Ezra Schroeder turned away from the horrific scenes on the monitor and stood face to face with an equally shocked Tom Reid. "Tom, I don't know how it can be arranged, but I need to see the president. I believe this time she will listen."

Tom just stood there, unable to respond. Of all times to make such as an outlandish request, but inside his spirit Schroeder was right. The president had to be made aware that only her actions could bring an end to all of this devastation.

Wednesday, March 14*th*
4:18 *p.m.*
Jamkaran, Iran

Halfway around the world, a deafening cry from thousands of elated Shiite voices could be heard throughout Jamkaran praising Allah for the wonderful "miracle" they had just witnessed on the huge video display.

"Praise be to Allah!" shouted a euphoric Iranian President Ahmadinejad with tears of joy streaming down his bearded face. Standing at the podium with his arms raised upward, the president openly declared. "Right before our eyes, our beloved Madhi has destroyed America, the Great Satan! My Muslim brothers, this mighty miracle is just the beginning. I also pledge that before the next new moon, Israel, the little Satan, will be no more! Once our enemies are defeated, Allah's peace will reign throughout the earth.

Chapter Twenty-One

"And at that time shall Michael stand up, the great prince which stands for the children of thy people: and there shall be a time of trouble, such as never was since there was a nation [even] to that same time."

Daniel 12:1 KJV

On February 12, 2003, a month before America's invasion in Iraq, a secret mission went virtually unnoticed by the watchful eyes of the world's surveillance community. Under a cloak of darkness, over a dozen heavily armed Iraqi military trucks poured over the Syrian border. The last of Saddam Hussein's vast arsenal of weapons of mass destruction (WMD) had now crossed the Iraq/Syrian border destined for safekeeping in a temporary storage site somewhere in central Syria. Someday in the very near future, Saddam's deadly arsenal will move once more to a clandestine location high in central Syrian mountains. Once it has arrived at this final destination, these instruments of death and destruction will be mounted at the top of designated long-range missiles and rockets. Satan himself will then give the orders to launch the most lethal combination of chemical, biological, and nuclear weapons known to mankind at the deceased Iraqi dictator's original intended target, the Jewish State of Israel.

Thursday, March 22nd
12:46 *a.m. Israeli Standard Time*
Jerusalem, Israel

Try as he may, sleep would not come to Yacov Ben Yizri. For the past several hours he lay awake in bed beside his sleeping wife of forty-four years, Sybil, just staring at the clock on the nightstand. There were too many unsolved issues, too many unknowns to think about in order to give his sharp analytical mind the peace it needed to fall asleep. He kept agonizing over the same thoughts. *If only I could go back and undo what's already been done. We are sacrificing too much with so little in return!*

The very notion that he, Yacov Ben Yizri, the current Israel Prime Minister, would be the first Jew on record responsible for signing away a portion of God's covenant land, a land deemed militarily strategic to his nation's survival, to his sworn enemies was more than he could bear. All that was left was tomorrow's historic signing in East Jerusalem, a day he never dreamt in all of his sixty-four years.

The Israeli Prime Minister knew in his heart that there was no going back. The votes from the referendum were all counted and the results certified. His peace-starved people had voted by almost a two to one margin to accept the Arab League's terms. At noon Greenwich time tomorrow, with the Western Wall as a backdrop and all the eyes of the world watching, he was scheduled to sit down with his Palestinian and Syrian counterparts and sign a treaty relinquishing Israel's sacred land in exchange for peace with its Arab neighbors. Once all the papers were signed, the Palestinians would finally have their promised state with borders that included all the lands of Judea and Samaria up to the Jordan River. The Israelis would also relinquish a large section of East Jerusalem designated to become the new Palestinian Capital. The Syrians, on the other hand, would once again possess the whole of Golan Heights with its southern borders on Lake Kinneret.

If only we could have waited just one more week! his tortured mind again reflected. *I know the people would have voted differently!*

No one could have foreseen it coming. A little over a week after Israel's referendum vote, the United States of America, by far Israel's greatest financial backer, was devastated by a catastrophic earthquake of unimaginable proportions. The morning headlines of the Jerusalem Post read, "How can a devastated America fulfill its financial commitment toward Israel's disengagement plan?" This alone sent aftershocks of unsettling doubt throughout the Israeli community.

Even more disturbing were the secondary headlines describing leaked Mossad intelligence reports of eminent missile attacks on Israel by the Iranian-backed Islamic terrorist groups. Headlines read, "Hezbollah and Hamas militants pin America's woes as a sign of Allah's divine intervention. Attacks will soon follow on unprotected Zionists!"

As the prime minister made one more attempt to find a comfortable sleeping position, a luminous hand reached out of the darkness and imperceptivity touched the restless human on the side of his head.

"Peace be to your troubled mind, Yacov Ben Yizri," spoke the commanding voice of Michael. No sooner had the Archangel declared those words, than the Israeli Prime Minister was fast asleep.

"Guard him well!" Michael charged the large dark-skinned angelic warrior standing to his right.

"You have my word, Commander," assured Ramiel, Ben Yizri's angelic guardian. "The prime minister will never leave my sight."

The two massive angels now stood side by side, gazing out a large balcony window at Jerusalem's darkened skyline. Sensing concern in his commander's voice, Ramiel turned toward him and commented, "Commander, you seem troubled."

Ramiel stood shocked to see a visible tear in the Archangel's crystal clear blue eyes.

"I am troubled," Michael admitted, "but it is not about the outcome. I have no doubt we will be victorious!"

Michael, God's appointed Captain of His Heavenly Host, the Prince and Guardian over Israel, turned away from the window and looked down at the sleeping Prime Minister and his wife.

"My tears are for the thousands of innocent victims who are about to die without ever knowing the truth about their Messiah."

"When will it all start, Commander?" Ramiel quietly asked.

"In less than three hours from now," Michael replied. "I must leave now and join our fellow warriors."

Placing his massive hand on his subordinate's shoulder, Michael gave the prime minister's guardian one parting command.

"Let him sleep until then. It may be the last sleep he receives for a very long time."

Thursday, March 22nd
4 a.m. Israeli Standard Time
Jerusalem, Israel

Ever since Israel captured the Golan Heights plateau from Syria during the 1967 Six-Day War, tensions between Syria and Israel have continued to escalate, almost to the brink of war. As far as Syria was concerned, the Golan was theirs, no questions asked.

To Israel, this strategically positioned plateau, which was annexed as Israel's northeastern border in 1981, was indispensable. With it elevations ranging from 2,900 feet in the south and 7,100 feet in the north at Mt. Hermon, the Golan Heights has provided Israel essential defensive observation posts and excellent offensive firing positions to deter any concerted Arab attack. But just as essential to Israel's security, the Golan's snow-fed springs and rivers furnish over one third of the tiny nation's fresh water supply. The Golan watershed is also the only source of water for irrigating the Hula Valley below, Israel's richest agricultural area.

Standing guard along a high ridge-top plateau overlooking the Syrian border, a lone Israeli soldier checks the time on his watch. *Who would have thought,* he smiled to himself, *tomorrow night at this time a Syrian soldier might be assigned guard duty at this very spot.*

Come tomorrow, his tiny Israeli Outpost 8, located only meters from the Syrian border, was schedule to be decommissioned. Such would also be the fate of over a dozen more Israeli observation posts strategically positioned along the 20 kilometer wide Israeli/Syrian border. Within an hour of the signing of the historic peace treaty, Israel was required to surrender its almost forty-year control of the entire Golan ridge to the Syrian military forces.

The six Israeli soldiers of Outpost 8 had spent the previous day dismantling and packing up their surveillance equipment in anticipation of tomorrow's order to relinquish their high ground positions. Some soldiers would be redeployed elsewhere along Israel's newly established borders. Others had already been reassigned to assist Israeli citizens from the over thirty Jewish towns and kibbutzim scattered throughout the Golan Height to resettle safely within Israeli's newly assigned borders.

Tonight's moonless sky was exceptionally dark and clear. Standing alone along a chest-high stone wall, the Israeli guard marveled at the spectacular inky black star-lit sky above, a scene that he knew he would never be witness to again. Below his ridge-top position could be seen the lights from Syrian towns and cities as far away as Damascus.

"Uzi?" quietly projected a familiar voice from behind their stone bunker.

"Beny, I'm over here," Uzi Ebban commented, keeping his voice low enough as to not awaken his sleeping comrades inside the bunker.

"The sun will be up in a couple hours," Beny Rosen commented as he approached his fellow soldier and childhood friend. "Why don't you go in and get some sleep?"

"Thanks anyhow," Uzi replied as he placed his hand his friend's shoulder. "My duty ends in a hour," he commented as he again looked at the vast expanse of stars above, "and besides, I'm enjoying the view! And what gets you up a 4 a.m.?"

"I couldn't help it," Beny responded with a childish giggle. "I woke with my bladder ready to burst from all the beer I drank at last night's going away party."

"Wow!" Uzi excitedly remarked as he pointed in wonderment

at a streaking flash across the sky. "I've never seen a meteorite so large!"

"There goes another!" shouted Beny, loud enough to arouse some of the soldiers sleeping inside the bunker.

"What's going on out here?" shouted the small company's commander, 2nd lieutenant Ephraim Sneh.

"Sir, you needed to come out here and see this!" shouted back an utterly stunned Uzi.

In less than a minute's time, the beds inside the stone bunker were empty. All six Israeli soldiers assigned to Outpost 8 stood shivering out in the cold night air along their ridge-top position watching in horrified awe as what appeared to be over a dozen streaks of intensely bright light moved upward out of the darkened Syrian landscape below. Now high overhead, the bright objects crossed the border into Israel.

"They appear too large to be Katyushas!" observed corporal Moshe Kaplinsky as the rockets whizzed toward their location.

"Sir, they're even bigger than the Iranian Fajr-5!" Uzi commented as he turned to observe the thunderous fiery plumes passing overhead.

"They're Iranian-built Zelzal-2," shouted out the lieutenant as he followed the large cigar-shaped objects appearing to be destined for somewhere deep within Israel's heartland. "They can carry up to a 1,300 kg warhead as much as 200 kilometers."

"My God," shouted out an emotional Beny Rosen. "They could be headed for our central and southern cities!"

"Why are they doing this?" cried out Uzi Ebban. "Weren't we giving the Syrians everything they wanted!"

"Not everything," Lieutenant Sneh sadly replied as he shook his head in disbelief. "They obviously want all the Jews dead!"

Thursday, March 22nd
4:06 a.m. Israeli Standard Time
Jerusalem, Israel

After several hours of wrestling with his thoughts, the prime minister's troubled mind had finally surrendered to a deep sleep. Unfortunately, his deep state of sleep came to an abrupt end with the ringing of the telephone on the nightstand beside his bed.

"Yes?" responded the groggy Prime Minister holding the receiver to his ear.

"Yacov," replied the familiar voice of Avi Timar, his Minister of Defense.

"Avi?"

"Yacov, we are under a rocket attack!"

The prime minister instantly sat up in bed and looked around the darkened room. *This can't be! Tomorrow we sign a peace treaty,* the prime minister quickly thought to himself. *I must be having a bad dream!*

"Yacov, what's wrong?" pleaded his concerned wife beside him.

"Sybil, I don't know," announced her confused husband. "Avi Timar is saying we are under a rocket attack."

"Yacov, please listen carefully," interjected his defense minister. "The intelligence reports are still coming, but at approximately 4 a.m., over a dozen Zelzal-2 rockets were launched from a site somewhere along the Syria side of the Golan border."

"What were the targets?" demanded the prime minister.

"We have two confirmed strikes on the Haifa oil refineries," the defense minister replied. "We have reports of rockets striking Haifa's port, and a direct strike on Haifa University. The remaining rockets struck through out the city of Tel Aviv."

"What about our defense missiles?" the prime minister again demanded. "Our Arrow-2s should have destroyed any incoming Syrian rockets."

"Yacov, they caught us unprepared. Don't you remember—we were in the process of repositioning and reprogramming all of our missile defense systems to match up with our new borders."

"My God, Avi, this is insanity," the prime minister cried out. "Why would the Syrians do this now of all times?"

"Yacov, we don't believe the Syrians are directly responsible,"

Avi Timar responded in a firm voice. "We think it was a desperate attempt by Hezbollah to derail today's signing."

"Avi, it may very well be Hezbollah that launched those rockets," interjected Ben Yizri in an equally firm voice, "but I hold Syria directly responsible for allowing them the freedom and capabilities to perform such as a despicable act of war."

"Yacov, I'm afraid there's more," Avi announced.

Silence

"At the same time the Syrian missiles were launched, Hamas released a barrage of over one hundred Katyushas and Qassam rockets from both the Gaza and the West Bank, striking our southern cities of Ashdod, Sederot, Ashqelon and Natanya along the central coast."

"So much for peace with your neighbors!" commented the frustrated Prime Minister.

"Yacov, what would you have me do?"

With a look of determined resolve, Yacov Ben Yizri quickly responded, "An eye for an eye."

Avi Timar stood totally speechless. He was fully aware of the potential consequences of an eye for an eye response.

"We have no other choice," the prime minister soberly declared. "The Syrians attacked our cities. We will attack theirs. Launch surgical strikes against the Syrian refineries and against all known Hezbollah targets and identified rocket and missile sites throughout Syria."

"What about today's treaty signing?" asked the defense minister.

"There will be no signing with the devil!" responded back the resolute voice of the Israeli Prime Minister.

"Well said," proudly commented the prime minister's guardian Ramiel, observing from the background.

Thursday, March 22nd
6:00 a.m. Eastern Standard Time
Washington, D.C.
Oval Office

West Wing of the White House

Like clockwork, the first person seen by the president every morning was her tall, lanky Director of National Intelligence, Jonathan Burgess. From 6 until 6:30 a.m., no one else was permitted access to the Oval Office until the president's chief intelligence advisor had thoroughly briefed America's Commander and Chief on all matters related to national security.

Due to the explosive events unfolding in the Middle East, the president deemed it necessary to invite three other strategic members of her own cabinet to be present for this morning's daily Presidential brief. Joining the DNI chief was the Vice President, Neil O'Sullivan, the Secretary of the State, James Metloff, and the Secretary of Defense, Leslie Schaeffer.

Each man entered quietly through the Oval Office's side entrance door and proceeded to sit at prearranged chairs, which contained top-secret folders with their names labeled on the front cover.

"Good morning, gentleman," the president announced as she entered the room through the front entrance and made her way to her Oval Office desk.

"Good morning, Madame President," all four men stood and respectfully greeted their Commander and Chief.

"Gentlemen, forgive me for my appearance this morning," the president commented as she proceeded to walk past her trusted advisors, not stopping to give her customary cordial handshake greeting. "I haven't had much sleep in the past twenty four hours."

Looking aged and vulnerable, the person presently standing behind the desk of the most politically powerful human on earth stood in stark contrast to the person who sat there only a month earlier—a vibrant, self-assured person who genuinely felt that she could change the world all by herself.

"Gentlemen," the president announced, "due to the seriousness of the unfolding events in the Middle East, I have deemed it necessary to invite all of you to be present with me for this morning's intelligence briefing. Time is short so I will now turn this briefing over to our Director of National Intelligence, Jonathan Burgess."

"Good morning, everyone," the DNI chief commented with a brief smile and a welcoming handshake extended to each of the three men standing to his left.

"Thank you, gentlemen," the president acknowledged. "We can all be seated."

"Even though as cabinet members we possess the highest security clearance," Burgess cautioned, "the information I am about to share must never leave this room. Only the president has the authority to say otherwise."

Each man nodded, affirming the DNI's explicit terms of secrecy. They knew Burgess as a straightforward man who never minced words. Each man also knew Burgess well enough to sense a slight uneasiness in his voice. The president also appeared nervous as she silently sat behind her desk fiddling with her fingers.

"Will everyone break the seal on your folders and open to the first paragraph found on page one," Burgess commented as he too proceeded to unseal the top-secret folder on his lap.

The DNI chief waited a moment longer while the president and her secretaries opened their folders. After adjusting his glasses, he directed his attention once more to the gentlemen on his left.

"Gentlemen," Burgess continued, "my role as Director of National Intelligence is to meet with the president every morning at 6 a.m. and read to her verbatim every word that is in this intelligence brief. When I finish reading, I then proceed to answer to the best of my knowledge any questions the president may have in respects to the report. I answer only to the president. This is the protocol we will follow here today."

Again, each man nodded, agreeing to the DNI's terms.

"Please refer to paragraph one as I read it aloud.

"At approximately 9 p.m. Eastern Standard Time last night, a total of twelve Iranian built Zelzal-2 medium range rockets were launched from mobile units along the Syrian side of the Golan border. Half were launched within a five-mile radius of the northern Syrian border town of Hadar. Their intended targets were the oil refineries north of the Israeli coastal city of Haifa and the city of Haifa proper. The remaining six rockets were launched within the same five-mile radius of the central border town of Jaba with an intended target being the Israeli city of Tel Aviv. Basing their information on actual ground damage, Mossad, Israel's intelligence agency has estimated that each rocket was armed with a conventional half-ton warhead. Two of the six rockets made a direct hit on the Haifa Oil Refinery with a production capacity of 80,000 barrels a day of high-grade crude. According to current Mossad estimates, the Haifa refinery sustained irrevocable damages. Two other rockets made direct strikes on the Port of Haifa and another struck the Haifa University on top of Mt. Carmel. A final rocket fortunately landed in a playground in an eastern residential area. Due to specific targeting and the early morning hours, casualties in Haifa attacks were estimated to be less than a hundred, mostly nightshift workers at the refinery and dock-workers at the port. Early damage estimates in Haifa range from a over a billion to five billion dollars."

The DNI chief paused briefly to turn the page before continuing. "Such was not the case in Tel Aviv. All six rockets made scattered direct hits throughout the city, leveling two high-rise apartment buildings, destroying the heart of the business district, and almost destroying an entire block of residential homes. It will take days to account for all the dead and injured. Thousands still remain trapped and unaccounted for under tons of collapsed debris."

Burgess stopped momentarily to look up from his folder and address the president directly. "Madame President, it was the unanimous consensus of the intelligence agencies I represent that the unprovoked actions taken this morning against the state of Israel were not random acts of terrorism. We have sufficient evidence to believe that the rocket attacks on the Israeli port cities of Haifa and Tel Aviv were part of a carefully planned conspiracy by specific Islamic groups scattered throughout the region to derail the signing of today's Middle Eastern peace treaty.

All evidence points toward Hezbollah militants based in Syria, fully supported and sponsored by the government of Iran, as the sole Islamic group responsible for launching this morning's rocket attack against the sovereign state of Israel. What's more, we also find the Syrian government directly responsible by proxy for allowing such radical groups as Hezbollah to operate within their borders as a legitimate militia. "

"Jonathan, this is sheer madness!" the president cried out in frustration. "We were about to deliver them everything they wanted. Why in God's name would they do this now, of all times?"

"Madame President, I whole heartedly agree," Burgess affirmed. "In our Western way of thinking, what they did this morning makes absolutely no sense. To literally destroy years of hard-fought negotiations defies all logic. But Madame President, what we in the West view as an acts of sheer madness, those in the Islamic world see as heroic acts guided of divine inspiration."

Jonathan Burgess paused momentarily to stare directly into the eyes of the president. "Madame President, may I speak candidly?" the DNI asked.

"By all means," the president replied with an affirming nod.

"I believe we in this room share some of the responsibility for what has taken place over night," Burgess boldly proclaimed.

"You need to explain yourself, Mr. Burgess," the president responded scowling.

"Please, don't get me wrong, Madame President," Burgess clarified. "Our nation's attempt to achieve a lasting peace between Israel and her Arab neighbors was truly a noble cause. But in our own zeal to facilitate this outcome, we ignored the fact that one of the basic tenets of radical Islam has been and still is the complete annihilation of Israel from the face of this earth. In retrospect, pressuring the Israelis into believing that a peaceful coexistence with their surrounding Arab neighbors was in their best interest was wrong. We inadvertently prompted the Israelis to drop their guard and play right into hands of the Islamic terrorists."

"Mr. Burgess, what is your point?" demanded a clearly irritated president.

"Madame President, were you aware that as of two days ago, the entire nation of Israel has had virtually no protective missile shield on its borders?

"No Mr. Burgess, I wasn't aware of that fact," the president replied.

"Well, Madame President, Iran was aware of it. So was Syria, and every radical Islamic group in the Middle East. In fact, their entire plan hinged on the fact that Israel would be forced to reposition every one of their Arrow and Patriot defensive missiles to conform to their new borders. By deceiving the Israelis into accepting a brief sense of false security, the Islamic militants ingeniously planned for this window of opportunity to fire medium-range rockets deep into the heart of Israel without being first destroyed by Israeli defensive missiles."

Burgess' words appeared to strike a chord with the president. She stood to her feet and proceeded to walk around her desk to confront Burgess head on. "My God, Jonathan," the president declared as she sat on the Oval Office couch positioned directly behind her DNI. For the first time, Analise Devoe eyes were opened to the truth about the Muslim's true intentions. "If what you are saying is true, then I allowed myself to be setup."

"We all were setup, Madame President," Burgess consoled.

One thing Analise Devoe was not good at was admitting when she was wrong. Without saying another word, she promptly walked back to her chair behind the Presidential desk.

"What has been the Israeli response at this point?" the president asked in an attempt to hurriedly change the subject.

"I can answer your question in two words, Madame President," Burgess replied as he proceeded to remove his glasses and place them in his shirt pocket. "Surgical restraint!"

"Please explain?" the president asked.

"In Israeli military terms the tactic is known as 'an eye for an eye,'" the DNI chief declared. "Even though the Israelis have every right in the eyes of the international community to go into Syria and level everything in sight, they chose instead a course of restraint, reducing the chance of innocent losses and striking hard only at known tactical targets.

"I applaud the Israelis motives!" declared an impressed president.

"To be specific," the DNI continued, "at approximately 1 a.m. Eastern Standard Time this morning, a squadron of Israeli F16s fighter jets struck the Syrian port of Baniyas completely destroying Syria's main coastal oil refinery in retaliation to the unprovoked rocket attacks that destroyed Israel's Haifa's Oil Refinery. According to reliable intelligence sources on the ground, Israeli jets also severely damaged the Syrian coastal pipeline that receives over 400,000 barrels per day of top grade light crude from the Jebisseh oil field to the north."

Jonathan Burgess stopped briefly to look at the gentlemen to his right.

"Even as we speak, Israeli F15 and F16 fighter jets are scouring the Syrian countryside carrying out surgical strikes on all known Hezbollah weapon sights and strongholds."

"I'll be frank with all of you!" the president once again interjected. "Even though the Israelis are showing remarkable restraint up until now, my worst fear is that they will inadvertently strike a target that will ignite this entire crisis into something far worse."

"The president's fears are well founded," Burgess affirmed. "The Russians have a naval base stacked to the hilt with every conceivable defensive and offensive weapon imaginable in Tartus, less than fifty miles south of Baniyas. All we need is one misguided Israeli strike to come anywhere close to the Tartus and instead of having a limited regional conflict, we will be looking at a possible Armageddon."

"May I interject?" asked the Secretary of Defense, Leslie Schaeffer.

"By all mean, Les," the president replied.

"The way I see it, the Israelis are too smart to target anywhere close to Tartus. The last thing Israel wants is to draw the Russians into this conflict. My fear is that the Iranian masterminds behind all this were hoping to use their Hezbollah pawns to draw the entire Arab league into a regional war against Israel."

"Mr. Secretary, that's precisely my opinion and the opinion of the CIA director James Meyers!" Burgess affirmed. "An attack on Syria by Israel, whether provoked or unprovoked, could be viewed as a violation of article 2 of the Arab League Defense Treaty that states, 'an attack on one member Arab state is considered an attack on all.'"

"Jim?" the president turned next to her Secretary of State, James Metloff and asked, "What do you suggest?"

"Unfortunately, Madame President," the Secretary guardedly replied, "due to our own present crisis here at home, we are extremely hard pressed in offering Israel any direct assistance either financially or militarily. As we speak, my fellow members at the State Department are working feverously through every diplomatic channel available to resolve this situation. We are in contact with the heads of all the moderate Arab countries asking them to intercede with a voice of reason into the situation. I am happy to say that we are getting the full support of our allies in NATO and also in the European Union. I've heard reports this morning that European Union President Giulio D'Alema has verbally committed over twenty thousand European ground troops to help secure the Israel's borders once the hostilities are over."

The president once again turned her full attention to her DNI. "Jonathan, I have one final question to ask you."

Everyone present had a good idea of what the president was about to request. It remained the only question everyone had avoided asking. All eyes were now focused on the president as she asked her Director of National Intelligence, "What about Russians? What role do you see them playing in all of this?"

Burgess had anticipated the question. He had been struggling with it all morning long before he had arrived at the White House. The Russians had always been the wildcard when it came to taking sides in the Middle East. They have always been viewed by the West as riding the fence of opportunity. In the past, the Russians had succeeded in undermining almost every attempt by the West to keep Iran from developing nuclear weapons. The Russians not only supplied all the components needed to build the Iranian nuclear reactors, they have also supplied both the Iranians and Syrians with the world's most technologically advanced offensive and defensive weapons.

"Madame President, I have no hard core answers to either of your questions," Burgess admitted. "All I can offer you is my gut feelings."

"Go ahead," the president quietly accepted.

"Madame President, the Russians smell the strong scent of American blood in the world's waters. They view America as mortally wounded and they are presently circling around our dying carcass. The Russian's perceive that the only thing stopping them from stripping us clean from our title as the 'world's only remaining superpower' is Israel."

The Director of National Intelligence knew he had said all that was needed. Before making his closing remarks, he looked directly into the eyes of everyone in the room. With the most penetrating stare he could muster, he clearly and poignantly expressed the most declarative statement in his entire career as a public servant,

"Regardless of our present situation, America must do everything in her power to never abandon the state of Israel!"

Thursday, March 22nd
6:45 a.m. Eastern Standard Time
Washington, D.C.
Oval Office
West Wing of the White House

Sitting all alone in a room where others have sat contemplating decisions that were at times too overwhelming for even the most brilliant of human minds, a broken president looked up toward the ceiling above her desk and began to cry. Always the overachiever, she never allowed life situations to get the better of her. Throughout her youth, she was always selected as the one most likely to succeed. As captain of her high school lacrosse team, her determination and competitive zeal helped inspire her team to two consecutive state titles both her junior and senior years. As a young lawyer, she approached each new case and legal challenge as a champion prize-fighter would an opponent. More than just winning, she wanted to prove to both the world and herself that she could do it all on her own. Finally, after reaching the pinnacle of human success, a feat only few other humans had ever achieved, Analise Devoe, the first female President of the United States, had come face to face with a challenge she could not conquer, and a challenger she could not defeat.

Carefully observing the president from behind stood two angelic giants, Yahrieh, the angelic prince of prophetic wisdom and worldly affairs, and Muriel, the Archangel charged with making sure God's prophetic message of Truth is fulfilled.

"Now, that is a first!" Yahriel announced with a surprised looked. "Not once have I seen this strong-willed human ever shed a tear!"

"Well," Muriel responded to his fellow Archangel's observation, "I've heard it once said that humans are a lot like nuts."

"Now how can you compare a human with a nut?" Yahriel asked with a puzzled look.

"Well, some humans have a thin shell covering over their spirit or inner man. For them to receive God's Truth of Salvation, all the Holy Spirit has to do is tap a little and their thin shell will crack. Most others are like this human."

Muriel proceeded to walk over and placed his hand on the president's shoulder.

"It's a shame!" Muriel commented as he looked down in pity at the sobbing human. "They have encased themselves inside thick walls composed of self pride. In order for them to receive the Truth of God's salvation, their hard outer shell must first be crushed in order to expose their soft inner spirit. Every shred of their pride must be stripped away from them before they are ready to listen to the Spirit of Truth."

"Do you believe Analise Devoe is now ready to listen?" Yahriel asked with a look of sincere hope.

"Perhaps!" Muriel replied with a smile. "Now that her shell's been removed."

"And with less than a week left before Passover, you need to bring Schroeder back for his final visit to the Oval Office."

Muriel shook his head in agreement.

Chapter Twenty-Two

"Watch ye therefore, and pray always, that ye may be accounted worthy to escape all these things that shall come to pass, and to stand before the Son of man."

Luke 21:36 KJV

When it comes to Bible prophecy, what most humans fail to take into account is that God's promises are eternal and inevitable. Whether we like it or not, God's promises will come to pass according to His prophetic timetable. Even with the foretold biblical events unfolding right before their eyes, humans continue to totally discount, marginalize, analogize, and reinterpret God's promises to fit their own personal belief systems and time schedules. Like the three proverbial monkeys who see no evil, hear no evil, and speak no evil, humans go about their daily lives acting as if the inevitable will never happen.

Thursday, March 22nd
2:45 *p.m. Israel Standard Time*
The 9,000 *foot Summit of the Jabal Ash Shanin Ridge*
Central Syria

Patience may be a virtue for some, but not when applied to nervous demons. For the past several hours, like an expectant father awaiting the arrival of his first child, Apollon paced back and forth across a metal platform that overlooked the over one-hundred-foot-deep, fifty-foot-wide missile silo below. Like clockwork, every thirty seconds or so, the impatient demon commander would blast out obscenities that resonated throughout the entire nine-level steel- and concrete-reinforced underground facility.

"What is taking those Russian idiots so long?" Apollon screamed, this time directing his seething wrath toward several midlevel demons standing among their host humans only one platform below. "By the time they decide to launch, the Israeli b-tards will have already programmed their arrow missiles to shoot them down!"

"They're just about ready, Commander," returned a shout from Orbez, the demon assigned to head missile engineer Dimitri Lischinsky.

Orbez was just as nervous as his commander. He, along with over a dozen other demonic specialists assigned to the clandestine Jabal Ash Shanin missile facility, were acutely aware that time was now their main enemy; every second now wasted meant the Israelis would be that much closer to reprogramming and repositioning their nation's defensive missile shield.

In a large, brightly lit room located on the opposite end of the nine-level underground facility, a rather stout, white-haired Russian military officer smiled as he and three of his fellow comrades visually scanned the black screen of a radar display.

"Colonel Ivanovich, the skies are now clear for launching," declared a jubilant radar specialist, Andrei Nikolaevich.

Those were the very words the Russian commander was waiting to hear all morning. The decision to launch the two nuclear-tip SHEHAB-4 missiles at the Israeli nuclear facilities located outside the cities of Tel Aviv and Haifa was put on hold until this very moment. For the first time this morning, not one radar blip was visible indicating no Israeli jets are flying within 150 kilometers of their airspace. This was not the case just an hour earlier when the entire screen appeared lit up like a swarm of mad hornets flying in every conceivable direction.

"Launch!" shouted an equally elated Colonel Ivanovich.

"Prepare for missile launch in silos one and two!" announced the missile control center's head engineer, Yuri Novgo, to his fellow engineers on the opposite end of the underground facility.

Every human engineer and technician immediately vacated the missile site seeking safety behind the steel- and concrete-reinforced blast lock area. In their absence, they left behind two Iranian

SHEHAB-4 missiles and two solos full of jubilant dancing demons. For the demons, the scorching heat released by the blast of the missile was nothing compared to the indescribable intensity they were accustomed to existing in their hellish inferno.

The demon celebration immediately ceased when an ear-piercing crack vibrated from above. As they looked up in wonderment, each of the twin silos' 740-ton steel- and concrete-covered doors began to slowly retract. The demons stared in awe as daylight penetrated each of their cylinder-shaped cavities hewed out of the solid rock mountainside. In less than twenty seconds, the dozen or so demons standing below were marveling at a perfectly shaped circular opening exposing the blue skies above.

Extremely hot gases began venting out from the bottom of each missile pushing hard against the solid rock floors below. As the human control room engineer announced the ten second countdown to launch over the facility's intercom, the silo walls began to vibrate tremendously from the extreme force from each missile's exhaust. The demons once again began to dance and celebrate for they knew their mission at Jabal Ash Shanin Ridge missile site was almost over. In less than fifteen minutes in human time, when the last of the fiery missile plumes had exited the skies above, Apollon's demons would know whether to continue to dance and celebrate, or bow low in shame. They would soon know if all their efforts over the past ten years had accomplished their goal of eliminating the Jewish state's nuclear missile deterrent, Israel's last hope of survival.

Thursday, March 22nd
2:45 p.m. Israel Standard Time
Tel Hai, Israel

An entire legion of over five thousand fully armed angelic warriors assigned to guard the northern Galilee settlement of Tel Hai were gathered around a large stone monument of a lion. With thousands of blazing swords raised high, their voices combined in unison, shouting out one single name.

Removing his sword from its sheath, the highly esteemed Archangel looked out in humility at all the fearless warriors who served under his command. Tal Hai was the final stop on his whirlwind cross-country tour. He had just spent the entire morning traveling the length of Israel's borders with Egypt, Jordan, Syria, and Lebanon, both encouraging and preparing his warriors to do battle with a formidable enemy.

"Some of you should vividly remember the heroic battle that was fought on this very spot not so long ago," declared Michael, the Commander of the Heavenly Host. With his brilliant golden sword held high over his head, he recounted the events of that fateful day.

"Eight Zionist settlers valiantly fought and died here on March 2nd in the human year 1920. Fighting along side of the humans were also a dozen of our finest warriors."

The renowned Archangel, respected by his warriors for his insurmountable strength and valor, was also known for his passion to serve. Instilled within the being of this exalted servant was the freedom to demonstrate the same range of heartfelt emotions as His Creator.

"Unfortunately," Michael paused briefly to muster enough inward strength to continue, "my warriors found themselves also vastly outnumbered and totally overwhelmed by the ferocity of the enemy attack. Four of my best warriors were lost on that day. A day after the battle, I stood right where I am standing now, vowing to myself, 'never again!'" declared the humble Archangel with tears in his eyes.

"Never again!" his warriors returned the same charge.

"Six months later," Michael continued, "a group of over twenty fellow Zionists returned to Tal Hai to bury their loved ones and to resettle the land given to them under the covenant. Once again, this small group of Zionist settlers was attacked from all sides by overwhelming numbers of Arabs."

Michael paused once again, lowering his sword to chest height. "I was there on that day," he openly declared. "Once again, my warriors and I were also outnumbered, but unlike the previous attack, we were prepared!"

Pressing his sword across his chest, the Commander of the Heavenly Hosts thundered a declaration to all the warriors standing before him, "I stand here now as a witness before my Lord and Creator to testify to the valor and determination on that battlefield. When humans and war-

riors stand together united, prepared to do battle and to hold fast to the promises found in God's Holy Covenant, then no powers on earth or in hell can stop them!"

"Never again!" the warriors again shouted in unison.

"Together, we won the battle that day!" Michael declared. "It marked the first time in over two thousand years that the Abraham's covenant descendants living in their covenant land fought back from insurmountable odds and defeated their enemies!"

Turning to face the monument erected in back of him, Michael continued, "This stone lion was dedicated on this site in remembrance of that hallmark battle. Since that day, we have fought many battles alongside Abraham's descendants, each time outnumbered and each time victorious! What is our charge?"

"Never again!" the warriors answered in unison.

"The lion not only represents the valor and courage demonstrated here so long ago. It is a monument dedicated to the true Lion of Judah, the Holy One, Our Lord and Creator who's Name is above all names. This is His covenant land. We will fight and defend Israel with all of our strength and all of our might!"

Raising his sword once again high into the air, Michael vowed one last charge to his warriors, "All the powers of hell will not prevail against us!"

"Never again, Amen!" thundered the combined voices from a legion of angelic warriors.

"Amen!" calmly repeated their Commander Michael as he replaced his sword in its sheath and prepared himself for the impending battle.

Thursday, March 22nd
2:58 p.m. Israel Standard Time
Onboard an Israeli F15 Jet Fighter

An exhausted Major Dani Weisman looked out to the left of his F15's cockpit window and smiled. There on the eastern horizon was a familiar sight to Israeli Air Force pilots, Mt. Hermon, a snowcapped beacon welcoming home the present commander of the Israeli's Air

Force's first and most honored jetfighter company, Squadron 101. With his tired mind craving sleep, all he could think about as he entered Israeli air space for the second time in one day was the status of two of his fellow fighter pilots, possibly shot down by surface to air missiles while performing their missions somewhere over central Syria.

Thirty-nine fellow members of Weisman's squadron out of Sedot Mikha Airbase were the first to take to the skies over Syria only minutes after this morning's unprovoked rocket attacks. As far he knew, he and his men had successfully accomplished their main objective: to eliminate all possible enemy missile sites found throughout Syria.

Look to your far left, a thought flashed through the tired pilot's wandering mind. Blessed with the eyesight of an eagle, Weisman focused in on two distant vapor trails rising at what he guessed to be a 70-degree angle above the Syrian horizon and headed straight for the Israeli border.

"Contact Sedot!" Jehriel spoke again to Weisman's thoughts.

Jehriel, along with hundreds of other angelic warriors, had been assigned by their Commander Michael to accompany all Israeli pilots on all missions since the conception of the Israeli Air Force back on May 29, 1948.

Without hesitation, Weisman followed Jehriel's orders contacting his home base, Sedot Mikha Airbase located south of Tel Aviv.

"This is Thunder 1 calling Python 1. Do you read?"

"Yes, Thunder 1," Sedot acknowledged, "we have you on radar."

"Python 1, there appear to be two incoming . . ."

"SHEHAB-4s!" Jehriel shouted into Weisman's thoughts

"Repeat again, Thunder 1?" Sedot requested.

"Python 1, there appears to be two incoming SHEHAB-4 missiles presently estimated at 32.60 north and 35.3 west traveling southwest with trajectory of 70 alpha delta nine omega."

Thursday, March 22nd
3:00 p.m. Israel Standard Time

Sedot Mikha Airbase Control Tower

"General Ben-Nun!" shouted First Lieutenant Moshe Levi.

The piercing shout instantly got everyone's attention, including Major General Eliezer Ben-Nun, Commander and Chief of the Israeli Air Force. Every person in the circular air traffic room immediately stopped what they were doing and looked up to see a terrified flight control specialist standing by his radar screen waving his hands in all directions.

"General Ben-Nun," Lieutenant Levi shouted again from across the room.

"I am in contact with Major Dani Weisman. He just reported spotting two incoming SHEHAB-4 missiles located at 32.60 north and 35.4 west traveling southwest with trajectory of 70 alpha delta nine omega."

The words "incoming SHEHAB-4 missiles" struck panic on the faces of everyone in the room.

"General," called out another flight control specialist. "I did some quick calculations. They're headed right for us!"

"How much time do we have?"

"Sir, if those numbers are right, ten minutes max!"

"My God, get the prime minister on the phone!" the general ordered.

Thursday, March 22nd
3:02 p.m. Israel Standard Time
Prime Minister's Office
3 Kaplan St. Hakirya, Jerusalem

From the moment he arrived shortly before daybreak, the Israeli Prime Minister had not left his Jerusalem office, not even to eat. He had spent hours on the phone speaking with influential world leaders and meeting with his cabinet members behind closed doors, attempting to do everything humanly possible in to avert an all-out regional war. He was in his office having a private long-distance discussion with European Union President Giulio D'Alema when his secretary, Mira Halbani burst into the room.

"Yacov! Air Force General Ben-Nun is on line two," announced his flustered secretary.

"Mira, can't this wait?" the prime minister asked.

"Yacov, there are more missiles headed this way!"

"Giulio?"

"I heard my friend," President D'Alema acknowledged, "my prayers are with you!"

The Israeli Prime Minister wasted no time switching lines on his speaker phone.

"General Ben-Nun?"

"Mr. Prime Minister," a deep firm voice resonated throughout the small ten- by twenty-foot conference room. "I am afraid I have some bad news!"

"I'm listening," the prime minister affirmed.

"Mr. Prime Minister," the general continued. "We have confirmed reports that two SHEHAB-4 missiles, originating out of central Syria, are presently in flight over our northern Israeli air space. It is my firm belief that each missile has nuclear capabilities and their intended targets appear to be the city of Tel Aviv and our underground facilities of Toresh and Soreq."

General Ben-Nun paused briefly before asking the next all important question.

"Sir, what would you have me do?"

At that moment, all time seemed to stand still for Yacov Ben Yizri. *How can one person alone answer such a question?* he asked himself. *I need more time!*

"Detonation time?"

"Unless our defensive shield is ready, no more then six minutes, sir," replied the impatient voice of the general. "

OH God in heaven, I beg you, flashed the prime minister's thoughts, *please, let the shield be ready!*

With time quickly running out, the impatient General again asked the head of his nation for what kind of swift military response, if any, was warranted for such an unspeakable act. "An eye for an eye," the prime minister calmly proclaimed.

"Sir?" the general quickly followed.

"You heard me right, General," a defiant Prime Minister responded. "The Syrians seem to be hell bent on destroying our people. I am ordering you to take out Damascus!"

"Mr. Prime Minister, am I hearing correctly?" repeated the general, "Are you asking me to nuke Damascus?"

"You have your orders, General," the prime minister reiterated. "Now carry them out!"

"That's affirmative, sir!"

Thursday, March 22nd
3:03 p.m. Israel Standard Time
Onboard an Israeli F15 Jet Fighter

For Major Dani Weisman, the decision was easy. No longer fatigued, a surge of pure adrenaline now directed every nerve and fiber of the IAF Squadron's Commander toward his new objective: to do whatever it takes to prevent the two SHEHAB-4 missiles from striking their intended targets.

In human terms, Major Weisman knew the challenges set before him were impossible. The fact that he was low on fuel with only one missile left was not going to stop him from carrying out what he knew could very well be his final mission. *Besides,* he thought to himself, *I have been in impossible situations before, and somehow I've always made it through!*

Adoni, I need your help one last time, he silently prayed. Before he could finish his prayer, his thoughts were interrupted by a familiar voice coming over his headset.

"Major Weisman, we heard you may need some help?"

"We!" Major Weisman exclaimed.

"Look out you cockpit, Major!"

Before looking out, the grateful pilot looked up and finished his prayer, *Thank you, Adoni. You came through again!*

Flying parallel on each side of his F15 fighter jet were two fellow members of his squadron, Captains Micah Cohen and Elon Kaufman.

"You guys are truly angels!" a happy Major Weisman responded with a thumbs up.

"Just call us Michael and Gabriel!" jokingly commented Captain Cohen.

"Now that was really funny!" Jehriel laughed to himself from the back of the cockpit.

"What's our plan, Commander?" asked Captain Cohen, the F15 pilot flying to Weisman's right.

"The missiles should be crossing the 'Homa' any second now," Weisman replied. "Pray to Adoni that the 'Fence' is up and running!"

Thursday, March 22nd
3:04 p.m. Israel Standard Time
Hillside north of the Golan village of Banyias

The term "Homa" or "Fence" alluded to by Commander Weisman were the codenames given to the first battery of Arrow 2 ballistic missiles set up along Israel's Northeastern border with Syria. First deployed in 2000, this first line of defense was hoped to provide an impenetrable shield against any incoming enemy missile or rocket. Two other defensive batteries of arrow missiles had since been strategically positioned outside the cities of Haifa and Tel Aviv.

The order to deploy Israel's Theater Missile Defense system (TMD) to its original Golan site was received shortly before daybreak by Major Abram Herzog, the senior engineer assigned to the IDF's 91st Northern Command Division. Immediately after receiving the phone call from the Secretary of Defense, the monumental task of transporting Israel's protective missile shield to its original position over 70 kilometers to the northeast went into high gear. This meant breaking down and transporting an entire systems battery consisting of eight launch trailers, each with six launching tubes containing ready-to-fire two-stage missiles back over the Golan's steep mountainous roads. Three trucks in all accompanied each battery, one transporting a 20-by-60-foot large radar display and the other two, a complete communications and launch control center.

An Arrow 2 system can detect and track incoming missiles as far away as 500 kilometers and can intercept missiles 50–90 kilometers away. The Arrow 2 used a terminally-guided interceptor warhead to destroy an incoming missile from its launch at an altitude of 10 to 40 kilometers at nine times the speed of sound. Since the missile did not need to directly hit the target, a detonation within 40–50 meters was sufficient to disable an incoming warhead. The command and control system was designed to respond to as many as 14 simultaneous intercepts.

The caravan of eleven trucks had arrived at their destination high on a level hilltop overlooking the Golan village of Banyias shortly after 1 p.m. For the TMD team of over two dozen engineers, their job had just started. The last time they assembled the entire battery, it required over six hours. Now, they were asked to attempt the impossible. They were ordered to have the entire battery up and running in just two short hours. As the minutes rapidly ticked away, tempers and emotions among the team of highly trained specialists ran thin. As the 3 o'clock deadline loomed near, the battery commander approached his radar chief engineer, Major Ezra Elam.

"How much longer?" ranted the impatient battery commander, Major Herzog.

"Is my name Moses?" curtly replied a partially bald, gray-headed man crouching under the radar trailer. Holding two unconnected wires in his hands, a frustrated Major Elam looked up toward his old friend of over twenty years and said, "Abram, I am not a miracle worker! Unless we do everything right, nothing will work. Give me five minutes, ten at the most."

Without warning, an ear-piercing explosion similar to a very loud sonic boom captured the attention of everyone on the ground. The TMD team of engineers looked up and viewed in horror as the first stage of the twin SHEHAB-4 missiles separated high overhead of their Golan Heights position.

"Dear God," declared a shocked Abram Herzog as he looked down at his equally stunned radar specialist, "We don't have five minutes!"

Thursday, March 22nd
3:04 p.m. Israel Standard Time
Onboard an Israeli F15 Jet Fighter

The three Israeli F15 pilots also watched in horror as their prayers went unanswered. As the first of two ballistic missile stages separated and dropped to the ground, a decision was made.

"It's up to us now," declared Major Weisman.

"How fast do you think they are going?" asked Captain Cohen.

"Mach 2, maybe close to Mach 3," Weisman approximated. "The birds are also flying past our upper limits of 20 kilometers (65,000ft)."

The pilots knew that at speed Mach 2.5, or 1,875 mph, they would be pushing the limits of their aircrafts, but they also knew there was no other option. They could not let the missiles pass over central Israel.

"Full throttle!" commanded Major Weisman as he, as well as his fellow pilots, applied a steady downward force to the floor mounted throttle handle located directly in front of their seats.

"I don't know where I'm getting the extra thrust," Captain Kaufman announced, "but my gauges are showing Mach 3."

"Mine, too!" declared Weisman.

"That makes three!" chuckled the elated voice of Captain Cohen.

The three fighter pilots were well aware that regardless of what their console instruments were showing, it was virtually impossible for an F15 Eagle aircraft to obtain speeds approaching Mach 3. Some other external force, maybe an exceedingly strong tailwind, had to be at play.

Little did the humans inside the cockpit realize that their aircrafts were receiving a supernatural push in the direction of the fleeing deadly targets. As they rapidly approached the twin missiles, the mission commander made an important announcement. "Guys, we need to take inventory! I have one sidewinder and one sparrow left over."

A sidewinder missile was a heat-seeking, short-range, air-to-air missile that had the ability to twist and turn and stalk its intended target until detonation was made. The radar-guided sparrow missile had the same capabilities, but was tipped with a larger, more explosive warhead.

"I have one sparrow left!" stated Captain Cohen, followed by the same response by Captain Kaufman.

"Then let's make every one of them count!" Major Weisman declared. "We cannot let those birds fly out of their cage!"

Captains Cohen and Kaufman knew exactly what their commander meant by not letting the birds out of the cage. Each pilot knew that once the ballistic missiles passed over the sparsely populated Golan, their path would next take them over some the most important agricultural and population centers in all of Israel.

"Since I have one more bullet than the two of you," commented the confident voice of Major Weisman, "I'll take the left bird and leave you two the right. Just follow along until I give the command."

"That's affirmative, Major," acknowledge Captains Cohen and Kaufman.

As planned, Weisman's jet veered hard to the left, disappearing out of sight.

While his fellow squad members continued gaining precious distance on their assigned target, Weisman skillfully positioned his jet a safe distance behind the left missile.

"Gentleman," the 101 Squadron Commander announced, "I believe you both know as well as I that these birds may be nuclear. The good news is, we are still in the interception phase and we are at a relatively good height to shoot them down!" The interception phase was the last phase in a missile trajectory before it made its decent. Once the missile began its descent, it was too late to shoot it down.

"Let me know the moment you both are locked in," commanded Weisman. "Fire on my signal and get the hell out of there!"

"Affirmative, Major."

There's no time left. Any second now, the missile would be over the agriculturally rich Galilean countryside. A nuclear explosion there would instantly eliminate Israel's only means of feeding its six million plus population.

"Target locked," affirmed Cohen, followed by Kaufman.

The green target lock light was also flashing on Dani Weisman's console.

Major Weisman paused ever so briefly to offer up a quick prayer. "Lord, let this work!" he asked.

"Amen!" followed Captains Cohen and Kaufman.

"Fire!"

As four missiles from three directions accelerated forward, the three Israeli Air Force F 15 Eagle jetfighters veered opposite to the right and left in a desperate attempt to distance themselves from the potential thermo-nuclear blast. The same supernatural forces that earlier aided the human pilots in intercepting their targets was now at work assisting them out of harm's way.

A large orange flash, followed only moments later by a second blast of the same intensity, was visible as far away as the Lebanon border to the north, the Syrian border to the east, and North Galilee to the south.

"They weren't nuclear!" declared a shocked Captain Cohen as he throttled down his F 15 fighter to a safe cruising speed of Mach 1 (650 miles/hour) and veered south toward his home base Sedot Mikha Airbase.

"I would have bet my entire paycheck they were!" reiterated an equally surprised Major Weisman.

"They were nuclear!" cried out a totally confused Jehriel, still holding fast to the tail end of Weisman's aircraft. "Lord, what happened?"

If the angelic warrior had turned around, he would have noticed two devilish beings dancing in the midst of the dissipating reddish brown smoke from the missile explosion.

Jehriel was absolutely correct in his assumption that the missiles were nuclear. They were nuclear when launched and nuclear right up until the moment they were destroyed. What Jehriel and his fellow angelic warriors failed to take into account was the full scope of Apollon's ingenious plan. Secretly concealed within the tip of each missile was a chimera (a small midlevel demon), ordered to immediately disarm their respective warheads if fired upon by enemy missiles.

Within seconds now, Apollon and demon hordes would be celebrating their greatest achievement since the collapse of the twin World Trade Center Towers on September 11th, 2001.

Without notice, the skies over Northern Israel brightened beyond human description. Immediately following, a shockwave of scorching heat and hurricane-force winds radiated out from the source of the intense light in all directions, destroying everything in its path.

"What the hell was that!" cried out Captain Kaufman moments after regaining control of his wind battered F15.

"It was a nuclear shockwave!" declared the frantic voice of his fellow pilot, Captain Cohen.

"I don't understand!" Kaufman questioned. "Did Syria fire more missiles?"

"That wasn't from Syria," interjected the emotionless voice of Major Weisman. "It exploded north of our borders."

"My God," Captain Kaufman exclaimed as his mind quickly rationalized what had just taken place. "It was one of ours!"

"Elon, Micah."

"I think we know, Commander!" one of the two pilots calmly responded.

"My God," Weisman declared. "I believe we just nuked Damascus!"

Silence.

For the remainder of their return flight back to their home base, no more words were exchanged among the three pilots. Only their innate piloting skills got them back safely. Their minds were numb knowing that for the first time since mankind had witnessed the devastating effects of nuclear weapons, at least one such weapon had been detonated over a major civilian center. At the speed of digital technology, it wasn't long before every corner of the globe had heard the incredible news.

Within minutes, the political shockwaves that followed were exactly as Apollon had planned. World War III was about to commence and unless God Himself intervened, the tiny Jewish state would be no more.

Chapter Twenty-Three

"This is what the Lord says: I have heard my people crying; there is no peace, there is only fear and trembling. Now let me ask you a question: Do men give birth to babies? Then why do they stand there, hands pressed against their sides like women about to give birth? In all history there has never been such a time of terror. For my people, it will be a time known as Jacob's trouble. Yet in the end, Israel will be saved!"

Jeremiah 30: 5–7 NLT

Friday, March 23rd
8 a.m. Eastern Standard Time
Providence, Rhode Island
Main Studio
Gospel Broadcasting Network (GBN)

Nobody took notice of the warm southerly breezes, the blooming yellow daffodils, or the dazzling early morning sunshine as spring returned once again to Providence. Like the rest of the outside world, the horrific events over the past month have cast a deep, dark shadow over this once bustling vibrant New England city. In Providence's busy downtown center, people made their way to work passing by emotionless stares void of any expression of joy or happiness. The only glimmer of hope that these "shell-shocked" individuals shared in common with the remainder of the nation is that they would soon wake up to discover that this hellish month-long nightmare was all a bad dream.

Not everyone living in Providence had immersed themselves in a dark caldron of doom and despair. Though the outside world appeared to be rapidly spinning out of control, true hope could still be found shining within the walls of the Gospel Broadcasting Network. With last week's announcement of the lifting of all travel restrictions, a full audience now patiently waited inside PTW's main studio for the start of this morning's show.

With every seat in the auditorium filled, PTW's director, Charlie Bennett, alerted his technicians that today's show was about to start, "Cameras roll on 5 - 4- 3–2- 1 . . ."

For the first time since its first broadcast, today's show didn't begin with a musical introduction. The initial images appearing on the viewer's screens were more reminiscent of an old black and white video documentary taken from ground zero after the bombings of the Japanese cities of Hiroshima and Nagasaki. The viewers, both in the live audience and at home, sat in silent awe, finding it difficult to accept the horrific sights they were now watching didn't happen over a generation ago. Completely void of all color and life, the high-rise buildings, the businesses, and restaurants, an area where over four million Damascus residents had once called home, had completely vanished, all wiped clean by the intense heat of a thermonuclear blast. For only the third time in the entire history of mankind, human beings felt it necessary to resort to the ultimate weapon of mass destruction to settle their differences.

Superimposed over the shocking scenes were the words taken from a verse in the Bible.

"Look, Damascus will disappear! It will become a heap of ruins forever. Isaiah 17:1."

The cameras switched to the show's host seated beside his returning guest, Dr. Ezra Schroeder. Displaying his ever-present smile, PTW's host, Tom Reid, began the broadcast with a reassuring quote from the Bible, "Folks, regardless of what you might be hearing or seeing right now, God tells us in 2nd Timothy verse 7, 'For God has not given us a spirit of fear, but of power and of love and of a sound mind.' "

As the camera zoomed in to get a close up of Reid's face, he quotes another familiar Bible verse. "Remember Jesus' very words recorded in Luke Chapter 21 where He admonishes those living in the future who might be witness to the same kinds of mind-boggling events that we are seeing right now: 'And when these things begin to come to pass, then look up, and lift up your heads; for your redemption draws nigh!'"

The cameras zoomed out showing both host and guest. "I have asked my good friend, NSA code breaker and prophetic Bible scholar Dr. Ezra Schroeder, to come back on today's show and to share with us his insight as to how the rapidly changing events in the Middle East fit into Bible prophesy. Dr. Schroeder, we at PTW are honored once again to have you on our show."

After a brief handshake, Tom Reid wasted no time asking his guest a question that was on everyone's mind. "Dr. Schroeder, is the Israeli bombing of Damascus prophetic?"

Schroeder quoted directly from an opened Bible on his lap. "Dr. Reid, the verse shown on the television during the opening scenes of the show comes from Isaiah Chapter 17 verse 1. Let me read that verse again from the New Living Translation. 'This message came to me (Isaiah) concerning Damascus: Look, Damascus will disappear! It will become a heap of ruins.'"

"Dr. Schroeder," Tom Reid interjected, "Has that ever happened before? In other words, has there ever been a time in the past when the Syrian city of Damascus was destroyed?"

Schroeder smiled before answering with the inward assurance that the Holy Spirit was in complete control over every thought, and that no question would be left unanswered.

"Up until yesterday, Damascus was considered one of the oldest recorded continuously inhabited cities on earth," Schroeder declared. "Archeological excavations at Tel Ramad on the outskirts of the city have demonstrated that Damascus had been inhabited as early as 8000 to 10,000 BC. And yes, the city of Damascus has been invaded many times in the past by foreigners, by the Greeks, the Romans, and the Muslims, but there was never a time recorded in the past that Damascus was completely destroyed."

A message flashed across the bottom of home viewer's screens warning them that the same horrific introductory scenes broadcasted early were about to be shown. With stark images of a scorched earth shown in the background, Schroeder continued, "Isaiah tells us that this prophecy is not only about the destruction of Damascus, but after this oracle is fulfilled, there will never be a city called Damascus again. If Isaiah had only said, 'Damascus will be destroyed,' then presumably, it could be rebuilt. But the impact is stronger than that. Isaiah says specifically, 'Damascus will be negated from being a city.'"

"Dr. Schroeder, please explain to our audience why Damascus, and why now?"

"Absolutely, Dr. Reid," Schroeder affirmed as he turned to face the stage camera. "It is imperative that we all understand this one simple fact: until yesterday, Damascus was the central hub of Islamic terrorism. Several of the most prominent terrorist organizations, Hezbollah, Hamas, and the Islamic Jihad had their central headquarters in Damascus. We believe these were the very groups responsible for yesterday's bombings of the Israeli cities of Haifa and Tel Aviv that killed an estimated 4,500 people. To paraphrase God's sacred covenant found in Genesis 12:3, 'Any one person or groups responsible for attacking His chosen ones will be dealt with harshly and severely!'"

"Dr. Schroeder," asked Reid, "according to the Bible, what happens next with Israel?"

"To answer that question, I will continue reading from Isaiah Chapter 17 starting with verse 3." As the verses flashed on the screen, Schroeder again read from the Bible on his lap.

"The fortified cities of Israel will also be destroyed, and the power of Damascus will end. In that day the glory of Israel will be very dim, for poverty will stalk the land. Israel will be abandoned like the grain fields after the harvest. Their largest cities will be as deserted as overgrown thickets. They will become like the cities the Amorites abandoned when the Israelites came here so long ago.

"Why, because Israel has turned from the God who can save them. They have turned from the Rock who can hide them.

"Look! The armies rush forward like waves thundering toward the shore. But though they roar like breakers on a beach, God will silence them. They will flee like chaff scattered by the wind or like dust whirling before a storm. In the evening Israel waits in terror, but by dawn its enemies are dead. This is the just reward of those who plunder and destroy the people of God. Then at last the people will think of their Creator and have respect for the Holy One of Israel."

"Dr. Schroeder," Reid interjected, "some will say that the verses you just read have already been fulfilled thousands of years ago. How do you answer them?"

"Excellent point, Dr. Reid. I would agree with those who argue that these events had already taken place. It is a well-documented fact that Israel was twice taken into captivity by the Assyrians in 722 BC and Babylonians in 586 BC. But there is one crucial factor that must be taken into account when interpreting biblical prophecies: the Bible is filled with prophetic events that have dual fulfillments."

"Dr. Schroeder, what do mean when you say that prophecies have dual fulfillments?"

"I believe the best way I can answer your question, Dr Reid, is with an example," Schroeder replied. "About a week before Jesus was crucified, his disciples approached him and asked 'Tell us, what will be the signs of your coming and of the end of the age?' Jesus went on to describe specific events that would precede his Second Coming such as the destruction of the Temple, upcoming wars, false prophets, and the mass persecutions of believers. There are biblical scholars who believe that these events were completely fulfilled when the Roman General Titus sacked Jerusalem in 70 AD. Once again, I agree with those who say that Jesus' predictions were fulfilled forty years after his death, but I go one step further and say that Jesus' prophetic statements in this case were indeed dual fulfillments. Jesus specifically stated that 'this gospel of the kingdom shall be preached in all the world for a witness unto all nations; and then shall the end come.' That specific event wasn't possible thousand of years ago; but with our present technology, it is today!"

"Point well taken!" Reid declared as both he and the studio audience gave his guest a round of applause.

"Dr. Reid, it is my firm belief that Isaiah 17 is a prime example of an ancient prophesy having dual fulfillments. I say this because, up until yesterday, Damascus had never been totally destroyed and rendered uninhabitable."

Schroeder turned once again toward the camera and declared, "I believe that this event has now been fulfilled right before our eyes!"

Once again, Schroeder's last statement was followed by applause.

"As we have just read," Schroeder continued, "I believe the people now living in Israel are also under God's judgment for their blatant sin of disbelief. The Bible makes it clear that Israelis will abandon their large fortified cities in fear of being attacked. This is precisely what will happen if Israel's enemies attack her large cities with missiles and rockets!"

"Dr. Schroeder," Reid once again interjected, "I know people will ask this question: if the Jews are truly God's chosen people under His covenant with Abraham, then why would God allow them to suffer such a terrible fate?"

"Another good point, Dr. Reid." Schroeder paused and look directly into the cameras.

"I have two answers that will help your viewers understand. First, the Bible clearly states that God never goes back on His Word. Regardless of our actions as humans, His Word will always come to pass.

"And secondly, I cannot emphasize this point enough, our God is a Holy God! He exists in a Holy state, totally void of sin. Now that being the case, it is impossible for sinful man to approach a Holy God on his own. In ancient Israel, a person, such as the High Priest, could only approach God through a sacrificial sin covering made possible by the shedding of innocent animal blood. This practice of animal blood atonement ended with the destruction of the Jerusalem Temple by the Romans in 70AD. From that day until this present moment, the only way a Jew, or anyone else for that matter, could approach a Holy God is through the one and only sin atonement made available to all mankind by Jesus' blood sacrifice on the cross at Calvary."

"Amen," Dr. Reid affirmed.

"Dr. Reid, I believe there is something else revealed here in Isaiah's prophesy that will help shed light as to why America has experienced such devastating events over the past month."

"Please go on, Dr. Schroeder," implored Reid. "I believe right now you have the complete attention of all of America!"

Both guest and host felt God's strong presence. Schroeder once again looked down at his Bible and read, "Isaiah 17, verse 4 states that Israel will be abandoned like the grain fields after the harvest. Isn't this precisely what has happened?" Schroeder asked.

"But Dr. Schroeder," questioned Reid, "how does this tie in with America's problems?"

"Dr. Reid, it is by no coincidence that America's phenomenal rise to superpower status after World War II corresponded to the formation and establishment of the tiny state of Israel on May 14, 1948. Since that famous date, foretold thousands of years earlier by the prophet Isaiah, America has remained Israel's staunchest ally and loyal supporter both financially and militarily. During that same time, God had continued to honor the promise He made so long ago, 'to bless those who bless the descendents of Abraham.' As long as America maintained her supportive role as Israel's protectorate, her blessings have continued right up to the middle of last month."

"And what happened last month?" prompted Dr. Reid.

"Unfortunately, on February 13th our government made a terrible error. On that fateful day our president announced to the world that America would no long support Israel's right to exist within the prescribed borders dictated by God's everlasting covenant. I believe it was at that very moment when God had no other choice but to remove His protective hedge of blessings from America!"

Everyone in the studio including the audience, the technicians, and Dr. Reid sat on the edge of their seats listening intently to Schroeder's every word.

"The very next day, an unprecedented plague that still defies all medical explanations struck 'only' America. In a little over a month, a series of devastating economic and natural disasters have reduced this once great prosperous nation to third world status! Our country is not in a position to help Israel or anyone else for that matter. As of this moment, the United States of America is financially bankrupt! Even if America wanted to step in and help Israel right now, I'm afraid it's fiscally impossible!"

"Dr. Schroeder," Reid abruptly interjected, "I need to interrupt you at this time."

Reid then tilted his head slightly to the right, placing his hand against his hidden earphone. As he paused to listened to the incoming message, everyone, including the audience, noticed an expression of concern on Reid's face.

"Folks," Reid commented as he looked directly into the camera, "I just received some breaking news from our Jerusalem correspondent, Joel Klein."

Reid paused briefly to look toward his program manager, Charlie Bennett. On Charlie's signal, Reid continued, "We will be switching now to Joel Klein standing by live in Jerusalem."

The transition from PTW's main studio in Providence to their reporter standing on the streets of Jerusalem with the famous Wailing Wall as his backdrop was instantaneous.

"Joel, can you repeat for our PTW audience what has just happen?" asked Tom Reid.

"Yes, Dr. Reid," the reporter acknowledged. "At exactly 2:45 p.m. Jerusalem time, 7:45 a.m. eastern time, the Arab League of Nations voted overwhelmingly to declare all-out war against Israel!"

"What about Iran?" Dr. Reid interjected. "They are not part of the Arab league."

"The Iranians are wholeheartedly backing the Arab League's decision!" the reporter declared. "Dr. Reid, allow me to put this into perspective for your viewers. With the Iranians included, the tiny nation of Israel, with a current population of only six million, is facing the combined forces of over twenty-four Arab nations, over five hundred million strong."

"I believe those are the most insurmountable odds I have ever heard!" Reid acknowledged.

"Wait, Dr. Reid!" Klein abruptly stopped, as people, who were once standing in the background appeared to be running away from the direction of the Wailing Wall.

"As I speak," Klein continued, "I am hearing the distinct sound of air raid sirens over the city of Jerusalem!"

The reporter again paused. He appeared to be looking up, as if something in the skies above had gotten his attention. "Dear Lord!" shouted the reporter. The millions of PTW viewers sat in suspense watching the Jerusalem correspondent looking upward shielding his eyes with his hand from the sun's glare. "Dr. Reid, I believe I am presently viewing the vapor trails of either large missiles or rockets heading westward toward the coast."

With that said, the reporter's cameraman immediately repositioned his camera upward to scan the skies above Jerusalem in order to capture the incredible images.

"Did you see that?" Klein asked as the camera captured what appeared to be missiles exploding in midair. "I believe Israel's missile defense systems are now up and running!" Klein gleefully declared as even more explosions were viewed from high above.

The sight of even more westward bound missiles soon tempered Klein's euphoric overtones. To Klein and millions of viewers watching from thousands of miles away via satellite, the sobering images of incoming missiles portrayed one inevitable fact: it wouldn't take long before Israel's protective missile shield would be overwhelmed.

PTW's technicians once again switched back to the show's host and his guest in their Providence studio.

"Dr. Schroeder," a visibly shaken Tom Reid asked of the gentleman seated to his right, "What do we do now?"

"There is only one thing we can do, Dr. Reid," his Jewish guest declared with all the confidence of an ancient prophet of God. "We pray—but not an ordinary prayer. We pray a prayer that God Himself specifically recorded in the Book of Psalms over three thousand years ago."

Before continuing, Schroeder stared intensely into the camera lens as if his eyes were fixed on every viewer. "At this very moment in time, I believe God is calling His corporate body of millions of believers to pray Psalm 83 out loud in its entirety."

"Dr. Schroeder," Reid interjected, "while our technicians format the verses to Psalm 83, could you give us some background into this Psalm?"

"Absolutely, Dr Reid," Schroeder agreed. "Psalm 83 was written over 3000 years ago. It is also one of the few unfulfilled prophecies still remaining in the Bible. I personally believe Psalm 83 was written specifically for our generation to proclaim its words in order to frustrate an Arab conspiracy to destroy Israel."

Charlie Bennett signaled both Reid and Schroeder that the verses were ready to be presented. One by one, Schroeder read each of the first five verses presented at the bottom of the screen.

"1. Do not be silent, O God! Do not hold your peace, and not be still, O God!

For behold, your enemies make an uproar; And those who hate you have lifted up their head.

They have taken crafty counsel against Your people, and consulted together against Your protected ones.

They have declared, 'Come, and let us cut them off from being a nation, that the name of Israel may be remembered no more.'

With one mind they plot together. They form an alliance against you."

Schroeder looked up to give his commentary on how each verse pertained to Israel's present dilemma. "Just keep in mind everybody,"

Schroeder commented with a broad smile, "these verses were written well over three thousand years ago!"

From his position on the stage, Schroeder looked out to observe the astonished looks on the faces of those seated in the audience. Feeling the strong presence of God, he continued, "Let's once again go back 3000 years and discover who these conspirators mentioned specifically in verses 6 through 8 really are!"

One-by-one, Schroeder proceeded to name each of the ancient tribes and their respective present-day descendants: the Edomites, the descendants of Esau, are the present-day Palestinians living in Gaza, Israel and Jordan. The Ishmaelites, the descendants of Abraham's oldest son, now populate the entire Saudi Arabian Peninsula. The Moabites and the Ammonites, descendants of Lot's sons by his oldest and youngest daughters, are the present-day Jordanians. The Hagarenes, the descendants of Hagar, are today's Egyptians. The descendants of Ge'bal are today's Lebanese. The Amalekites, also descendants of Esau, populate the Northern Sinai and Jordan. The Philistines are descended from Noah's son, Ham. Their descendants are presently found living in Gaza. The ancient people who inhabited Tyre are today living in Lebanon. Assur is descended from Noah's son Shem. His descendants comprise the present-day nations of Syria, Iraq, and Northern Iran.

"Who would ever have imagined?" Tom Reid declared. "Just ten short minutes ago, we were all witness to the fact that these ancient biblical prophecies, foretold thousands of years ago, had come true! We heard first hand reports from Jerusalem that the descendants of these ten ancient nations, the present-day League of Arab Nations, had today conspired together not only to declare war on Israel, but to literally wipe Israel off the face of the Earth!"

Realizing that time was growing short, Tom Reid turned toward his guest and politely asked, "Dr. Schroeder, will you now lead all of us in prayer asking God to intercede for Israel?"

"It will be my honor, Dr. Reid," Schroeder humbly accepted.

"Will everyone in the audience please take the hand of the person sitting next to you, and those of you sitting at home please do the same," requested Reid. "I am asking everyone hearing my voice to read aloud the words from Psalm 83 projected on your television screens."

Friday, March 23rd
3:10 p.m. Israeli Standard Time
Highway One, 18 Kilometers Outside of Tel Aviv, Israel

Israeli Highway 1 was no exception. As with every eastbound land route leading away from Israel's major coastal cities, traffic on this major highway was at a complete standstill. Fearing more missile attacks to come, thousands of residents from Tel Aviv and other Israeli coastal cities literally stuffed their cars with nonperishable food items and personal belongings and fled inland. The mass exodus away from the Mediterranean coast started immediately after yesterday's bombings of Haifa and Tel Aviv and accelerated into high gear with the Arab League's declaration of war. With no other agenda but to escape harm's way, well over half of Israel's six million citizens were trapped in their cars with nowhere to go.

"Mother, look up at the sky!" commented a young boy sitting on the hood of his family car. Following her son's instructions, the young Israeli mother turned toward the eastern sky.

In a matter of a few short moments, thousand of stranded motorists along Highway 1 were pointing at the same incredible sight.

"My God," someone shouted, "those are missiles, hundreds of them, and they're heading right for us!"

Not even in their worst nightmares could they image such a terrifying sight. With nowhere to go and no shelter to seek, millions of fear stricken Israeli citizens dropped to their knees, crying out to a God they had long since forgotten.

Friday, March 23rd
3:20 p.m. Israeli Standard Time
Along Israel's Northern, Eastern, And Southern borders

All was ready. The borders were now secure. Michael's warriors, armed and protected only with golden swords and breastplates, took up their assigned positions. As a radar dish scanned the distant skies for signs of an impending storm, a million angelic eyes searched the cloudless horizon from Lebanon and Syria to the north, the Sinai to the south, and along the Jordanian border to the east for the signs of an approaching enemy.

One by one, hundreds of angelic scouts concealed deep within enemy territory began returning to their command post all reporting the same exact message, "The enemy is coming!"

From his command post strategically positioned high over the city of Jerusalem, Michael consulted his captains.

"Our warriors are ready!" confidently declared Archangels Uriel and Kiel, captains of the northern and southern front, respectively.

"So are our enemies!" the Angelic Commander Michael emphatically stated. With that said, Michael's entire physical character instantly transformed into that of a luminous being. His crystal blue eyes appeared now as flames of fire and his skin radiated as brilliant as the sun.

Turning to the captain on his right, Michael charged, "Uriel, never again underestimate the cunningness of your opponent! You, of all my captains, should have known that Gog is more formidable an opponent than all of Satan's demonic princes. Concealing chimeras inside those missiles tips to disarm the warheads was ingenious! Never forget, every move Gog makes is thoroughly calculated!"

"Commander, my warriors and I are ready for anything Gog has planned!" stated the embarrassed angelic prince. "I pledge, it will not happen again. Gog and his demonic hordes will not get past our northern flanks!"

"Commander!" shouted an angelic warrior stationed along the Jordanian border. "I see them coming on the eastern horizon!"

Michael ordered, "Tell our warriors to draw their swords, but do not attack until I give the command!"

Michael then proceeded to lift his sword high above his head followed by entire legions of millions of his warriors. In less than a twinkle of an eye, a brilliant golden outline of Israel's borders was visible all the way to heaven.

With one mighty shout, the Angelic Prince of God led his warriors in a unified cry, "To our King and His Messiah, Amen!"

It wasn't long before the distant skies above the entire length of Israel's borders appeared darkened as if by a swarm of advancing locusts. Approaching rapidly were the combined demonic armies of Gog's forces to the north of Israel's borders and millions of Apollon's demons from the south and east.

The foretold epic battle between the forces of good and evil was about to commence. At stake was not only the claim to Israel, God's covenant land, but more importantly, the entire outcome of God's prophetic plan for mankind on planet earth. As the deafening sounds of metal contacting metal began erupting above the skies over Israel, some unexpected assistance for Michael's battling warriors was soon to arrive from thousands of miles away.

Friday, March 23rd
The Moment Israel Is Attacked
Spanning All American Time Zones

All over America, millions of believers in Jesus, young and old, rich and poor, from every race and ethnic group, many kneeling in front of televisions in the privacy of their livings room, some in their places of employment, and many others viewing on large screens set up in schools and college auditoriums all across America, followed along with Ezra Schroeder and corporately read aloud every verse of Psalm 83.

In Jacksonville, Florida, watching PTW projected on a large screen setup in their school's auditorium, the principal of Jacksonville's Word of Life Christian Academy stood at the stage's microphone before an auditorium filled with over 400 faculty and students. With all heads bowed and eyes closed, she began to pray, "Lord Jesus, "We have just prayed Psalm 83 with that man on television. We now come together as a collective body of believers asking you Lord to protect Israel in her time of need. Please, Lord, place your mighty angels around her borders and keep her from all harm. We also ask you to open the eyes of the Jewish people. Please remove the blinders that prevent them from seeing the truth that Jesus is their true Messiah."

In Richmond, Virginia, over a dozen employees of Larry Johnson's Auto World gathered around a TV in the dealership's customer waiting room. After reciting the words of Psalm 83 shown on the television screen, each employee sat silently praying for God's intervention in Israel's time of need.

In San Diego, California, a small 84-year-old prayer warrior, watching the show on a small television mounted above her nursing home bed, prayed, "Father, in the mighty name of Jesus, I beg you, please put a supernatural hedge of protection around Israel. I pray the blood of Jesus over all people living within its borders, both Arabs and Jews, that not one hair on their heads will be harmed. Again, in Jesus' name, I come against all forms of weapons and attacks of the devil, that the devil's plans will not prosper, but will be trampled under God's mighty feet."

In PTW's studios in Providence, Rhode Island, at the completion of reading aloud Psalm 83, Schroeder cried out toward heaven, "Lord, hear our plea! O God, we beseech you now, destroy the present crop of Israel's enemies as you destroyed Israel's enemies of the past. Pursue them until they have acknowledged the name of Israel's God. Father, I beg you now, open the eyes of my people. I pray the same words that Paul prayed so many years ago, 'My heart's desire and prayer to you O Lord is for Israel, that they may be saved!'"

Friday, March 23rd
3:20 p.m. Israeli Standard Time

"Attack!" Michael shouted as the first wave of Apollon's demons made haste to cross the designated battle line drawn directly over the Jordan River. As Michael's warriors charged forward to intercept their sword-welding enemies, something astonishing occurred. The instant the angelic warriors' swords clashed with those of their enemies, each demon's weapon

exploded into a million dazzling pieces, leaving their terrified holders completely defenseless.

Friday, March 23rd
3:20 p.m. Israeli Standard Time
Highway 1, 18 Kilometers outside of Tel Aviv, Israel

"Look toward the skies!" shouted out the voices of those motorists stranded along the eastbound lane of Israeli Highway 1. All looked up toward the eastern skies to view a sight never again to behold. As if watching the most magnificent fireworks display ever staged, millions of Israeli citizens stared in awe as what appeared to be hundreds of dazzling, high-altitude explosions simultaneously occurring above their heads all at the same time.

"It is our arrow missiles shooting down the enemy's missile!" declared one of the onlookers.

"No, it is Adoni!" declared another. "He has heard our prayers and He is the One destroying the enemy missiles!"

"Praise Adoni!" shouted out a chorus of others.

In less than a minute's time, millions of Israeli citizens, both old and young, dropped to their knees and began crying out praises of sincere thanks to their long-forgotten Sustainer and Benefactor. As all of Israel knelt down crying out to their God, there came a bright light accompanied by a thunderous voice from the heavens above saying, "Look up, O Israel, and behold my beloved Son!"

Surprisingly, each person hearing these words was able to obey its command and look up. Without blinking or refraining from staring directly into the intense light, all were able to behold a sight long ago prophesied by the ancient Prophet Zachariah: "They will look on Me whom they pierced. Yes, they will mourn for Him as one mourns for his only son, and grieve for Him as one grieves for a firstborn."

As millions of tear-filled eyes remained fixed on their Messiah, God's thunderous voice proclaimed one final declaration, "O hear O

Israel, children of my covenant with your father Abraham. From this moment, trust only in the name of Yeshua for your salvation."

Instantly, the blindingly intense light vanished and blue skies returned over Israel. For well over any hour, every Israeli citizen continued staring upward, both repenting and mourning for their sins, but at the same time praising and rejoicing over their new found Messiah, Yeshua.

Friday, March 23rd
8:20 *a.m. Eastern Standard Time*
Providence, Rhode Island
Main Studio
Gospel Broadcasting Network (GBN)

"Folks," Reid interjected, immediately following Schroeder's prayer, "I just heard once again from our Jerusalem correspondent Joel Klein with some truly miraculous news. We will be switching now to Joel standing by in Jerusalem."

Once again, with Jerusalem's famous Wailing Wall as his backdrop, an obviously overjoyed Joel Klein stood ready to report on what would soon prove to be the most miraculous event that had taken place in the streets of Jerusalem since the time of Christ.

"Dr. Reid! I don't know how to properly articulate what I am about to say."

"Just take your time, Joel."

"Dr. Reid," the excited reporter continued, "the very moment the enemy missiles entered Israeli airspace, we witnessed them exploding into a million vanishing pieces right before our eyes. Following that, my camera man and I heard what sounded like loud rumbles of thunder."

"Thunder?" interjected Reid.

"Dr. Reid," Joel commented as he bent over to catch his breath, "now this is the most amazing thing of all! The very moment we heard the sound of thunder, every Jewish person within our sight looked up toward the sky as if they were watching something amazing occurring."

"Maybe they were staring in the direction of the exploding missiles?" Reid asked.

"No, Dr. Reid," Klein interjected. "The explosions occurred in the eastern skies behind us. The Jews were staring almost straight up!"

"What about the other ethnic groups present?" Reid asked. "Did you observe any of their members staring up?"

"No," Klein immediately replied. "I specifically watched a group of Muslim Arabs walking toward us."

"What was their reaction to the Jew's behavior?"

"They were marveling at the Jews just like us! Hold on, Dr. Reid," Klein again interjected. "Here comes one of the Jewish men we were observing running up to us now."

"Yeshua! Yeshua is the Mashiach!" the man declared into the camera.

"Are you a Messianic Jew?" Joel Klein asked the excited man, who was wearing a black hat and a prayer shawl.

"I wasn't five minutes ago," the man exclaimed, "but I am now!"

"By your dress, you are a Hassidic Jew!" the thoroughly astonished reporter declared. "What made you change your mind?"

"I heard God's voice with my own ears and saw Yeshua's pierced body with my own eyes. What more proof do I need?"

With only seconds remaining on the control room's clock, PTW's technicians switched back to their Providence studio. In the studio, words alone could not describe the jubilant feeling among the hundred or so people gathered in the large auditorium. Each person present knew in their hearts that they had just witnessed one of the greatest miracles of modern times. With the cameras still rolling, the show concluded with everyone, from the control room technicians to the entire audience, dancing and celebrating to the fast-paced rhythm of a lively Jewish song. Even the most reserved persons like Charlie Bennett and Bill Pierce, the chief control room technician, were seen dancing in a circle while praising the name of Jesus.

Joining in on the human celebration were two equally elated angels. Muriel and Ariel were both dancing and praising the name of their Lord and Creator along with a group of over a dozen ecstatic humans on the stage.

"Ariel, it's time!" Muriel shouted out over the music.

"Do we have to leave now?" complained his jubilant angelic companion, dancing alongside Ezra Schroeder and Tom Reid. "I was just learning the steps to this Jewish song!"

"Sorry, my friend," Muriel replied with a big grin, "I would love to stay and celebrate, but Passover begins tomorrow at sundown. We need to have Schroeder at the White House by 3 p.m. today."

"That only leaves us a little over two hours to get Schroeder to the airport!" Ariel remarked after looking down at the digital clock mounted at the edge of the stage. Hastily, Ariel leaned forward and spoke directly into Schroeder's thoughts.

"Look at the clock. It is time to leave!"

Responding as if to his own thoughts, Schroeder turned toward Reid and said, "Tom, I'm afraid I have to be leaving. My flight leaves at 11:30. Have all the arrangements been made?"

Schroeder could sense Reid hesitate.

"Ezra, I'm afraid there's been a slight change of plans!" Reid replied.

Instant panic replaced joy. To Schroeder, there was no time left for changing plans. "Tom, I don't like the look on your face!"

"I didn't want to say anything to upset you before the show," Reid sheepishly responded, "but I'm afraid my brother is not cooperating."

"Tom, for God's sake, Passover begins tomorrow!" Schroeder cried out loud enough to gain notice of those still celebrating nearby. "If I don't see the president today, you can forget all this celebrating. Israel will be toast!"

Pulling his upset guest to the side, Reid looked Schroeder directly in the eyes. "Ezra, listen to me. I have a plan!" Reid declared. "After talking to John last night, I was able to book myself a ticket on your flight. I am going with you!"

"I don't understand," Ezra commented. "Without your brother's help, how can we gain access to the president?"

"Ezra, John and I are identical twins!" Tom replied with a broad smile.

"Are you saying you're willing to impersonate your brother?" Schroeder asked with a surprised look.

"Possibly, as a last resort," Reid calmly replied. "With the fate of Israel right now hanging in the balance, I'm willing to do whatever it takes to get you in to see the president!"

"Is everything arranged in Washington?" Ariel turned to ask his angelic superior.

"That is Yahriel's responsibility," Muriel replied with a smile. "It is our job to make sure these humans arrive safely in Washington."

Chapter Twenty-Four

"Then Jesus said to him, 'Away with you, Satan! For it is written, 'You shall worship the LORD your God, and Him only you shall serve.'"
Matthew 4:10 NKJV

Far more accurate than any prophecy the so-called prophets of the world have to offer, the 2600-year-old Book of Ezekiel has recorded in its chapters the most amazing series of prophesies found anywhere in the Bible. In exacting details, Ezekiel foretells a convergence of times, places, and people groups who have and will play major roles in intricately shaping future world events.

Written over seven centuries before the birth of Christ, Ezekiel Chapter 35 predicted a future time when the Israelites would be driven from their land. This major event in Jewish history was fulfilled in 70 AD when Roman legions under Titus destroyed Jerusalem, burned the Temple, renamed the land Palestine after the Jew's enemies, the Philistines, and led millions of remaining Jews off into exile and captivity.

Ezekiel 35 also details this Jewish Diaspora, a vast period of time spanning two millennia when the descendants of Abraham would be scattered to the four corners of the earth, but would miraculously remain intact as a distinct people group. During their extended exile, the descendants of Esau and Ishmael would confiscate Abraham's covenant land. Known also as Arabs, these people groups would maintain a perpetual hatred of the Israelites until the end of time.

In its closing verses, Ezekiel Chapter 35 describes the land of Israel during this time as a desolate wasteland, not responsive to the agricultural efforts of the usurpers. During his visit to the Holy Land in 1867, American author Samuel Clemens (Mark Twain) describes Palestine as follows: "…A desolate country whose soil is rich enough, but is given over wholly to weeds…a silent mournful expanse…a desolation…we never saw a human being on the whole route…hardly a tree or shrub anywhere. Even the olive tree and the cactus, those fast friends of a worthless soil, had almost deserted the country."

Ezekiel Chapters 36 and 37 precisely predicted a future time when the Israelites would miraculously return to their land, becoming a nation after two millennia of dispersion. The land would once again respond to its rightful owners and flourish. During this time, the surrounding Arab nations would conduct a series of unsuccessful wars against Israel. All of these prophecies were fulfilled when Israel was awarded nation status in May of 1948. From that moment until the present, Israel's agriculture and economy has continued to thrive, rewarding Israelis with the highest standard of living in the entire Middle East. Also during this time, its Arab neighbors have repeatedly attacked Israel.

Ezekiel Chapter 38 foretells a future catastrophic assault led by a Russian/Persian confederacy of nations, unified with the sole purpose of destroying Israel once and for all. The question you should ask yourself right now is whose report will you believe, that of the soothsayers of the world or that of God? As for me and my household, we shall believe the report of the Lord.

Friday, March 23*rd*
11:15 *a.m.*
Onboard US Airways' Flight 720

No flight in aviation history could possibly be safer. Until it arrives at its destination at Washington's Reagan National Airport, the US Airways' Flight 720 airbus that had just departed Providence's Green International Airport would be protected by the most elite force of demon slayers found anywhere in the universe. Under Archangel Muriel's orders, Kiel and over two dozen of his best warriors had been given a dual assignment: to escort this daily 1 hour and 37 minute nonstop flight from take off to landing, and to safeguard one of the passengers onboard from the wrath of Satan himself. Ariel would now be joined by a host of Kiel's most elite warriors. Their mission would be to protect the only human who had in his possession the knowledge to expose Satan's last remaining plan to destroy the Jewish State of Israel.

Friday, March 23rd
7:17 p.m.
The Russian Naval Base
Tartus, Syria

Where armed Russian guards stood just 24 hours prior, sea gulls now strolled undisturbed up and down the docking pier searching for tidbits of discarded food. For the first time in months, all was quiet along the entire length of Docking Pier 7. Its secretly guarded Iranian-manned submarines had vanished sometime during the previous night under the dark blue Mediterranean waters.

A dozen or so sea birds suddenly took flight, seemingly spooked by something unseen. With their parting, an unnatural cloak of darkness descended over the entire pier and its surrounding waters. So dark was its presence that even the pier's automatic floodlights could not penetrate its aura. Where only moments before sea gulls perched watching the setting sun, now a host of shadowy figures appeared, their glowing yellow eyes fixed on the large expanse of open water beyond the pier.

"Michael's victory will be short lived," stated the shortest of the five figures.

"It will be his last, my Lord!" emphatically declared a darkened aberration standing to the group's far right. "Israel will be no more!"

One by one, the demonic princes took turns confidently boasting to one another about the final outcome of their next mission. They were too self-absorbed to notice a deepening scowl had formed on each of their leader's three faces. In a fit of rage, Satan proceeded to grab the throat of the demonic prince standing to his immediate right, lifting his twitching body high above the pier.

"Allahzad, you miserable excuse of putrid disgust!" Satan seethed,

squeezing the demon's throat so hard his yellow eyes bulged far from their sockets. "You assured me that your plan to destroy those dirty Jews was completely foolproof!"

Except for one, instant dread gripped the remaining princes. In all their eons of earthly existence, Satan's demonic princes had never been witness to the possible demise of one of their own. With his fellow princes Apollon and Amducious shaking in fear, Gog stepped forward, observing in awe-filled wonderment the sight of possible demonic obliteration.

To Gog's delight, his malevolent expectations were instantly rewarded. Exploding outward from Satan's grip in all directions was what appeared to be billions of infinitesimally sized reddish brown bat-like spirits, all screaming in woeful unison, "We are destined for the pits of hell!"

With the strong stench of burning sulfur roundabout, the Prince of Demons turned now toward his remaining princes and calmly asked, "Does anyone else want to join him?"

Once again, Gog maintained his crafty composure while his fellow princes stood by, quivering in silent terror.

"Good!" Satan said with a smile, as his adjacent heads both laughingly scoffed, "It was about time that we had a change in command."

With the same instrument of destruction used to crush the very existence out of the former Prince of Persia, Satan now reached out his clawed hand and affectionately stroked the shoulder of Allahzad's newly chosen successor.

"Gog, above all my princes, you have proven yourself worthy," Satan avowed. "Lord of the East, your plan had better work, or you'll face the same fate as your predecessor."

With his two rivals sneering on, Gog accepted his newly proclaimed title with a prideful grin. At long last, his patience was rewarded. The Prince of the North had finally received his coveted title of Lord over all Eastern domains. His realm had now doubled, extending from Russia's frozen tundra to the north to the warm, oil-rich waters of the Persian Gulf.

"Lord, Satan, words alone cannot express the great honor you have bestowed upon me. I will not let you down like these others," Gog pledged with a smirk. "My plan is foolproof!"

"What about Schroeder?" scoffed Apollon, standing in the background. "As we speak, he and that televangelist Reid are onboard a flight to Washington to tell the American president every detail of your 'secret plan.'"

The mere mention of that mortal's name sent Satan once again into a raging torrent. "Schroeder!" Satan thundered. So intense was his wrath, an explosive surge of energy burst out from his body, causing hundreds of overhead electrical transformers to explode into a colorful pyrotechnic display. In a matter of moments, the entire Russian port and city of Tartus were cast into total darkness.

"Schroeder must die!" Satan again shouted as his adjacent heads repeatedly declared, "Death to the dirty Jew."

"My Lord," Apollon interjected. "The Jew is now protected by Kiel and a host of his seasoned warriors."

With all three faces firmly fixed on his second in command, Satan calmly asked, "What is your plan to rid me of this Jew once and for all?"

"Have patience, my Lord," Apollon boldly replied. "Once Kiel is out of the way, I will rid you of this Jew once and for all. But for now, I must now concentrate all my energies on preventing Schroeder from meeting with the president."

"And how do you propose to do that since Kiel's warriors are watching Schroeder's every move?"

"That, my Lord, is the easy part," Apollon commented with an evil grin. "I will simply allow Kiel and his idiots to expend all their energies watching over the Jew. We, on the other hand, will unleash all the powers of hell against his unguarded Christian travel companion. Without Reid, Schroeder has absolutely no chance of accessing the White House."

"Isn't Reid guarded by Muriel himself?" Satan inquired.

"Not on this flight," Apollon declared. "Only Schroeder's guardian, Ariel, was seen boarding."

"Then where the hell is Muriel?" a frustrated Satan shouted out loud.

"He's already in Washington," Apollon proclaimed with an evil sneer.

"I don't care how you do it; I want you to find that archangel!" Satan charged. "Apollon, do everything in your power to keep him as far away from Reid and Schroeder as possible."

"At your command, my Lord."

Raising his clinched left fist high, Apollon instantly vanished, leaving Satan and his two remaining counterparts behind.

"Gog!" called Satan.

Showing not the least bit of fear, the newly appointed Lord of the East stood face to face with his master and boldly declared, "I will never let you down, my Lord. I pledge to you, before the Jews have a chance to blow their ram's horns announcing tomorrow's Passover, their beloved Israel will be no more."

"Then go now," Satan ordered. "Join your demons aboard their vessels."

Before departing, Satan issued Gog a stern warning. "Cunning Lord of the East, if you fail me now, I swear on myself, the remains of Allahzad will enjoy your company in hell for eternity."

With Gog's departure, only the demonic prince of America remained in Satan's presence.

"Amducious," Satan calmly announced, displaying what appeared to be a smile of gratitude on each of his faces, "I have purposely chosen to have you remain here with me until last."

In what appeared to be a rare act of appreciation, the Lord of all Demons proceeded to rest his clawed hand on his prince's right shoulder.

"I want to thank you for remaining my most steadfast loyal prince," Satan affectionately declared. "I have one more request of your services."

Though extremely loyal, Amducious lacked the intuitive abilities of his fellow princes to discern the true motives behind Satan's kind words.

"I want you to personally kill both Schroeder and Reid for me," Satan requested. "Kill Schroeder," one head ordered. "Kill Reid," echoed the other.

"I swear by your name, my Lord, it will be done," Amducious declared, raising high his clinched left fist.

"You don't understand, my loyal friend," Satan interjected. "I don't want you to wait until after tomorrow. I want them both dead by sundown today, is that clear?"

"But, Lord Satan, how can I possibly get close enough to Schroeder with Kiel and his warriors watching his every move?"

"I don't care how you do it—just do it!" Satan demanded.

"Yes, my Lord," Satan's loyal prince reluctantly agreed. "Your will be done."

Friday, March 23*rd*
12:21 *p.m.*
Onboard US Airways' Flight 720

With New Jersey's southern coastline in their sights, the crew of US Airways' Flight 720 began making preparations for their descent. In less than thirty minutes, this 100-seat commuter airbus would be touching down on a runway within sight of both the Jefferson and Lincoln memorials. For the crew of six, today's flight would be logged in as completely routine. But for two of the 94 passengers onboard, this cross-state journey would mark the beginning of a nightmare far beyond their wildest dreams.

"Did you feel that?" a startled Tom Reid turned and asked the person sitting to his immediate right in the window seat.

"Feel what?" Ezra Schroeder asked.

"It's hard to explain," Reid replied with a confused look. "It actually felt as if someone had just poured ice water all over me."

Schroeder paused, looking directly at his obviously shaken traveling companion. "Tom, we need to pray!" Ezra emphatically stated.

"I agree," affirmed a relieved Tom Reid.

The two men instinctively locked hands and bowed their heads in prayer.

"Father God," Reid began, "we need your help now like never before. I can sense in my spirit a strong presence of evil attempting to stop us from reaching the president. God, with the authority of the name of Jesus, I call upon you to supply Ezra and myself a strong hedge of protection. Surround us now with legions of your mighty angels."

"Adoni," beseeched Schroeder, "I rebuke the devil and his evil cohorts right now in the mighty name of Yeshua! Satan, you have no power over Tom and me for it is written, 'Greater is He who is in me, than he who is in the world.'"

"Satan, you are a liar and the prince of lies! You have come against us to kill and destroy," Reid boldly declared. "But God's Word says, 'He will put His angels in charge over us and no harm shall befall us. God shall shield us with his wings and His faithful promises will be our armor and protection.'"

"Adoni, Tom and I humbly sit here before your mighty throne. Be with us now as we attempt to meet with the president. Direct our paths all the way to the White House. Touch President Devoe's heart and open her eyes to the truth that we bring her. And most importantly, protect Israel from all harm and all attacks from the enemy."

"Father, I have one final request," Reid asked with tears streaming down his face. "I pray for the soul of my brother. Lord, whatever it takes for John to enter into the Kingdom, I place him now in your hands. Do with my brother John as you will. We ask all this in the mighty name of Jesus. Amen."

"Amen," echoed an angelic voice from behind.

Friday, March 23rd
1 p.m.
The James Brady White House Press Briefing Room
Washington, D.C.

At exactly 1 p.m., everyone stood to their feet, applauding the President of the United States as she entered the room.

"Good morning, everyone," a beaming Analise Devoe announced, speaking into the podium's microphone. "Wow, what a difference a few hours of time can make!"

Her joking comments were followed by an outburst of cheering applause. For the first time in well over a month a real sense of relaxed tranquility returned to White House Press Briefing Room.

"Folks, I mean this with all my heart." the president commented, smiling as she looked around the room filled with familiar faces. "Words cannot describe the sense of relief I'm feeling right now. Are you all feeling the same thing?"

Her receptive audience of journalists responded back with resounding nods of affirmation.

If any person in the room appeared relaxed, it was Analise Devoe. More than anytime in her brief tumultuous tenure as President of the United States, she stood before her nation in a complete state of peace. Though they couldn't pinpoint it, even this room full of perceptive reporters could sense a change had taken place in their president. In a moment, they were about to find what brought about this change.

"Folks," the president continued, "before I start today's briefing, I would like to ask the entire nation and each and everyone of us gathered in this pressroom to bow our heads in a moment of silence, thanking God for rescuing the world from the brink of disaster."

Thank God! Literal shockwaves of disbelief raced through the room filled with skeptical reporters. *Who is this person standing behind the Presidential podium? Analise Devoe, calling on the name of God, never. She must have lost her mind!*

"I know exactly what you are all thinking at this moment," the president calmly stated, directing her attention to the cameras broadcasting this live national telecast.

"The Analise Devoe you have all known was a devout atheist. She would never in a million years acknowledge the name of God. But my fellow Americans, I have had time to reflect on the horrific events that have directly affected our nation over this past month. I also sat in awe this morning viewing, as did most of you, the miraculous events that have taken place in the Middle East."

Except for the president's voice, no other sound could be heard in the room. Everyone present either stood or sat fixed in silent awe ready to record the very next breaking revelation from the president's lips.

"Even with Israel's superior defensive missile shield, hundreds of deadly missiles and rockets do not explode in midair on their own," the president declared. "After everything I have witnessed, there is only one rational conclusion I can now make. I emphatically state that God is real and for the remainder of my presidency, I will affirm this fact. I have repented of my great ignorance and I pledge from this moment forward, I will do everything within the powers vested in me by the great people of the United States of America to beseech God to once again bless our broken country with abundant greatness."

Eyes literally popped and jaws dropped at the president's shocking statements affirming before the entire world a belief in a personal God. But of all the reporters present, one single person standing to the president's far left stood more amazed than any other.

"I don't believe this is happening!" mumbled an emotionally stunned John Reid.

Equally shocked was a pair of angelic beings standing directly behind Reid. "I must say, I am truly impressed," Muriel commented, turning to applaud his fellow archangel standing to his right.

"I believe 'bombs bursting in air' may have had some effect," Yahriel jokingly replied. "Did you take care of Beelazad and Zorah?"

"I expect Kiel's warriors are keeping Reid's demons in good company," Muriel replied with a smile as both Archangels turned their attention back to the human press briefing.

Friday, March 23rd
1:12 *p.m.*
Ronald Reagan National Airport
Arlington, Virginia

For the first time in aviation history, Reagan National Airport played host to the most bizarre gathering of supernatural entities ever to converge along the shores of the Potomac River. It was a parade from the pits of hell. Demons of all rankings, shapes, and sizes lined up along both sides of the airport's long concourse, taunting and screaming out gross obscenities at Kiel and his warriors.

"Kiel's warriors are a bunch of Jew-lovers!" screeched several ugly chimeras running parallel at a safe distance to the angelic escorts.

"Schroeder and Reid are dead meat!" screamed out a wide-mouthed aberration with a breath stench so putrid it would repel the filthiest of flies.

With the airport's exit in clear view, over a dozen midlevel demons made a surprise frontal charge on the small contingent of angels and humans. Kiel's warriors immediately responded by tightening their ranks around the two humans.

Without notice, a team of airport security guards blocked the airport's front entrance, not allowing anyone to enter or exit.

"Everyone stay exactly where they are and please—remain calm!" ordered a tall, muscular guard.

"I'm sorry folks for the inconvenience," another guard announced, "but we presently have a very serious situation just outside the concourse in the parking lot. I'm sorry to inform all of you but as of right now, National Airport is under a lockdown!"

Standing only feet away from the Airport's blocked exit doors were a stunned Ezra Schroeder and Tom Reid.

"What do we do now?" Tom Reid asked in frustration.

"We definitely need to pray!" responded Reid's traveling companion. "Without a doubt, Satan is doing everything in his power to keep us from meeting with the president."

Little did Schroeder realize how much truth was in his words. For just beyond his human senses, a battle was being waged in the supernatural to prevent his meeting with destiny.

Friday, March 23rd
1:23 p.m.
James Brady White House Press Briefing Room
Washington, D.C.

"The last question will go to Maggie Rowe," the president announced as she pointed to the *New York Times* reporter seated with her hand raised in the second row.

"Madame President, you said that except for the Iranian government, you have been in constant contact with the Israeli Prime Minister, the leaders of the Arab league, and European Union President Giulio D'Alema. As of this moment, has anything yet been resolved?"

"Maggie, I can answer your question with an unequivocal yes!" the president declared. "Since this morning's preemptive missile attack on Israel, President D'Alema and I have been in constant contact with all the parties involved calling for an immediate cessation of all hostilities."

"Are you saying we have an agreement, Madame President?"

"As of 12:45 p.m. this afternoon," the president replied with a broad smile, "we have a truce!" This brought a boisterous round of applause and cheers throughout room.

"Madame President," Ms Rowe shouted above the voices of her colleagues. "What about the Iranians?"

The persistent reporter's question captured the full attention of everyone in the room, including the president.

"I can't answer that," the president sadly confessed. "I pray they too will listen to reason and follow the lead of their Arab neighbors in seeking a peaceful solution to this conflict."

With that being her final comment, the president ended the press conference with her very first "May God bless America!"

As the president made her stage exit in the direction of her smiling press secretary, Archangel Muriel leaned forward and spoke directly into John Reid's mind.

"Ask her now about your brother's visit."

Gathering all the courage he could muster, John Reid boldly stepped forward and asked the approaching president, "Madame President, this might not be the right time, but I need to ask you a really big favor!"

"What is it, John?" the president paused and asked in a calm, unperturbed voice.

Nervously, John Reid made his request known, "Madame

President, as I speak, my brother Tom may be on his way to the White House right now to seek a meeting with you."

"Why would your brother want to meet with me?" a puzzled president asked.

"Before I answer your question, there's more, Madame President," Reid sheepishly announced. "He's being accompanied by Dr. Ezra Schroeder."

"The Newton man?"

The president's raised voice caused instant fear to grip Reid. He knew he could have retracted his request right then and there with minimal damage being done. Instead, Reid boldly decided that now was the time to follow through on the promise he had made so long ago while sitting in his father's church. No matter what the outcome, whether or not he was fired from his coveted position as White House Press Secretary, it didn't matter now. John Reid was not going to pass up this opportunity of making his Heavenly Father proud of him.

"Yes, Madame President," Reid boldly proclaimed. "I believe they are both headed here to supply you with information vital to keeping the Middle East peace process from collapsing."

The president paused for a moment, making direct eye contact with her press secretary. "John," the president said in clear firm voice, "I want you to contact your brother and Dr. Schroeder right now and to tell them from me to get their butts right over here! Is that clear?"

"Done, Madame President!"

Friday, March 23rd
1:36 *p.m.*
Ronald Reagan National Airport's
Public Parking Lot
Arlington, Virginia

At approximately 1:04 p.m., a crazed gunman indiscriminately opened fire on groups of innocent bystanders walking to and from their cars parked at Reagan National Airport's long-term parking lot. Initial police reports have two people killed and four others wounded before an airline security officer shot the lone gunman dead. Until the police investigations were over, returning travelers who had used the long-term parking lot as a safe haven for their parked cars would temporarily be denied access to their vehicles.

Reid and Schroeder were among the hundreds stranded travelers ushered to the far southern end of the airport, away from the ongoing police investigations.

"The way I see it, we have two options," Schroeder commented to Tom Reid. "We can wait here until the police have finished their investigation, or we can leave my car here and get on the metro. That way we will be downtown in less than thirty minutes."

"I say the metro," declared Tom Reid.

"I second that!" Schroeder agreed.

No sooner did Schroeder affirm his friend's suggestion, than the familiar sound of PTW's theme song could be heard coming from Reid's jacket.

"It's Cindy calling to find out if we made it here in one piece," Reid commented as he reached into his jacket's pocket to secure his cell phone.

"Hello, sweetie."

"I didn't know you thought of me that way," chuckled a male voice on the other side of the line."

"It's my brother!" Tom declared with a broad smile. "John, you are not going to believe what happened. There was a shooting in the airport's parking lot and we can't access Ezra's car until the police investigation is over!"

"Stay right there," John commanded. "I'm coming right over."

"John, you don't have to do that!" Tom interjected. "Ezra and I can catch the metro, and we'll be there in less than a half an hour."

"You are not taking the metro, is that clear, little brother?" John firmly instructed. "I'll be there in less then twenty minutes."

"John," a confused Tom Reid commented, "you aren't sounding like the same person I talked to at 7:30 this morning."

"That's because that person you talked to this morning is not the same person," John confessed with a smile. "Tom, hold on to something because I have some really good news to share."

After a brief pause allowing time for his brother to gather his thoughts, John Reid continued. "Tom, you and Ezra have a three o'clock appointment with the President of the United States!"

"Praise Jesus!" an overwhelmed Tom Reid cried out in joy.

"I second that motion!" replied the equally ecstatic voice on the other end of the phone.

The two human siblings were totally unaware that evil spirits were monitoring their entire conversation. Standing far enough away, just out of the range of Kiel's watchful eyes, three demonic beings finalized their latest scheme.

"This may have worked out better than I planned," Apollon announced to his smiling captains.

"A slight change in plans, commander?" asked Calazad, the demonic prince of Northern Virginia.

"Commander, what about our main mission?" questioned Amducious.

"That hasn't changed, just delayed," Apollon replied with an evil grin. "First, I personally want to take care of the only human who has direct access to the President of the United States."

"John Reid." said Calazad.

"Yes. And once Reid is out of the way," Amducious interjected, "I'll personally take care of Schroeder and the other Reid."

"But until then, my orders are for the two of you to keep Kiel and his warriors totally occupied," Apollon charged the demonic princes. "Under no circumstances are you to allow Schroeder to come anywhere near the president! Is that clear?"

"We swear by Satan!" both demonic princes avowed with clinched left fists held high.

Chapter Twenty-Five

"For we are not fighting against people made of flesh and blood, but against the evil rulers and authorities of the unseen world, against those mighty powers of darkness who rule this world, and against wicked spirits in the heavenly realms."

Ephesians 6:12 NLT

Friday, March 23rd
1:52 *p.m.*
White House's Southeast Gate
Washington, D.C.

Like a flock of hungry vultures hovering above the skies of Washington, D.C., scores of black-winged demons began landing on the tops of all the man-made structures surrounding the White House. In a matter of minutes, hundreds of yellow eyes were scanning every inch of the White House grounds for signs of their intended prey, White House Press Secretary John Reid.

Observing this ominous spectacle from the back entrance to the White House's East Wing, a concerned Archangel Muriel turned to his angelic companion and asked,

"How long have they been up there?"

"The first one arrived about 10 minutes ago," Yahriel replied, his own eyes transfixed on a single demon sitting alone on the edge of the adjacent Treasury Building.

"And who's the handsome one over there?" Muriel asked. "He looks too angelic to be one of Amducious' demons."

"I know exactly who he is!" Yahriel declared with a look of concern. "This is the first time I've seen him on American soil."

"Well, who is he?" Muriel again asked.

"He was the mastermind behind Auschwitz, Dachau, and Treblinka," Yahriel replied.

"Mekizad!" Muriel instantly recalled. "What is he doing here?"

Though Muriel had never set eyes on Mekizad, this demon's reputation as the evil force behind Heinrich Himmler's plan to exterminate every single European Jew was known to all angelic beings. Of all Satan's assassins, Mekizad had proven to be his brightest and most deceptive.

"The answer is simple," Yahriel replied. "He's been sent to kill Reid. We can't take any chances with him around."

"He will never get close to John Reid!" Muriel confidently stated. "We have warriors positioned along the entire route and I am personally accompanying Reid to and from the airport."

Suddenly, a car driven by John Reid exited the underground entrance to the White House's private parking garage.

"Time to go!" Muriel bid his angelic counterpart a quick farewell as he passed through the side of the passing car, supernaturally readjusting his massive angelic frame to comfortably fit into the backseat of the midsized vehicle.

Completely unaware of the presence of his angelic escort s, John Reid stopped to sign out at the White House's southeast gate.

"Leaving a little early today, Mr. Reid?" asked Frank Cooper, one of two secret service agents on duty at the White House's Southeast security checkpoint positioned directly across from the U.S. Treasury Building.

"I'll be right back, Frank," Reid answered with a beaming smile. "I'm headed over to National Airport to pick up my brother and his guest for a 3 o'clock appointment with the president. It shouldn't take that long."

"I don't know about that, Mr. Reid," Cooper cautioned. "Didn't you hear about the shooting in National's parking lot? Homeland

Security has the entire airport on lockdown. They're checking to make sure there weren't any terrorist connections."

"My brother Tom told me about it when I called, but I don't think the White House Press Secretary will have any problems getting in," Reid said with a confident smile.

"Better yet, Mr. Reid, I'll make a few phone calls over to National to tell them you're coming." Feeling a few drops of rain on his hand, Cooper looked up toward the sky and commented. "You better get going now. It looks like a big storm might be brewing."

"Thanks, Frank," responded the appreciative White House Press Secretary, "I'll see you back here in no time!"

The moment his car left the security of the White House grounds, an impending clash of supernatural forces would determine John Reid's final destiny.

Friday, March 23rd
2 p.m.
In Route to Reagan National Airport

With the advent of spring, it was not unusual for cold and warm air masses to clash over the skies of Washington, D.C., producing rain-laden storm clouds, but the ominous tempest rapidly approaching the city was far from usual. As Reid's car exited the fenced-in security of the White House complex, countless numbers of demonic spirits took flight in the air, darkening the skies above to near midnight conditions.

The moment Reid turned right onto Executive Avenue, a blinding torrent of rain burst forth from the skies above, making driving virtually impossible. *Where did this come from?* Reid questioned as he cautiously inched his way onto the tour bus service lane that wrapped its way around the eastern side of the National Ellipse.

At the same time, waves of demonic spirits welding bloody red swords attacked Muriel's angelic defenders from every conceivable direction. Metal clashing metal produced a thunderous display of brilliant flashes visible for miles around.

Never had a storm so ferocious struck the D.C. metropolitan

area. Blinding flashes of lightning and ear-piercing cracks of thunder could be seen and heard throughout the city. Within a five-minute period of time, an unprecedented four inches rainfall had emptied out of the skies above Washington, D.C., completely inundating the city's public drainage system. Power outages and flooded streets were everywhere with no letup in sight.

Taking the path of least resistance, a fast-flowing river of runoff was now following Reid's car down 15th Street. With the Washington monument barely visible out of his passenger's side window, Reid immediately jammed on his brakes, stopping just short of what appeared to be an endless sea of water that continued far out into the Tidal Basin.

With Independence Avenue, Reid's planned route to the airport, now partially submerged under several feet of water, the strong-willed, free-spirited son of America's first televangelist tried something he hadn't attempted since his childhood. With his bent elbows resting on his car's steering wheel, John Reid folded his hands and made one simple request, "Lord, what shall you have me do?"

Muriel smiled as he leaned forward to dictate specific directions into John Reid's mind.

Turn around and head toward the Holocaust museum. From there, take 14th Street southward to the Route 1 bridge across the Potomac.

"Thank you, Lord!" Reid looked up and smiled. "Now why didn't I think of that myself?"

With a quick look in his rearview mirror, the Presidential Press Secretary executed a perfectly illegal U-turn, crossing the centerline onto a lane completely void of any oncoming traffic. With that feat successfully accomplished, Reid slowly proceeded to drive eastward through huge pools of standing water toward the direction of the Holocaust Museum.

Unknown to Reid and his clandestine angelic passenger, a carefully concealed stowaway named Jalizad lay hidden among the important documents found inside the car's center console. The tiny chimera's mission was to keep his master Mekizad constantly aware as to any changes in Reid's route.

Now it was Jalizad's big chance. With the big angel in the backseat preoccupied in rerouting his own warriors to their new positions, Jalizad was able to transmit his own telepathic message informing his master of Reid's exact location.

The light just turned red as Reid pulled up to the corner of Independence and 14th Street. "Now Lord," Reid petitioned with a smile, "you know I don't have time to waste at this light."

"Praise the Lord!" Reid shouted out as the traffic light instantly changed from red to green. Not only did the light change prematurely, the moment his car turned right on 14th Street, the torrential downpours instantly stopped. For the first time since he left the White House, the road in front of him was completely clear and rain free. With a smile of gratitude, Reid looked up toward heaven and said,

"Thank you, Father. Thank you for taking me back!"

"Pray…Any second now you'll be seeing Him!" screeched an audible voice loud enough to catch Muriel's attention.

The Archangel wasted no time locating the source of the blasphemous cry. Thrusting his hand forward between the front seats, he instantly pulled out of the console what appeared to be a twitching little bat rapidly fluttering its clawed wings in a desperate attempt to escape.

"Who sent you here?" Muriel demanded, squeezing the tiny chimera's chest with just enough force as not to destroy him.

"You are about ready to find out!" Jalizad scoffed.

Out of nowhere, an impact indescribably powerful caused the driver's side door to instantly implode, thrusting both the human driver and his angelic guardian sideways and backward against the opposite side of the vehicle. Inadvertently, the explosive force caused the mighty archangel to loosen his grip on his tiny captive.

As Jalizad attempted to make a hasty escape through the heaps of twisted metal and broken glass, he turned to mock his former captor one last time. "Your God is a liar and His Son is a fool!" the fleeing chimera screeched before a blinding flash out of nowhere instantly disintegrated Jalizad into a reddish-brown puff of sulfurous smoke.

"That's one down, and one left to go!" declared a fiery eyed, sword-

welding warrior named Doriel. After slicing through the tiny chimera, Doriel joined five of his sword-drawn angelic companions all surrounding a late model van that broadsided the driver's door of Reid's car.

"Get out of the car now and face us, you scaly coward," commanded Artriel, the leader of the angelic team assigned to accompany Reid's car to the airport.

"My pleasure," responded a deep, melodic voice from inside the vehicle.

All six angelic warriors stepped back, allowing room for their captive to exit the crumpled van.

"He's passing through the center panel directly in back of the driver's side door!" Doriel shouted as his fellow warriors joined him in a tight semicircle each extending their golden sword tips toward the emerging demon.

In a matter of moments, an exceedingly handsome dark-haired demon was facing his angelic challengers, his sword drawn, with his back to the van.

"Well, look who we have here," Artriel boldly proclaimed, pointing his razor sharp sword tip at the demon's throat. "If it isn't Satan's chief assassin, Mekizad himself."

The smiling demon kept his sword at arm's length, twitching and twisting his weapon in a desperate attempt to ward off his captors.

"Sir, please allow me the privilege of being the first to run him through with my sword," requested Nefriel, one of five angelic warriors under Artriel's command.

"Let him go," ordered a familiar voice from behind. Stepping out from the crushed remains of John Reid's car stood their unscathed commander, the Archangel Muriel.

"Muriel, do you know what you are asking us to do?" questioned his puzzled captain, Artriel. "This demon was responsible for the deaths of over 6 millions Jews in the Holocaust!"

"Sir," Doriel pleaded, inching the edge of his sword ever closer to the neck of the smiling demon, "you can't just let Mekizad go! We may never have another chance like this again!"

Before responding to his warrior's requests, Muriel made a passionate plea, "I want all of you to listen! If it was up to me, this monster would be burning right now in the pits of hell where he belongs, but the Lord Himself has ordered His release."

Muriel didn't have to say another word. His obedient warriors never questioned a direct command from the Lord. They immediately girded their swords in their belt sheaths and stepped aside, allowing ample room for Satan's chief assassin to spread his black scaly wings and take flight, hovering at a safe distance just out of the range of their swords.

"I really feel bad about John Reid," Mekizad brazenly mocked while flapping his bat-like wings in a circular fashion to maintain his stationary position. "I guess there's no one left to arrange Schroeder's meeting with the president. What a shame!"

Muriel stood by totally unfazed by the demon's taunts. With a look of confidence, the Angelic Prince of Truth gazed up at the hovering demonic spirit and pronounced his final doom,

"Go back and tell your master that his days on this earth are quickly coming to an end. It won't be long from now before each one of you miserable cursed creatures are given an eternal dip into the Lake of Fire."

Before vanishing out of sight, Satan's demon assassin sneered downward at his former captors and stated his own prophetic claim, "And it won't be long from now mighty warrior before you say goodbye to your beloved Israel! "

Friday, March 23rd
2:14 *p.m.*
Intersection of 14th and C Street SW
Washington, D.C.

For the curious onlookers, it was truly a gruesome sight to behold. An ejected body, bloody and lifeless, protruded out through the shattered glass of the first vehicle's windshield. A second victim, bleeding profusely from a deep laceration extending down the left side of his head and neck, lay semiconscious, trapped under a tangled mesh of twisted plastic and steel.

Within minutes of the collision, the first police officer

arrived, Corporal Jerome Canady, a seasoned veteran on the D.C Metropolitan Police Force. But neither he nor the teams of trained emergency workers to follow were prepared for such a horrific sight. The officer wasted no time ordering people away from the accident scene in order to assess the situation first hand.

"My God!" the stunned policeman said to himself, staring in disbelief at the sight of two mangled vehicles jammed tightly against the corner wall of the Bureau of Printing and Engraving. Never had he witnessed in all of his years of patrolling the streets of D.C. an impact so devastating forceful as to meld one vehicle directly into another.

"This van must have been flying down C Street!" Officer Canady again mumbled out loud. As he cautiously walked toward the front end of the damaged van, the sight of a lifeless body protruding out from a shattered windshield was overwhelming.

I've never seen a T-bone collision so gruesome! he thought to himself, taking a moment to regain his composure. He next approached the crushed vehicle pinned against the marble wall of the Bureau of Printing and Engraving. Assessing first the extensive damage to the outside of the car, Officer Canady next looked through the shattered glass of the driver-side window carefully searching for any victims. He then spotted a second victim, possibly the driver, precariously jammed tightly against the car's front passenger side door.

"Sir, I am Officer Jerome Canady. Can you hear me, sir?"

"Yes, I hear you," replied a faint mumble from inside the car.

"Sir, you're going to be all right," Canady reassured. "Help is on its way!"

The officer immediately rushed back to his patrol car, contacting the nearest shock trauma center to his location. "Washington Hospital Trauma Center, Shelly speaking. How can I help you?"

"This is Corporal Jerome Canady from the First District Metropolitan Police," the officer hastily replied. "I am presently on the scene of a two-car collision at the intersections of 14th and

C Street SW, directly across the street from the Department of Agriculture. I need you to send a MedSTAR helicopter to this location ASAP. I have one possible fatality and a semiconscious victim trapped inside his vehicle bleeding profusely from lacerations along the left side of his face and neck."

Shortly after Officer Canady called for assistance, an entire fire battalion from D.C Station 16 arrived on the scene, accompanied by their own contingent of EMTs and rescue equipment.

"Artriel, I am having Doriel accompanying me to the airport," Muriel ordered. "I want you and the remainder of your warriors to accompany Reid to the hospital. Remain there until we return with Tom Reid and Ezra Schroeder."

"God speed, Commander," Artriel replied.

Friday, March 23rd
2:50 p.m.
Ronald Reagan National Airport
Arlington, Virginia

Tom Reid paced nervously back and forth, stopping at regular intervals to peer out the airport's south entrance door for a car driven by his brother. "I'm starting to get really worried," Reid commented, sitting down on a vacant seat next to Ezra. "John should have been here at least twenty minutes ago!"

"He probably got caught in that big storm we were hearing about," Schroeder reassured.

"But then why didn't he call and tell us?" Reid blurted out.

"Reverend Tom Reid and Dr. Ezra Schroeder?"

To their surprise, Schroeder and Reid looked up to see two very tall, meticulously dressed men wearing dark suits and ties looking down at them.

"How do you gentlemen know who we are?" asked an inquisitive Ezra Schroeder.

"Please allow me to introduce ourselves, Dr. Schroeder," the taller of the two men replied, pulling his suit jacket aside to display his official White House badge and nametag. "I am Special Agent Joseph Murray and this is my partner, Agent Abel Dory. We are both Secret Service agents assigned to the White House."

"We were expecting my brother, John Reid to meet us here," commented a confused Tom Reid.

"That is the reason why we are here, Mr. Reid," Agent Murray replied. "I'm very sorry to inform you that your brother has been involved in a very serious accident. He is presently being attended to by doctors in the trauma section at Washington Hospital."

"My Gosh, what happened?" a shocked Tom Reid demanded.

"From our reports," replied Agent Dory, "your brother was struck broadside by a van driven by a man driving under the influence of both drugs and alcohol."

"He was also driving on a suspended license," commented Agent Murray. "We are here to take the two of you directly to Washington Hospital."

"Is Tom's brother going to live?" asked Schroeder.

"We can't answer that question, Dr. Schroeder," Agent Murray responded. "We'll have to leave that up to the Lord."

The agent's last comment immediately caught the attention of both Reid and Schroeder. Turning to his traveling companion, Tom Reid declared, "We have to pray!"

"Absolutely!" affirmed Schroeder. "I'll start first."

As people passed by in every direction and scores of demonic spirits hissed in the background, four humans inconspicuously bowed their heads in prayer to intercede for the life of John Reid.

"Abba Father," Schroeder began, holding tight to the hand of Tom Reid sitting beside him, "we come before you with an urgent request. As we pray, Tom's brother John is in desperate need of a miraculous touch of your healing power. We pray the blood of Yeshua over John Reid's entire body. Give the doctors and nurses attending him your supernatural wisdom and insight to bind John's wounds and restore his body to total health. Surround that operating room with your peace and your protection, in Yeshua's name I ask."

"Please Lord, spare my brother's life," pleaded Tom Reid. "Your word promises in Psalm Chapter 90 verse 4 a lifetime of three score years and ten. Please grant John his full measure in years, Lord. John Chapter 10 verse 10 states that the thief comes only to steal, kill and destroy. Your word says that You have come that we might have life. Lord, please restore my brother's life. I ask this in Jesus' name.

Amen."

"Amen," affirmed both Agents Dory and Murray.

Friday, March 23rd
3:21 p.m.
MedSTAR Entrance to Washington Hospital Center
NW Washington, D.C.

A black Ford Crown Victoria with tinted windows and government tags arrived at the MedSTAR (Medical Shock Trauma Acute Resuscitation) entrance to Washington Hospital Center. A man in a black suit emerged from the front passenger side door of the car opening the rear door as a courtesy to the guests seated in the back. Instead of exiting immediately, the two backseat occupants remained seated, utterly transfixed in a state awe.

"I must truly commend you on your driving skills, Agent Murray," stated an impressed Tom Reid.

"I don't know whether to call it luck or perfect timing!" Schroeder declared. "Every light we passed was green! Agent Murray, I must admit, you are one phenomenal driver! I have never seen anyone maneuver so well through D.C traffic!"

Agent Murray responded to his passenger's compliments with a quick glancing smile in the car's rearview mirror and a humble "thank you."

"Dr. Schroeder and Reverend Reid," Agent Dory stated, holding open the rear passenger door as his guests exited, "Agent Murray and I are proud to have been of service to such fine outstanding American citizens as yourselves."

Agent Murray remained seated behind the wheel while Agent

Dory instructed his parting guests on how to locate the Hospital's ICU's unit.

"Reverend Reid," Agent Murray called out from inside the car.

"Yes, Agent Murray," Tom Reid replied, bending down to look through the opened front passenger window.

"Agent Dory and I will continue praying for your brother's speedy recovery."

"Thank you, Agent Murray," Reid responded, extending a handshake of gratitude through the opened window. "That means more to me than anything!"

With a parting handshake, Agent Dory returned to his vehicle while Reid and Schroeder proceeded in the direction of Washington Hospital Center's MedSTAR ICU entrance.

"Oh, my gosh!" Schroeder blurted out. Literally stopping dead in his tracks, Schroeder turned, remembering he had forgotten to thank Agent Murray. "Where did they go?"

"The car was just there!" exclaimed Tom Reid.

Both men stood no more than thirty feet away from where a black Ford Crown Victoria was parked only moments before.

"This is too much!" stated a mystified Reid, turning his head in every direction in a futile attempt to locate the missing vehicle.

"I knew there was something really strange about those two," Schroeder commented with a big smile. "There's no natural way anyone could drive from National Airport right through the heart of D.C. and make it here in under twenty minutes!"

"What are you trying to say to me, Ezra?" Reid asked with a serious look on his face. "That these secret service agents were really angels?"

"Angels, wow!" Schroeder shouted. 'Praise the Lord!"

"Ezra, I don't know about you, but I am getting a good feeling about all this," a giddy Reid declared. "Let's go see my brother!"

Muriel and Doriel stood by in the background amused at the sight of two excited humans making a beeline toward the MedSTAR entrance to Washington Hospital Center.

"Commander, why do humans react that way when they finally discover we are real?" Doriel asked.

"To put it simply," Muriel answered, "humans don't always trust in God's Word. If they truly believe what they read, they would have so much more peace knowing that we are always right there doing the bidding of the Lord."

Friday, March 23rd
3:26 p.m.
ICU Waiting Room
Washington Hospital Center
NW Washington, D.C.

No one seemed to be paying any attention to the CNN reporter discussing a new European Middle East peace proposal on the wall-mounted video monitor. For the twenty or so people seated in Washington Hospital Center's MedSTAR ICU waiting room, there were more important things than peace proposals to think about. Somewhere behind the wall supporting the video monitor, their loved ones' lives hung in the balance.

One of the two receptionists seated behind the ICU's public information desk looked up and immediately recognized a very familiar face staring down at her.

Placing both hands across her mouth to keep from screaming, she let out a very refrained "Oh, my gosh!" just loud enough to arouse the attention of all those around her. "Aren't you the Reverend Tom Reid?" she asked.

"Yes, I am," Reid replied with a smile. And your name is?"

"Molly Reynolds," answered the ecstatic receptionist, immediately extending her hand to greet the popular televangelist.

"Molly, I would like you to meet my friend, Dr. Ezra Schroeder."

"I know who he is!" Molly proudly announced. "I watched both you and Dr. Schroeder this morning on PTW before I left for work. Reverend Reid, what are you doing here?"

"My brother, John Reid, was flown in here not too long ago by a MedSTAR helicopter. We need to find out his present condition and where he might be located right now," Tom replied.

"Is your brother John Reid, the Presidential Press Secretary?" asked a voice in the background.

"Yes he is," Reid answered, turning around to be greeted by a small gathering of onlookers. A rather tall black woman dressed in traditional green hospital scrubs stepped forward.

"Reverend Reid, my name is Andrea James. I was the MedSTAR nurse called out to the scene of your brother's accident."

"Then you know John's condition?" asked Reid.

"I do," the nurse replied. "Your brother is a very lucky man, Reverend Reid."

"Do you mean he's going to be OK?"

Nurse James paused momentarily to smile before answering Tom Reid's question. "I don't know whether to call it fate or divine intervention," Nurse James reflected. "Believe me, I've seen my share of crash scenes over the years, but I can honestly say I have never seen a car sustain the amount of damage as the one your brother was driving and the person inside survive."

"So you are saying my brother is going to survive?" Reid once again asked.

"I'm going to leave that question up to you to answer for yourself, Reverend Reid," Nurse James replied, projecting a big smile on her face. "Please, gentlemen, follow me. I'll take you to see your brother."

Nurse James led Reid and Schroeder through a labyrinth of rooms and hallways leading away from ICU in the direction of the Hospital's emergency room. Instead of entering the emergency room through the hospital main entrance in the front of the building, the nurse escorted her guests through a door marked "emergency personnel only." Once inside, the hectic scene of a busy metropolitan emergency room greeted the threesome.

"Because your brother is what we consider here at Washington Hospital to be 'high profile,' we have him secluded in a private room in the back corner of the emergency room," the nurse commented as she led Reid and Schroeder through the large room filled with scores of injured and sickly patients being attended to by trained medical personnel.

"Your brother is right in here, Reverend Reid," Nurse James smiled, holding open the door to the room.

As he entered the room, Tom Reid was a bit apprehensive. His twin brother had been flown to a shock trauma center with possible life threatening injuries. At last, he would see for himself the extent of his brother's injuries.

"Hello, Tommy!"

In the center of the twelve-by-fifteen-foot room sat a man on an elevated hospital bed. His badly bruised face was barely visible through the thick layers of gaze and bandages.

"John, is that you?" Tom asked.

"Minus about fifty stitches or so, it's me," his bandaged brother replied, "alive and kicking!"

"Praise God!" Tom shouted out moving closer to his brother's bedside to inspect the extent of his facial injuries.

"It's not as bad as it looks!" John commented, forcing a painful smile. "The two EMTs who cut me out of the car also removed a large sliver of broken glass from the side of my head and neck. They informed me later if it was a half inch deeper, I would have been toast!"

"It's truly a miracle!" declared Miranda, seated beside her husband's bed. "The doctor said if it hadn't been for his side airbag deploying, he wouldn't be here today."

"That's the first time I've ever been called a side airbag!" Muriel commented from a duet of chuckles from his angelic companions, Ariel and Doriel.

"I'll leave you all now to celebrate on your own," commented a smiling Nurse James still holding open the door to the private room.

Before exiting, the nurse's attention was diverted toward some sort of commotion coming from the direction of the main entrance to the emergency room. "Wow, there must be something really big going on up front," she announced as she stretch forward to get a better look.

"Oh, my God!" Nurse James exclaimed. With a look of total shock on her face, Nurse James opened the door as wide as it would open and announced, "People, get ready. Do you ever have company on the way!"

All eyes in the room, both angelic and human, were focused on the opened door. The first person to enter the room was a man dressed in a black suit and dark tinted glasses. Stopping just inside the door, he turned and announced, "Ladies and gentlemen, the president of the United States!"

All eyes and mouths opened wide as Analise Devoe made her entrance into the small private room.

"John Reid, how dare you stand me up for our 3 o'clock appointment!" the president commented in a joking manner.

"Madame President, you didn't have to come all the way over here to see me!" remarked a totally overwhelmed John Reid.

"By the look of your face, Mr. Press Secretary," the president continued, winking in the direction of John's wife Miranda, "you are certainly in no condition to come visit me in the White House!" Turning now toward the two gentlemen standing to her right, the president declared, "I want to thank the two of you for opening my eyes to the truth."

"Madame President, I don't understand what you mean," commented a confused Tom Reid.

Looking Reid directly in the eyes, the president confessed, "I really don't understand it myself, Reverend Reid. All I can tell you is that I walked into the Oval Office this morning for a scheduled 8 o'clock appointment. Instead of discussing the latest intelligence reports out of the Middle East with the Secretary of Defense, I felt compelled to turn on the television and watch a segment of your show. I turned on the show at the point where you asked Dr. Schroeder, along with those in the audience, to pray on behalf of Israel."

Tom Reid just stood in silent awe, completely mesmerized by the president's last statement. *Praise you, Lord* was his only thought. *Thank you, Holy Spirit, for touching her heart!*

Everyone in the room stood astonished at the sight of tears welling up in the president's eyes.

"I can't tell you how long it has been since I last prayed and asked God for anything," the president admitted, "but at that moment, I felt compelled to pray for Israel's protection. That's when I witnessed with my own eyes deadly missiles exploding in midair for no rational reason or explanation!"

Stopping briefly to wipe the tears from her eyes, the president continued, "Needless to say, my blind eyes were instantly opened to the truth that God is real, and as I have stated before the nation, I plan to serve Him for the remainder of my life!"

"Praise Jesus!" shouted out a swollen faced John Reid, followed by his brother Tom and Ezra Schroeder.

Turning now toward Tom Reid and Dr. Schroeder, the president calmly asked, "Gentlemen, what was so important that the two of you felt compelled to fly all this way to tell me in person?"

Never in their wildest dreams could the two traveling companions have ever imagined a day like today. Flashing first through their minds were the miraculous events that took place earlier this morning in the Middle East. After their arrival at Reagan National, they were literally trapped in the airport with nowhere to go. They were next escorted through the congested streets of the nation's capital on one of the most bizarre rides of their lives by two probable angelic beings. Now, to top off their whirlwind adventure, they stood face to face with the president of the United States.

"Madame President," Schroeder boldly stated. "We believe we are in possession of information vital to maintaining peace in the Middle East."

"This information you are talking about wouldn't have been

passed down by Sir Isaac Newton, would it?" the president asked with a skeptical look on her face.

"Madame President, Sir Isaac Newton was a man of God," John Reid courageously declared from his bedside. "If God wanted him to pass along information vital to the world's future, I believe it to be entirely possible!"

Everyone in the room, including the president, was impressed with John Reid's bold declaration. Returning to Schroeder, the president said, "Very well, Dr. Schroeder, tell me what Sir Isaac Newton has to say after all these many years. And please, don't leave out a single detail."

With both Reid brothers looking on, Ezra Schroeder opened his brief case and handed Analise Devoe a copy of the matrix that both he and Isaac Newton had deciphered of Psalm 83. For the next few minutes, Ezra Schroeder had the complete attention of the president of the United States of America.

Standing only a few feet away from the president's side, Yahriel turned toward his three angelic companions and gave a big thumbs up.

Muriel responded back by raising his golden sword high above his head and declaring, "God's prophetic plan will now be fulfilled. All praises to the King of Glory and His Messiah forever and forever!"

"Amen!" responded thousands of surrounding angelic voices.

Chapter Twenty-Six

"He will confirm a covenant with many for one 'seven.' In the middle of the 'seven' he will put an end to sacrifice and offering. And on a wing of the temple he will set up an abomination that causes desolation, until the end that is decreed is poured out on him."

Daniel 9:27 NIV

Saturday, March 24th
8:35 *p.m. Passover Eve*
Officer's Wardroom
Aboard the USS Theodore Roosevelt
Just off the coast of Cyprus

A brightly glowing beacon in the darkness is the only way to describe the appearance of the USS Theodore Roosevelt at night-time. But tonight, America's premier nuclear-powered Nimitz class supercarrier shone even brighter than ever. It was party time aboard the floating fortress affectionately nicknamed by its crew the "Big Stick." After spending a total of 189 days away from their homeport of Norfolk, Virginia, its crew of just over 5,500 navy personnel had good reason to celebrate. Bar a presidential order, tomorrow they were scheduled to end their 157day Mediterranean deployment and steam back for home. Whether above or below its 333-meter long deck, every member of the Theodore Roosevelt's crew was out and about celebrating. That included the ship's usually reserved commanding officer, Captain Charles R. Bryant.

Seated at the head of a table surrounded by over a dozen of his fellow officers, Captain Charlie Bryant stood to his feet to propose a toast.

"For most of you," he commented, "tomorrow marks the official end of the USS Theodore Roosevelt's tenth deployment. For me, tomorrow begins the last leg of my tenure onboard a ship where I have literally spent the majority of my naval career serving our country."

"It's about time!" shouted the ship's executive officer, Lieutenant Commander A.J. Schmidt.

"A.J. just wants your job!" jokingly remarked Lieutenant Owen Empey.

"Gentlemen!" interjected Lieutenant Commander Michael Todd, "Would you all please be kind enough to allow poor Charlie to finish his speech. I'm late for another party starting right now on C deck."

"Lest we forget, the commanding officer of this vessel still has the power to demote," the captain continued with a smile, "I strongly suggest that all of you listen to Lieutenant Commander Todd's advice and allow me to finish my speech."

"Hear, hear!" responded his men with an approving applause.

"I stand here before all of you tonight humbly honored to have served along side of some of the greatest naval personnel our great nation has ever known. Tonight, I would like toast the thousands of men and women who have also faithfully served onboard the USS Theodore Roosevelt since it was first commissioned under Captain Dayton Ritt in 1988."

Raising his glass high, Captain Bryant was just about ready to present his toast when a noncommissioned officer, communication's Chief Petty Officer Juliann Durkee, rushed into the officer's wardroom with an important message.

"Sir, I'm sorry to interrupt. Your presence is needed immediately in the Combat Information Center."

"By whose request?" demanded the irritated captain.

"Sir," the Chief Petty Officer stated, "the request comes from the president herself."

"Excuse me gentlemen," the captain commented, placing his full glass of cider back on the table. "Don't anyone leave this room and that is an order! When I return, I will start exactly where I left off—after I find out what the president of the United States wants."

As with all onboard Navy communication centers, the USS Theodore Roosevelt's Combat Information Room was equipped with a crypto-secure L-band radio system called the Joint Tactical Information Distribution System (JTIDS). Every top-secret communiqué either sent or received using this closed computer-to-computer based system was done so without fear of being either intercepted or interpreted by enemy sources.

The Captain entered the large room equipped with the world's most sophisticate communications systems followed by Chief Petty Officer Durkee.

"Attention on deck!" Durkee announced.

"Carry on," said Captain Bryant, walking directly over to a computer station manned by the JTIDS specialist, Petty Officer First Class Lea Berry.

"Sir," Berry commented, looking up at her commanding officer, "I have just decoded the second of two communiqués sent here directly from the White House."

"Have they been verified?" asked Captain Bryant.

"Yes, sir," Berry replied, "they have each been verified twice. The first order was sent by the president herself."

"What was the gist of the president's message, Petty Officer Berry?"

"Sir, she has issued the Roosevelt an immediate search and destroy order."

For a brief moment, Captain Bryant raised his thick brown eyebrows, exhibiting a visible look of dismay. *Is this order coming from the same president who had us stand down during the entire Middle East conflict?* he thought to himself.

"Sir, the president has issued an immediate order for our entire

Trident Anti-Submarine Squadron to search for two missing Russian-built kilo submarines. They are believed to be presently positioned somewhere off the Israeli coastline."

"Were there any specific reasons given for this order?" the captain asked.

"Yes Sir," Berry quickly responded. "The reason for the order is stated in a second communiqué issued by Secretary of Defense Schaeffer. The Secretary's message states that there is sufficient evidence to suspect Iranian nationals hostile to Israel's existence man the two Russian made subs. The message strongly suggests that each sub may be in possession of some form of tactical nuke, possibly tipped at the end of a Russian Klub-3M54 missile or a Russian-made Shkyal rocket torpedo."

The room of over a dozen communication specialists became strangely quiet. Looking around at all the concerned faces, the captain calmly stated, "Well, so much for leaving tomorrow!"

After spending several more minutes thoroughly going over each communiqué with his JTIDS specialist, the captain looked up with a serious look on his face. "Hand me the MC.

"Attention to all personnel aboard the USS Roosevelt, this is Captain Bryant."

With the sound of their Captain's voice permeating every square inch of this city block long vessel, crewmembers immediately stopped whatever they were doing to listen.

"I am sorry to inform all of you, but we have just received a Presidential order canceling tomorrow's scheduled redeployment. Until further notice, our status has been changed to General Quarters. All personnel are ordered to immediately report to their assigned duty stations. Also, I want to see all Trident officers in the Mission Planning Room ASAP."

For the members of the U.S. military, disappointment was only a fleeting moment. As soon as the captain signed off the ship's intercom, the disciplined crew went into immediate action, shifting from a stand-down mode to that of combat ready.

Saturday, March 24th
9:20 p.m. Passover Eve
Mission Planning Room
Aboard the USS Theodore Roosevelt

All eight departments of the Trident Anti-Submarine Squadron, 27 officers in all, were present in the Mission Planning Room. The moment the captain entered the room everyone stood to attention.

"As you were," said Captain Bryant with Trident executive officer, Lieutenant Commander Aaron Carr standing at his side.

"Two things the navy has taught me after all these many years," the captain reflected with a smile. "First, never say never, and secondly, never bet on a sure thing."

The Captain's introductory humor was followed by an appreciative applause. "Gentlemen, we are about to embark on a mission code named by Washington, 'Newton's Riddle.'"

The moment the captain mentioned the mission's code name, everyone in the room looked dumbfounded at each other, as if thinking the same exact thought, *Who came up with such a ridiculous title for a code name?*

"Now please don't ask me how someone came up with that name, because I really don't have clue!" the captain admitted, reading the confused faces of the officers seated before him.

"What I can tell you is that we have been ordered to locate two missing Russian-made kilo submarines possibly positioned somewhere off the Israeli coast. According to satellite surveillance, both subs went missing two nights ago from a Syrian Russian Naval Base. Intelligence also suggests that Iranian crews with extremely hostile intentions possibly man both submarines. It is also believed the mission of the Iranian crew is to somehow disrupt the extremely fragile peace that presently exists between the state of Israel and their surrounding Arab nations. I will now turn over the remainder of this meeting to our Trident executive officer, Commander Aaron Carr."

Lieutenant Commander Carr was a tall, thin man in his mid-forties, with graying sandy blonde hair. He was considered among his peers as the world's leading expert in submarine warfare, having taught weapons and systems engineering at the U.S. Naval Academy four years prior.

"Ladies and gentlemen, Operation 'Newton's Riddle' commences right now!" Carr boldly announced, projecting a strong aura of confidence before his fellow officers.

"First and foremost," Carr stated, "we need to find those two missing submarines. To meet that challenge, Secretary of Defense Schaeffer has requested the assistance of Incirlik Air Base's 39th Air Wing located in Adana, Turkey. They will be sending us four Lockheed P-3C Orion aircraft equipped with rear-mounted magnetometers designed specifically for detecting submerged metallic objects. The P-3Cs are scheduled to deploy from Incirlik at 2200 hours and arrive at their destination about 20 miles off the Israeli coast around midnight. They will then be flying wide swaths over the open waters between the Israeli cities of Haifa and Tel Aviv. If they detect the slightest changes in the surrounding magnetic field, they will mark the coordinates of that area indicating a possible target. That's the moment we step in!" Before continuing, Commander Carr paused momentarily to allow a fellow officer time to display a map of the entire Eastern Mediterranean.

"We will divide up into two teams, five Foxtrot helicopters each. I will command our Alpha team and Lieutenant Commander Boyer will command our Beta team. Once we are over a targeted area, we will scatter over fifty sonobuoys (inflatable surface floats equipped with radio transmitters and sonic hydrophone sensors) over the entire surface. The moment we have made a positive ID of our two targets, we have been ordered by the president of the United States to blow them both to kingdom come!"

After a brief applause, Commander Carr asked, "Any questions, ladies and gentlemen?"

Several hands immediately went up. The first to be recognized was a young officer seated in the front row. "Sir, what types of ordinances are suspected onboard the subs?" Ensign Peterson asked.

"Ordinances of the worst kind, Ensign Peterson," Carr replied.

"We have been notified that the submarine may be equipped with nuclear-tip missiles or rocket torpedoes, maybe both."

"Sir," asked Ensign Shaunte Freeland, "you mentioned the Israeli cities of Haifa and Tel Aviv. Are they possible targets?"

"It is believed that one submarine has been sent to Haifa. The other, somewhere off the coast of Tel Aviv."

"Commander, have the Israelis been notified?" asked Lieutenant Commander Kevin Levine.

"That's affirmative. They were the first to be notified. We will be using their airspace to carry out the entire mission."

"Will the Israelis be taking part in the mission?" Levine again asked.

"The answer to your question is no," Carr firmly stated. "The Israel government agrees that in order for this mission to succeed, this operation must remain entirely clandestine. One thing we have to avoid at all costs is igniting this into a major conflict, especially where the Russians might be involved."

"Sir, is there an announced deadline for a possible attack?" asked the same ensign.

"Yes," Commander Carr affirmed. "We believe it is sometime between now and sundown tomorrow, the beginning of the Jewish Passover."

Saturday, March 24th
10:44 p.m. Passover Eve
12 Kilometers off the Israeli Coast

Totally concealed under the cloak of darkness, twin metallic monsters penetrate the surface of the vast expanse of open waters found just off Israel's coastline. With only the faint illumination from Israeli coastal cities barely visible in the eastern sky, two Iranian Captains stood alone on the bridges of their respective vessels exchanging their final plans.

"Praise to Allah!" declared Saeed Rashid, the captain of the twin submarine nicknamed the Klub. "He has chosen us to present the

Jewish pigs illegally squatting on our sacred land such a wonderful Passover gift."

"Only Allah could have planned an event so perfect," responded Rahim Mohammad, the Iranian captain of the sister kilo submarine named the Granat.

"Let's synchronize our watches," suggested Captain Rashid. "At my mark, it is now exactly 10:45 p.m. and 30 second…Mark!"

"Done!" declared Captain Mohammad.

"At midnight," Captain Rashid continued, "we will submerge to a depth of 100 meters and maintain speeds of 30 knots until we arrive 10 kilometers out from our appointed destinations. At exactly 1:45 a.m., we will maintain a depth of 50 meters, during which time we will ready our Passover surprises. At 2:15 we will travel full speed in the direction of our destiny. When we are exactly five kilometers away from our targets, we will launch our rocket torpedoes and make a hasty retreat back to our original position, 10 kilos off the coastline. At 2:45 a.m., we will launch our final Passover surprise, our Klub-3M54 missiles, at Israel's inland missile bases."

"To Allah be all glory!" each captain defiantly stated before retreating below their respective decks to join their crews.

"To Satan be all glory!" mocked a blackened figure remaining on the deck of the Klub, his squinty yellow eyes restlessly searching the inky black skies above. A nagging feeling kept telling him that all was not well. Instead of joining his fellow demons inside the large metal hull, he unfurrowed his large, scaly wings and took flight, scanning the choppy black waters below and the starlit skies above for any signs of trouble. After a short period of time, the restless spirit returned to the deck of the submarine, satisfied that his evil plans remained undetected. Smiling, he looked out toward the illuminated eastern horizon and vowed, "Before this night is through, all of Israel will know what it is like to taste the intense flames of hell!"

Saturday, March 24th
Midnight Passover Eve
20 miles off the Israel coast

At the stroke of midnight, four Lochheed P-3C Orion aircraft, code named the "Mag Force," arrived at their appointed destination, 20 miles off the central Israeli coast. Air Force Major Brian DeChant, the group's commander, piloted the lead plane of the group of four. Glancing down at his brightly lit instrument panel, the major announced, "Well, gentlemen, we have arrived!"

"So has the navy!" declared pilot Lieutenant Emilo Vasquez, pointing to a brightly lit formation of ten Sea Hawk helicopters flying only a few hundred feet above the water to the left of his plane.

"Commander Carr, this is Major Brian DeChant, United States Air Force, at your service."

"And what brings the United States Air Force out at this fine hour in the morning?"

"Something about helping our navy friends locate some missing Russian subs."

"What is your itinerary, Major DeChant?"

"Starting immediately, my pilots and I will scour every square inch of over four hundred square miles of open waters between the coastal cities of Haifa and Tel Aviv. Lieutenant Vasquez will take the outside perimeter starting here at the 20-mile mark. Captain Dan Nelson will make a parallel swath starting at 15 miles. Lieutenant Royal Baker and I will assume the inside perimeters from the coastline out to 10 miles. If there are any subs out here Commander, we will find them for you within the next three hours."

"Good hunting, Major DeChant. Find us some subs!"

1:45 *a.m. Passover Eve*
Aboard Iranian Submarine One
10 *Kilometers off the Coast*
Haifa, Israel

It was standing room only in the Klub's torpedo room. While over a dozen humans and their respective familiar spirits stood along the side of the seven-by-four-meter chamber, four burley men carefully positioned what appeared to be a small black space rocket into its launch tube resting place.

"Lord Gog?" inquired Aznod, a midlevel demon assigned to oversee the dozen or so familiar spirits assigned to each Iranian crewmember. "Will these humans be a safe distance away after they launch the torpedo?"

Gog portrayed a rare smile as he stood along side his scaly skinned overseer. "The probability of them escaping the power of a nuclear blast at close range is highly unlikely," answered the demonic Lord of the East.

"Then how can the Iranians be a safe enough distance away to launch their nuclear missile?"

"Change of plans," Gog declared displaying his evil sneer. Once they release my beautiful torpedoes, I will have no further use for these Iranians. I have already arranged for each missile to be automatically launched the very moment the rocket torpedoes are fired."

2 a.m. Passover Eve
10 Kilometers off the Coast
Haifa, Israel

"Lieutenant Vasquez, any metal detected yet?" asked Major DeChant.

"That's a negative, sir. I'm presently on sweep four with one more to go.

"Same here, Major," followed Lieutenant Nelson. "I've just completed my fourth sweep. I'm turning now at the 10 mile mark.

"Look's like these waters are metal free, Major DeChant," radioed Lieutenant Baker.

"You may be right," DeChant replied. "I'm flying within two miles off the coast of Tel Aviv and right now there's nothing out here."

"Hold on, Major I'm getting something!" Lieutenant Baker declared. "Bingo, I see a large chunk of metal directly below me. I'm presently flying at 32° 6' N 34° 44' E. Mark!"

"Lieutenant Baker, I have that position marked," affirmed Major DeChant. "They are closer to the coast than I thought!"

I bet you all a month's pay the other one is just as close," Lieutenant Baker stated with confidence. "I'm only six miles off the coast of Haifa."

"Commander Carr, we have found you a possible target," Major DeChant proudly declared, contacting the Alpha Team leader.

"Major DeChant, my team is just five miles away and closing," Carr answered back.

"Major," radioed 'Mag Force' pilot Dan Nelson. "Are you changing our orders?"

"Cease and desist immediately," answered Major DeChant. "Head straight for Tel Aviv and find me that other sub!"

2:13 *a.m. Passover Eve*
10 *Kilometers off the Coast*
Haifa, Israel

As the seconds ticked down, the tension mounted for both demons and humans alike aboard the twin submarines. Their crews were acutely aware that in less than two minutes from now, they would be well on their way in changing the destiny of planet earth. At exactly 2:14, the large diesel engines powering each of the twin submarines started, their deafening vibrations exciting the members of each vessel. Gog was still taking no chances. With only seconds left before each submarine throttled full steam toward their intended targets, Gog turned toward his overseer Aznod and ordered, "Take my place until I return. I want to check the surface one more time to make absolutely sure nothing goes wrong!"

Strange vibrations and splashing greeted Gog as he hurriedly ascended. Stopped just shy of the surface, Gog watched in wonderment as the choppy black waters above appeared to instantly flatten and brighten. In a matter of moments, dozens of metal cylinders began penetrating the surface above. The determined demon wasted no time reaching the surface. Hidden amongst dozens of floating cylinders, the Demon Lord of the East screamed out," Damn you, God!" With military helicopters hovering above, Gog shook his clawed hand toward heaven and declared, "You are not going to stop me this time!"

Wasting no time, Gog instantly reversed direction using his scaly wings to fly through the dark Mediterranean waters below as easily as he could fly through the skies above. In a matter of moments, the determined demon penetrated the submarine's back hull, passing directly into the torpedo room. Once inside, the frantic demon located the nearest human host to do his bidding. Piercing his clawed hand deep inside the human's back torso of the torpedo specialist, Gog screamed out, "Fire the torpedo!"

"What are you doing!" shouted the torpedo room's head engineer, Mular Hussein. Hussein made a desperate attempt to intercept the torpedo specialist before he prematurely pressed the firing button. "Only the captain can give the orders to fire!"

"Screw his orders," screamed the charging human, his mind and body under Gog's complete control.

2:15 *a.m. Passover Eve*
100 *Feet above the Surface*
10 *Kilometers off the Coast*
Haifa, Israel

Piloting the lead Alpha Foxtrot helicopter, Commander Carr carefully positioned his craft directly above the fifty or so floating sonobuoys scattered across the targeted area. Acting as one single transmitter, the buoy array relayed the digital acoustical data to an onboard computer based monitor viewed by each of the Alpha team's four (ASO) acoustic sensor operators.

"Commander Carr, I have conformation!" declared Seamen First Class Jason Forbes, the ASO onboard Commander Carr's Foxtrot helicopter. "We have a Russian kilo submarine directly below us."

"Is our target moving or stationary?"

"Sir, this sub sounds like its ready to rock!" replied an excited Seaman Forbes. "If we don't move now, it's going to be history!"

Commander Carr knew if he didn't act immediately, the submarine would vanish without trace. Turning to his copilot, Commander Carr gave the order to launch the only anti-submarine weapon specially adapted for the use on a helicopter.

"Fire the Mk-46 torpedoes, now!"

Meanwhile, 50 meters below the surface…

"What are you doing," screamed Captain Rashid, throwing open the torpedo room door. "Don't you dare press that button!"

"Press it you stupid idiot, fire that torpedo!"

The expression "fire and water don't mix" couldn't be more true. A rapid upsurge of what appeared to be boiling water mixed with bellows of fiery black, oily smoke burst through the surface almost directly below the hovering helicopters.

"A bull's eye, Commander!" shouted an ecstatic Seaman Forbes.

"That's one down and one to go!" declared the relieved Alpha Team's Commander. "I just pray our Beta Team can soon make the same claim."

No one onboard the Alpha Team helicopters took notice of a small group of blackened figures flying aimlessly above frothy waters. With the remains of their human hosts trapped inside the sunken vessel on the bottom of the sea, these tiny spirits desperately searched above and below the sea's surface for the leader. Little did they know that Gog had abandoned them a split second before the exploding torpedo pierced through the metal exterior of their vessel.

Knowing only an approximate location, Gog flew southward toward Tel Aviv in a desperate attempt to locate the second submarine. With the distant lights from Tel Aviv's harbor growing brighter on the eastern horizon, Gog's squinty yellow eyes strained hard to see any signs of military aircraft flying above the waters.

"There they are," Gog smiled, spotting the distant Beta Team's searchlights aiming in the wrong location. "They're heading the wrong way!"

Instantly out of nowhere, a light brighter than the sun momentarily blinded the hurried demon.

"Going somewhere?" asked the massive luminous being hovering directly in front of the demon's path. Instant fear filled the normally cool collected demonic Lord of the East.

"Get out of my way, Michael," seethed Gog, lowering his clawed right hand to secure his sheathed sword.

"Go ahead, Gog, remove your sword," taunted the Commander of the Heavenly Host. "You know you don't stand a chance against me."

With a huge archangel now blocking his way, Gog knew he had to act fast before the American anti-submarine team could foil his plans. In desperation, the demon folded his wings, diving straight down into a freefall. With Michael flying behind in fast pursuit, Gog strained every fiber of his being to out maneuver his angelic arch-rival.

The demon's superior flying abilities paid off. Quickly spinning his body around 180 degrees, Gog felt relieved, not seeing one trace of his pursuer. He once again smiled, sensing the nearing presence of his fellow kindred spirits. With supernatural perception, Gog could now see the entire outline of the rapidly moving sub.

"Praise Satan!" Gog openly declared. "Any second now it will reach the launching point and there are no American helicopters in sight!"

"That's what you think," stated a commanding voice from behind.

Instant panic filled Satan's third in command. A searing pain radiating out from his lower right leg once again halted the demon's pursuit. To Gog's horror, two mighty, sword-drawn angels, Pethel and Riel, were hovering directly in back of him, one holding a severed leg cut off directly below the knee.

"This wouldn't happen to belong to you, would it?" asked the smiling warrior, Pethel, extending with his left hand the demon's still twitching appendage.

"Keep it as a souvenir," Gog seethingly mocked. "Unfortunately, you're both too late. Any moment now your precious Tel Aviv is going to become burnt toast!"

"Unfortunately, you are wrong again!" stated as very familiar voice from behind.

"Now watch and weep, Lord of the East!" commanded Michael, using the tip of his sword to direct the demon's attention toward a bright spot illuminating the distant surface waters.

The moment Gog turned, the skies above the distant waters brightened. His squinty eyes widened to the size of yellow cue balls at the sight of a rising column of boiling smoke and fire jetting upward above the blackened sea's surface.

"I can tell by the look on your face that you are a little disappointed right now," Michael commented, displaying a slight smile.

"Destroy me, now!" the defeated demonic prince cried out, bowing his head low before his captors.

"You have no idea how much I would love to honor you request," Michael responded, pressing his sword's razor sharp tip deeper into the side of the demon's head. "Unfortunately, the Lord still has further plans for you."

Michael proceeded to lower his sword to waist height.

"Let him go!" the Archangel commanded.

As Pethel and Riel lowered their swords, the demoralized demon again cried out.

"I can't face Satan. Destroy me now, Michael, I beg you!"

"I'll leave that up to Satan to decide," Michael smiled. "And Lord of the East, the next time you see your boss, tell him for me, it's now T-minus seven years and counting."

Epilogue

Sunday, May 14*th*
12 *Noon*
Jerusalem, Israel

Never in the history of world had anyone witnessed an event such as this. Kings and queens, presidents and prime ministers, a who's who of world leaders, celebrities, and religious leaders from every nation on earth all gathered in one place to watch history being made. With the Temple Mount's Western Wall as his backdrop, the man who brokered this remarkable agreement stepped up to the stage microphone to a thunderous round of applause. Everyone, including the Pope, who was seated directly behind the stage podium, stood to their feet applauding the man credited with bringing an end to the longest lasting conflict between two diametrically opposing people groups the world had ever known. There was almost a carnival atmosphere in the streets of Jerusalem.

People of all nationalities, faiths, and creeds had traveled here from every corner of the earth to personally experience an elusive phenomenon called peace. As the cheers and boisterous applause continued, President Giulio D'Alema stood behind the stage podium smiling and waving to the crowds below. Standing firm and proud, the president of the European Union began his speech with an old but very familiar story.

"It is altogether fitting that we, the corporate body representing world humanity, meet here at this special place. Today's date also has significance. It was on this date back in 1948 when Israel was declared once more a nation after 2000 years of dispersion. It was also here over 3900 years ago that Abraham, a man known for his extreme faith, was tested beyond human measure. Because Abraham had absolute faith in what he believed, he passed his test of faith. As part of his reward for not wavering, Abraham was granted all the land presently under our feet. He was given a land blessed with milk and honey, big enough to support all of his future descendents."

Another round of cheers and applauses erupted from the crowds below.

"Abraham was also promised countless descendants who would one day outnumber the stars found in the sky. Unfortunately, the future descendants of Abraham's two sons, Ishmael and Isaac, refused to share in their joint inheritance. For the next 3900 years, their intense rivalry produced only bloodshed and misery for the descendents of Abraham. Hundreds of wars have been fought and millions of innocent have died, and for what purpose?" D'Alema asked. "Everything given to the sons of Abraham has since been lost, nothing has been gained!"

The European President paused, shaking his head in disgust.

"Standing here before you today," D'Alema continued, "almost in the exact spot where Abraham stood so long ago, I now say to the world, Abraham's dream is still alive! The descendents of Ishmael and Isaac are once again brothers. They are now joint heirs to their Father's dreams and their Father's promises. After two months of hard negotiations with the present-day descendents of Ishmael and Isaac, I now have the honored privilege to stand here before the world and say, we have an agreement."

The massive crowd once more erupted into cheers and applause. President D'Alema allowed them all a few more minutes to vent their excitement before continuing.

"On the table before me is a peace treaty that both Israel and all twenty-two members of the Arab League have agreed to sign. Part of this agreement gives the Palestinians immediate statehood and complete autonomy over the entire West Bank and Gaza Strip with Ramallah as the Palestinian Capital. The Palestinians will also receive a generous monetary settlement backed by the World Bank.

These funds will satisfy the Arab League's requirements for dropping, once and for all, their demands for 'right of return.'"

The large contingent of Arabs in the crowd cheered vigorously at the announcement of a Palestinian state, but then booed when told the "right of return" was removed.

"In exchange for these guarantees," President D'Alema continued, "the Arab League has agreed to end all hostilities with Israel. They will normalize relations with the Jewish state by allowing for the mutual exchange of ambassadors and the opening of free trade between their borders. As far as the status of Jerusalem is concerned . . ."

An instant hush covered the crowds below. For decades, the final status of Jerusalem was the one topic no one dare discuss. Everyone stood silent, waiting for the president's next word.

"...Israel has agreed to relinquish all rights to the one square kilometer area known as the Old City in exchange for international recognition of greater Jerusalem as Israel's Capital. The Old City will then be declared a sovereign UN enclave with guaranteed international protection. Within the Old City's borders, the Muslims will be granted full autonomy over the Dome of the Rock and the al-Aqsa Mosque. The Christians will have complete authority over the Church of the Holy Sepulchre. There is only one new stipulation to this entire agreement: by a majority agreement of all parties involved, the Jewish authorities have been granted for the first time in over two thousand years permission to rebuild a Jewish Temple on a designated sight adjacent to the present al-Aqsa Mosque. Permits to begin construction of what will be known to the world as the Third Temple will be granted immediately following today's signing."

The very thought of construction beginning on a Jerusalem Temple sent rams horn shofars blasting throughout the entire city. Jews everywhere in the city began shouting and screaming at the top of their lungs. The streets of Jerusalem literally erupted into a wild celebration with dancing and singing everywhere. Never in their wildest dreams could the Jews have imagined having a Temple to once more call their own, a Temple to both worship and make sacrifices once again to the Holy G-d of Israel.

The world watched in awe as the Prime Minister of Israel sat down in the midst of twenty-two Arab League leaders. With pens in hand, each leader cordially took turns signing and dating their names on lines designating their represented country at the bottom of each page. The very moment the final name was signed, twenty-three white doves were released above the stage, signifying a new era of tranquility and peace had finally come to the Middle East.

Sunday, May 14*th*
6:30 *a.m.*
229 *Chevy Chase Court*
Rockville, Maryland

On a typical Sunday morning, Rachel and Ezra Schroeder would still be fast asleep, but this morning they set their alarm clock to awaken them shortly before six a.m. For the past half hour they sat up in their bed, totally captivated by the events viewed on their small bedroom television. With the signing of the treaty now history, all that was left to watch on television were the wild scenes of jubilation taking place throughout the streets of Jerusalem. Turning to his wife, Schroeder asked, "Seen enough?"

With a true look of concern on her face, Rachel Schroeder turned toward her husband and asked, "Ezra, is this what I think it is?"

"I truly believe it is, my dear." Schroeder somberly answered. "There is only one way to know for sure, my dear. Come with me."

Putting on her bedroom slippers, Rachel Schroeder followed her husband out of their bedroom and down the hall in the direction of Schroeder's office. Once unlocked, she proceeded to follow him behind his office desk as he sat down and booted up his computer. In a matter of seconds, the large computer screen brightened displaying the NSA emblem.

"Here we go!" Schroeder commented, releasing a deep sigh. Once he had typed in his personal access code and password, his desktop screen turned blue, revealing all of his top-secret software programs. In a matter of a few seconds, he was able to access the same program he had used earlier to crack Isaac Newton's Bible codes.

Looking up at his wife, he asked, "Are you ready to find your answer?"

Rachel Schroeder shook head in agreement.

"Father, I ask you now for your supernatural wisdom and guidance to reveal to both my wife and myself the truth behind the events that have taken place today in the Middle East. Reveal to me now the exact words I need to type into this program. In Yeshua's mighty name I ask. Amen."

With his eyes closed, a small still voice inside Schroeder's head clearly spoke, *"Type in Daniel Chapter 9 verse 27 and today's date."*

Instantly, a brightly lit matrix consisting of two lines of colored Hebrew characters appeared across the screen. Schroeder leaned forward, slowly translating the crisscrossing Hebraic message into English. "Daniel's 70th week has begun. Seven years left before Yeshua's return."

With tears in their eyes, both husband and wife looked up at each other and smiled, confirming each other's thoughts.

Standing in the background, Schroeder's guardian angel turned toward his angelic superior and asked,

"Now that the truth of God's prophetic plan has been revealed, is my role as Schroeder's guardian over?"

"Not quite yet," Muriel replied with a big smile. Placing a comforting hand on Ariel's shoulder, the Archangel charged with spreading God's prophetic Truth throughout the earth turned toward his angelic companion and said, "Lest you forget, mighty Ariel, there are still seven years remaining until the Lord's return. Schroeder's role in spreading God's prophetic truth is just getting started!"

Newton's Riddle

Reference page
God's past warning to America

- On January 16, 1994, when President Bill Clinton met in Geneva with Syrian President Hafez el-Assad for the purpose of pressuring the Israelis into giving up the Golan Heights. The morning after the meeting, the powerful 6.9 Northridge earthquake rocked Southern California, becoming the second most destructive natural disaster to strike the United States, right behind Hurricane Andrew.

- On January 21, 1998, Israeli Prime Minister Binyamin Netanyahu was coldly received in the White House by President Bill Clinton. After the meeting, both the president and his Secretary of State Madeline Albright snubbed the Israeli Prime Minister by refusing to have lunch with him. That was the very day the Monica Lewinski scandal broke into the headlines that eventually led to the impeachment and the disgraceful downfall of President Bill Clinton.

- On September 28, 1998, as Secretary of State Albright worked on the final details of an agreement in which Israel would give up 13% of Judea and Samaria, a hurricane named Georges with winds of 110 mph gusting to over 175 mph slammed into the United States Gulf Coast. As PLO Chairman Yasser Arafat addressed the United Nations declaring an independent Palestinian state by May 1999, Hurricane Georges pounded the Gulf Coast causing over $1 billion in damage. At the exact moment Arafat departed American soil, the storm dissipated.

- On November 30th of that same year, Arafat returned to Washington again to meet with President Clinton to raise money for a Palestinian state with Jerusalem as the capital. A total of forty two other nations were represented in Washington. All agreed to give Arafat $3 billion in aid. Clinton promised $400 million and the European nations $1.7 billion. On that day, the Dow Jones average dropped 216 points, and on December 1st, the European Market had its worst day in history. Hundreds of billions of market capital were wiped out in the U.S. and Europe.

- Six months later, on May 3, 1999, the very day Yasser Arafat was scheduled to declare to the world a Palestinian state with Jerusalem as its capital, the most powerful tornado storm system ever to hit the United States swept across the states of Oklahoma and Kansas. It destroyed the suburbs of Oklahoma City with winds clocked at 316 mph, the fastest wind speeds ever recorded. God's list of warnings to America goes on and on. Up until that fateful day in September of 2001, it was only Israel who had to contend with the Muslim wrath of suicide bombings and terrorist attacks. That all changed when the White House openly declared that on September 23, 2001, America would announce to the world its two-state solution with God's land being divided into Israel and Palestine. That announcement never happened. On the morning of September 11, at exactly 8:46:30 a.m., the wrath of Muslim suicide bombings and terrorist attacks came to the shores of America.

- God's final warning to America came on August 23, 2005. As the world watched, the last of the Jews were forcefully evicted by their own countrymen from their homes in the Gaza strip. This was all due in response to tremendous pressure being exerted

> by our president and his Secretary of State on Israel to disengage from "Palestinian land." On that very day, a weather system formed off the coast of Florida. This storm grew to become Hurricane Katrina, which destroyed not only the city of New Orleans, but most of the state of Mississippi as well. Imagine, just one single storm completely wiped out an area the size of Great Britain, rendering thousands of Americans homeless, causing over a hundred billion dollars in damage, and leaving thousands dead.

"What America has done to Israel, God has done to America. One year after they were forcefully removed from their former Gaza homes, thousands of evicted Israeli Jews still remained in makeshift governmental housing. So too, one year after powerful Hurricane Katrina struck the Mississippi and Louisiana Gulf Coast, thousands of evicted American citizens were still living in government-provided housing. Every single time, at the exact moment that America pressured Israel into dividing their God-given land, disaster has struck America. Just as God sent prophet after prophet and judgment after judgment to warn ancient Israel to return to Him and forsake the world, America has been warned and now the warnings are over."

Neill G. Russell